SEVERANCE LOST

A FRACTAL FORSAKEN BOOK

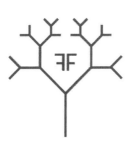

J. LLOREN QUILL

Published by J. Lloren Quill
www.jllorenquill.com

Publisher's Note: This is a work of fiction. Names, characters, places, and incidents are a product of the author's imagination. Locales and public names are sometimes used for atmospheric purposes. Any resemblance to actual people, living or dead, or to businesses, companies, events, institutions, or locales is completely coincidental.

Cover design and map by Abby Haddican
Editing by Ben Barnhart
Book Layout © 2015 BookDesignTemplates.com

Severance Lost/J. Lloren Quill -- 1st ed.
ISBN 978-0-9979887-1-0

For the wonderful Quill girls,
who are more amazing and fantastical than anything you will read in
this novel.

PILLAR

THE KINGDOM OF
MALETHYA

MINOT

THE
NOMADIC
TRIBES

Ispirtu

Rue St.

Regallo
Estate

Darik's Palace

RAVINAI

Bellator

Arena

Slate's
Apartment

Infirmary

Catalpa
Grove

PORTSWAIN

THE
DISENITES

CONTENTS

REFLECTION OF REGRET

A single ray of light entered the room and carried with it the hope of a new day. The light warmed Slate Severance's eyelids, gently rousing him from tortured dreams. In this moment when the nightmares end and the day begins, mistakes of the past are stripped away, leaving behind one's true self. Slate felt honest, virtuous, and determined to protect the defenseless.

Slate rose from bed, but wakefulness followed slowly and so the mingled moment remained. Aspirations for the day mixed with memories of yesterday. *Yesterday wasn't so bad. Memories of yesterday would not ruin today. He was destined for great things.*

He staggered toward the bathroom on waking legs and relieved himself, but memories from the week prior tainted the simple pleasure. *It wasn't his fault. He didn't have a choice. The drunken soldier had attacked him and he had to defend himself.* There is no dishonor in self-defense, his father would have said.

He cleansed his hands in the basin. *These hands killed that soldier.* Memories poured into his head. Last month, a squadron tracked him to his campsite in the middle of the night and attempted to collect the bounty on his head. They failed. *Were these hands good for anything but killing?*

Slate looked in the mirror. He shouldn't have looked in the mirror. His muscular physique, born of life-long training, was drained of color and laced with scars that crisscrossed his torso like ribbons. More memories came back at the sight of his injuries, memories he wanted to forget, memories of pain. He could withstand any pain suffered. He could tolerate the memories of pain inflicted; he was destined for great things.

His gaze rose to meet his eyes in the mirror. These were not the eyes of a righteous man. Blood vessels emanated from the accursed eyes in deep red reminders of his failures. These were the eyes that inspired fear throughout the kingdom. They called him demi-god.

They called him a Shadow of the Night. They had once called him Stonehands. They told stories of him to frighten children at campfires. And the stories were true.

Slate clung to the hope carried on the rays of the day's first light, but he couldn't escape the binds of regret. *If only I could re-live my life... If only I could make it right...*

CHAPTER ONE

A LEAF IN THE WIND

Slate stood in the depths of the Arena, awaiting his introduction. From the tunnel entrance he could see a small portion of the crowd, and it comprised the largest congregation of people Slate had ever seen. Noble families proudly displayed their house symbols from elevated seats, but Slate barely registered their presence. He absently spun the staff from hand to hand to check his grip. He felt as if all the moisture in the air had been removed and sent straight to his palms, leaving him with a dry mouth and a healthy appreciation for the leather grips wrapped around the middle of his staff.

"Ladies and Gentlemen of Malethya, welcome to the opening match of the Guild Tournament," the crier yelled, and the musicians quieted their instruments. "Our first contestant comes to the city of Ravinai from the far reaches of the kingdom. Born in the northwestern mining village of Pillar and wielding a staff, here is Slate Severance!"

Slate ran through the tunnel and controlled his breathing to calm his nerves. Deafening clapping, stomping, and shouting resonated through the stone around him and urged him toward the sunlit entrance of the dueling courtyard. The brilliance of daylight blinded him, and he failed to notice the step down to the sandy courtyard. His instincts responded quicker than his feet, and he planted his staff in the sand and vaulted overhead. A slight over-rotation during his flip caused him to drop to a knee upon landing and swing his staff back into position. What the crowd witnessed was an acrobatic, staff-flourishing entrance. Applause erupted, and Slate unwittingly became a crowd favorite in the eyes of the raucous citizens.

He counted his good fortunes and waited for his opponent. Most contestants in the tournament were seasoned from service in the King's army but hadn't yet reached their physical prime. The crier announced, "His opponent hails from the nomadic tribes of the Southern provinces, Rainier Tallow, who has chosen two short swords for this contest." An unimposing figure, both short in stature and boyish in looks, entered the courtyard. He did not entertain or even acknowledge the onlookers, so the applause died quickly. Despite minimal enthusiasm from the crowd, Rainier's lithe and confident gait reflected much experience. Slate didn't see him adjust his grip on his short swords or lick his lips to combat the dry air, so he presumed the fighter came by his confidence honestly.

The crier outlined the rules of the match for the crowd. "A bugle signals the start of the contest, and the two combatants fight with magically blunted weapons within the confines of the dueling courtyard. The first combatant to knock down his opponent is the winner. Contestants, turn and acknowledge the members of the Crimson Guard in attendance."

In the seats of honor above the commoners and nobility sat the Crimson Guardsmen. An impressive showing in the tournament could earn an invitation to train for the Crimson Guard in one of the guilds. Citizens of Malethya and members of the King's army could participate in the Guild Tournament, requiring Slate to win dozens of preliminary fights in the outlying provinces before making it to the Arena.

Slate and Rainier bowed to the Crimson Guardsmen and faced each other. Rainier's darting eyes locked on Slate and a nearly imperceptible smirk found its way to the tiny fighter's mouth. They crossed staff and sword and a bugle sounded.

Rainier advanced in a series of feints and testing blows, forcing Slate to use the longer staff defensively as he kept the short swords at bay. Rainier darted left and right, changing forms fluidly and keeping Slate on the retreat. Slate kicked dirt from the ground to daze Rainier, but Rainier anticipated the trick and struck Slate's unguarded ribs. Rainier backed away before Slate's counterattack could reach its mark.

A backward glance marked the approaching edge of the dueling courtyard. Slate gave ground more rapidly to counterattack with more forceful blows in the space created, but Rainier deflected the counterattacks and pushed Slate even closer to the edge of the dueling courtyard and victory.

Slate decided on a painful gambit. He kicked sand at Rainier once more, purposefully leaving his wounded ribs exposed. He had difficulty predicting Rainier's position during his offensive flurry, and by exposing his wounded ribs, he was hoping the aggressive nature of the fighter would leave him vulnerable. Rainier avoided the sand and came at Slate with a high-guard on his right side, expecting a blow from above by his taller opponent. It was exactly what Slate wanted, and he thrust his staff into the right leg of Rainier. He felt his blow land just as a blinding pain spread across his ribs.

Not trying to be a hero, Slate distanced himself from Rainier. He assessed the damage his blow had done to Rainier and saw he clearly favored his left leg. Slate took the offensive, swinging his staff from a distance that left Rainier unable to counter with his shorter weapons and loss of mobility. The skill of the nomadic tribesman prolonged the match awhile longer, but then Slate landed a sweeping blow to Rainier's left leg, and his wounded right leg could not support his weight. Rainier fell to the courtyard and a bugle sounded, signaling the end of the match.

Slate reached down and offered his hand to his opponent. Rainier shook off his disappointment in the loss before accepting help onto his feet. They both soaked in the applause of the crowd before making their way across the courtyard. Rainier then surprised Slate by following him out of the tunnel, outside of the Arena, and into Slate's camp.

Each fighter returned to his tent to rest between fights. Slate's tent was nearly empty. He had traveled to the tournament by foot, carrying rations for the trip and a sleeping blanket. In addition to the tent, the tournament had provided a cot, armor, and a stand of blunted weapons. Slate returned the staff to the weapon stand, sat on his cot, and started the slow and painful process of removing his armor. Rainier hauled a discarded crate into the tent and used it as a chair.

"That was well fought, Slate. Many of these soldiers trained in the King's army stick to their forms with too much rigidity. This makes them predictable and unable to turn the tide of battle if they are outmatched. They don't take risks like you did," he paused, "You fight like a tribesman."

Slate smiled at the backhanded compliment that valued cunning over might. But Rainier had also clearly stated that Slate had won with a fair amount of luck. "I fight like my father," Slate replied.

As they talked, Rainier's servants entered the tent. Each had the olive skin associated with the southern provinces and dressed in silks wrapped and tied at the waist. Ornate tattoos covered their hands and feet. Within a matter of minutes, the servants transformed his tent into a room fit for a nobleman. Blankets and lounge pillows covered the dirt floor and hanging silks provided privacy for bathing. Rainier ignored the changes around him, so Slate didn't acknowledge them either.

"...then your father should be proud. I thought I was the only remaining fighter without formal training in the King's army."

The tent flap opened and two people entered, and Slate understood the servants' preparations. The first was a man dressed in simple traveler's robes with a well-worn woodcutter's axe hanging from his side. He carried himself with the self-assuredness of a king. "My name is Lucus. I am a wizard currently traveling with the Tallow tribe." Slate had never met a wizard, but enough tales had reached the small village of Pillar for him to know of magic in Malethya. Lucus' simple attire did not fit Slate's preconceived notions of wizards gathered from campfire stories. Lucus said, "Rainier has resisted the traditions of the Tallow tribe up until this point by refusing to name a Teacher, but it is with great pleasure that I formalize Rainier's acceptance of your offer to serve in this esteemed position."

"I didn't intend to offer anything…"

"You extended your hand to Rainier when he was fallen. He accepted your hand, sealing the pact." Rainier remained silent and Lucus contributed little in the way of explanation. "I believe I can shed some light on tribal customs, but first I offer a gift to celebrate your honorable victory and help you prepare for your next match. Would you allow my apprentice Sana to treat those injured ribs?"

"I thank you for the offer, Lucus, but magic is not allowed in the tournament," Slate responded, temporarily ignoring the misunderstanding in favor of keeping the tournament rules. But the pain in his ribs became sharper and made breathing more difficult now that the adrenaline of the match had subsided. Slate feared that several of his ribs were broken rather than just bruised or cracked.

Lucus gave a knowing smile. "Magic may not be applied during tournament matches. There are no stipulations preventing healing between matches. The tournament is intended to showcase our most talented warriors, not to leave them bloodied and broken."

Slate nodded his acceptance with some trepidation at having magic used upon him, but his fear dissipated when Sana lowered the hood of her robes. She likely had suitors from the highest courts, but she approached with a purposeful stride that implied she was unaware of her beauty or purposely dismissive of it. "Healing is easiest when I have direct contact with the wound," Sana told Slate as she started removing his leathers without bothering to ask permission. When she unhooked and pulled away the last of his leathers, the pain in his ribs spiked as his chest was allowed to expand, making the full extent of the wounds apparent. Thankfully, his inability to draw a deep breath made it impossible to scream in agony, and he only managed to produce a stifled grunt. Sana turned her gaze from the wound to Slate and lectured, "Your leather armor distributed the force of the blow over a large area and prevented puncture of the skin, but the red color and immediate tissue swelling suggests internal damage. I am going to touch the wound and probe its extent. You will feel a slight tingle."

Slate needed to stare at something to ignore the pain and found Sana's face convenient for the purpose. Her eyes fixated on the wound and reminded Slate of the focused state he entered in battle preparation, but it differed in a manner he couldn't quite place. Her lips articulated an inaudible conversation with herself that her clenched jaw resisted. Sana placed her hands on his side, closed her eyes and a warm tingling sensation radiated from her cool touch. The warm sensation moved around through his chest, always probing deeper and never staying in the same location. After several minutes, Sana opened her eyes and explained her diagnosis. "You have two broken ribs with multiple fractures of each. They have damaged the surrounding muscles and connective tissue but have not impacted your lungs. I will realign your bones and then stimulate them to grow and reconnect. There will be pain as the bones realign and travel through the damaged tissue. The growth of the bones and the final healing of the surrounding tissue will leave you fatigued but should not cause significant pain. Try to remain still until I have finished. Are you ready?"

Slate grabbed the edges of the cot for support, clenched his teeth, and nodded. As promised, the pain of the bones realigning was excruciating. When they were broken, it had happened in an instant. Realigning the bones required more time and exacting focus. Slate began to worry that if it took any longer he would lose consciousness and Sana would have a perfectly still patient to work upon.

Finally the pain abated, but Sana's continued concentration told Slate that her work continued. Sana's lips moved inaudibly as she worked and Slate realized why the nervous habit bothered him. When he first learned to fight, his father told him to concentrate. He squinted his eyes, clenched his jaw, and tightened his muscles. Later in his training he understood these reactions were counterproductive and that true concentration required an open mind to read your opponent and the control to use only the muscles necessary to prevent fatigue. If training to use magic was anything like his experience with combat, then Sana had not yet gained this experience. This realization coincided with Sana straightening up with a smile on her face, leaving Slate to feel foolish for questioning her talents. But before he could thank her, a new pain throbbed in his sides. It felt like his skin was being stretched from the inside. He gasped in pain.

Sana probed the wound again, but Lucus intervened. "What did you find?" he asked his apprentice calmly.

"I have properly aligned the bones, but they continue to grow." Lucus casually took her place near Slate and within seconds the warm feeling returned and the pain subsided. Sana hid her frustration behind a mask of professionalism. "You are healed and will require some rest before your next match. I wish you the best, but I have other matters to attend." Sana abruptly left the tent, leaving the impression that her early exit had more to do with her failed attempt at healing than anything else on her agenda for the day.

Lucus explained. "Sana has immense potential but struggles to control her spells. Unfortunately, this can be the most difficult part of being a wizard. The use of magic is not difficult if you have the ability. If you apply the correct techniques, the spell is cast, but applying it in the correct dose for the situation is what differentiates a wizard from a simple traveling magician and his tricks." Slate intended to ask Lucus about the Tallow clan, but fatigue ran over him like a wave. He fell asleep in his cot before he could verbalize his questions.

Rainier awoke Slate by gently shaking his shoulder. "Teacher, the crier is announcing your semifinal match. Prepare for battle." Slate jumped out of bed and suited up with Rainier's help as he offered information on his opponent. "I have sparred with this contestant. He is powerful and relentless, but slower than you. Your staff will not withstand a direct blow from his broadsword. Try to deflect his blows rather than block them. Good luck, Teacher." So far, Rainier seemed to be the Teacher in this relationship.

Slate grabbed his staff and ran for the Arena entrance as the crier announced his name. Slate sprinted through the tunnel, flipping over his staff and landing on one knee in the dueling courtyard. The crowd cheered loudly at his now familiar entrance.

"Weighing in at 260 pounds and wielding the broadsword, Magnus Pudriuz!"

An equally large cheer arose for Magnus as he stepped into the courtyard and extended his broadsword into the air. Slate saw why it would be easy to cheer for Magnus. He was a physical specimen and looked the part of a tournament champion. His arms were the size of Slate's legs and his leather armor needed to be specially made to fit his large frame.

Slate and Magnus bowed to the Crimson Guardsmen in the Arena and turned to face each other. Magnus glowered and remained standing during Slate's bow, impressing Slate. Many contestants attempt to rattle their opponents with fear, and Magnus had a talent for it. It was a valuable trait, but it was a gimmick. Rainier's quiet confidence threatened Slate much more than Magnus' glowering. Slate extended his staff to cross Magnus' broadsword. Magnus swung at Slate's staff in a display of strength rather than simply crossing it. Slate loosened his grip on his staff and allowed it to fly through the air upon contact, landing ten yards away. Magnus and the crowd laughed at his expense while he went to pick it up, but his feint allowed Slate to judge the power behind Magnus' blow and found that Rainier's advice was correct. He would need to avoid direct engagement.

As the laughter died down, Slate entered into a defensive fighting stance and tried to appear frightened. He considered pissing his pants to heighten the effect, but the look on Magnus' face showed that his acting was convincing enough without that embarrassing ploy. The bugle sounded and Magnus rushed Slate. Slate took a few shuffling steps backward in a continued display of fear as Magnus began to lower an overhead swing that would have snapped his staff in two. Before it found its mark, Slate launched himself to the side, easily avoiding the slow powerful swing. He planted the staff into the ground and altered the momentum of his body, swinging toward Magnus's backside. Before he could turn, Slate delivered a powerful kick to the back of his knee. Magnus didn't drop, but his balance faltered. Slate swung the staff into his other leg and toppled the large fighter with one final, well-placed blow to the back. Magnus landed face-first in the sand and the bugle sounded. The crowd applauded after coming to grips with this quick change of events. Slate ran back to the tunnel entrance and left Magnus cussing and swearing after Slate as he picked himself up from the ground. Before he reached the tunnel, he heard the crier say, "Let's hear it for Slate Severance, who just won his tournament match in record time!" Slate raised his staff for the crowd but didn't slow down.

Rainier met him at the tunnel and fell into a jog at his side. Slate thanked him for his insight about Magnus but found Rainier quiet on their return to the tent, where Lucus awaited.

"Let us talk quickly before the headmasters of the guilds arrive. Our time is short."

"The headmasters of the guilds are visiting?" Slate questioned.

"It is tradition for the heads of the guilds to meet each of the final contestants before the championship bout. It is a great honor, but you must handle these meetings correctly. The Crimson Guard is filled with people whose skills and talents are only exceeded by their egos and personal agendas. You must tread carefully during these meetings. Do not promise anything to the headmasters until you have a better understanding of the consequences. How much do you know of the Crimson Guard?"

"Nothing," Slate acknowledged. "Most people from Pillar spend their entire lives working in the mines. My father was enlisted in the King's army and taught me to fight, but I know little of the guilds or the guard."

"King Darik commissioned the Crimson Guard to train the land's most promising warriors in the guilds. No member of the king's army can question or accuse a member of the Crimson Guard since their directives come directly from the king. All Guardsmen belong to one of three guilds: Bellator, Sicarius, and Ispirtu.

"Bellator specializes in various fighting techniques and the use of weaponry. Its headmaster is the famous war hero, Villifor. He will undoubtedly be interested in having you join his school regardless of the outcome of the championship bout. Magnus was his prized recruit and your showing in the semi-finals will have piqued his interest.

"Ispirtu trains all of the mages that enter the Crimson Guard. Their headmaster is a powerful wizard named Brannon. I advise added caution when speaking with Brannon. He is not only the headmaster of Ispirtu but also the father of your finals opponent.

"Sicarius is the last guild. It teaches stealth, strategy, and the art of deception. I do not know the name of Sicarius' headmaster and if you learn it, I suggest you promptly forget it for your own safety. Members of Sicarius gather information for the king and conduct covert operations." Slate heard a large commotion of people approaching outside of the tent. Lucus said, "That will be Villifor. His fame draws large crowds and his personality does little to discourage the practice. May your tongue be as swift as your staff, Slate Severance." Lucus raised his cloak and discreetly exited the tent, leaving Slate to feel like a leaf blowing in the wind. Unsure of the proper protocol for meeting a war hero or a headmaster, Slate waited outside the tent entrance.

Villifor struck an impressive figure on his approach, surrounded by admirers and greeted by well-wishers. Upon identifying Slate, Villifor hailed, "Good show! Well fought, Slate Severance!" Villifor grasped his forearm and continued loud enough for his entourage to hear, "Let us make our introductions in private. I promise to be brief because I know the importance of preparing for battle." Villifor strode into the tent leaving Slate and Rainier to follow in tow. Slate wondered if Villifor's last statement was meant to discourage his entourage from following into the tent or to encourage them to wait outside until Villifor emerged.

The blankets and lounging pillows spread across the tent floor by Rainier's servants provided the best place to meet despite its informality. Villifor relaxed against a pillow and gestured for Slate to join him. Rainier sat next to Slate without an invitation to join the conversation. Villifor continued with a raised eyebrow in Rainier's direction, "You defeated Magnus by mixing guile, cunning and decisive action to overcome physical inferiority. Had you faced Magnus in ten consecutive fights, he would have bested you nine times." A twinkle appeared in his eye. "In battle, you only get one opportunity. Identifying weakness and exploiting it is often the difference between life and death. Commit to Bellator and your teachers can instruct you in the forms and techniques required to master your weaponry of choice. Master these forms to decrease the weaknesses in your fighting technique and more importantly . . . survive situations in which you should not." Villifor's eyes momentarily glazed, no doubt remembering some long past battle, before returning to focus on Slate. "There is no better place for a tournament champion to hone his skills than Bellator. You belong in Bellator, an instrument of the king's will, and a protector of Malethya." He stood up to depart and rejoin his mob of adoring citizens, finishing the conversation with, "Excel as a member of Bellator, and find your name sung in songs of valor with fame that precedes your arrival in every town."

Could this day become any more confusing? Lucus warned about the dangers of speaking too openly with the headmasters, and yet Villifor didn't even provide the opportunity to speak. "What do you make of that?" Slate posed to Rainier.

"You would be fortunate if your remaining two meetings proceed as smoothly. You learned that you are welcomed in Bellator, and I believe Villifor spoke plainly. Either he knew you had little experience in these types of encounters, or he did not wish to speak in front of me."

"Why wouldn't he wish to speak in front of you?"

"Because I will not be joining any of the guilds . . . I have other obligations to my tribe." A complex mixture of pride and duty indicated a long conversation would be required. Switching subjects back to the battle ahead seemed the best course of action. "Do you know anything of my opponent in the finals?"

"You will be facing Lattimer Regallo, the son of Brannon. He has the potential to become a powerful wizard like his father, but he has been training for the tournament determinedly. His forms are well practiced but without the physical prowess of Magnus. I believe he will stay within his capabilities as a fighter, utilizing a stout defense to wear you down. He favors a long sword and shield."

"When is the championship match?" Slate was beginning to understand that the tournament ran according to its own timetable.

"I am not certain, but I could inquire."

Desiring some quiet time to clear his head after a whirlwind day, Slate nodded in affirmation and looked toward the ground. Rainier understood his desire and stepped out. With the tent to himself, Slate sat against a lounging pillow and sorted his thoughts. He had landed a lucky blow to win his match against Rainier and now found the tribesman pledged to his tutelage without direction as to what should be taught. The terms and duration of this teacher/student relationship would have been cleared up by Lucus, but the meetings with the headmasters were a pressing priority. Villifor had praised him in one sentence and told him he would have lost nine of ten contests against Magnus in the next. His father would have told him to clear his mind and focus on his upcoming match against Lattimer or to prepare for meeting the headmasters from Sicarius and Ispirtu, but Slate could not concentrate on any of these things. He kept picturing Sana, the apprentice with the same drive and determination that reminded him of his early days of training.

A knife blade touched his neck and he froze. His attacker whispered, "Only an idiot meets an opponent on an equal field of battle. Villifor can teach you a thousand ways to kill a man and yet the most junior member of Sicarius could have joined his group of admirers, killed him and left before that pompous figurehead even knew he was dying. Sicarius teaches you to master your surroundings. No door will bar your way. You could sit next to your own mother and she wouldn't know it was you. Most importantly, no one will ever slip into your tent unnoticed and place a knife against your throat again. Sicarius is not for everyone. If you are successful in your missions, there will be no public glory. No one will tell your tale. If you are truly talented, the world may even forget your name . . ." Slate felt a slight electrical twitch against his neck before his eyes rolled up and he blacked out.

When Slate awoke, he waited a few seconds for the fog to clear from his head. He resisted the urge to bolt upright out of worry that the headmaster of Sicarius could still be in the tent. Whatever the Sicarius headmaster had done to him left no lasting effects, but it was impossible to tell how long he had been unconscious. Rainier was not present so Slate presumed that he'd only been unconscious for seconds or minutes, not hours. Slate checked for signs of how the headmaster had entered and exited his tent. There did not seem to be a mark of any kind indicating entry under the tent walls or tears in the canvas. It was unsettling. During his search he noticed a note folded neatly on the pillow of his cot with a coin shaped object set atop.

Slate,

I offer my apologies for the details surrounding our first encounter, namely the knife and shock stick. Information is more valuable to the right people than any treasure and my identity qualifies as valuable information.

For your first lesson from Sicarius, I will explain how I entered your tent and left you incapacitated, since it is undoubtedly on your mind. I used Villifor's grandeur to blind you. You and Rainier turned to follow Villifor, which allowed me to slip into your tent unnoticed. I bided my time until I had you at a disadvantageous position. There are a number of more elaborate methods at my disposal, but I chose this simple plan to drive home a point; you are defenseless.

In preparation for your training in Sicarius, I suggest utilizing your newfound role as a teacher to implement a game of stealth called Stratego. The game is quite simple in nature but complex in practice. You or Rainier will hold this token at all times. The other can earn the token by stealing it or through surprised incapacitation of the person holding the token. Incapacitation through direct confrontation is not allowed. Leave the frontal assaults to Bellator.

From time to time I will check on you. Try to make it more difficult for me than it was this afternoon. If you decide to join Sicarius, I expect you to report to the guild with the Stratego token in your possession.

Slate examined the Stratego coin. One side of the coin had the same insignia as the letter, and the second side was devoid of any markings. Its heft identified it as iron ore but not the typical hematite mined in Pillar. The coin intrigued Slate. The deformities within the iron ore gave the coin a dull reddish hue and yet the shape was perfectly formed. To be molded and engraved with the Sicarius symbol, the iron needed to be melted down, which would separate the iron from the stone deformities. Since this hadn't happened, this seemingly simple coin was anything but simple. Not knowing the consequences of failing to heed the rules in the letter and the ease with which he had been incapacitated convinced Slate that maintaining possession of the token would be prudent. He wrapped it in a strip of cloth and tied the cloth around his arm.

Rainier stepped into the tent and reported the championship bout was scheduled to occur just after sunset, leaving about one hour to meet headmaster Brannon and prepare for the match. Slate decided not to recount his introduction to the Sicarius headmaster for now, opting to prepare for his next battle instead. Slate gestured for Rainier to join him in the open area of the tent and began transitioning between several of his battle stances. The familiarity of the forms gave his brain a rest from the headmasters and helped keep his muscles limber prior to his final match. It also made him feel like he was at least attempting to live up to his newfound role as Rainier's teacher, although Rainier easily followed the progression of forms.

Toward the end of the progression, Brannon entered the tent. His entire being radiated a sense of superb confidence bordering on narcissism, and his elaborate robes enhanced the impression. The layered black and purple robes bore insignias of both Ispirtu and the house Regallo, signaling that his pride in the family name equalled his station as headmaster, a bold and unconventional statement. Brannon stood to the side and quietly waited as Slate completed his training forms, though he did so with an openly hostile stare. The reason for his angst was unknown to Slate; he knew that one never interrupted a soldier's forms or a mother's prayers.

After his forms were completed, Brannon began, "If you are fit to join Ispirtu, you will follow proper etiquette. Typical punishment for failing to address the head of your order, in this case me, involves serving as a personal attendant until proper respect can be learned through servitude. Of course this assumes that you are able to join Ispirtu. Unlike the other guilds that will accept any farm boy capable of yielding a sword, training in Ispirtu requires the ability to perform magic. "

Brannon stepped forward and laid his hand upon Slate's forehead. Similar to the way Sana had probed his injuries, Brannon's touch did not end at his fingertips. It extended into every muscle limbered up from his forms and into the deepest cells of his deepest organs. Naked didn't adequately describe the sense of exposure. Thankfully, Brannon's probing lasted for the shortest of time periods, after which he spoke to Slate.

"The champion of the tournament gets to choose his guild, but you do not have the spark required to be trained in the use of magic. If you win the tournament and choose Ispirtu, you will be the lowest member of the guild without the ability to conjure the simplest of spells. For this reason, we have nothing left to discuss. I bid you good luck in your remaining match and in your studies in one of the other guilds."

The Ispirtu headmaster exited the tent, and Slate drank a glass of water thinking it might cleanse the places soiled by Brannon's probing, but time would prove to be the only effective cleanser.

Rainier noticed Slate's discomfort and attempted to refocus his Teacher on the upcoming match. He grabbed a long sword and shield and stepped into the open area of the tent. "I'll show you Lattimer's favorite forms." Rainier's expertise with these weapons no longer surprised Slate, and they sparred for a few minutes until the crier's voice, magically enhanced to be heard throughout the arena's grounds, drifted into the tent.

"The final match of the tournament will begin shortly. Come take your seats to see the surprising upstart, Slate Severance, pit his skills against the tournament favorite, Lattimer Regallo!"

CHAPTER TWO

STONEHANDS

Glowing orbs danced in the darkening sky, illuminating the multitude streaming toward the arena. The lights intermingled and darted while changing colors in a dazzling and unpredictable show. The orbs danced to pulsating changes in color and moved to the silent song being sung overhead. The effect was overwhelming and beautiful, and Slate realized the championship match would be an entirely different experience than his previous bouts.

The skyward performance of the orbs was so spectacular that it distracted Slate from the other changes made to the arena for the championship match. Though the arena was elliptical in structure, it had been constructed in quadrants and each of the quadrants expanded outward by some magical means. The ground between each of the now disconnected quadrants had risen up to seamlessly connect one section to the next. The end result was that the arena had doubled in size to accommodate the masses wishing to watch the championship bout. Even to Slate's untrained eye, the transformation of the arena must have required an exorbitant amount of magic.

As Slate approached the tunnel entrance to the arena, the crowd around him made way at the sight of his leather armor and weaponry with chants of "Ho, Slate!" and "Fractal's blessing to you, Slate Severance!" Small crowds formed behind Slate, making him feel a little bit like Villifor. Slate waved and greeted the well-wishers before entering into the relative solitude of the tunnel entrance.

Slate turned to Rainier. "This looks like an entirely new place. Do you know of any other surprises?" But the noise of the crowd drowned out any attempt at conversation. Rainier clasped him on the shoulder, gave a reassuring squeeze, and left Slate to his thoughts. Slate recollected the anticipation of waiting within this tunnel for his match against Rainier. Then, the crowd noise had come from above him, reverberating through the walls. Now the tunnel became alive with noise from above, below, and every direction, reverberating through his entire body until he felt like the entire arena was just an extension of his will.

Bugles trumpeted and the crier's voice rang out over the crowd. "Citizens of Ravinai and travelers from all parts of Malethya, thank you for joining together to celebrate the best warriors in our lands. Before we enjoy this entertaining match, I ask that all of you pay tribute to the sacrifices made by members of the Crimson Guard in their service to us all." Enthusiastic applause broke out and the crier continued on the decrescendo. "Special gratitude is due to the Ispirtu Guild and visiting delegates of the Wizard Council who have transformed the arena for tonight's championship bout. Without further ado, let us meet tonight's combatants. Please welcome the upstart from Pillar whose staff is almost as quick as his victories…Slate Severance!"

Slate trotted down the tunnel, picking up speed as he went. He kept his eyes focused on the top step exiting the tunnel so he wouldn't be blinded, planting his staff and leaping overhead in his now familiar entrance. Slate tucked his head during the forward flip over the staff, but where he expected to see the solid ground of the arena, Slate saw only air. Below him, a huge bowl had been carved out to provide seating for additional spectators. Slate's awe at the magnitude of this magical feat was immediately nullified by the sheer panic about the open air below him. Slate would be fortunate to survive the fall.

Slate continued his flip as usual, rationalizing that a broken leg would be preferable to a broken skull. His feet came underneath him and a jolt brought him to his knee as he felt solid ground beneath his feet at the exact location he had expected the ground to be. But this fact was in stark contrast to the information provided by his eyes. Below him, spectators filled the bowl structure, easily outnumbering the spectators from the earlier matches. But where was the dueling courtyard where he would fight? Slate raised his eyes from the air that supported him and saw the crier in front of him, seemingly floating. Rising to the thunderous ovation of the crowd, Slate took a tentative step forward, felt the air hold his weight, and continued in what he hoped was a confident gait to stand beside the crier.

Once Slate reached the center of the arena, the crier chronicled his previous bouts for the spectators. "Slate Severance began his tournament run with an exhilarating match against Rainier Tallow." The orbs overhead coordinated their movement to show a perfect image of Rainier crossing swords with Slate prior to their match. "Rainier's quickness put Slate at a disadvantage early, as he gave ground and was forced to maintain a defensive stance before a well-timed counterattack slowed Rainier, allowing Slate to take the offensive and eventually subdue his opponent." The orbs reenacted the final moments of the battle, then showed Slate helping Rainier from the ground. "In his semi-final match, Slate set a tournament record by toppling the heavily favored Magnus in only 8 seconds! Let's hear it for Slate Severance!" Slate soaked in the applause and noticed that his orb-image displayed him from a vantage near his feet. As they slowly panned around him, the orbs recreated a slightly exaggerated and grandiose view of his actual physique...perhaps it was his imagination or a slight modification for the entertainment of the spectators.

"And now, let me introduce Slate's competitor, Lattimer Regallo!" boomed the crier. Lattimer emerged from the opposite tunnel holding a long sword and a shield bearing the family crest. Lattimer banged the long sword against the depiction of a raven on his shield and jogged toward the crier. When he got closer, Slate stared into a rather plain but unreadable face with fierce grey eyes that exuded utter confidence. The crier continued, "Lattimer demonstrated his technical prowess with victories over Jak Warder's broadsword and the short swords of Cirata Lorassa." Slate studiously observed the orbs as they replayed Lattimer's previous matches. Lattimer rarely attacked early in the bout, counterattacking just enough to keep his opponents honest. Both Jak and Cirata became more aggressive as the match wore on, and Lattimer waited for his opponent to make a mistake before striking. Slate resolved to not become frustrated with Lattimer's strong defensive tactics and compromise his own defenses in the process.

"Would the combatants please acknowledge the members of the Crimson Guard?" Slate and Lattimer both bowed toward the section of the arena containing the guard. "Tournament rules prohibit the use of magic by contestants during the bout. This rule will be monitored by the esteemed headmaster of the Ispirtu Guild." Brannon stood and acknowledged the thunderous ovation from the crowd. "Finally, King Darik would like to address the combatants."

King Darik rose from his seat of honor to address the crowd and the combatants. He dressed in formal robes appropriate for the public function, but still wore his long sword at his side, refusing to give up the weapon that had earned him the crown. "Ladies and gentlemen, with great pleasure I present to you the final bout of the tournament. Fine fighters from throughout Malethya have pitted themselves against each other in a quest to claim the title of tournament champion, and the field has been whittled down to these two extremely gifted combatants. Let us appreciate their combined skill during the upcoming battle and sleep easy at night knowing that these men will use their talents to protect all of us through their future service in the Crimson Guard. Now, let the battle begin!"

Slate crossed his staff with Lattimer's long sword under another round of deafening applause. A bugle sounded and the tense combatants rushed into motion. Slate feinted to his right and quickly slid to his left, attempting to engage Lattimer on his sword-hand, where his defenses were lighter. Lattimer did not appear overly quick, but his technical skills with the shield and sword compensated for any physical advantages Slate possessed. Slate couldn't land a solid blow, so he continued to circle and test Lattimer's formidable defenses.

While circling, early signs of fatigue entered his legs and arms. The prior matches and the healing performed by Lucus and Sana must have affected him more than he thought. As minutes passed and Slate circled, the effect magnified. Instead of just fatigue, heaviness slowed the motions of his arms and legs. Slate was tempted to overwhelm Lattimer with his remaining strength, but the recreated battles from the orbs stayed Slate's hand. So far, this match was playing out exactly as the others had, and Lattimer would be expecting an offensive charge at any moment.

Slate's arms tired with each swing but not in a way he had ever experienced. He felt again the sense of invasiveness when Brannon had tested his magical aptitude, except this time a persistent feeling probed his entire body and pushed something into the muscles of his arms and legs. Magic was being used against him.

Slate disengaged by stepping back and regrouping while Lattimer continued to hold his defensive position. Slate hoped to appeal to Lattimer's obvious pride in the family name and force a break in his defensive techniques. With Lattimer opting not to engage him, Slate held his staff in one hand and rested one end on the invisible ground, a sign of disrespect toward his opponent. He then yelled to the arena, "See the famous Regallo crest! Its prominence hides my opponent perfectly! When our enemies attack, the Regallo family will safely defend themselves while the rest of us actually engage our enemies in battle!" Wanting to emphasize his point, Slate worked up a good bit of spit and launched it toward Lattimer; it landed square in the middle of his shield bearing the family crest.

Lattimer rushed him, but Slate underestimated his own fatigue. He took up a defensive stance that required as little foot movement as possible, but it was still difficult to keep his staff moving fast enough to repel Lattimer's offensive blows. The magical intruder within his body still pushed the fatigue-inducing elements into his arms and legs. Frustration rose within Slate. He did not train this hard or come this far to lose in an unfair fight. In his anger, landing a blow with his staff and causing Lattimer to fall didn't feel sufficient. The intimacy of connecting his fist against Lattimer's jaw held much more appeal. He hated the fact that something within his own body hindered him and he had no defense against it. He hated being in a hopeless situation and his frustration boiled over. Slate transferred his staff to his left hand, blocked an overhead blow from Lattimer's sword, and then threw all of his remaining energy into a punch that was sure to fail. Slate didn't care. To the punch he added all his emotion as he transferred his weight from right foot through his hips and into his arm. As he felt the power of his punch move past the traitorous parts of his body that were causing him fatigue, he felt them get swept along with his emotions. Slate's fist came forward and Lattimer easily raised his shield. The shield met his fist at the very moment that all of Slate's energy and emotions transferred from his arm to his fist. The wooden shield splintered and shattered as his hand burst through and connected with Lattimer's jaw in a surprising and utterly satisfying thud. The jaw-bone gave way, Lattimer fell, and blood pooled on the invisible ground as a bugle sounded in the arena. With his adrenaline pumping, Slate raised his bleeding fist in the air and the spectators showered applause onto him.

Amongst the cheering, several members of the Ispirtu Guard who specialized in healing ran toward the combatants. They first checked on the unconscious Lattimer before turning their attention to Slate. Slate wasn't concerned about his hand. If Sana and Lucus could heal and reset a broken rib, a couple scratches from the wooden shield shouldn't be a problem. He was wondering how he had managed to punch through a shield and break his opponent's jaw when he noticed the wizard examining his hand grew quiet. Slate looked into the wizard's eyes and saw a mixture of confusion and anger as he examined Slate's hand; the sight invoked the same emotions in Slate. His hand and forearm had a mixture of scratches and a gouge from the shattered wood, but what lay beneath the broken skin and muscles of his hand was what drew his attention. The bones of his hands looked like the iron ore mined in Pillar.

What had happened to him?

The crowd grew quiet and an orb looked over his shoulder. The image of his hand displayed in the sky above the arena for everyone to see. The crier, feeling the need to fill the deafening silence, quickly trotted over to Slate. He grabbed Slate's wounded arm, lifted it in the air, and proclaimed, "The winner of this year's tournament is a champion with mining in his blood and iron in his bones....let's hear it for Slate 'Stonehands' Severance!"

The crowd again erupted with chants of "Stonehands." Brannon and the attending wizards circled Slate and paraded him out of the courtyard. Slate soaked in the praise of the spectators honoring their new tournament champion, but he got the sinking feeling the attending wizards were less of a parade escort and more of an armed guard synonymous with their name. Whatever happened to him during the match caused great concern to the wizards and his ignorance would not sufficiently answer the pointed questions they were about to ask.

CHAPTER THREE

INVESTIGATIONS

The guardsmen led Slate through a seldom-used tunnel and his exultation dimmed as the lights of the arena faded. The little conversation that did exist between the wizards quickly died away in subservience to Brannon's silence as he guided the group forward. Slate applied pressure to his untreated hand to prevent additional blood loss. Victory provided a temporary boost of energy, but battle fatigue returned quickly as Brannon entered a small room. Several of the guardsmen stayed outside the door as Slate and the others followed.

The room consisted of a basic table and chairs, with some unimpressive artwork depicting arena victors adorning the walls. No one sat. No one offered congratulations. No one offered his tired legs a chair. Brannon grabbed his arm and looked at the open wound with the odd mixture of iron mixed into the bones of his hands. He addressed the wizard who first observed Slate's wounds.

"Did you probe the wound? Is this how it looked immediately following the match?" Brannon demanded.

The wizard, despite her status as a member of the Crimson Guard, answered demurely, "It does appear unchanged from the time of my examination. Upon sight of the unnatural wound I did not probe it further. I did not want to tamper with any residual magic from the spell used to create it or impede any subsequent investigation." A sense of foreboding hung upon Slate with the weight of pick axe after a day in the mines.

Brannon nodded his dismissal and the openly relieved guardsmen left the room. Next, Brannon called forth an elderly mage by the name of Ibson. Ibson approached at a slow yet confident speed and Brannon addressed him. "As the appointed member of the guard responsible for maintaining the integrity of the tournament by monitoring the use of magic, I have failed, warranting an investigation into the matter. Will you lead the investigation on behalf of Ispirtu and the Wizard

Council?"

Ibson accepted and turned toward Slate. "I know you are weary, but would you allow me to use magic to investigate what happened to your hand? After that, you may rest before answering some questions."

Brannon interrupted, "Questioning should occur immediately and this investigation should not draw out unnecessarily."

Ibson casually turned to Brannon. "I am an old man and doing things quickly becomes more challenging at my age. Please pardon my lack of expediency. I promise I will make up for my shortcomings in this area with thoroughness." Brannon's neck started to turn red, but he held his tongue and turned to leave. Before exiting, Ibson stated, "Please do not travel too far, Brannon. I have a few questions for you as well, and I don't travel very well at my age. In fact, I don't lift very well anymore either. Please have one of your men fetch a cot for the champion." Brannon's back straightened before he stormed out of the room. Turning his attention back to Slate, the old man began to investigate his hand.

Ibson probed his hand in the same manner he had addressed Brannon, calmly, confidently, and as promised, quite thoroughly. Ibson danced from cell to cell, tissue to tissue and advanced so slowly it barely felt as if he were advancing at all.

The contrast in styles between Ibson and Brannon reminded Slate of peddlers traveling through Pillar. Some set up shop for one day, only interested in selling their goods and moving on. When these peddlers left town, no one noticed. Others stayed for a week and took the time to have dinner with the families in Pillar, despite their relative poverty and unimportance to the vast majority of the kingdom. These peddlers left as a member of the community and were often given gifts of food and drink for the road ahead.

Ibson finally probed the bones in his hands after spending extensive time in the tissues surrounding them. His findings disrupted his typically calm demeanor and caused him to move his probe completely away from his hands and into his blood. When he was done, he looked sadly at Slate.

"I'm afraid you are going to be very sick in the coming days. I can tell you are tired, but unfortunately it will get much worse. I am stopping now so that I do not fatigue you further. You require a blood transfusion and rest. We all have iron in our blood, but yours is absent.

The iron in your blood currently resides in the bones of your hands."

The shock on Slate's face answered the question of whether or not he knew that this was the case. Ibson continued, "I am sorry this has happened to you, Slate Severance. For the matter of the blood transfusion, direct access to the donor's blood is preferable." He produced a knife from his robes, nicked his finger, and touched the open wound on Slate's hands, joining the two bloodstreams. While blood transfused from Ibson to Slate, Ibson concluded, "Normally I would transfuse portions of several healthy donor's blood into your own, but I cannot risk it because of the investigation. Having too many donors will cloud my ability to probe your blood adequately. Over the coming days, I will transfuse you with my own blood, and you will begin to gain strength again. Meanwhile, you will experience light-headedness, a headache, and potentially a host of other less common symptoms." He then gently clasped Slate's damaged hand and promised, "I'll get to the bottom of this. Sleep well, Champion." When he released Slate's hand, the damage was completely repaired, but the fatigue remained and Slate collapsed onto the cot.

Agony gripped Slate for days. The majority of the day was spent asleep, while a throbbing headache and nauseating dizziness greeted him upon awakening. The first day, Ibson didn't ask him any questions, giving him a transfusion each time he awoke and urging him to eat and get back to bed. The second day was slightly better than the first, and Ibson asked Slate to describe the events in his day leading up to the championship match.

Slate summarized all the pertinent events: his fight with Rainier, the healing of his ribs by Lucus and Sana, the fight with Magnus, meeting the headmasters, and the final match. Even with his attempts at brevity, the oration required numerous breaks to sleep and regain strength. Sometimes he would awake to find Ibson conversing with other wizards or interviewing people related to the chain of events Slate described. Recalling the Sicarius headmaster and the power of information, Slate remained still and caught pieces of the questioning. On one occasion, he heard Ibson conversing with Rainier.

"...the Wizard Council has long respected the customs of the nomadic tribes, both in support of a relatively independent existence from the crown and in...privacy...for the practice of those beliefs."

Ibson continued. "Rainier, I ask your cooperation in confirming or providing additional detail to the events leading up to the final match of the tournament, since you were the only person with Slate the majority of the day."

"Matters of the Wizard Council or the crown rarely coincide with the mission of our tribe." Rainier answered. "But in this instance, I see no areas of conflict either, so long as the teacher/student relationship between myself and Slate is not interfered with. Slate accurately described the events of the day. Are there any specific details that interest you?"

"Let us begin with your match against Slate. He struck a blow that caught you by surprise. To do this to...you...would seem to be a difficult task. Is it possible that magic was involved, in any form?"

"The blow did indeed catch me by surprise, but I do not believe magic was involved. He fought fairly and honorably."

Ibson paused, contemplating his final question. "Did Slate mention a medallion or totem to you? It appears to be made of stone and was strapped to his arm..."

"I was present for the healing of his ribs following our match, and there was no such medallion strapped to his arm at that time. I do not know how it ended up there or when."

Ibson thanked Rainier for his time and Slate began to stir, being careful not to cause suspicion. Opening his eyes, he found Rainier by his side. "Rest and recover Slate. My tribe grows restless staying in one place for too long, but I will remain behind to begin my studies." Rainier maintained the stoicism of a diplomat as he departed.

Ibson slowly made his way toward Slate's bedside. "Are you regaining any of your strength?" the old wizard inquired. He was regaining strength even though the splitting headache remained and he acknowledged as much to Ibson. "Good, good. Your recovery is progressing as expected. I believe we are ready to recommence the investigation of your hand." Slate nodded his permission and Ibson probed throughout his body, spending the majority of his time on Slate's unwounded hand and the location on his arm where he had strapped the medallion. Upon completion, Ibson ordered him to eat and return to bed.

A pounding on the door woke him. "Let me see the champion!" The boisterous voice of Villifor resonated through the door. The door swung open before it could be answered. Villifor's voice and animated expression were offset by the hulking figure of Magnus positioning himself respectfully behind the Bellator headmaster.

"Well fought, Slate! Fractal's fortune to you! A true champion uses all the weapons at his disposal, even if your choice of words was rather…distasteful for some members of the audience. Nonetheless, I have the joy and honor of proclaiming you the tournament champion." Each time Slate's name was mentioned as the champion, Magnus' eyes grew a little darker. "On behalf of the three guilds, you are given the privilege of choosing your areas of training. Having proven your prowess within the arena, I trust you will hone your skills within Bellator."

Slate's silence was met with unfazed confidence from Villifor. "I look forward to you joining us in a few months when you report for training. For now, I will leave you to Ibson to wrap up this little Ispirtu embarrassment and to restore the name of our champion so that you can walk the streets of Ravinai and bask in the glory you have earned. Few have their names spoken throughout Malethya, and I have heard nothing but the tales of Slate 'Stonehands' Severance since your bout." The final compliment was given with a twinkle in his eye that was one part possessive and one part predatory. Slate got the unshakable feeling that Villifor would settle for nothing less than having the now-famous Stonehands as his protégé. Feeling weary from the exaggerated praise, Slate was relieved when his two visitors left him alone to sleep once again.

"You must have reached some conclusions by now!" Slate was jolted awake by the forcefulness of Brannon's voice.

"I have learned some very interesting facts," replied Ibson between sips of tea. "For instance, did you know the mission of the nomadic tribes rarely coincides with the matters of the crown? …a fascinating people indeed. Perhaps when the investigation is done I will spend some time learning more of their culture."

An exasperated Brannon rephrased his question, "Have you reached any conclusions regarding the manner in which Slate circumvented tournament rules?"

"As of yet, I have not. Perhaps if I could ask you about the wards you placed prior to the match I could gain some insight into the matter." Ibson replied.

"For fractal's sake, Ibson! I placed the standard wards for the detection and prevention of magic surrounding myself, Lattimer, and Slate, per tournament rules. The wards detected no magic spells within the dueling courtyard. Slate has less magic in him than I have in my morning crap, and Lattimer would hardly cast a spell giving his opponent the ability to punch through his shield and break his jaw! Even if my untrained son did cast that idiotic of a spell, it would have been detected by any number of wizards within the arena who had cast their own protective wards, including you. Whatever form of magic caused this incident; it was a result of something that happened prior to the championship fight. Now enough games, Ibson! What have you learned?"

"You have a sharper mind than I, Brannon. I fear conclusions take a bit longer for my old mind to reach. However, I take nightly walks that tend to clear my head. Would you care to join me tonight? I believe I will take a walk around the arena. I greatly enjoy the view of the setting sun from the arena heights as it sets upon the city."

"I'll meet you at sunset. If you walk the same speed that you work, you should leave this room now to make it through the tunnels in time." Brannon replied bitingly and left, majestic robes flowing.

Turning to Slate, Ibson said, "As is typical with most wizards, I find myself in agreement with the ever-wise headmaster of Ispirtu; I should start my walk soon. Since you are regaining your strength, could you find Lucus for me and ask him to accompany me on a walk this evening as well?"

Seizing the chance to leave the room he had been confined to for days, Slate answered, "I would gladly find Lucus in partial repayment for your kindness. I thought he would have left with the Tallow tribe. Where might he be?"

"No repayment is needed, Slate. Unfortunately, I do not know where Lucus is located. If I knew that, I wouldn't need you to find him, now would I?" Ibson stated matter-of-factly. "However, if I were looking for him, I would try the grove of catalpa trees south of town. They are flowering this time of year and he is likely seeking such a place following days in the city and the mindless prattle of its people. I'm sure the guardsmen outside will know the way..." Ibson then shook his head in a manner that showed his opinion of having guard members keep an eye on his activities. As Slate rose to leave, Ibson called back to him.

"Yes, Ibson?"

"This is yours, and it should be returned to you." Ibson tossed the Stratego medallion in the air, and Slate caught it. "Being on the Wizard Council, I am not a member of the Crimson Guard and know little of Sicarius, but I do recognize the insignia. Later, I will want to ask you a few questions regarding its import. For now, just consider this: I have been in this world for quite a while and very few people keep their endeavors as secretive as the members of Sicarius. This is not inherently bad, but secrets kept closely are often guarded from outside view because the morals of most people would judge the activities harshly. Be careful in your dealings with them…and in your choice of guilds."

The statement caused Slate to pause, and he felt relief at getting the medallion back. Slate did not want an encounter with the headmaster of Sicarius in which he needed to explain how he had lost the medallion before even starting the game of Stratego. Slate pondered Ibson's comments while leaving, ordering the guardsmen stationed outside his room, "Take me to the catalpa grove south of town by the authority of Ibson." The guardsmen reluctantly acquiesced, telling Slate something about Brannon's standing orders and Ibson's place in the hierarchy. Still, they led Slate down the tunnels.

As they exited the arena, Slate nearly ran headlong into Lattimer Regallo, with Magnus trailing him. Lattimer spoke as he passed by. "There are more deeds done in the Regallo name than there is mining dust in Pillar. You disgrace yourself by your actions in the tournament."

Slate stopped and said, "I don't know the deeds of the Regallo family, but I know how much mining dust is in Pillar. Most people work the mines all their lives and they learn from an early age to set their pride aside before it consumes them. Your pride was your weakness and it made you unworthy of the championship. "

"Tournament champion is simply a title. Once we enter the guard, your title will mean nothing. I look forward to evening the score with you, Slate. I'm sure Magnus would like a chance to spar with you as well." Lattimer smiled and Magnus clenched his jaw, revealing muscles Slate didn't know existed. Lattimer and Magnus retraced the path Slate had just taken with the guardsmen. Could Lattimer and Magnus be meeting with Ibson? Did Ibson ask Slate to find Lucus just to get him out of the room for this meeting? If Ibson didn't mind meeting Brannon in front of Slate, why did he want to question Lattimer in private? Was Ibson even questioning Lattimer, or was he jumping to conclusions? His mind raced as Slate followed the guardsmen out the tunnels of the arena and into the city.

CHAPTER FOUR

AN ALLY LOST

The sunny afternoon infused energy and excitement into the city of Ravinai. The marketplace bustled with patrons searching for fresh vegetables from outlying farms and peddlers selling their wares. Young and old men purchased flowers; the young men attempted to gather favor from the girls at their sides, and the old men tried to pacify their spouses for past transgressions. Merchants yelled, banged pots, and generally did anything they could to garner attention.

Slate took in the sights, sounds, and lively atmosphere while occasionally smiling and waving at citizens who recognized him from the tournament. It was strange and exciting to have complete strangers know your name. The guardsmen tolerated the brief encounters of celebrity and ushered Slate toward the southern outskirts of town.

As the city died away, the added weight in Slate's hand reminded him that he still carried the Stratego medallion. He casually tossed it in the air and the bright sunlight caught the surface. The Stratego medallion now consisted completely of stone, devoid of the iron present before his match. Slate nearly fell on his face, faster than even Magnus had gone down.

He needed to discuss the implications of the medallion's change, but with whom? Ibson was the obvious choice, but he could have switched the original medallion with a stone replica while Slate slept, although the motive for such an act was beyond Slate. Lucus and Sana seemed trustworthy, but he knew so little of them. Rainier? After his conversation with Ibson, the Tallow clan was a bigger mystery than the wizards. If the medallion truly had lost the iron from within, had it ended up in his hand? Was that what the Sicarius headmaster intended? For now, it seemed most wise to keep the information hidden until he knew who was trustworthy.

A few minutes out of town, a simple dirt trail through the woods led to a large glen and a grove of trees at its center. The trees stood nearly fifty feet tall and were covered with groups of trumpeting flowers. Slate assumed these were the catalpa trees, although he had never seen such a tree in Pillar. A man leaned against the trunk of a catalpa tree in the middle of his own private sanctuary, awaiting their arrival.

"Ho, Slate. It's good to see you up and about again. I trust Ibson has healed your wounds." Lucus greeted Slate.

"He has indeed. It's been a difficult few days, but I am feeling much better. Do you know Ibson well?"

Lucus smiled. "You could say that. Ibson was my teacher, and now he remains a friend for whom I have great respect."

"I am to relay a message to you on his behalf…"

"Let us speak privately." Lucus interrupted. "Guardsmen, would you leave us?"

One Crimson Guardsman set her feet defiantly in the ground. "Brannon gave us orders to accompany Slate if he were sent somewhere by Ibson. We will remain."

Lucus responded, "I would not expect you to disobey a direct order, but this investigation is being conducted under the authority of the Wizard Council as requested by Brannon, in order to retain impartiality. This conversation may contain confidential information, so I need to temporarily eliminate your ability to hear our conversation."

The Bellator Guardsmen begrudgingly agreed. "That's acceptable, but don't try any trickery, wizard." Lucus clasped his hands over the ears of a guardsman and looked up to the leaves of the trees. Shortly thereafter, he repeated the procedure for the second guardsman.

Slate began, "You didn't need to go to all that trouble…Ibson just asked for you to accompany him on a walk this evening."

Lucus smiled, "It was no trouble, and now we can speak openly without word of our conversation going directly to Brannon or Sicarius. While we talk, let's help out the catalpas a little bit."

Slate walked with Lucus into the center of the grove and glanced back to find the guardsmen following at a respectful distance. Lucus noticed Slate's interest in the guardsmen and asked, "Are you wondering what I did to them?"

"In the past few days, I was healed using magic three times, had the iron in my blood fused with the bones of my hand, and I am under investigation for something I know nothing about. Yes, you could say I'm interested…"

Lucus laughed and gave Slate his first lecture on magic. "Magic requires two components, the spark and a pattern. Did you notice that I maintained physical contact with the ears of the guardsmen? This is not required, but it reduces the amount of power or spark that the spell requires. The amount of spark that each wizard has is inherent and cannot be changed. Did Brannon test you for the spark when you met him?"

"Yes, he did. He told Ibson his morning crap has more spark than I do."

"That sounds like Brannon," replied Lucus. "I'm afraid that means you won't be able to learn magic. Nonetheless, if you are interested, I will continue to explain the best I can."

"Please, continue…even if I can't practice magic, I would still like to understand it."

The lesson continued. "To cast a spell the spark must be linked to a pattern in which the wizard has a level of understanding. This is best explained as an example, such as our Crimson friends back there. When I looked up at the leaves, I was focusing on the pattern of the wind blowing through the leaves. It tumbled upon itself after encountering a leaf, causing the leaf to move and the wind to change directions. My understanding of this pattern, linked with my spark, recreated the phenomenon within the ears of the guardsmen. The air surrounding their ears tumbles upon itself and prevents sound from entering. I did not deafen the guardsmen. I simply made it so the only sound they hear is tumbling air, much like the rustling of leaves in the trees above."

"Then what happened when Sana tried to heal my broken ribs?"

"Sana understood the pattern to grow bones, but she tied too much spark to it, causing your bones to grow more than she intended. I reversed the pattern and adjusted the spell to counteract the effects. She is still learning, but one day she will be an excellent wizard."

"She let her mistake affect her too greatly. Where did she go?"

"Our relationship is rather loose. I enjoy time alone, and Sana keeps her own schedule. When she is here, I teach her. It is an unconventional match of wizard and apprentice, but in our case, it works quite well. Now, let's help out the catalpa and get back to Ibson."

The flowering trees towered overhead and reformed Slate's view of his place in the world, while Lucus looked upon the trees as he would a long-time friend. The wizard approached a tree that had fallen recently;

its large, heart-shaped leaves were still green. With one powerful swing of his axe, he buried the blade into the heart of the tree trunk. The green leaves turned a sickly brown, falling to the forest floor while the axe blade began to glow. Lucus removed his axe and knelt in the center of the grove, resting his free hand on the forest floor. The remaining buds of the catalpa flowers bloomed before Slate's eyes. First a few flowers, but as the spell radiated outwards, hundreds and then thousands of petals opened. Lucus analyzed the wind passing through the trees and swung his arm in a circle. The wind followed the movement of the axe, creating a gentle breeze that carried pollen from flower to flower. After the flowers pollinated, he thrust the axe upwards and sent the remaining pollen high into the air, where it would disseminate and settle upon distant catalpa flowers.

Lucus lowered his axe and hung it from his belt. The wizard preempted Slate's questions and astonished expression. "An explanation of that spell is beyond your first lesson in magic, and I have other things to discuss. Let's walk."

Slate gathered his senses from the display he just witnessed and matched Lucus' pace on the way to Ravinai and the arena. The Crimson Guardsmen dutifully followed, albeit at a further distance given their newfound respect for Lucus.

Lucus ignored the reactions of the guardsmen and addressed Slate. "I owe you an explanation regarding the Tallow tribe. Do you know what it means to become a teacher?"

"So far, Rainier deserves the title of teacher more than I. He knew my arena opponents and their fighting styles. Rainier made a mistake in choosing me as his teacher."

Before answering, Lucus decided to broaden the conversation. "Do the people of Pillar tell stories of the nomadic tribes to the South? They have developed a certain…reputation."

"No. Merchants and peddlers travel through town occasionally, but we've heard nothing of the Tallow tribe. What reputation?"

"You should form your own opinion, but most villages consider the nomadic tribes to be cut-throats and thieves. They have vast personal wealth and their abilities as fighters lead many to believe it was gained through improper means." Lucus paused to emphasize his point. "I do not believe this is the case. In my time traveling with them, the Tallow tribe exhibited the most admirable of qualities. However, the Tallows are extremely guarded about their beliefs. Very few people understand the nomadic tribes or their motivations. They are cunning fighters and astute merchants, but they do not look for battle or seem interested in attaining additional wealth." Finally, he added, "I must admit though, there is much I do not know of the tribes…"

In Ravinai, the marketplace quieted with the setting sun and the smells of dinner wafted from open windows. Since his time to question Lucus was running short, Slate dug for more information. "You have not mentioned what the nomadic tribes expect from their teachers."

Lucus answered, "I have only witnessed two other teachers being named: a cobbler within Ravinai and a mother of two from an outlying village. This is what brought me to your tent in the first place. I wanted to meet you to understand the tribe better, but I still haven't been able to link any commonalities between you and the other teachers. Whatever reason Rainier chose you for this honor, it does not relate to battle tactics. What are your plans following the tournament?"

"I don't have the means to stay within the city, and the quiet of Pillar could help me sort through life's recent events."

"That is wise. Reflection reduces mistakes, and you have many decisions ahead of you." Lucus ended their conversation. "Ibson is waiting for me." Slate squinted into the setting sun to see the old wizard pacing back and forth in one of the arena's many entrances. The woodsman made a twirling motion with his hand to restore the hearing of the guardsmen and left to meet Ibson.

The guardsmen led Slate back to his empty room and took up post outside the closed door. "Slate, we need to talk." the raspy voice of the Sicarius headmaster floated to him, alternating in both pitch and inflection, leaving no clues to identify the headmaster. Startled, Slate spun and chopped downward where the shock stick had previously touched his neck.

"I'm in the room next to you. After finding where Brannon was holding you, I took up a temporary residence in the adjacent room. I've listened to some of Ibson's conversations through the wall. He is conducting a very thorough investigation, but even taking into account the old wizard's penchant for details, the investigation should be complete by now. Something is amiss."

"Why are you doing this? Are you trying to help me? It is difficult to trust someone I have never met." Slate questioned.

"I don't care whether you trust me, Slate. In my line of work, I am often the bearer of ominous news based on vague and incomplete information. You must be patient and then act decisively according to the information at your disposal, as I do. People are impatient by nature, and that trait is heightened in wizards with magic at their disposal. I'm worried that Brannon's patience with Ibson is ending. If you have any indication that Brannon will assume control of the investigation, find Ibson or Lucus and leave. Investigations conducted under the rule of the Wizard Council are very different from investigations conducted by Ispirtu. It is not an experience I would wish upon anyone..." The Sicarius headmaster ended the one-sided conversation. "My time has run out, as other business in the city requires my attention. If you require a covert escape from Ravinai, use what little skill you have in this area, and I will help where I can. Good luck, Slate."

Slate threw open his door, trying to catch sight of the mysterious headmaster. The surprised guardsman barred his way, and with their attention diverted, a fully cloaked figure slipped out of the adjacent room undetected. The figure bowed slightly to Slate for the diversion he hadn't intended to create, but he suspected the headmaster anticipated his actions from the beginning. The guardsman shouldered Slate back into his room, and the headmaster disappeared into the night.

Alone in his room again, Slate reflected on his encounter with the Sicarius headmaster, the most recent of the puzzles in his life. He understood the headmaster's point...information was information. It was not good, nor bad. It didn't require trust. The holes in the information and the validity of the information was what required trust. Did he trust the headmaster? The alternating voice could have belonged to a man or a woman. The full cloak and a slightly hunched posture left Slate with only the vaguest of physical descriptions. Even the actions of the headmaster were contradictory. A knife to the throat was followed by an apologetic letter placed upon his pillow. The headmaster found him in a guarded room within the depths of the arena to deliver a message of impending danger and the promise of aid if needed. Yet knowing the headmaster had been eavesdropping on him and Ibson for days left him with a sour taste in his mouth.

Before he finished contemplating the morality of the headmaster or devised an ingenious plan of escape, Lattimer entered his room flanked by guardsmen. "Guardsmen, escort the *champion* to my father and don't hesitate to teach the cheater a lesson or two as we go…just don't leave any marks."

A few painful minutes later, Slate entered the arena and located Brannon in the twilight sky. He knelt at the bottom of a set of stairs, but the object of his attention didn't come into view until he got closer. Drops of blood descended the steps and turned into a pool at the bottom. Brannon knelt over an unidentifiable body, his resplendent robes soaking in blood. Brannon placed one hand on the head of the recumbent and a second hand gripped an ornate scepter made of petrified black wood that cradled a large orb upon the distal end. Brannon looked up as they descended toward him and revealed the identity of the fallen figure. The ashen face of Ibson stared lifelessly into the night.

"Get Slate down here!" Brannon barked. The guardsman nearly shoved Slate down the rest of the stairs, while Lattimer stood behind his father and gazed down at Ibson in shock.

"What happened?" Slate managed to spit out.

"He lost a lot of blood from a head injury. I closed the wound, but he needs more blood than I can give. You hold some of his blood within you from your recovery. It is time to repay his kindness."

Brannon grabbed Slate's hand and touched the orb to Ibson's body. The orb glowed. Slate gladly helped heal Ibson, but as time went on Slate weakened. Light-headedness followed and Slate fought to maintain consciousness. Just as his vision began to narrow, the feeling subsided and the orb dimmed. Slate knelt to recover.

"I was able to save his life, but his mind may be irreparably damaged. I will send him to the infirmary in the hopes that they can do more. A pity…" Frustration appeared on Brannon's face. After the brief moment of near humanity, Brannon continued. "This investigation has continued for too long. It has claimed one of the kingdom's best minds and you are not worth that cost. Let us be done with this."

The Sicarius headmaster's warning about Ispirtu investigations came crashing back and a cold fear swept over Slate. The imposing wizard extended his hand toward Slate, blood dripping from the sleeve of his robe. The futility of the Sicarius headmaster's warning struck Slate. A canary had a better chance of escaping the mines of Pillar than Slate had of escaping Brannon.

"Wait." Lucus' voice descended the staircase and Slate never felt so grateful. "What are you doing?"

"What I should have done a long time ago...I'm going to figure out what secrets Slate has been holding."

"This investigation is under the authority of the Wizard Council, is it not?"

"Ibson is unable to carry out his duties. I plan to put this mess behind us." Brannon spoke with finality.

Lucus tried to temper Brannon's resolve. "You were the last person to see Ibson before his accident. How would it look if you closed out the investigation? Even the Regallo name would not sufficiently withstand the criticism and scrutiny of such an act. Would you agree to let me investigate? I already tire of the incessant chatter of the city and wish to leave. I would be most expedient in the manner involving Slate."

The sound logic convinced Brannon. "Be done with it then."

"To do the job properly, I'll need some help." Lucus inclined his head toward Brannon's scepter.

Brannon laughed a joyless laugh accentuated by the silence in the air that followed. "I suppose you do need help, woodcutter. Hold up your axe."

Lucus ignored the condescension in Brannon's voice and held up his axe.

Axe touched scepter and the orb glowed brilliantly, transmitting an orange hue to the axe. When the axe reached a steady but dim glow, Lucus took back his axe and spoke to Slate. "This spell will give me access to all of your memories, feelings, and thoughts leading up to the championship bout, as well as your conversations with Ibson. I apologize for the invasiveness, but it will help us to conclude the investigation." The look on Lucus' face was truly apologetic. He did not wish to do this.

More than anything, the anguish of Lucus convinced Slate that this was the best course of action. With the axe dimming slightly, Slate provided his answer quickly by meeting the eyes of Lucus and nodding. Lucus touched Slate's hands.

Ripping. Pain. Confusion.

Instantaneously, it was done. Slate collapsed to his knees. Touching Lucus, Slate felt he lost part of his self. He was not just exposed or naked, but part of him had been *taken*. His memories were intact, and he couldn't pinpoint anything physically wrong, but Slate understood the anguish on Lucus' face before the spell began. Lucus collapsed as well, remaining on his knees even after Slate recovered. Lucus eventually opened his eyes and Slate helped him to his feet. The man had been through a lot.

Brannon's patience was at an end. "What did you uncover, woodcutter?"

Lucus gained strength in his voice as he spoke. "The iron in Slate's blood merged with the bones in his hand. Ibson had decided to exonerate Slate from any wrongdoing since his lack of spark precluded the ability to cast such a spell. Slate should retain the title of tournament champion. Whatever was done to Slate was done by a third party and without his knowledge. The identity of the third party has been lost along with Ibson's mind."

"Pitiful. Two of the Wizard Council's most prominent wizards have failed to identify Slate's accomplice. Meanwhile, the Regallo name has been irreparably damaged by these proceedings." Brannon sneered at Lucus and then turned toward Slate. "All past champions earned the right to choose training in Ispirtu, Bellator, or Sicarius. Ispirtu is open to you, but you will not be welcomed there. Now leave me as I tend to Ibson."

Lucus had recovered a great deal in the short time Brannon addressed him with some of the gauntness disappearing and the color returning. The wizard helped Slate back to the arena exit before saying, "You planned to return to Pillar. I would travel with you if you allow it."

The request surprised Slate, but of all the mystery and intrigue building in his life, Lucus was the one person who had provided some answers. He didn't want to miss the opportunity for a few more. "It would be an honor, but I fear Pillar won't offer much to your liking. It is a small town that survives by the rock beneath it. The people are as simple as the soup they make for lunch."

Lucus smiled. "After all this, a good cup of soup and simple conversation sounds pretty nice. I've had my fill of Ravinai, wizards, and cleverness for a while. Let's find Rainier and prepare to leave. Is there anything you need from your room?"

"I left my travel sack and staff. The guardsman took me before I could grab it." The wizard and the famous fighter now known as Stonehands took a short detour to Slate's room before exiting through the maze of arena tunnels.

Slate stopped and looked back at the arena. The four quadrants had moved back to their original positions and the floor consisted of normal, everyday sand. Everything appeared as it had the first time he laid eyes on it, and yet it looked completely different to Slate. The arena was the site of his greatest triumph, a place where people from all of Malethya had cheered his name, but the victory came with consequences. He could live with the changes to his hand, but the investigation introduced a whole host of questions and Slate was at the center of it all. Even with the investigation officially closed thanks to Lucus, Slate felt like the journey was only beginning and the questions were coming faster than the answers.

CHAPTER FIVE

ESCAPE FROM RAVINAI

"Where should we look for Rainier?" Slate asked Lucus as they walked the lamp-lit streets of Ravinai.

"You don't find a tribesman by looking for them." The wizard offered no further explanation. "Let's get out of the city as fast as possible."

"Should I expect trouble?"

"Brannon's name carries more import than every name other than the king's, and some say more. Many will seek to avenge your achievement in the championship bout to curry his favor. We should leave until some other perceived slight has arisen and dulled people's memories of your own."

The Sicarius headmaster's promise to master his surroundings made Slate wonder if the first step was the realization that he was completely exposed in the well-lit streets. "If what you say is true, anyone on the lookout for us would spot us quite easily on this lamp-lit street."

"What do you suggest?"

"Let's slip through the darkened alleys and exit the western part of the city. The alleys will help avoid notice and people would expect us to take the main road to the north."

Lucus agreed to Slate's plan and they entered into the first alleyway. Slate stopped to adjust his eyes to the darkness, staff at the ready. After a moment the crates and refuse of the alley came into view, and the two companions made their way forward. Shuffling feet identified an attacker behind the crates. Slate swung his staff only to connect with wood and send the crates tumbling along the alley floor. An agitated cat hissed up at Slate before leaping to a windowsill and eyeing Slate suspiciously. A muted chuckle from Lucus forced Slate to swallow his pride and calm his nerves. There were many alleyways in the city, and he needed his instincts intact.

Slate and Lucus traversed the alleyways of Ravinai slowly, but with each street crossed, Slate became more confident in his abilities to navigate the city and distinguish the sounds of rats and alley cats from more dangerous foes. Most importantly, they avoided contact with people, any one of whom could be a supporter of Regallo. The buildings decreased in size and spread out as they neared the outskirts of the city, consisting mainly of pubs and taverns in which the locals appeared to be excellent patrons.

Slate peered at a tavern entrance from the cover of darkness when a drunken argument spilled into the street. Steel flashed, but no alarms were raised, indicating this was a common event in this region of the city. The fight drew a crowd of revelers, however, and Slate wanted to circle around the commotion. He signaled to Lucus and reversed course.

Retreating through the alley, a silhouetted figure appeared ahead with a sword unsheathed. Before Slate attacked, Lucus mimicked the shrill cry of a meadowlark and the figure ahead returned the song of a sparrow. Lucus' hand fell on Slate's shoulder and he whispered, "Relax. Rainier has found us."

Relief flooded Slate. He could handle a single attacker, but the sounds of fighting would have drawn the attention of the drunken mob in the street. "Ho, Rainier," Slate greeted the tribesman in low tones.

"Ho, Teacher. The city is still abuzz with talk of Stonehands Severance. I even heard a few peddlers advertising trips to Pillar with promises of tours into the depths of the iron mines to find the secret to your success..." Slate flashed a smile at the thought but hoped people didn't spend their hard-earned money on such lies. If they did, they almost deserved to lose it. Rainier asked, "Why are you leaving like a thief in the night rather than the champion you are?"

"I'm a champion that has made some enemies. One of them has gravely injured Ibson, the wizard in charge of investigating my Stonehand and I may be next on the list. I've offended the Regallos, and their supporters might hope to avenge the family name in the form of a battered and bloodied tournament champion."

"Ah, offend you did, and it worked beautifully. Well fought! Now, let's get out of this city." Rainier greeted Lucus and the group went down a few alleys to gain some distance from the drunken crowd. Slate found the quietest section of the tavern-filled street and, despite being better lit than he preferred, darted across the street. A jovial patron exited a nearby pub as Slate was fully exposed in street light and recognition spread across his face followed by a boisterous greeting. "Ho, Stonehands! Fractal's grace! Let me buy you a drink!" His exuberance was only surpassed by the volume of his voice. It drew the attention of the nearby crowd and Slate fled. Preferring speed to stealth, Slate led the group through the city streets until they reached a small park that provided plenty of darkness in which to regroup and strategize.

Rainier spoke first. "A group left the crowd to chase us, but we distanced ourselves from them."

Lucus added, "Unfortunately, our pursuers gave away our direction of travel to Brannon's supporters. Our night is not done yet…"

On cue, a group of ten men appeared from a side street brandishing lights and an amalgam of weaponry. The leader of the group carried a mace in one hand and a lamp in the other. They appeared too surly to have been drinking. His followers had less intimidating short swords, but Rainier had already proven they were formidable weapons if used correctly.

Slate had chosen this spot to see their attackers coming, but there was nowhere to escape unseen either. Streets surrounded the park on all four sides and the low shrubbery didn't provide adequate cover to sneak away.

"We have to face them. We are outnumbered, but we don't have enough cover to hide or escape. Lucus, do you have much experience in battle?"

"I prefer not to engage in battle, but I've picked up a few tricks during my travels. My greatest asset in these circumstances involves using magic on both of you." The Regallo supporters crossed the street to search the far corner of the park. Slate knew they had only a few seconds to finalize their plans.

"Absolutely." Slate answered for both him and Rainier, eager for the wizard to provide him with extra strength or speed or anything that would give a physical advantage in the coming fight. Lucus touched Slate's leather armor and an area of exposed skin. After Lucus completed his spell, Slate flexed his muscles and was disappointed to feel convincingly normal. He was unsure what the wizard's spell had accomplished, but then he looked across to Rainier and saw the astonished expression on his face.

Lucus repeated touching Rainier's armor and skin. Seconds later,

Slate understood Rainier's reaction; Rainier disappeared. Slate strained his eyes into the darkness and was able to locate Rainier, but he blended into the shrubbery and park bushes.

Lucus whispered, "I have studied animals in the woods and I know their patterns well. Some are able to blend into their surroundings quite remarkably. Be thankful their secrets are yours tonight. I have enough strength left to also hinder our attackers. I will place the wind in their ears as I did to the guardsmen. These spells will take the majority of my remaining strength, so I will hide in our current location and maintain the spells as long as I can. Fractal's fortune." The wizard lay in the bushes.

Their attackers whispered from their location in the middle of the block-long park, presumably about the noise in their ears, and soon were shouting their frustrations, angered at their inability to hear their own voices. Slate took the left side of the group and Rainier the right, dropping two assailants immediately with well-placed blows. Slate jabbed his staff into the base of his opponent's neck, knocking him out. Rainier cleanly sliced the hamstrings of an unsuspecting swordsman. His wails were deafening to all but his compatriots as he writhed upon the ground.

The remaining Regallo supporters recovered quickly considering their circumstances. They formed a circle with their backs to each other, drawn weapons facing out. One of them was a bit slow and Slate took out his knee, followed by a blow to the head. The group of seven swung defensively in front of themselves, attempting to survive attackers they took to be prey, prey that silently blended into the night.

The leader of the brigands had more wits than Slate gave him credit for. He snuffed his lamp, throwing the entire park into near darkness and reducing the advantage of Lucus' spell. Slate tried to slip his staff between the twirling mace and short swords but did not connect. From the clashing of metal opposite of him, it sounded as if Rainier was having the same issue until one of the soldiers screams filled the night air. Six left.

Slate tried to sweep the leader's feet, but the large brigand jumped and brought the mace down directly toward Slate's head. Slate rolled away, hearing the air whoosh past him. His body had reappeared, signaling Lucus had tired of holding the spells. Any warning to Rainier would have to wait as the Regallo supporters retook the offensive.

Three brigands set upon Slate, and he was overmatched. He used his staff to keep some distance, but the leader managed to flank him. He threw an overhead blow with his mace that Slate was forced to block with his wooden staff, snapping it in two. The large man lifted Slate up by the neck with one hand and squeezed. Slate looked directly into the eyes of his unknown attacker and saw a mix of joy and satisfaction. The revulsion Slate felt for this man was overpowering and yet he knew he was at an end. The pressure increased behind his eyes and his eyelids closed for the last time.

Slate awoke on the ground and found Rainier kneeling over him. "You saved my life..." Slate forced painfully from his throat.

"Not this time, Teacher." Rainier slowly helped Slate to his feet and he saw the mace-wielding brigand lying on the ground. A dart was embedded deep in the side of his neck.

"I was fending off the short swordsmen when they suddenly dropped to the ground. I didn't see where the darts came from..." A throwing knife plunged into the ground between their feet, burying itself to the hilt and pinning a note with the now familiar insignia of Sicarius emblazoned upon it.

Slate and Rainier looked in the direction of the knife throw. A dark figure stood atop the rooftop of the closest building, basking in the dim ambience of the city at night. The figure gave a slight bow and then leapt gracefully to an adjacent rooftop, landing softly and gaining speed as the headmaster attended whatever other matters were of interest in the darkness of the night.

Slate reached down and dislodged the throwing knife. The weight of the simple blade was offset by the intricate hilt displaying engravings of flowering catalpa trees. Slate pocketed the perfectly balanced weapon and opened the note.

Dear Slate,

I followed your progress during your covert exit of Ravinai. You are as predictable as Brannon's mood, as loud as Villifor, and slower than I thought imaginable. Currently, you appear perplexed by the thought of crossing a street full of drunken idiots. If you had dressed in something besides the same armor that you wore for the tournament, walked with a slow meander and sang a slurred song into the ear of Lucus and Rainier as they helped you cross the street, no one would have noticed you. You also seem to have a penchant for the grime and refuse of dark alleys and take sadistic joy in scaring cats. Personally, I find the night air and view much better from the rooftops of the city.

Oh good, you have conquered your fear of the drunken idiots and made a frantic dash across the street, hoping beyond hope that no one on the crowded street in front of you would notice. Alas, your plan failed and the inevitable mad dash across the city begins. Some drunkards are following you and others have gone to alert your true opponents for the evening. I will follow after I finish my thoughts and provide help if needed.

The world does not follow the rules of the tournament. No one carries a wooden sword. Your opponents will not be half-trained sparring partners. For whatever reason, this world has given you an important part to play, even if the exact role is still being defined. You will need every advantage afforded to you to compete in a world full of wizards. Take this time to train before you truly need it. If you have not started your game of Stratego before our next encounter I will take it as a sign that Sicarius, and my aid, hold little interest for you.

PS – catalpa trees have long been revered as symbols of wisdom within Sicarius. I do not believe your actions in the catalpa grove with Lucus were coincident, nor my choice in throwing knives for the evening. Consider it a gift.

Slate folded the note, letting his emotions tumble upon themselves as they usually did after an encounter with the enigmatic headmaster. His life had been saved but at the last possible second. He had been tracked effortlessly, and the entire battle could have been avoided if the headmaster provided aid navigating the city. Slate clenched his jaw and buried his frustrations, looking up to Rainier.

"Let's get Lucus and get out of here. I'm tired of this city and its people." Nonetheless, the Sicarius headmaster's words regarding wooden swords inspired Slate to retrieve a pair of short swords from their incapacitated foes.

"Agreed…He may need our help if he pushed himself too hard." Rainier checked on Lucus. The wizard breathed shallowly but his eyes focused when Rainier came into view.

"So we won? Hand me my axe." The woodcutter rasped.

Rainier lectured the wizard. "You should not have exerted yourself in that way. You won't be able to travel for days." Slate unhooked Lucus' axe and placed it in his hands. Lucus closed his eyes, and the color returned to his face as the axe drained of color.

"Thanks, Brannon. Well, let's go." Lucus jumped to his feet and smiled before explaining his sudden energy. "I have never had a very strong spark, and I know my limits very well. Brannon's limits are so high that he didn't notice when I stored a little extra from his scepter in my axe for just such an occasion. I will need several days to recover fully, but at least now I have the strength to travel." The three headed west and exited the city with the warmth of the rising sun against their backs.

CHAPTER SIX

CAMPFIRE STORIES

Lucus, the master woodsman, led the group into the forested countryside, paying no heed to roads, as they traveled cross-country toward Pillar. For several days, no one mentioned the events that had occurred in Ravinai. It was as if some mutual moratorium had been placed on all things related to the tournament, guilds, headmasters, or magic. Slate knew this was temporary, but the simple pleasure of traveling through the woods provided a welcome distraction from processing all the people and mysteries that had recently entered his life.

They ate breakfast in a wooded glen one morning, but when Slate began repacking his travel sack, Lucus stopped him. "If you aren't in too much of a hurry to get home, we might stay here a little longer."

Lucus had kept a steady pace since leaving Ravinai. Meals weren't rushed, but they didn't waste time either. They had covered nearly twenty miles each day, and taking an extended break after a meal wasn't a part of their established routine. "In a hurry? No, I suppose I'm not. What makes this glen different from the other sections of forest we have travelled through?"

A meadowlark cried within the heavy woods. "An excellent question…but I don't think we will have to wait very long after all." The woodsman mimicked the song of a sparrow and Sana emerged from the wood.

She managed to maintain her elegance as she unceremoniously dropped her travel sack and reclined on the grassy knoll. With all the life-threatening activities of the past few days, his initial impressions of Sana had been largely suppressed, but they came back quickly in her presence.

"Glad to see you received my message." Lucus welcomed his apprentice.

"You know I can't resist a cryptic message to meet at a time and place with a description indecipherable to anyone but me."

"I sent that message after meeting Ibson and hearing the worry in his voice," Lucus explained to the group. He turned to Sana, "His investigation of Slate became more complicated than he anticipated and if something were to happen to him he wanted me to clear Slate's name and get him safely out of Ravinai. Unfortunately, Ibson's words proved prophetic. He fell down the stairs of the arena while on his evening walk. Given that Ibson was the most careful and deliberate man I ever met, I find it unlikely that he forgot to look for the next step in front of him…"

"Why didn't you stay to investigate Ibson's accident?" Sana questioned.

"Ibson asked me to look after Slate, not to track down his attacker. I have no intention of letting the issue die, however."

"Where is Ibson now?" Concern for the old wizard was evident upon Sana's face.

"Brannon transferred him to the infirmary. If his mind is muddled as Brannon described, they have the only facilities available for treatment."

"I would like to visit him," Slate stated.

"And I'm sure he would appreciate the visit," Sana tried to catch up on recent events by addressing Slate. "How did you meet up with Lucus and Rainier?" Rainier and Slate recounted the steps of their final evening in Ravinai, embellishing slightly upon the retelling. In Rainier's version, he felled three Crimson Guardsmen in their battle to exit Ravinai. Slate caught a blade on his stonehand and broke it in two with a quick snap of his fingers. The two points of the story that remained without alteration were Lucus' intervention with Brannon and the heroic acts of the Sicarius headmaster.

Sana's face showed incredulity and amazement as she listened, and true pleasure at hearing the tale recounted. She seemed to easily ascertain the true parts of the story from the conjured ones and enjoyed the story even more for having to dissect the truth from it. Sana eyed Lucus meaningfully during the telling of how the investigation ended. His silence was response enough for her to refrain from asking questions at the moment. Instead, she focused her questions on the Sicarius headmaster.

"The headmaster followed you through the city, and you had no idea? I've heard stories of the Sicarius headmaster but most were as fantastical as Slate breaking a blade by snapping his fingers." Slate laughed. Storytelling was a fine art, and he appreciated when someone let him know he had taken it too far.

Rainier admired the prowess of the headmaster as well. "To stick a dart in someone's neck while engaged in battle is a formidable task. To do it at night from a rooftop is the sort of thing that inspires exaggeration."

Slate displayed the headmaster's throwing knife, which drew admiration from the group and reminded Slate of the note attached to it. Slate wasn't ready to forego aid from the headmaster, so he pulled out the Stratego token.

"The Sicarius headmaster gave me this token during the tournament for use in a game called Stratego. Rainier, the teacher/student relationship is foreign to me, but I'd like Stratego to be the first lesson for both of us. The objective is to obtain the Stratego token. You must catch the other unaware, either by stealth, thievery, or unexpected incapacitation, but it cannot be forcefully obtained through direct combat."

Rainier pondered his first task as a student and asked, "Can I see the token I'm supposed to steal from you?" Slate handed him the Stratego token. Rainier turned the stone over in his hands a few times while asking more questions. "How does the game end? How does one win Stratego?"

"I need to have the Stratego token in my possession if I enlist in Sicarius. I haven't chosen a guild, so it is merely competition until then."

"Ok, that sounds simple enough, and it wouldn't be the first time someone tried to steal from a tribesman."

Slate reached for the token. "Let's start."

Rainier continued turning the token in his hands. "I thought we'd already started."

"I was just explaining the rules..." answered Slate.

"Did you expect me to keep the token when you handed it to me?"

"No"

"Then I caught you unaware."

Slate was about to argue when a mischievous laugh from Sana interrupted him. Lucus, too, chuckled and Slate realized he had been tricked. "Well played, Rainier. You make the Tallow tribe proud."

Lucus offered cordially.

"It appears the mighty tournament champion has not only hands of stone but the wits of one too," Sana said.

Slate wanted to change the subject from his failed attempt at Stratego. "Speaking of stones and hands, I need to find out what this thing is good for. I didn't dare use it when we left Ravinai because I didn't know its capabilities." Slate made a fist with his stonehand.

"I'll help you incorporate your stonehand into your fighting technique. Combat seems to find you on a regular basis, so you should prepare." Rainier suggested.

Sana added, "And I can help test the limits of what you can do…and help mitigate risks in the testing. It is a subject I spent time considering while away and have already devised my first test." Slate accepted both offers and Sana continued, "We could begin now. The test requires a flat stump that sits under a large, overhanging tree and a stone." Trees and stones were abundant in the heart of the woods, so they began their morning walk and promptly located such a setup. "Lucus, could you level the stump?"

The woodcutter lived up to his name by taking out his axe and cutting through the stump in one fell swing. Lucus needed several cuts to clear the surface of the large stump, but when he was done, no marks distinguished where one swing ended and the next began. The stump was as level and smooth as a tabletop.

Sana then put on her own display of magic. Walking to the underbrush, she located a vine and held out her hand. The vine untangled its chokehold and wound up Sana's arm into a perfect coil. Sana's next directions came before the vine finished coiling. "Could you and Rainier lift up that stone?" Sana pointed to a moss-covered boulder in the nearby forest. Forces of nature had failed to move that rock for ages, but Slate didn't want to concede defeat.

"Of course we can…" Rainier refused to display weakness as well, so the two begrudgingly walked to the boulder. With effort driven by pride, they heaved the stone upward and held it a few shaky inches off the ground. Sana motioned them toward the stump and the two waddled over, managing to position the stone several inches above the flattened surface.

Sana went to work. The coils of vine flew off her arm at an astonishing rate, laying down an intricately woven pattern upon the stump. Slate would have been impressed if he could think about anything besides not dropping a boulder on his foot. Sana finished. "All ri….thump…ght, you can put it down now." Rainier and Slate dropped the boulder onto the net of woven vines at the first sign of completion. "Good…now we just need a pile of stones roughly the weight of the first stone."

After scavenging the woods to collect stones, Slate returned to see Sana's plan come together. The vine web enclosed the stone and formed a rope that wrapped over a large tree branch. The other end of the grapevine formed a second web in which he placed his collection of stones. Sana created a pulley system like the ones used in Pillar's mines, with the small stones used as a counterbalance to the large stone, but how it would help test his hand he had no idea.

"Rainier, your job for this test will be to add in or take out the small stones as I request. You can start by adding in a few until the large stone is suspended above the stump." Rainier added stones to the basket and eventually the large stone lifted off the stump, just as Sana described.

"Great…now Slate, the test begins. Please place your hand on the stump."

Slate assessed the potential damage of a falling boulder. "I thought you said I should mitigate the risks of testing my hand." Sana was unwavering. "Your hand now has stone in it. We need to find out if it is as strong as stone or not. The test is perfectly safe and controlled. We can place as much or as little weight as we need to on your hand by adding or subtracting small stones into the basket at Rainier's end. I have triple checked my calculations for the strength of the vine rope that is needed and, as you can see, it holds the weight of the stone just fine."

Logic and trust don't always agree with each other. Even Sana's arguments and his own observation did nothing to encourage his participation. In the end, he decided he needed to trust someone, and Lucus, Sana, and Rainier had been more helpful to him than anyone else in Ravinai. Slate knelt by the stump and laid his hand flat.

Sana consulted briefly with Lucus, who appeared content to let his apprentice take the lead on testing Slate's hand. She then asked Slate, "May I probe your hand during the test to monitor what is going on?"

"Yes, if it will make the experiment safer…" Slate felt Sana begin to probe his hand. She signaled Rainier to remove stones, dropping the boulder toward Slate's hand. The boulder applied slight pressure upon his hand, but no pain accompanied it. Sana spent a few minutes probing the bones, stone, and soft tissues of his hand before she was satisfied. She signaled additional stones to be removed. Slate's hand began to go numb and Rainier added stones to raise the boulder.

"The stone embedded in your bones is supporting the weight of the boulder. The numbness occurred because the vasculature of your hand compressed, eliminating blood flow to your muscles and the soft tissues surrounding the bones. Once you regain the feeling in your hand, we can modify the test and begin again." Slate flexed his hand a few times and placed it back on the stump. This testing wasn't so bad after all.

"Rainier, do you remember how many stones were in the basket when we stopped the test?" Rainier nodded. "Lucus, can you pull down on the rope until Rainier gets the right number of stones in the basket?" The wizard played the part of apprentice and did as he was told, pulling down the rope until it raised a foot above Slate's hand.

"Lucus, please let go of the rope." The rope rubbed against the tree branch as the boulder descended.

"What?!" Slate managed to ask before the boulder fell onto his hand. The weight was immense, but his hand felt only slightly more pressure than during the previous test.

"It's the same amount of weight as last time but with a dynamic load. I believe your hand can withstand a large load for a short period of time, and this is one way to test my theory." They continued until the boulder was nearly at the height of the tree branch. Rainier had helped Lucus to pull it up that far and Sana signaled to let go of the rope. The noise of the rope sliding over the tree branch was interrupted with a loud "Snap!" The full weight of the boulder crashed down onto the stump, pinning Slate's hand against the stump and popping his shoulder out of socket as his body dove away from the boulder and his arm stayed still. The boulder rolled off his hand and everyone rushed toward him.

Sana, already probing the hand, extended her search into his shoulder. "It's dislocated." Slate didn't need magic to tell him that. He sat up and looked to Rainier. "Do you know how to do this?"

"I've seen it done before, but I've never done it myself." Before a magical solution could be offered up, Slate responded. "Good enough for me. Go for it." Rainier put one hand on Slate's shoulder and pulled while applying pressure against his collarbone. The relief was immediate and left him with only soreness surrounding his shoulder.

Sana refused to acknowledge failure and turned defiant. "This test exceeded my expectations and proves my theory correct. Your hand can withstand a great amount of weight, but if the weight is applied for extended periods of time you stand the risk of damaging the soft tissues in your hand." She left to repack her travel bag before anyone dared to contradict her stated results of the study.

Slate inspected the vine rope. It had frayed on the tree branch and finally snapped. Lucus explained, "Sana calculated how much force the vines could hold and created the rope accordingly. For the original test she planned that was sufficient, but when she altered her test plans to include dynamic loading, she failed to consider that friction from the tree branch would cause abrasion of the rope. It was a clever test, and it was an understandable mistake, a mistake I don't think she'll make again. Besides, she is right. We learned a lot about your hand today, and you're walking away good as new." The woodcutter clasped him on the shoulder and the soreness instantly melted away.

"If that was successful, I'd hate to be a part of a test that went wrong," Rainier commented with a shake of his head.

"I think I prefer fighting…it's a lot less dangerous."

The two returned to camp and found Lucus packing next to a silent Sana. They took their cue from the wizard, packed their travel sacks and resumed the morning march without further agitating the temperamental apprentice. The silent walk eased Sana's tensions and by the time their empty stomachs forced them to stop for lunch, she broke the silence in the group. "Slate, tell us about Pillar. I have never been to that part of the kingdom and prefer to know something of a place before I visit."

Rainier and Lucus lean forward to listen. There weren't many reasons to talk about Pillar and even fewer to be interested. "As we get closer, the forest floor will turn rocky. Eventually the dense forest will lose the battle with the hard earth and only the hardiest trees will remain. The only thing tougher than the trees of Pillar are the people who live there. The town sits in the foothills of a small mountain range. The winters, when the winds change course and blow to the west, are fierce, as the mountains tend to increase the snowfall. The warming spring temperatures cause flooding of the rocky ground and make farming difficult. The people in Pillar mine iron ore, which is sent to King Darik's refineries to the east. It was said the King wanted to build the refineries in Pillar, but he couldn't find enough people willing to live there." Slate finished with a prideful smile. Most people could not understand why anyone would live in Pillar. For the people that chose to make Pillar their home, it came with a strong and innate sense of community pride. They lived where most people could not, and there was honor in that.

"Does your family work the mines?" Sana asked.

"No, my father does some basic iron working for the townspeople and makes trips to the forest to gather wood and hunt in preparation for winter. My mother repairs the machinery in the mines when something breaks down and salts the meat of any animal that can be caught. I live on my own now, but I am learning the trades of both my parents. Everyone in Pillar has several jobs within the community. There aren't enough people for it to be any other way."

"How did you learn to fight?" Lucus, the pacifist, asked to Slate's surprise.

"My father served in King Darik's army during the Twice-Broken Wars. In my younger years, I collected wood with my father and would always be swinging a stick at something. He tired of watching me flail around and decided to teach me proper technique. Fighting was discouraged in Pillar because training took time away from more essential tasks, but my father reasoned if we completed our obligations to the community, then our time was our own. We sparred on a regular basis without anyone in town knowing."

"Do you know much about the Twice-Broken Wars?" Lucus asked.

"No one talked about them."

"The people of Malethya often speak of the Twice-Broken Wars as one war because the fighting never stopped. Ships arrived on the southern shores of Malethya bearing strangers called Disenites. They landed and awed the citizens with technology that couldn't be understood in terms of the link and spark of magic. The Disenites took offense to the use of magic and the peaceful encounter turned violent, with the Disenites quickly capturing the port cities. The independent nobles fell one-by-one to the invaders, losing their land to weapons they could not match. Except for one group. Villifor led a small group of soldiers that stemmed the tide, attacking the Disenites quickly and then disbanding into the countryside before a counterstrike could be coordinated. The villagers of Malethya welcomed and hid his soldiers and with his success in defying the Disenites, the name Villifor became legend. Villifor's success gave Darik time to band the remaining nobility and form an army, but more ships arrived and it became clear that they were fighting a losing battle. Darik ordered the wizards in his command to attack the invading army directly, spewing fire and roiling the earth beneath their feet, leaving death and scorched earth in their wake."

"The success of the wizards against the Disenites caused much relief and controversy in Malethya. Darik believed magic should be used in the protection of Malethya and support was widespread due to the recent attacks. A smaller group of wizards and soldiers who saw the destruction firsthand tried everything within their power to prevent the use of magic in battle again. They saw a distinct difference between enchanting weapons or armor and using magic directly as a weapon. Factions broke away from the King's army and the Civil War erupted in an attempt to supplant King Darik. The fighting was the most brutal the kingdom had ever seen, but in the end, the use of magic in battle gave King Darik an advantage that proved insurmountable for ordinary soldiers. The war ended, but it has not changed the beliefs of everyone in Malethya. Ispirtu and the Wizard Council were established after the Civil War as a place of study for wizards that either agreed or disagreed with the use of magic in battle. Since that time, other disagreements have arisen between the two groups, but that is the main difference."

"Is that why you chose not to fight in Ravinai the other night?" Rainier asked.

"Yes, but without any training in its use during battle I would have been as likely to kill you as hurt your opponents."

"Does the Wizard Council want to see King Darik supplanted?" Rainier asked.

"He has kept the peace for decades, as your father said. For me, that is enough. We have enjoyed a peaceful, if not altogether pleasant, relationship with Ispirtu and it is because of King Darik."

"Slate, I'm confused about part of your story. If no one in Pillar was supposed to know you could fight, how did you end up in the tournament?" Rainier asked.

"I traveled to a neighboring, albeit distant, village to trade for some gears to replace a few that had chipped teeth. I took my staff in case I ran into a bandit in my travels. When I got to the town, they were hosting the preliminary matches. I thought it would be fun, but then I kept winning. I returned home with an invitation to fight in the arena. I packed my things and told the townspeople the news. I knew fighting was against Pillar tradition, but they seemed even more irate than I'd expected. Even my father remained reserved at the news of the arena, despite his obvious pride. As he sent me on my way toward Ravinai, his only advice was to remember the lessons learned in Pillar and to remain true to my beliefs."

Lucus eased Slate's concerns. "Time eases tensions and everyone will be excited for your return. There will be time for more stories on the road ahead." The subtle hint cued the group to resume their travels.

After a long afternoon and a hearty dinner, Rainier told Slate it was time for sparring. They found some open space and donned leather armor. Each brought their short swords, but Slate wanted to hear Rainier's plan before starting. If it involved boulders he was going right back to camp.

"Well, Teacher, I've been thinking the entire day's march about how your stonehand could help you in combat. I don't believe it is any benefit while wielding short swords."

"There must be something I can use it for…"

"I also realize I will not convince you this is true without devoting our first session to proving my point. Let's fight. No heavy blows or head shots. Stop at the loss of a weapon or an open blow."

Slate couldn't think of anything better. He had come to Ravinai to fight, but since the tournament ended, everything he knew had been turned upside down. It was oddly comforting to get back to something he knew he was good at.

They touched swords, and the comforting feeling disappeared as Rainier proved his proficiency with his preferred weapon. Time after time, Rainier disarmed Slate or ended the match with a light touch of his armor.

Slate tried to figure out ways of incorporating his hand into his technique, but punching or catching a sword were the only options. He tried punching once or twice, but the motion was much slower than the wrist flick it took to defend it with a short sword. Catching a moving sword seemed like the definition of idiocy, but it did give him an idea.

When Rainier swung from his right side, Slate dropped his sword and caught Rainier's incoming blade. The sharp blade snapped in two, but Slate looked down and saw blood dripping from his enclosed fist.

"What were you thinking?!?" Rainier dropped his weapons and rushed over to Slate and inspected his cut hand.

Rainier bent over to examine the wound, and Slate's plan came to fruition. He brought the pommel of the short sword in his left hand down lightly on the back of Rainier's neck...just enough of a blow to knock him out. Slate bent down and extracted the Stratego medallion from Rainier's care. Rainier woke up a few seconds later with a headache fueled by angst. Slate flipped the medallion in the air. "Sorry about the knock to the head. I saw an opportunity and after all, it is within the rules of Stratego."

"You're right. It is within the rules." Rainier's tone left no doubt about his feelings concerning Stratego's rules.

Slate then walked over to Sana, who had quietly watched match after match. "Would you heal my hand?"

"I am not some bar wench who brings you drinks after you have already proven yourself inebriated. You continue to hurt yourself in idiotic ways. This display was the worst of all; you betrayed the trust of your friend to get some stupid medallion. Well, you've damaged Rainier's trust and hurt your hand for the sake of possessing the Sicarius toy. Heal yourself." She got up and left.

Later that evening, the group huddled around their small campfire, with contention all around. Slate didn't completely understand why he was no longer in Sana's good graces, but he understood why Rainier was sore with him. Rainier gave him a quick glare as he left to get firewood.

Slate contemplated the Stratego incident. His life had taken a very serious turn since the tournament, and he needed every advantage afforded him to survive in the world of the Crimson Guard. Right now, the Stratego medallion, and the help of the Sicarius headmaster, fell into that category. He wouldn't apologize. He did what he had to do. Rainier would understand in time.

Crack! The world went dim as he rolled forward, coming to rest just outside the fire ring.

Heavy eyelids opened and Slate picked himself up from the ground. He felt the back of his head and found his hair matted with blood from where Rainier had struck him with a piece of firewood. Rainier stoked the fire and tossed the Stratego medallion in the air. "Like you said, rules are rules."

Slate reconsidered his position. He had enough people trying to bash his head in to add Rainier to the list. "I'm sorry for my actions during training. I took advantage of your willingness to help me...worse, I took advantage of our friendship. Fractal's grace to you."

Rainier sat back down across the fire. "If I would have known that swinging a piece of firewood at the back of your head would knock some sense into you, I would have done it earlier. Apology accepted." The tribesman smiled. "Now that we've had a little bit of practice at Stratego, maybe it makes sense to add a few rules of our own. Neither one of us will make it out of these woods alive if we knock each other senseless every chance we get."

"I agree, but how do you think the headmaster will view your change in the game's rules?" Slate was silent for a moment before answering his own question. "The purpose of Stratego is to be aware of your surroundings and develop skills to infiltrate your opponent's guard, even when it is up. How about this? If either of us can sneak up and tap the back of the neck, we agree that counts as incapacitation. We can maintain the spirit of the game without inflicting permanent damage."

"My head thinks that is a very good idea...in more ways than one. Since you will be the one explaining our version of the rules to the headmaster, I am in full agreement."

"It's about time you two came to your senses," Sana admonished. With the Stratego understanding, order was restored amongst his traveling companions and the good-natured telling of tales began once again. Tonight, it was Slate who picked the topic and he addressed Lucus.

"Why weren't you able to maintain the camouflage spell during the attack in Ravinai? Could you tell the spell was fading?"

Lucus answered after a moment of reflection. "I ran out of spark. It is similar to running a long distance and finally collapsing. The runner can endure a lot of pain, and it can be difficult to know when to stop. Similarly, a wizard can feel the energy draining, but there aren't any other indications of when you will run out."

"What about the probing of my wounds? You must have felt something in order to know how to heal me properly."

"Do you remember that spells need both a pattern and the spark to work? Probing allows a wizard to search for patterns. A trained wizard can sense where changes in patterns occur. In the case of healing, your injury altered your body's normal patterns and the wizard restores them."

"Then what about the investigation that Brannon made you perform?" That spell had certainly felt different to Slate than a probing spell.

Lucus frowned. "That spell is based on the pattern of sharing experiences with another, sitting down and discussing events in your life, much as we are doing now. However, the spell is only loosely related to that pattern. It allows the spellcaster to not only share experiences but to relive the actions and thoughts of the person who experienced them." Lucus elaborated as he noticed their questioning looks. "That spell requires a lot of spark because it relies upon a pattern that is loosely tied to it. It is why I needed to borrow some energy from Brannon and why I was hesitant to use the spell. The Wizard Council teaches that spells loosely tied to their original patterns should only be used if other options are not available. The Crimson Guard and Ispirtu originated from the need to use magic in combat. They teach that the best spell is the one that works the quickest and most efficiently, the two attributes needed most during combat. In your instance, I conducted the spell because I felt there were no other options. I apologize for the intrusion of your memories, and I tried to speak only what was necessary to Brannon in order to close the investigation."

Slate looked at the group. Lucus was one of two wizards he had met who seemed to have his best interests at heart, and the second was currently in the infirmary. Rainier had foreign habits and beliefs compared to the people of Pillar, but had so far proven to be a good friend. Similarly, Sana had offered to help test his hand and had healed him. With all the uncertainties and troubles he was wrestling with in his mind, he needed to discuss and make some sense out of them. This seemed like the best group in which to place his trust. He asked a question that had been bothering him during Lucus' explanation.

"You said a wizard can't feel magic, but you have my memories.

You know that I felt every probe, healing spell, or other conjuring people have used on me in the last few days. Is that normal?"

The only noise that could be heard was the crackling of the campfire and the spitting of the meat as it roasted. "That is not normal. I have never heard of someone with that ability, but what it means, I can't say. I know you have questions, but I do not have answers for you." Lucus finally responded.

Sana processed the information the fastest. "I've used magic for years and it is uncomfortable to use something so powerful and not have any feeling associated with it. Does all magic feel the same?"

"Everyone's magic feels a little different," Slate said, "but it is difficult to describe. It can be warm and soothing, like when you healed me, or it can be a thunderhead waiting to light up the sky. Sometimes the feelings are far worse…" How could he describe the feeling of being stripped naked from the inside or having your memories ripped out of your head?

Lucus finished for Slate. "Slate endured more than just broken ribs in the past few days. He will describe the experiences when he is ready." This quieted any further questions, but it didn't stop Rainier from stealing confused glances at Slate throughout dinner. Slate wished he understood the tribesman better…his look had definite meaning, but its meaning was lost upon Slate.

It was a quiet camp that evening as the group laid to rest. Slate stared sleeplessly at the night's stars and decided a walk in the woods would help clear his head. He stepped through camp, but Sana must have been fighting a similar bout with insomnia and joined him. She walked silently and companionably at his side while Slate tried to comprehend Lucus' revelation. Finally, she stopped and looked him in the eyes. "I don't know what you and Lucus experienced in Ravinai. I can't make the memories go away," she took his bandaged hand and lifted it up, "but I can ease your pain." She probed his hand and healed the wound from Rainier's blade.

Slate studied Sana's face and saw concern for him masking her own pain. "My father said painful memories aren't meant to be erased. They motivate us to right our past wrongs. We need to learn from them without letting them change who we are. I will not let the past define the person I will become and neither will you. I don't know what you have been through, but you have demonstrated honesty and compassion to me." Slate wrapped Sana in his arms, but she gently pushed away. "Your intuition is sharper than your wits, Slate Severance. My life is complicated in ways I hope you never understand."

CHAPTER SEVEN

AN ALLY LEAVES

A comfortable pattern of testing, combat training, and evening campfire tales developed while travelling to Pillar. The repetition put Slate at ease with his traveling companions, but he stayed silent on the topics weighing heaviest on his mind. Who was responsible for turning his hand to stone during the tournament? Was it the same person that hurt Ibson? Which guild would he choose? Slate thought of these issues constantly, but answers eluded him.

Through Sana's efforts, Slate learned his hand could support large amounts of weight but only for a short duration. He could withstand a direct hit from a blade but not without slicing his hand to the bone. Sana created a test that bent his hand, hypothesizing that stone was susceptible to fracture when bent or put into tension. Thankfully, the two materials worked well together, and the flexibility of the bone prevented fracture of the stone.

Sana's tests also resulted in a newfound hatred for swimming. Sana insisted he swim in a creek to determine if his hand's added weight made it difficult. It didn't take long to give her an answer. Unfortunately, his admission only sparked Sana's curiosity and led to a whole host of tests. How long could Slate tread water? How much could he carry while treading water? Slate decided the boulder dropping on his hand was preferable to another swimming test.

His time with Rainier was educational as well. The tribesman taught him new forms and techniques, particularly improving Slate's proficiency in the short sword. In return, Slate created two staffs from tree branches and trained Rainier in his favorite style of fighting. They also found that, unlike fighting with short swords, his hand offered considerable advantages when wielding the staff. The staff was quick, had a long reach, and a large surface for deflecting opponent's blows, but it was less effective against heavy armor or defensive tactics. Slate could use the staff to occupy his opponent's defenses and then strike a pounding blow with his fist. Rainier didn't have heavy armor to test their new techniques, but the strategy seemed sound. Slate's incorporation of his stonehand into his fighting style highlighted his lack of progress in the intricacies of Stratego. Despite numerous efforts and thoroughly laid plans, Rainier retained possession of the medallion.

Lucus continued his role as guide and fountain of knowledge concerning Malethya, but he became more reclusive and eccentric as the days went on. Animals began appearing near him, most of which were of the shelled variety: snails, turtles, beetles and the like. The animals were around for a while and then would leave, seemingly of their own accord. Then one day Lucus ran into a strand of spider silk strung between trees. The rest of the trip, spider webs appeared in multitudes, starting in a typical circular pattern and then changing into miniaturized, tightly woven, and complex patterns. Slate gave the wizard his space.

This was the way of things as the forest ground became rocky and the trees became sparse. After weeks of walking, they were only a few days' from Pillar. In late afternoon, the group set up camp at Lucus' order. He requested Rainier and Slate forego their nightly training in lieu of a discussion around the fire. He didn't waste time with pleasantries.

"I will leave in the morning. I promised Ibson to escort you safely from Ravinai and you are now within two day's walk to Pillar. My obligation is fulfilled and the circumstances surrounding Ibson have weighed greatly on me. I wish to return to Ravinai to speak with Ibson in the hopes he has a moment of clarity. If he has not recovered, I will conduct research into Ibson's comments prior to his incident. They related to the investigation of Slate, but I feel the culprit is the same in both instances. I would share Ibson's comments with you now, limiting my conversation to topics shared with me by Ibson. Slate, I will not discuss information gained from your memories."

The whole group was taken by surprise. Slate had become accustomed to travelling with Lucus, and it never crossed Slate's mind that he might leave. "I wish you would continue with us, but Ibson deserves justice for what happened to him on my account. I've avoided discussing the events of the tournament, but I agree it is time."

Lucus began with Ibson's insights, "Slate met with relatively few people during the tournament and Ibson interviewed all of them, save the Sicarius headmaster. Ibson probed Slate's hand and found iron had fused with his bones, as you know, but there was a discrepancy he kept hidden. Everyone has iron in their blood, but the amount of iron in Slate's hand was too great to be the only source."

Slate asked Rainier to show the stratego medallion to the group. "When the Sicarius headmaster gave that to me, it was a mixture of stone and iron. When Ibson returned it to me following my recovery, the iron was gone."

Lucus explained, "Yes, Ibson was highly interested in the Stratego medallion because it was tied to your arm during the match. As you've seen with my axe, objects can have enchantments. One possibility is that the Stratego medallion released a spell during your match. The headmaster only needed to know the time of the championship bout and to ensure your contact with the medallion."

Sana questioned that possibility. "Why would the Sicarius headmaster interfere with the tournament or be interested in Slate? What would Sicarius have to gain?"

Lucus shook his head. "I don't know and neither did Ibson. Regardless, that was only one possible explanation and there are several problems with it. The most pertinent is that magic is taught in Ispirtu. Students with the spark are not given the opportunity to join Bellator or Sicarius. While I have no doubt the headmaster possesses the skills to obtain a rare magical artifact such as the one we speak, without the spark or aid from someone in Ispirtu, it would be useless."

Sana continued her systematic deductions. "Does that rule out Villifor then?"

"He does not contain the spark, but Bellator works closely with Ispirtu. Ispirtu wizards are incorporated into the ranks of Bellator Guardsmen to care for the wounded or attack if needed. Since the Sicarius headmaster gave you the medallion after your meeting with Villifor, the order of events would seemingly absolve the Bellator headmaster of guilt, but Ibson did not rule him out of his investigation. The Sicarius headmaster gave you the Stratego medallion with a note while you were incapacitated and anyone could have switched the medallion before you awoke, framing the Sicarius headmaster."

"Brannon cast the spells to detect magic in the championship bout. Could he have tampered with the fight?"

"...this is a disturbing possibility. Brannon met you after receipt of the medallion and could have enchanted it prior to the match. Brannon possesses the ability to do so, but a motive is unclear. His pride in the Regallo name is well-known. He wouldn't cast a spell that damaged Lattimer's chances of victory. Similarly, Lattimer has the spark, but he did not meet with you prior to the match and if he cast the enchantment spell during the bout, a number of wizards within the arena would have detected it."

"Ibson's investigation seemed to end with countless possibilities but few conclusions." Rainier generalized.

"Ibson's efforts mean you need to be wary of all the headmasters. Their games of power and politicking have, for whatever reason, involved you. You are like the pollen of the catalpa trees that I sent into the air, tumbling among the clouds and hoping to land in a distant grove to lay your roots. Learn quickly, Slate, before the soil turns barren and the weeds choke you out." Silence fell over the group as the generally optimistic wizard spoke these ominous words. "I have not yet shared the last and most dangerous possibility. Slate's incident may not have been caused by the medallion or the headmasters but by a mage of the worst sort."

Sana, the wizard's apprentice, understood the reference. "What you suggest is no longer possible. There hasn't been a mage of that sort in ages."

"It is possible...simply forgotten. Slate, do you recall that magic consists of two parts, the spark and the pattern? Wizards blend these two components in varying amounts to create similar spells. You probably noticed that my spark dims in comparison to Brannon or Sana. However, I have spent my life studying the complex patterns of nature, which allows me to cast powerful spells. Brannon relies heavily upon his spark to cast complex spells with only loose associations to related patterns." Slate failed to see how this lesson pertained to their situation, but he trusted the point of the story was coming if he remained quiet. "The probing spell detects changes in your body's pattern. The safeguards to prevent magic in the tournament are similar. A wizard can detect magic because the patterns used to cast a spell are the wizard's interpretation of the pattern and are inherently wrong. The spark is used to bridge the gap between the true pattern and the wizard's interpretation of it. We cannot detect the spark used to cast a spell, but a trained wizard detects magic by association with changes in the pattern surrounding a wizard. When a spell is cast, the pattern surrounding a wizard is disturbed. Do you see where I am going with this?"

Slate could not but guessed because Lucus expected a response. "Well, in order to avoid detection, a spell would need to call a pattern perfectly or be called without the pattern." Rainier clenched his jaw, apparently knowing how this story would end. Slate needed to wait for the explanation.

"Precisely. Calling the pattern without the spark is impossible because the pattern is too complex. It consists of all patterns in the body, nature, and time. However, a wizard named Cantor discovered a means to cast spells using only the spark. He shared his discovery with some of his trusted colleagues and the Golden Ages of Malethya began. Without being constrained by the pattern, the wizards could bestow properties to people and objects that were previously unimaginable. The hungry were fed by changing basic grain into vast feasts for the populace. Money was plentiful as the wizards turned iron into gold when needed. Eventually, the limitless power corrupted the wizards, leading to wars conducted and won by the cruelest creations of the wizard's imaginations. Cantor watched as his discovery created nefarious tools of destruction. Rain was enchanted to enflame anything it landed upon. Minds were twisted and enslaved or subjugated. People lived in fear of the death and destruction wrought around them, bestowing the name Blood Mages upon the wizards in power.

"Cantor decided the world would be better off without spark-based magic. He invited his former colleagues to celebrate the anniversary of his discovery. At dinner, he raised a toast and everyone praised his brilliance. The enchanted wine coated the stomachs and warmed the spirits of the Blood Mages, right before they convulsed and died as the wine-tasting arsenic took effect. Cantor destroyed any evidence or accounts of spark-based magic and left a note. It said,

> The world of man will be at peace when we cease our attempts to control it and understand our place within it. My discovery drove pious and studious wizards into corruption and greed. Their actions left me no recourse but one that leaves me most aggrieved. While the people recover from the terror that has enveloped the land, I can only hope they forgive me. Bless you all. I will remain indebted to society for longer than the

perimeter of a two dimensional fractal.

Cantor was never found and, as years passed, his story and discoveries were largely forgotten outside the world of wizards. Indeed, the only remaining parts of this story in common lore have manifested themselves as campfire stories and as a formal blessing. "Fractal's pattern" and "fractal's fortune" are spoken as good tidings and to prevent ill omens. "Blood mages" remain popular villains for local storytellers. Before his fall in the arena, Ibson speculated that if a blood mage cast a spark-based spell, it would go undetected and implicate one of the headmasters. He said it was probably the fears of an aging mind, but if something unnatural happened to him, I was to investigate it more seriously, so I must leave now that you are safe in Pillar."

Headmasters, magic, blood mages…Slate had enough. "You warn of an evil as limitless as the imagination and in the next breath you tell us you are leaving?"Lucus sighed, "I am leaving, but I am not leaving you empty handed."

The woodcutter reached in his travel sack and produced a simple leather glove Slate recognized as his own. "I have been thinking of ways to protect the soft tissues of your hand. After your first training session with Rainier, I thought the most practical application would be a glove that allowed you to catch a blade during battle."

Now Slate was interested.

"At first I studied the patterns of animals such as snails and beetles that create a hard shell for protection. Unfortunately, their shells cracked or shattered if a large enough force was applied. Then I ran into a spider web. The silk clung to my face and although I could peel it away, it remained intact. After playing with several different variations, I found the silk could be woven into a tight pattern, creating an extremely strong and lightweight fabric of sorts…you may have noticed some interesting spider webs in the past few weeks. I wove the silk pattern into your leather glove trying to match the pattern and blending of the iron with your bones. Would you care to test it?"

Rainier didn't wait for Slate to answer. He jumped up and wielded a short sword. When Slate had placed his hand within the glove, Rainier unloaded a powerful overhead blow. Slate grabbed the blade in midair and managed to bring it to a stop. The force of the blow was felt through his entire arm, but when he let go of the blade, he saw the glove was still intact. More importantly, so was his hand.

Rainier smiled. "How do I get one?"

Lucus chuckled. "It wouldn't do you any good. The glove is able to prevent the blade from cutting into Slate's hand, but it is the stone in his bones that absorbs the force. If you tried to use the glove to catch a blade, it would prevent your hand from cutting, but your bones would be crushed."

Slate wanted nothing more than to train with Rainier that instant, but he came to his senses. Lucus would leave in the morning and he needed to soak up all the knowledge he could from the wizard before his departure. He was making a mental list of questions for Lucus when the wizard cut him short. "I have told you what I know of the headmasters, the investigation, and blood mages. I have given you all the help I can offer for the trials ahead in the form of your glove. Let us spend the rest of our time as friends do, with tales and spirits." The wizard then pulled out a bottle from his traveling sack, drank and passed it around the campfire, surprising his friends and signaling the beginning of the night's end.

CHAPTER EIGHT

HOMECOMING

A headache and a rather empty feeling greeted Slate in the morning. The wise and eccentric wizard who led their group during their travels was gone, Rainier was stoking the fire, and Sana remained asleep. In his absence, Lucus ordered Sana to accompany the group back to Ravinai, a kindness for which Slate was extremely grateful.

Anticipating the completion of their journey, Slate gently shook Sana awake. When he touched her shoulder, Sana flung back her blanket, grabbed Slate's arm, and rolled on top of him, pinning Slate to the ground with the flash of a knife. The knife looked dangerous, and Sana looked like she knew how to use it.

Slate tried to calm her nerves. "…um…good morning to you, too…?"

Sana kept her face serious, but Slate detected a hint of embarrassment at her actions. "I'm sorry. Old habits die hard." Sana stood up and returned the knife to a hidden pocket in the sleeve of her robe. Looking to change the subject, she said, "Are we going to Pillar or are you two planning to sit around this campfire all day? Go fetch some water to douse the fire. Lucus must have taken the sense right out of you when he left." Rainier got up and went toward the stream, laughing at the entire course of events and the all-too-serious Sana. That did little to brighten Sana's mood, but Slate was in high spirits with thoughts of home.

"So how long have you been looking for an excuse to roll around with me?" Slate gave a smirk. She had already pulled a knife on him. What else could she do?

"Did that line work for you in Pillar? I don't fantasize about rolling around on a bed of rocks." Sana's response discouraged Slate, but the sons of Pillar had great reserves of persistence.

"In Pillar, we make do with what we have. Opportunities to be alone in a small town are scarce, but a bed of rocks can always be found." Sana looked unimpressed, so Slate tried honesty. "…but to answer your question, no. The girls in Pillar didn't like that line either."

"I hoped you had more to offer than lousy attempts at flirtation." The condemnation didn't discourage Slate.

"I've had little use for a sharp tongue in my life, but a simple tongue does not equate to a simple person." Slate finally coaxed a smile from Sana.

"You're right, Slate...and simple comments like that make me believe you could handle a little complication in your life."

Stopping while he was ahead, Slate gathered his things and the three left for Pillar, with Slate leading the way through familiar territory and the group discussing their arrival.

"What are you looking forward to the most?" Rainier asked.

"When I first see my father, he will be reserved out of respect for the town rules I broke by fighting in the tournament, but later on he will want to know the details of every bout. He might even ask us to recreate our match, Rainier, so be prepared to lose again."

Rainier countered. "What did Villifor say? You would lose to Magnus nine fights out of ten? Well, even those odds are favorable in comparison to a rematch against me."

"Are you excited to end our journey?" Slate asked in return.

Rainier stretched and cracked his back. "The tribe travels constantly, but that doesn't mean I'm used to sleeping on the ground every night. Let's try to make it to Pillar tonight."

With their goal set, the group made good time through the sparsely vegetated ground and reached the foothills of the mountains at sundown. The most common way for travelers to reach Pillar was from the Northeast, in the direction of the only road, but Lucus' direct route through the woods had them approaching from the Southeast. Slate took a little known and seldom used path past Old Man Leatherby's farm. He was as tough as the stone around him and found Pillar to be too metropolitan for his tastes, preferring the solitude of the village outskirts.

"I thought you said no one farmed in Pillar?" Rainier queried Slate.

"I said farming was difficult. Old Man Leatherby has planted crops in this rocky ground for years, but even with his devoted attention, he never grows more than enough to feed a few half-starved cattle through the winter." The persistence of Leatherby was admirable, if nothing else.

"I don't see any cattle," Sana stated and Slate saw she was right. Even in the low light, the cattle should have been visible. There wasn't light in Leatherby's windows or smoke from the chimney either.

"Let's pay Leatherby a visit." The group approached his home and knocked but got no response. Slate peered through a window and saw no signs of recent activity. Did Leatherby die while he was in Ravinai? He was often short of breath and his mother expressed concern for Leatherby living alone. "We'll find out what happened to him in Pillar."

Rainier gave Sana a sideways look and asked Slate, "Did Old Man Leatherby leave his property very often? You've had a way of attracting trouble lately."

"Well, no, but this is Pillar. Trouble doesn't find its way out here."

Sana added, "Maybe we should take a lesson from the Sicarius headmaster and try to get a view from on high? Is there a foothill around here with a clear view of town? I'd rather arrive a little later and be sure it's safe."

Slate appreciated their concerns, but people didn't contrive nefarious plots in this far corner of the world. Sana and Rainier were just too accustomed to the corruption in Ravinai. Nonetheless, he wanted to appease his traveling companions. "There is a ridge that overlooks the town with large rock formations to provide cover. With the moon out tonight, we should have enough visibility to scout the town."

The conversation quieted as the group left Old Man Leatherby's farm to ascend the foothill, a term Sana and Rainier found debatable. It may have been a foothill compared with the mountains towering over Pillar, but it still qualified as the most perilous climb the nomad and apprentice had ever undertaken. Recognizing their trepidation, Slate moved ahead slowly, pointing out moss and lichen covered areas on the sloped faces of rock that could give way if stepped on, leading to a nasty fall. There were several steep sections of the foothill that required a short climb and Slate patiently helped Sana and Rainier. They stood on his shoulders at times, leaving him to climb up afterwards, or he would climb up first and then reach down to help them up. He had first climbed this hill when he was five.

Finally, the group reached the crest of the hill. Slate took up a position in the rock formations that gave him a clear view of Pillar. The western mountains rose up as a mighty backdrop, with a small stream winding toward the valley. The mine was set up near the stream and its modest entrance hid the deep caverns beyond, giving no indication that this was the sole reason for interest in Pillar from the outside world. Farther down the valley, stone houses were built into the mountain as a matter of practicality. Small footpaths connected the homes and a modest meeting hall to the stream and mine entrance. It was a small but solidly built town and its sight would have brought Slate much joy…

…but smoke didn't rise from the chimneys.

Slate frantically scanned the town he knew so well. All the homes were dark and lifeless, but the moonlight didn't provide additional detail. His eyes followed the largest path through town, the cart path from the mine entrance toward the northern exit. At the narrowest section of the valley pass, Slate saw a makeshift camp. In the camp's torchlight Slate could barely make out the glistening armor of the Crimson Guard.

"What have they done?" Slate whispered under his breath and dropped reflexively into an attack form, his hands tightening around the staff. Before he could sprint down the hillside in a fit of rage, Sana's hand rested on his arm comfortingly and reason reentered his brain.

Rainier provided his strategic assessment of their situation. "Those are trained Crimson Guard down there. We can't go barreling into them with a full frontal assault consisting of two untrained warriors and a wizard's apprentice."

Sana added her own advice, "We took the Sicarius approach by coming up here and I think we should continue to gather more information before acting. Let's locate and incapacitate any guardsmen in this area. Then we can look around in the houses below." It was hard to argue with Sana's logic, but the application of it would be difficult.

"How do we locate the guardsmen on watch? They've undoubtedly taken a position with good visibility and it would take a fractal's blessing to locate them before we were seen." An answer wasn't readily available and Sana broke eye contact with Slate, pondering a solution. She kicked a rock back and forth, probably in frustration…which gave Slate an idea. "We need to draw their attention and get them to leave their post to investigate without raising an alarm. Then we'll learn their positions and gain the advantage. Even something as simple as a rock landing against the stone walls of a house would do the trick. On a clear night like tonight, the noise would echo off the rocky landscape and funnel up to whatever vantage points the guardsmen have taken."

"We're far enough away to escape discovery, but the town is much further than a stone's throw away. There are machines of war that throw objects large distances such as catapults, but we are short on supplies to build something like that…" Rainier contemplated. "Would a sling work? That's pretty simple…"

Sana, who had already displayed her aptitude for mechanics by building various test stations for Slate, took over. She pulled out a length of the grapevine rope she created and used her knife to cut it into two equal lengths. Then she took an old shirt from Rainier's travel sack and ripped it into a wide strip, causing Rainier to frown. None of them had clothes to spare. The strip was tied between the two vine ropes, creating a pocket to hold a stone and the two ropes were affixed to Slate's staff. The result was a sling of similar design to that of a trebuchet. "Weapons of this type take a lot of adjustment to work accurately. We don't have that option, so I'll use magic to control the release of the rope while it is swinging."

Rainier loaded a rock into the sling, and Slate heaved the staff overhead with all the force he could muster. Halfway through his swing, the load lightened considerably and the rock disappeared into the night sky. A few seconds later, a thud sounded from within the town, even if its exact location couldn't be determined. Slate strained his eyes into the moonlit night for signs of motion.

Seconds turned into a minute and then a shadow passed from one house to the other. He pointed for the benefit of Rainier and Sana but didn't take his eyes away for fear of losing his mark. The moonlight reflected off the Crimson armor just enough to track the guard as he investigated the town and then followed the mountain stream above the town and returned to his post. It was a rock formation similar to the one where they were currently hiding.

"They are in the rock formation near the stream above town. I know the location well."

"Great, let's go pay them a visit." Rainier's overly confident tone reappeared. Sana remained uncharacteristically quiet, with pride upon her face as she removed the sling from Slate's staff and packed it in her travel sack.

Slate walked a circuitous path toward the rock formation to avoid the sightlines of the guardsmen. The climb took them until the deepest dark of night, but they eventually positioned themselves with a view of the guardsmen. Within the rock formation, two guardsmen sat motionless, resting against the rocks. Apparently even Crimson Guardsmen got bored on watch, especially in such a remote location as Pillar.

"We need to knock them out. Sana can you camouflage us like Lucus did?"

"I'm afraid not. That's a difficult spell I have yet to master." The apprentice admitted. "But I do have an alternative. Grab some moss and I'll affix it to your shoes. It should mask your approach." Slate and Rainier both gathered some of the plentiful moss from the rocky ground. Sana then explained, "Moss loves to grow on trees, so I use the spark to make it grow on the soles of your shoes instead. You'll lose traction but gain stealth." They held the moss against the soles of their shoes and Sana cast her spell. Slate tried out his new boots. He would have to be extra careful of his footing, but his steps were as quiet as death.

Rainier didn't waste time. "I'll circle around to the far one and you take the closer one. Let's knock them out simultaneously." They slipped down from their elevated perch and positioned themselves outside the rock formation, in view of each other. Slate held his staff in hand and his blood ran hot with the thought that these two could be responsible for the disappearance of the townspeople. Slate nodded to Rainier and then channeled his anger and frustration into a swing at the resting, helmeted soldier. Halfway through his swing, he heard Rainier land a quick blow to the thick neck of the other soldier, dropping him to the ground. Slate's guard awakened at the sound of the muffled blow and reacted with astonishing speed, reaching for his sheathed sword while deflecting Slate's blow with his other hand. Slate threw a punch, and the guardsman ignored the unconventional tactic in favor of unsheathing his sword and letting his helmet absorb the blow. It was a mistake he would regret as Slate's stonehand shattered his jaw and dented his helmet against the rock behind him. It was a little messier than he had intended, but he managed the job without an alarm being raised.

Sana climbed down and tied up the guardsman with her grapevine rope. Rainier began removing the guard's armor. "We don't want to attract attention from the main guard camp. At least from a distance they'll assume we're patrolling."

"Wait, what about me?" Sana asked.

Rainier answered matter-of-factly, "The armor belongs to two male guardsmen. Besides, if we are discovered, we will need to fight, in which case I'll be of more use than you." Sana, despite her aptitude for logic, decided against using it on this occasion, souring her mood.

Slate tried to placate her, "We'll need a lookout anyway. Can you keep an eye on things from here and hoot like a night owl if someone is approaching?"

Sana jutted out her jaw. "Get the armor on and get back as quickly as possible." She then took up her post overlooking the town, ignoring Slate and Rainier.

Slate put on the Crimson armor and tried not to laugh when he saw Rainier. The diminutive nomad looked ridiculous. The armor on Rainier jutted out at the shoulders and pretty much everywhere else.

"Don't say a word." Rainier warned Slate and started down the mountainside toward Pillar, oversized armor fighting his movements every step of the way. A smirk appeared on Slate's face as he followed Rainier down the mountain.

The smirk faded as they approached the first house belonging to the Lampitts. A small garden grew next to the house, a small area of land painstakingly cultivated over the years to provide a few vegetables during the short growing season. Approaching the midpoint of summer, the vegetables should have grown above the soil, with leafy green rewarding all the cultivation. Instead they lay trampled in the ground. Rounding the corner of the stone house, they saw shattered windows and the wooden door barely hanging from its hinges. Slate thought of the difficulty it took to get enough wood transported from the distant forest to make that door, and it turned his stomach. He touched the splintered door, and his heart stopped. The splintered surface of the wood was dyed red in areas. Slate didn't want to look in the door, but he had to know what was inside.

The stone floors were darkened, and the stench of dried blood permeated his nostrils. His eyes quickly scanned the room, hoping beyond hope that the Lampitts were hiding in a bedroom or under the dining room table. When no one came running out to meet him, Slate steeled himself and started looking for clues. There were no bodies, but when he found little Lucy Lampitts's hair tie still holding a lock of blond hair he vomited on the spot and then left the house to sit on the mountainside, breathing in as much fresh air as he could inhale.

After an indeterminable length of time, Rainier came out of the house and found Slate. "I'm sorry you had to see that. Do you want to continue?"

"No…yes, yes I do. I need to know what happened. What did you find out?"

"There was quite a battle in that little house, but everything has been cleared away. There were streaks in the floor leading out the doorway. The bodies must have been loaded up and removed. I would like to look in one more house to see if it is similar, but I think we will find the same thing throughout the town."

"If we are only going to look inside one more house, it needs to be the one I grew up in. As much as it pains me, I need to see what happened to my parents."

"Which house is it?"

"The small one by the well…" Slate pointed to a nondescript house next to the meeting hall. Rainier nodded and helped Slate to his feet. Slate marched down the small path in the mountainside as he had done countless times before. Mrs. Cleary would tell him to hurry home or that he was late for dinner. Her house was as empty and broken as the Lampitts's. Mr. Raisedale would tell him he needed extra help in the mine, because the mine always needed extra help. No voice called after him as he passed by another broken home. Mother would look up from her small workbench set outside so she could work in the sun, gears and machine parts spread across the top and smile as he came home. The bench but intact taken inside and flipped up against the solitary window, blocking the opening. His solidly built home had been turned into a defensive stronghold. Every opening had been sealed, save for the stone door. Slate had often questioned why his father insisted on having the impractically heavy stone door, but he had just said, "We are a simple people and we will use what is plentiful." Slate now saw the other purpose. With the stone door closed, the house was nearly impenetrable…nearly. Slate's mother created metal hinges for the door, but they were battered until they had given way. The heavy door had then been pulled outward, and it lay cracked on the uneven ground outside the home.

A dozen bodies lay atop the stone door near the entrance to Slate's home. Slate expected to see armored or uniformed bodies but instead saw peasants with simple clothing. They held hammers and rock picks and other tools turned into rudimentary weapons. Even more confusingly, the peasants were mutilated. Dismembered arms and legs lay scattered alongside decapitated heads on the ground. The stack of bodies and body parts reached a summit in the doorway. An old sword pointed skyward, held in place by the armless body of a dead peasant.

The hoot of the night owl pierced the sky, which Slate noticed but didn't act upon.

"We need to leave," Rainier whispered tersely. Slate didn't want to leave. Everything he knew was gone. Every person from his childhood was dead. His parents, the only family he had, were killed. Why wasn't he here to help fight off the attackers? Maybe he could have saved them. The beating of hooves grew louder and Rainier grabbed his arm, pulling him back.

Slate allowed himself to be pulled, too shocked to put up a fight. Rainier pulled Slate inside a house with a view of Slate's boyhood home. It smelled of dried blood and death. In his current state, Slate found the room fitting and he stared out the window in a daze. The hoof beats stopped on the main path from the mine, forcing the approaching contingent to walk the rest of the way upon foot. Their voices penetrated Slate's preoccupied mind.

A feminine voice filtered through the night air. "We didn't find any villagers alive to question. The bodies were brought to the mine for your examination. We thought the cold mining caves would prevent decay better than leaving them out here. It appears most villagers were taken by surprise and killed in their sleep. However, there was one notable exception, and we are bringing you to that house now. We left the scene intact for you…"

"You did very well, guardsman. I traveled as quickly as possible from Ravinai when the report came in." The voice of Villifor was unmistakable, even in Slate's stupor. It snapped Slate to attention, with his eyes burning a hole through the figure of the approaching headmaster. They reached Slate's house and Villifor quietly looked at the bodies of the attackers. "Who has seen this?"

"There are two guardsmen on watch in the mountainside above the village."

"Please wait for me by the horses." All four guardsmen turned to leave, along with one cloaked individual. "Magnus, stay with me."

The hulking figure with a broadsword across his back returned. "Yes, Villifor?" The headmaster waited until the guardsmen were safely out of earshot before continuing.

"What do you see?"

"A weak and pathetic miner overwhelmed by peasants without weapons."

"Why would these peasants attack a man so heavily fortified in his home? He has modest belongings and many lives were lost breaching his door."

"I can't think of any reason."

"Then you still have a lot to learn." Villifor reached down and pulled the armless body from the top of the pile, exposing Slate's father beneath. "I know this man, although I'm sure most people in Malethya have forgotten him."

"Was he a hero from the war like you?"

Villifor appeared conflicted before answering. "He was a stubborn fool who doesn't deserve to be remembered. I hope his son has inherited his mother's judgment. We already know he inherited his father's prowess with weaponry…this is undoubtedly the father of Slate Severance."

Magnus looked down on Slate's father and spat. "Hero or not, he is nobody to me."

Villifor slapped Magnus across the face. Magnus' eyes flared, but he said nothing. "I said he didn't deserve to be remembered. Did you hear me say he deserved to be disgraced? It's time for you to learn another tough lesson. There is something unnatural about this attack. Peasants don't continue to attack in this manner after losing an arm or leg. The northern villages already speak of increased raids and armed bandits. If news of this attack gets out, it will lead to chaos in the kingdom. We can't allow that to happen. Back in camp, there is a package of explosive orbs. Tell the guardsmen on watch to help load the bodies from here and take them into the mine. While they are loading the bodies, go set the orbs in the mine. Make sure you come back to camp in one piece…and alone."

Magnus lifted his chin slightly and clenched his jaw. "What about the guardsmen?"

"Guardsmen stationed in this part of Malethya don't deserve to wear crimson. They've been sent here for various crimes or flaws in character. They'll aid the crown more by staying silent in the bottom of a mine shaft....do you have a problem with that?"

"No sir. I want to serve the crown."

"Excellent, and don't forget to enlist the *help* of the two guardsmen up the mountainside. I'll see you back at camp alone, and if I do, you will have earned my mentorship in Bellator."

Magnus stood silent for a second as the gears of morality turned slowly in his head. Apparently they needed more oil, because the gears seized and any question of morality stopped with them. Magnus made eye contact with Villifor and said, "Yes, sir!" in a commanding voice. His lips twisted into a nearly imperceptible smirk, causing Slate to shiver. Was he looking forward to carrying out Villifor's sadistic command? The two men walked back to their horses.

"Excellent. After the explosion, ride into camp at a gallop and breathlessly explain there was an accident in the mine. The exploding orbs should be powerful enough to give us a valid excuse to leave this fractal-forsaken outpost and get back to civilization." The two men mounted their horses and rode away.

As soon as they were out of earshot, Rainier whispered hurriedly. "We've got to get back to Sana. Magnus will be looking for those guardsmen as soon as he gets the explosive orbs from camp." Slate and Rainier scrambled up the hillside and reached Sana in the rock formation just as they heard the sound of Magnus' horse riding up the main path to the mine entrance. Sana met them with a flurry of questions.

"What's going on? Were you spotted? Who is getting off that horse down there?"

"Magnus is coming to order these two guardsmen to bring the dead, with my parents among them, into the mine where the other townsfolk have been kept. While the guardsmen are in there, he plans to collapse the mine to eliminate anyone that has seen what transpired in Pillar." Slate looked down at the still unconscious guardsmen, then at the approaching figure of Magnus. They wouldn't have time to hide the bodies and if Magnus informed Villifor that the guardsmen were incapacitated, they'd have every guardsman in camp looking through the mountainside for them.

"Rainier, Magnus is looking for inept guardsmen. Let's live up to his expectations. Sana, stay hidden and figure out a distraction. We might need the extra time if we're still down there when Magnus blows the mine." There wasn't time for a better plan.

Slate told Rainier to sit with his back against the rock formation. "Pretend to sleep...and snore...loudly!" Even with the darkness giving them extra time, Magnus would be within view in seconds when he turned a corner of the small mountain path. Slate hurried to a spot just before the bend in the path, leaned against a tree for balance and started peeing.

When Magnus rounded the corner, Slate pretended to be startled. He slurred a few drunken curses as he jumped in surprise, delivering a satisfyingly large amount of urine onto the meticulously cared for cloak of Magnus. "Drunken fool!" Magnus shouted as he assessed the damage to his clothes. Slate ran up the footpath to Rainier, kicking the snoring guardsman awake with the furious Magnus on his heels. Slate spun to face Magnus, dropping into a pitifully inept interpretation of a battle stance. Rainier jumped up and reached for his short sword, only to get it stuck in its sheath while attempting to pull it free. "Stop in the name of the Crimson Guard!" Slate commanded in a terrified voice.

"Don't call yourselves that. Crimson Guardsmen do not drink while on duty or fall asleep at their post." Magnus wound up and slapped Rainier upon his helmet. "Pitiful. Improperly fit armor and weak bladders. You can call yourselves Crimson Guardsmen, but make no mistake. You are all but ostracized from the ranks of the guard, sentenced to a meaningless life in a forgotten part of the kingdom. " Slate's shoulders slumped in relaxation. Magnus had not recognized them in the darkness. "Villifor requested you personally transfer the bodies in town into the mine. There is a cart near the mine entrance for the task. Do it quickly to prove your worth and maybe you will curry his favor. I will wait for you by the mine."

"Yes, sir!" Rainier and Slate answered simultaneously. They put on a good show of running as quickly as possible down the narrow mountain trail. Magnus could be heard following them down at his own self-assured pace, undoubtedly proud of his natural ability to command the fully trained guardsmen. The ruse had worked. Sana remained safe in the rocks above Pillar and they remained undiscovered.

They found the cart at the mine and pushed it down the trail. After putting enough distance between themselves and Magnus to whisper, Rainier asked, "What's the next part of the plan?"

"That's as far as I got before Magnus showed up."

Rainier groaned. "So the plan was to get ourselves blown up in the mine? You need to work on your lesson plans, Teacher." Rainier's odd sense of humor surfaced and he chuckled at his own joke. "Are there any ways out of the mine beside the main entrance?"

"There's a ventilation shaft, but we'd never get to it in time. The whole mountain would cave in before we made it out."

"Then we'll have to go out the front," the tribesman whispered with a smile. They left the cart as close to Slate's house as the path would allow and Rainier set to work, grabbing the dead attacker from the top of the pile and hefting him off the impaled sword. Slate looked down upon the still face of his father. Emotion threatened to overwhelm him, but he managed to steel himself for the moment. There would be time for emotion later. Right now he needed to get out of town alive. Slate closed his father's eyes and carried him to the cart.

How would he get out of town without alerting the guardsmen? Could he prevent Magnus from blowing up the town? His mind raced and the pile of bodies in the cart grew higher. Rainier was right – the only way out of the mine was through the front entrance where Magnus would be stationed. Slate walked into the tomb he had once called home and discovered his mother. She had died rushing toward the door, presumably to take his father's place when he fell to the attackers. "I'm sorry for leaving, Mother," Slate whispered as he gently picked her up. Slate laid his mother in the cart, unable to understand why this massacre had happened.

"It's time to head back." Rainier whispered, resting his hand on Slate's shoulder. "Are you ready?"

"There's nothing we can do for them now, and this mountain was a big part of their lives. It's fitting they will be buried beneath it. The town is dead. Let Magnus bury it. We just need to get out alive."

"We'll get out alive," Rainier met Slate's eyes with resolve. "Consider it a test for your student."

The two pushed the cart toward the mine and found Magnus leaning against the entrance. Slate could make out a bulge in his cloak pocket that looked to be the same shape as the orbs from the arena. That must be the trigger to detonate the explosive orbs in the mine. "There's a large cavern about five minutes into the mine. Unload the cart there, where you see the bodies of the other peasants. As a reward for your hard work, you can take your time unloading the cart. I'll make sure to let Villifor know of your devoted service."

"Yes, sir!" Rainier promised before pushing the cart past Magnus.

Inside the mine, the temperature cooled considerably and Slate hoped he wasn't blindly following Rainier to his death. He looked over his shoulder and saw Magnus walking away from the mine, fingering the orb within his pocket. Sheltered from his view by the added darkness of the mine, Rainier pushed the cart down a slightly descending path in the direction of the cavern. "...just in case he's listening for the sound of the wheels on the stone," Rainier said in explanation. "Now, take off your armor and grab anything you want to keep."

Slate disrobed and grabbed his staff. "Now what?"

"We walk out the front entrance and face Magnus. I'm tired of acting inept." Rainier unsheathed his short swords and smirked.

"We'll have guardsmen upon us in minutes if they hear the sounds of battle."

"We face certain death in this mine. There is no other way out, so we need to go out the way we came...besides, I have a feeling Magnus won't want to fight us." He offered no further explanation before striding out of the mine as if he were entering an arena duel. Magnus faced the mine entrance a hundred yards away, turning the orb over in his hands. He dropped it into his pocket and reached for his broadsword at the sight of Rainier exiting the mine with swords drawn. Slate followed Rainier's lead and ran for the exit of the mine. He planted his staff outside the entrance and flipped overhead, landing on one knee. Recognition flashed on Magnus' face but Rainier spoke before Magnus charged, "If you want to leave this town alive, stop right there."

Magnus laughed into the night. "This isn't the arena, little man, and this isn't a practice sword. You are unarmored and I could snap Slate's staff in two with one swing."

"...if you are able to connect, Magnus. As I recall, you didn't land a single blow in our last encounter." Slate countered, trying to appear more confident than he was. Rainier began circling to his right, trying to flank Magnus.

"Let's find out." Magnus unleashed a mighty swing across his body. The horizontal swing prevented Slate from leaping to the side as he had during their initial encounter and the reach of the blade was sufficient to keep Rainier from countering as he engaged Slate. Slate jumped back, narrowly escaping the sword's reach and Rainier dove to the ground. The only way Slate could think to stop Magnus without the sounds of their battle reaching the Crimson camp was to catch his blade. He transferred his staff to his left hand and flexed his right hand within Lucus' glove…time to see if all this testing would pay off.

Whoosh. A throwing knife with a catalpa tree on it flew by Slate's head and buried itself in Magnus' foot. Magnus stopped in mid-swing, dropping the blade tip to the ground in agony. Rainier darted within range of his short swords and pressed his blade against Magnus' throat. "Drop it." Rainier commanded. Sana stood silhouetted on top of the mine entrance, holding the exact pose Slate used in his description of the Sicarius headmaster standing atop the rooftops of Ravinai. "I told you not to fight. That is the blade of the Sicarius headmaster in your foot. I would be very still if I were you." Terror appeared in Magnus' eyes and he dropped his sword. Slate caught it before it hit the ground. "Here's how this is going to work." Rainier spoke in a dangerously quiet tone to Magnus. "We want to get out of here without guardsmen chasing us all the way to Ravinai. You need to get back to camp alone and with the mine blown up. It seems to me that both can happen."

Slate turned the large sword over in his hands. It had a blade notched from use and a family crest at the hilt. Images of Magnus spitting upon his dead father resurfaced and Slate let them smolder. He casually walked up to Magnus, reached within Magnus' cloak pocket, and pulled out the trigger orb. Inside the orb, two colors shifted with respect to each but never mixed. "How does this work?"

"Break the orb by striking it with your sword. When the colors mix, the exploding orbs detonate."

Slate looked to the sword in his hands. "Did your father give this to you?"

"I peeled that sword from the hands of a dead nobleman who placed his bets poorly. It means nothing to me." Despite the declaration, Slate sensed a connection between Magnus and his sword.

"The people of my village didn't believe in fighting. Since they were caught defenseless in life, it would be fitting to protect them in death. This sword would be a good start…"

Slate walked up to the mine entrance, sneaking a glance at Sana above the wooden support structures, still holding her best Sicarius pose. He laid the sword within the mine and walked back to Magnus. His eyes were bulging from his head in anger, but the threat of the Sicarius headmaster held him in check.

Rainier finished the conversation. "The only thing left to discuss is what happens when I pull this sword away from your throat. The Sicarius headmaster will stay within striking distance as we go and untie the captive guardsmen up in the mountain. I won't have their deaths on my head. They will awaken in short order and undoubtedly make their way to the Crimson camp. You will stay right here and not move because you wouldn't want to find another knife streaking toward you in the night. Once the other guardsmen are clear of the mountaintop, we'll detonate the exploding orbs. Do you understand?"

Magnus looked to the knife in his foot. "I understand. I also understand that I won't forget this." His anger seemed to focus as he settled his gaze upon Slate.

"…neither will I…" Slate spit in his face, as Magnus had done to his father, and stepped on the catalpa knife, burying it further into Magnus's foot.

Slate walked up the mountain trail toward the rock formation and the guardsmen and Rainier joined him shortly after. They cut the grapevine ropes and slapped their faces a few times. They'd be lucid in a few minutes, alarmed after that, and adrenaline would bring them to their feet and running toward the Crimson camp. They collected their travel sacks and Rainier gave the call of the sparrow. Sana met them and they headed toward Old Man Leatherby's farm, stopping to look down on the town when they were a safe distance from the mine.

Slate pulled out the trigger orb. "How did you make that throw, Sana? Maybe you should be the one joining Sicarius."

"Falcons capture their prey by diving incredibly fast and true, even through buffeting winds. I applied that pattern to my knife with some spark. It flew straight, but my aim was off. I tried to hit him in the head."

"Then you have the best bad aim in the world. That was perfect." Rainier said.

"…and those two guardsmen should beat Magnus back to camp." Slate smiled.

In short order, two men came running down the mountain path as the sun's first rays hit the valley that nestled Pillar. Slate took one last look at his hometown and triggered the orb. Colors swirled and an explosion came from deep within the mountain. Rocks and dust spewed from the mine entrance as deep cracks appeared in the stone houses and roofs collapsed. The two guardsmen were thrown to the ground. Magnus, who had been prepared for the blast, ran to the defenseless guardsmen and disposed of them with a rock thrown from the mountain. He knelt by the corpses for a moment and then galloped toward the Crimson camp on his horse.

Rainier kept watch of the Crimson camp in case Magnus sent guardsmen in search of the trio. Slate wasn't concerned. If Magnus was willing to kill for placement in Bellator, he wouldn't jeopardize his status under Villifor by admitting defeat at the hands of Slate and Rainier.

The horror of what Slate saw this night finally overwhelmed him and he broke down. "Who would kill everyone in a defenseless town?" Slate asked the early morning air. Sana comforted him with a hug and a gentle kiss upon his cheek. It barely registered to Slate, as his mind raced.

He had only sought a little glory by fighting in the tournament. Everything since had brought him heartache and agony. If the values of the Crimson Guard led to these atrocities, Slate wanted no part of it, but that was no longer an option. Whoever harmed Ibson had also coordinated the attack on Pillar, miles upon miles from Ravinai. Every bit of life he had known before the tournament had been taken away from him. His parents and his friends were gone, even the town itself was destroyed. He was all that was left and he vowed to make sure their deaths weren't quickly forgotten.

He would go to Ravinai.

He would join the Crimson Guard.

He would find who killed his parents…and make them regret it.

Slate straightened and Sana pulled away, sensing a change within him. He looked down upon his ruined town. He would need to improve his fighting skills in Bellator so that he wasn't outmatched every time he faced a Crimson Guardsman. He needed to understand how Ispirtu used magic in battle so that he could avoid it or counteract it. Most importantly, he needed the skill of Sicarius to investigate and avenge the deaths of his parents.

Slate reached his staff out until it touched the back of Rainier's neck, who was watching the Crimson camp. "Stratego medallion, please...I'll be needing that now." A startled Rainier looked into the hardened face of Slate and handed over the medallion. "The tournament champion wins the right to choose his guild. There is no one I can trust within the Crimson Guard. Any of the headmasters could have orchestrated the attacks on me, Ibson, or my parents. I'll need access to all of them, so I will not choose Ispirtu, Sicarius, or Bellator. I will join all three guilds and take lessons from each. I will learn their secrets and put an end to the evil I have witnessed here."

REFLECTION OF REGRET

Red eyes refocused and stared back at him from the mirror. Blink. *They're still there.* Slate grabbed a towel and rubbed his face. He tossed the towel at the mirror, hoping to avoid his reflection as he left the wash room.

The naked body of a bar wench sprawled across his bed. What was her name? It didn't matter, but somehow regret was worse when coupled with forgetfulness. She had served him in the tavern the night before and recognized him...smart girl...without disguising his red eyes and white skin he wasn't exactly incognito. Girls like her confused Slate. The most feared man in Malethya walks into a bar and girls would do one of two things, run and hide or throw themselves at him. This one had flirted with him all night and the more he ignored her, the harder she tried. By the time he went up to his room to retire for the evening, she followed him up and never left. Now she lay peacefully sleeping and Slate hoped she would stay that way until he left.

He buried the regret in the place he stored every other painful emotion. Last night temporarily relieved the pain of the wrongs he had caused, momentarily replacing the pain in the form of satisfaction with this wench. In return, she could brag to her friends that she had seduced a demi-god, or whatever name she decided to call him. She would exaggerate his physical gifts and prowess, making the story more exciting and Slate infamous for even more reasons. The story would spread and more wenches would follow him up to his room on future nights. That's the funny thing about being a legend. The stories pile on top of each other, mix together, and change altogether.

A noise from the window caught Slate's attention. Down on the street, an innkeeper taught his boy basic forms with the sword. That was good...the boy would have need of the sword. Attacks on villages were rampant nowadays, with the aftermath of Pillar all too common.

The young boy deflected a slow overhead blow from his father. For both their sakes, he hoped they practiced diligently before this village met a similar fate. Had they been in Bellator, they would have been forced to learn as quickly as Slate…

CHAPTER NINE

GUILD LIFE

Slate stood at attention with the members of Bellator, waiting for the early amber rays of the autumn sun to reach the courtyard and signal the start of their training. The sun flirted with the dirt of the courtyard, hovering at the bottom of the guild's ornate pillars and archways that supported the offices and lecture halls overlooking the training ground. The guild was constructed with five such courtyards as centerpieces, each signifying an increased level of skill. Slate had yet to progress from the first courtyard despite several months of training.

The sun's rays touched the sand of the courtyard and Hedok emerged from the school. Their trainer was a large, grizzled man. He swore constantly at their technique, their family's stock, and even himself on occasion.

"No bloody weapons today! Your mockery of the sword tires me. You don't deserve to use one. Find someone your size and prepare to fight...and for fractal's sake don't throw any blows that could cause permanent damage!" Hedok limped toward the center of the courtyard, waiting for his trainees to form a circle around the edges. "You let a decrepit old man beat you into position? Maybe I'll need to bring some throwing knives out here and see how fast you move!"

Slate looked for someone his own size to match up against. He was taller than most of the students and strong by most standards, but did not carry the muscle of the others. Members of Bellator worked out aggressively and most had added weight to their frames quickly since joining the guild. Slate fell behind in training because of his commitments to Ispirtu and Sicarius. The morning training was his only lesson within Bellator. All the other students matched up, leaving Cirata Lorassa scrambling to find any partner other than Slate. She was too slow and hustled over to where Slate stood.

Slate's skill in hand-to-hand combat dwarfed Cirata's skills and she knew it. Cirata could have humiliated any number of fighters in the first courtyard with the exception of Jak Warder. She would be looking to impress Hedok with a strong showing in the hopes of joining Magnus in the second courtyard.

"People facing away from the circle…attack!" Hedok bellowed. Slate threw a quick left that Cirata deflected and then brought a roundhouse kick from the right. Cirata dove inside his attack and grabbed his leg just below the knee. She then twisted in the direction of Slate's motion and drove her shoulder downward on his hamstring. Slate received a face full of sand for his efforts as Cirata twisted his knee and finished him off with an elbow to the kidneys.

Slate picked himself up and scanned the courtyard to see that he had lost quicker than anyone else, a frequent event that frustrated Slate. If he committed his time to Bellator he could have advanced to the second courtyard as Magnus had done.

"Cirata and Jak, you look like your mothers bedded the right soldiers…heck, maybe it was even me!" Hedok laughed at his own joke and bellowed again. "People facing the circle…attack!"

Cirata dove for his left leg, going for a takedown. Slate held off the basic move by planting his right foot to keep his balance. Then Cirata altered her grip to swing her body around and drive into Slate's right leg. That was definitely not a basic move. He fell on his back, facing skyward. Cirata delivered a finishing blow to his exposed neck with a little more force than was necessary for a training match.

As the sun rose higher in the sky, the continual beatings became educational. Slate began to read Cirata's motions and even successfully defended one of her attacks when Villifor walked onto a balcony overlooking the courtyard to observe the newest members of Bellator. Magnus stood stoically behind Villifor on the small balcony and passed judgment upon his inferiors.

"The progress exhibited during your training session is unsatisfactory," Villifor said. "I believe additional motivation will help you reach your potential. Tomorrow we will hold a contest similar to today's training. The prize, should you be skilled enough to win, is to advance to the second courtyard and receive personal training from me."

The prospect of advancing to the second courtyard stunned everyone, but the opportunity to train with Villifor was nearly unprecedented. Magnus was the first person to receive training directly from the headmaster in recent memory and his face spiked with envy at the announcement.

"I believe some of you are ready for advancement…" Villifor let his eyes linger upon Jak and Cirata, "…while others have been lax in their training." He didn't need to look at Slate for the reference to be understood. "Tomorrow you will defend against two armed opponents of my choosing. Whoever withstands the onslaught for the longest amount of time will be the winner. Hedok will supply weapons. You are dismissed."

Slate walked gingerly back to the changing room and Jak fell in beside him. He was larger than any fighter Slate had encountered, save Magnus. Thankfully, that's where the similarities ended. Jak was a popular figure in Bellator. He was personable and quick to offer help in learning proper technique during training sessions. Slate had benefitted from his tutelage numerous times.

"After working so hard, it's difficult to believe I could advance to the second courtyard as early as tomorrow," Jak mused. "I wouldn't mind getting a shot at Magnus again either." Competition was fierce in Bellator and defeat in battle, even during sparring sessions, was remembered for a long time.

"I hope you beat Cirata, Jak. You deserve to advance." Slate said, finding that he genuinely meant it.

"Cirata will have to wait in the first courtyard a little longer. I'm not worried about her. You are my toughest competition."

"Ha! You must have been too busy clobbering your opponent today to notice I spent the majority of the time on my back."

"These are just basic, regimented drills. Without the constraints of a drill, you'll showcase your natural ability for the unexpected. If the tournament proved anything, it's that you are unpredictable."

"Thanks, Jak… I just hope Villifor chooses someone other than you or Cirata as my opponent tomorrow." Slate donned Ispirtu robes in preparation for the next part of his day. The other members left to discuss battlefield strategies and learn the lessons of Malethya's past. "Have fun upstairs and good luck tomorrow."

"We're discussing the roles of pikeman and cavalry today. It should be enlightening…" Slate didn't share Jak's interest in battlefield strategy. Slate planned to face his parent's murderer in a more intimate setting than a battlefield. He just needed to figure out who it was.

Slate left the Bellator complex and walked through the streets of

Ravinai ignoring the stares of citizens. Members of Ispirtu were unmistakable in their black robes, and citizens treated them with a combination of deference, respect, and fear that ultimately led to avoidance when possible. In the untimely event they needed to interact with him, they would appease his wishes and shower him with praise while trying to extract themselves from the situation. Magic had a strange effect on people who didn't understand it and most members of the populace had very little knowledge of it. The mystery of magic served to increase the power of Ispirtu and wizards in general, so they felt little need to educate the ignorant masses.

Wrought iron gates allowed a view of towering Ispirtu, a dramatic view even though Slate saw it on a daily basis. He wasn't impressed by the towering peaks or architectural detail. The Bellator complex was built just as intricately, but it lost its grandeur with familiarity. What made Ispirtu unique were the orbs surrounding the structure. They flew from peak to peak, served as lookouts around the guard towers, and simultaneously put on a visual display for anyone within view. A group of orbs that appeared as a crimson banner bearing the Ispirtu insignia morphed into ivy and covered the stone wall, wrapping around columns and projecting an air of academic excellence. On a different tower, the orbs morphed into a catwalk spanning the courtyard to an open window of a distant tower. These were the reasons Slate had studiously memorized the way to his lessons. If he mistook the orb illusions for reality, it was a long drop.

At the gates, one of the orbs flew down to eye level and circled him. In the security house, a low-ranking member of Ispirtu viewed the orb's projected image of him and compared it against records on file. Since few members of Ispirtu needed to leave on a regular basis during their training, the security detail recognized Slate and quickly opened the gate upon his arrival.

"Ho, Slate. How was Bellator this morning? Did you show them we know how to fight in Ispirtu too? How many shields did you punch through today?"

That was Tommy. By all accounts Tommy was failing his training within Ispirtu and stood very little chance of actively serving in the guard. Like many in Ispirtu, he signed up for training in the Crimson Guard with intentions of joining a different guild...in Tommy's case it was Bellator. He was placed in Ispirtu after testing positively for the spark, and now he lived vicariously through Slate's stories of Bellator.

"Good morning, Tommy. We were one person short in the duels this morning…we could have used you." Slate clasped Tommy on the shoulder, unwilling to crush his Bellator fantasies that made his days in Ispirtu bearable.

Slate neglected to join the stream of people entering Ispirtu and instead peered inside a first-story window. Inside, a squadron of Disenites attacked a reconstruction of a noble's estate. Members of Ispirtu took up positions on the roof of the manor and mercilessly rained fireballs upon the attacking soldiers. Orbs worked in concert to project the images of the attacking Disenites, simulating the attack formations of some past battle in the Twice-Broken Wars. The attacking Disenites didn't cause physical injury, but the simulation recreated the damage of the battlefield as well. The orbs would explode portions of the estate as chronicled during the real battle. The members of Ispirtu cast a tracking spell that signaled the orbs not to detonate if a wizard was within the blast radius. Since Slate didn't have the spark, he couldn't be tracked, and these recreated battles were as dangerous as the real thing. He would need to find a different route to his lesson in Magic Defense.

Slate looked up to the second-story window and hiked up his robes to scale the exterior of the building. The nice thing about the intricate stone architecture of Ispirtu was that it was as easy to climb as the foothills of Pillar. Slate reached one hand up to the window and hauled himself over the threshold.

"It looks like we'll have to start locking the windows again. You never know what will crawl through these days." The voice of Lattimer Regallo welcomed Slate to Ispirtu.

"I see the infirmary was able to set your jaw, but I think it's a little out of place…if you ever want it readjusted, let me know." Lattimer subconsciously touched his reconstructed jaw before turning his attention to the ring of sycophants drawn by the celebrity status of the Regallo name.

Brannon entered the classroom, black and purple robes flowing behind him. "To your seats!" Magic Defense was the only class instructed by Brannon, and Slate made sure he was enrolled. He needed to find more information about the headmaster, but he also needed to understand how to face a wizard in battle.

"Is there such a thing as a counter spell?" Brannon asked the class but silence followed. "Slate!"

"No, headmaster."

"…and why is that, Mr. Severance?"

"Some spells counteract the effects of other spells, but in a battle, there is no way to know which spell your opponent will cast. It would be a fool's errand to try to block an opponent's spell. The best defense, or counter spell, is to attack quicker than your opponent."

"Excellent. Now the best way to attack quickly is to use a familiar pattern so that you don't waste time creating a link to your spark. Use a pattern you already know and then pour your spark into it until the spell is cast." Brannon strode back and forth across the room. "The recreated battle of Loring's Gulch in the hallway has inspired me to add a practical element to today's lesson. Everyone line up in two lines."

The students easily divided with Lattimer's followers forming one line while Slate and the other leftovers formed the second line. Slate wasn't amongst friends, but at least he wasn't amongst enemies.

In the middle of the two opposing lines, Brannon placed two candles. To the first students in each line, he instructed, "On my mark, push the flame from the candle toward your opponent. I will counteract the effects of the fireball before it reaches the loser."

Live fireballs and Slate couldn't conjure a hairball…great.

"I fought in the Twice-Broken Wars. Many powerful wizards died because they could not cast spells quickly enough. You will not meet the same fate if the Disenites return. Go!" Brannon ordered. The two students concentrated hard and Slate counted. *1…2…3…4…5…whoosh.* A tiny ball of flame shot from one candle toward the poor wizard at the head of Slate's line. Right before it reached the wizard, the fireball dissipated in a cloud of steam. The wizards in Lattimer's line offered congratulations to the victor.

"Terrible! You must be faster, faster, faster! It is the best defense in battle. Strike before you are struck!" Brannon's voiced rose and echoed around the room. "Next two in line…Go!" Slate counted to four before another fireball shot toward their line. Brannon berated the students again, and the process continued. Slate finally neared the front of the line and realized that Lattimer had positioned himself to face him.

"Next two students, step up!" Lattimer stared malevolently at Slate. Defeat wasn't quickly forgotten in Ispirtu either. The fastest time Slate had counted was three seconds and he estimated the distance at ten paces…it would be close. "Go!"

Slate sprinted ahead while counting in his head. Seven paces left, but he was picking up speed. … *1* he passed the candles and was closing fast. …2 Slate launched himself into the air toward Lattimer.

Lattimer lost his concentration when Slate jumped to strike and failed to cast his spell. Slate reeled back, putting on a good show of intimidation while never intending to throw the punch. Ispirtu rules strictly forbade physical violence within its walls, something Slate found to be a stark contradiction to their sometimes ambivalent rules regarding the use of magic. As his fist moved forward, aimed just to the left of Lattimer's head, Lattimer ducked and Brannon sent a concussive wave at Slate, throwing him into the wall. Brannon stormed toward him, hauled him up by his robes and screamed in his face.

"While you are in Ispirtu you will follow my instructions to the letter! Get out of here before I lose my temper…Master Primean will be expecting you tonight. Once he finishes with you, report to my office. You can serve as my attendant to learn obedience." Brannon released him from his grasp.

As Slate left, he heard Brannon berating Lattimer and the remaining students. "Let this be a lesson to all of you! When you think your opponent is outmatched, that is exactly the moment he will do something unexpected…then you'll find yourself cowering on the ground and disgracing the Ispirtu name on your soiled robes…" The door closed behind Slate, but the muffled lecture continued on the other side. Slate wasn't looking forward to a visit with Master Primean, but it wasn't his first punishment, and the look in Lattimer's eyes was worth it. The order to report to Brannon was new, however, and Slate was a little worried about it.

Footsteps approached around the corner of the hallway, bringing Slate back to his immediate situation. His stunt forced him to exit the school via the hallways. Orbs formed the appearance of patrolling Disenite Guardsmen that attacked wizards on sight.

Slate avoided the guardsmen and surveyed the hallway from the relative safety of the building's ornate alcoves and architectural accents. Statues of famous wizards lined the corridor in a slightly haphazard manner. Some were set into alcoves while others stood in poses of action in the middle of the hallway. Directly in front of him, a wizard held his hand out in defiance of attacking soldiers. The soldiers were frozen in time as the land roiled beneath their feet. Further away, a mage stood in regal robes, presumably addressing the eager minds of Ispirtu. On and on the statues progressed, providing hope to Slate's dire situation.

Slate dashed from statue to statue, hiding as the Disenites passed. Slate saw a girl dart into an alcove ahead, but she failed to see one of the patrols. The Disenite projection called an alarm and three more patrols converged on the trapped girl. She began to concentrate.

1...Slate could use the distraction to break for the exit, but his conscience tugged at him. 2...While the orbs didn't physically injure students, pain was used as teaching tool. 3...A wizard needed to be able to attack from a distance to maintain an advantage in battle. 4...Four patrolmen would certainly overwhelm a wizard who wasn't fully trained yet.

The patrolmen attacked in pairs. The first two drew swords and entered the alcove as 5... the girl released a feeble attempt at a fireball. It hit the metal chest plate of the Disenite guard and dispersed. Slate slid behind the pair of attackers in the rear and chopped at the base of the guardsmen's necks. The projections crumpled to the ground silently and disappeared. Slate silently dispatched the final two guardsmen before they could reach the girl hidden behind an artist's rendering of a catalpa tree. Before she realized what happened and ran off, Slate pinned her arms against her side with his left arm and covered her mouth before whispering in her ear.

"Sicarius has taught me to blend into my surroundings and appear behind my prey at the moment of my choosing. If you let anyone in Ispirtu know I attacked these guardsmen without magic, I will find you again and teach you the lesson more forcefully. Do you agree to remain silent?"

"Fractal's truth, I agree." Slate released the girl, who remained in a minor form of shock. Slate recalled his first encounter with the Sicarius headmaster and felt a small amount of guilt for replicating the situation. At least he hadn't incapacitated her. Slate left for the stairwell while the hallway was free of danger.

"Teach me, Slate!" The voice startled Slate enough to turn around and the girl rushed on. "I came to the Crimson Guard to join Sicarius. Now I'm stuck in Ispirtu as a weak wizard unable to fend off a single

Disenite. I walk the hallways in fear and stand little chance of escaping this prison. Teach me to blend into the surroundings as you do…please…you are the only one with the skills to help me survive here." Her head hung ever so slightly at the word please, with her dark hair falling in front of her face. Her large eyes continued to stare at him and her jaw clenched, showing her determination. A slight quiver in her lips proved she was genuine.

How could Slate tell her that he lived in fear of these hallways too? "What's your name?"

"Annarelle."

"Meet me at the security station tomorrow morning. Look for Tommy. I don't know if I'll be of much help, but I'll do what I can…"

To Slate's surprise, Annarelle ran up to him and hugged him. In the distance, a door opened and wizards poured into the hallway. Slate took off at a full sprint for the stairwell, knowing he had already taken too much time. At the bottom of the steps he stopped cold. Between him and the exit, a full battalion of Disenite projections streamed from their ships during an invasion of a southern port. He didn't know what to do next when Annarelle raced down the steps after him. "The tracking spell tells the orbs not to explode anything within a few feet of us. If you stay close to me, you should be safe."

Slate unabashedly clung to Annarelle while inching through the recreated battle. Cannons from the ship smashed the nearby buildings to shrapnel, which all stopped in midair inches from causing his death. Slate crowded even closer to Annarelle as he tried to ignore the real dangers around him, exhaling in relief when he crossed the threshold of Ispirtu. "Thank you, Annarelle." Slate clasped her shoulder in appreciation and headed for the guardhouse, where Tommy recorded his exit.

In the streets of Ravinai, Slate ducked into an alleyway and removed his Ispirtu robes, using the city's bustling streets to transition his mind from the dangers of Ispirtu to his next task for the day. Slate prepared by familiarizing himself with the city's activities, viewing them as someone with training in Sicarius, rather than the naïve young man who had been overwhelmed by the intricacies of the city when he'd first arrived in Ravinai. Innocuous events and subtleties in action taught him more of a person's character than the clothes they wore or the tales they told. Slate thrived on walking within the city and deciphering its ebbs and flows.

The busy street opened into an expansive city square and with it came the purpose of his stroll through the city. Within this square, Slate would meet someone with the skills of Sicarius. Slate held something valuable, and for him to maintain possession of it, he had to stay alert.

Slate scanned the crowd, memorizing every face he passed and mentally sifting through them for potential danger. A merchant passed with a facial tic, but his hand hovered by his money pouch, indicating his anxiety had a financial origin. A courtier made eye contact with him, a beggar didn't lift his head as he passed by, and a clerk followed him more closely than was typical. All of these garnered more attention than the majority of people Slate passed, but Slate hadn't found his mark yet. The activity exhausted him mentally. He needed to maintain an outwardly calm appearance to blend into his surroundings while still positioning himself to see and evaluate everyone he passed. With practice, he had gotten more efficient at the process, but in a setting with this many people, his skills were tested.

Balconies overlooked the busy city square and buildings housed a variety of restaurants in the lower levels. Citizens of Ravinai lounged in outdoor seating and enjoyed their noontime meals in the picturesque setting. An intricate fountain featuring lions, from the family crest of King Darik, sprayed a light mist into the air. Slate ignored all of this and kept scanning the crowd as quickly as possible.

Two people to his right perused a merchant's shop, but their faces were hidden from view. Slate continued monitoring the shoppers as he passed. One entered the shop and the other lingered. Slate gazed unceremoniously at the fountain and then let his eyes follow a good-looking girl walking in the opposite direction. The maneuver turned him in the direction of the lingering shopper. The build was about right and the clothing was a bit too nondescript for the fashions of the other customers at the shop. He had him.

Slate approached. "Hello, Rainier."

The figure turned around and smiled. "Good afternoon, Teacher. What gave me away? It was the clothes, wasn't it? I should have chosen a less affluent shop."

Slate laughed. "Yes, the clothes were out of place, and you hid your face from me twice. That was more than coincidental." Slate reached in his pocket and pulled out the Stratego medallion. "I guess I'll keep this for another day. Now let's grab some food. I'm starving."

The Sicarius headmaster had encouraged Slate and Rainier to continue their game of Stratego to hone their situational awareness. Slate taught Rainier techniques from his Sicarius missions, and they used the city square like a dueling courtyard. The large number of people created an appropriately challenging environment, and the Stratego medallion changed hands on a regular basis. After the game was completed for the day, the restaurants within the square provided a chance for Rainier and Slate to catch up on the day's events while enjoying this most perfect of seasons. The summer heat had receded but the bitterness of the approaching winter was yet to arrive.

Slate grabbed an open table at a restaurant, making sure to order before the waitress left. "I'll take your largest steak, some chicken, and a side of potatoes." It was amazing what a morning of battle and scaling the walls of buildings did to your appetite.

"So what did you find out today?" Slate asked Rainier.

"I helped a few travelers entering the city with directions and got some news of the surrounding area. Attacks in the northern villages have increased, but details are hard to obtain because the tiny villages scarcely receive visitors. People complain of relatives suddenly losing contact and one merchant claimed a town disappeared that he had visited the previous year. It was a small hunting village within the woods. He didn't find any buildings, but he also admitted he could have mistaken the location within the forest."

"Villifor remains adept at hiding evidence of the attacks then…"

"That is possible, but I haven't heard rumors fitting the description of the Pillar attack."

Slate sighed. "Okay, Rainier…thanks for checking. Sooner or later we'll get a lead on what happened."

"Have you found any new information about the headmasters?" Rainier inquired after deciding on a sandwich and some fresh fruit…no wonder Rainier was the size of Magnus' leg.

"Villifor returned to Bellator today. He watched our lessons and declared a competition to advance from the first courtyard. The winner receives personal tutelage from Villifor."

"Do you think he is pushing fighters through training quickly for some reason?"

"My contact with him has been pretty limited, but it must relate to these secret missions. Advancement has been more frequent than years past, so it does seem like he is pushing students through training."

"We need more information. Could you discreetly ask someone who has advanced if they've noticed anything amiss?" Rainier said.

"Students of the first courtyard don't have access to the higher courtyards. I only see them if they decide to watch our lessons, which is rare."

"We'll have to create our own opportunities then. If you win the competition tomorrow, you'll have greater access within Bellator...so how do we win this thing? You could use your glove from Lucus..."

"No one at Bellator or Ispirtu knows that I have that glove and Sicarius has taught me the value of information. I don't want to use it until the time is right. I'll have to figure out a different way of winning tomorrow...somehow. I'm behind in my training compared to some of the other students. They are bigger, stronger, and now they have more practiced techniques...with two of them attacking me at once, my chances for victory are slim." Slate described the rules of the competition to Rainier.

"Remember, today you were trying to beat your opponent. Tomorrow you don't need to beat anyone. You just need to survive the longest. Survival is something that you have shown an innate proficiency for...and it's not something that can be taught in a lesson. What about Brannon?" Rainier changed the subject before Slate could comment on their student-teacher relationship status and the ridiculousness of it. Rainier was starting to sound dangerously close to Lucus at times.

"He hasn't missed a day of lecture. If he is behind the attacks, he's been orchestrating them from within Ispirtu. Today his lecture took a more practical turn though, complete with flying fireballs. Do you think he is pushing his students harder than usual for the same reason as Villifor?"

"Possibly, but Brannon would push his students hard regardless..."

"That's true. My actions in class today may have earned me an avenue for new information though..."

Rainier groaned. "What did you do this time?"

"Lattimer was going to shoot a fireball at me, so I charged him before he could let loose."

"You mean the fireball that was part of the lesson? The fireball that

Brannon ordered Lattimer to create?"

"That would be the one. When you put it that way it makes a little more sense that Brannon sent me to Master Primean again tonight." Slate gave a smirk.

"Slate, your pride will be the end of you...now tell me where the good news comes in."

"I will be personally attending Brannon after my visit to Primean. I don't know what that entails, but it should be a chance to get some more information."

"Just try not to attack him if he asks you to clear his plate...personal attendant sounds very close to servant." Speaking of plates, where was his food?

"I think I can manage that, although I might be tempted to put him in one of my Bellator holds and ask him a few questions using the techniques I've learned in Sicarius." The thought of watching Brannon squirm put a smile on Slate's face.

"...and how is the most enigmatic of headmasters? Have you had any recent contact with Sicarius?" The waitress finally brought his order of food. She lifted the lid from the covered plate and revealed a sealed envelope nestled into the squash.

The waitress was immediately apologetic. "I don't know how that got there! Let me get you another plate!" She reached for the plate, but Slate stopped her from taking it away.

"I don't know how this got here either, but I know who arranged it. You can leave the plate." The waitress seemed even more perplexed than before and exited at Slate's request, likely to scold the cooks concerning pranks with her customers.

Rainier looked to Slate. "How much of our conversation do you think the Sicarius headmaster heard?"

"I don't think I'd classify it as private. Let's see what the letter says." He opened the squash soaked envelope and found inside a sealed envelope bearing the Sicarius emblem. Breaking the wax, he finally got to the letter.

Dear Slate,

Apologies for interrupting your lunch, but it is time for another lesson. Your situational awareness has improved dramatically since the tournament. Let's put it to use. On Rue

Street, there is a large mansion adorned with Ispirtu-inspired decor. On the top floor of this house, there is a locked trunk. You must locate the trunk, open it without damaging it, catalog the contents, and seal it back up. Do not steal anything from the trunk or the house. Leave that to the common thieves.

Complete this task and drop off your list of catalogued items. Judging by your impatience at lunch, I would not want to come between you and your next meal, so I ask you to complete this task before dinner.

Finally, be careful during your lesson today. Rue Street is in a district of Ravinai where members of Ispirtu take residence. I don't think you are ready for a direct encounter with a fully trained wizard, so make sure to be discreet.

Slate folded the letter back up and shook his head. Sicarius always requested difficult, seemingly random tasks to be performed in inordinate timeframes. The requests didn't usually make sense, but they continued to push his skills learned within Sicarius, which was a misnomer itself. If there was a building that housed Sicarius, Slate had yet to enter it. He had never attended an Ispirtu-like lecture or met another member of Sicarius. His entire training had come in the form of Stratego and missions delivered in notes. Slate found the practice frustrating upon reflection and exhilarating during execution.

"It appears that my afternoon plans have changed. I am to break into someone's house, determine the contents of a locked trunk, and escape undetected."

"Let's go scope it out." Rainier usually accompanied Slate on his Sicarius missions. The Sicarius headmaster never explicitly required Slate to accomplish his missions alone. Indeed, the Sicarius notes never gave directions as to *how* a mission was to be accomplished. The tone of their dictation always implied that there was *a* way to complete the mission, if he were only clever enough to sort it out. It looked like it was time to solve another riddle.

The two paid the waitress and offered a generous tip. The poor thing seemed rather rattled by the note appearing in Slate's plate.

Slate and Rainier made the short walk to Rue Street and along the way the houses turned from small residences into mansions with manicured gardens and sprawling estates. It made the rest of the city feel very confined in comparison.

Slate had difficulty telling which mansion the Sicarius headmaster's note referenced because most estates displayed allegiance to Ispirtu. They had stone statues or ornamental trees cut into Ispirtu-inspired shapes. At the top of a hill, Rainier discreetly gestured to his right. Slate let his gaze wander in that direction and the meaning of the headmaster's letter became apparent. This mansion had a small number of Ispirtu orbs dancing around a non-descript stone figure. The orbs changed appearance to give the stone figure the likeness of various wizards that Slate recognized from his Ispirtu training. The orbs indicated this was the correct target of his mission, but the mansion itself left no doubt. The stately home had purple banners hanging from every window, and each banner bore the Regallo family crest.

The estate had a sprawling lawn bordered by a six-foot wrought iron fence. Slate assumed if Brannon could spare some orbs for an ornamental statue, then he probably had a few working security similar to Ispirtu. The main gate was swung open in a gesture of inclusion to the citizens, but Slate took one look inside the gatehouse and knew the gesture was merely symbolic. The guard looking back at him struggled to appear relaxed, like he was more inclined to act than sit. This was a Crimson Guardsman with training from Bellator. Slate needed more information about the house and the security there, but he was already being watched.

They walked by the estate talking amiably, cognizant of the guardsman's eyes burning holes in the back of their heads. After disappearing from the guard's view, Slate strategized with Rainier. "That mansion is on lockdown. If we have any chance of getting in there, we need to know exactly where security is stationed and how they respond to an alarm."

Rainier continued Slate's thought, "...and we need the alarm to be completely innocent so that the guardsmen go back to their posts calm and unsuspecting."

Slate looked around and spotted two young boys playing catch with a ball. That was about as innocent as you could get. He gestured toward the boys. "I'll enlist their help. Can you circle around the back and scout the guard's response there?"

"I'm sure the Regallos have a servant's entrance so they don't have to interact with the help. I'll watch from there." Rainier disappeared through the lawn of an estate without the security concerns of the Regallos.

Slate approached the young boys. "Nice arm. Which one of you can throw it the farthest?" The older of the boys didn't need much encouragement. He wound up and threw the ball as far as he could, sending it into the neighbor's yard.

Slate walked over and picked it up. "Do you think I can get the ball over that fence at the top of the hill?"

"No way!" The younger boy proclaimed. Slate launched the ball into the air and easily cleared the fence into the Regallo estate.

"How are we going to get it back?" The older boy asked.

"You can climb that fence, can't you?" Slate challenged the older boy, who took it up defiantly.

"Of course I can!"

The older boy climbed the fence, and Slate observed the guard's response. The first guardsman signaled a security breach to the guardhouse and three alert guardsmen exited the main entrance of the estate. When they saw the nature of the security breach, one guard ushered the boy off the grounds with his ball while the others returned to their posts.

Rainier met up with Slate. "What did you find out?"

"Three guardsmen came out the front door at the alert. I was surprised not to see any security orbs, so we caught a break there. Unfortunately, that's where the good news stopped. Despite the estate's outbuildings to hide behind, the only visible entrance is the front door or one of the windows, and we'd be in plain view if we tried to use them to enter the house. Did you have any better luck?"

"The back of the house has two entrances. Four guardsmen emptied onto the back lawn from one entrance, but none exited the service entrance on the side of the house."

Rainier had done very well on this trip. If they were going to use the service door, however, Slate needed more information. "What about windows or a strategy for approaching the door unseen? How do you know there isn't a Crimson Guardsmen posted just inside the door?"

Rainier furrowed his brow before answering. "Well, I didn't see much security at the gate on the side of the house, but the neighbor's estate is immediately adjacent to the property. There was a baker's cart that was pulling up to the service entrance. We could wait until they get another delivery and sneak in…"

Slate had already turned toward the neighbor's estate. "We go now then. They may not have another delivery until tomorrow, and that is our only chance to get into the Regallo estate." He didn't leave time for Rainier to argue.

Infiltrating the neighbor's estate was child's play in comparison to the Regallos. Hedges lined the street and ran the perimeter of the lawn. Slate ducked through the hedges and gazed at the lavish house offset from the street. Immaculate gardens were laid in his immediate vicinity, with mature rosebushes providing cover. Slate crept along the rosebushes, darted behind a gardener's shed, and sprinted to the corner of the house, ducking beneath the windows as he waited and listened for any shouts of alarm. None came, Rainier joined him a second later, and Slate moved on without a second thought. After navigating the halls of Ispirtu, an estate lawn was hardly worth mentioning.

They moved toward the back of the house and Rainier stopped Slate when he thought they were at the closest point to the service entrance of Regallo's estate. "How are we getting across?" Rainier asked.

"I'm afraid *we* won't be…I need a lookout."

"But you don't know what you'll encounter in the house. You need me with you."

"If I get caught in there, there are enough guardsmen that backup won't matter." Slate continued before another argument could be made. "That is a six-foot fence. I could climb it, but the few seconds it would take to scale might be the difference between getting caught and fulfilling the mission. It'd be a lot quicker with your help…"

Rainier gave in. "Yes, Teacher." The last word came out with a bit more sharpness than it typically did. Rainier was not happy about being left on this side of the fence. That didn't stop him from dutifully ducking into the hedges, scouting the Regallo estate, and reporting back.

"The delivery cart is still there. It looks like a delivery from the bakery. One guardsman patrols the back lawn of the estate. I'll signal when her attention is drawn away…now."

Slate ran directly toward the fence, and Rainier squatted near the hedges. Slate launched himself into the air, tucking his legs, and landing on Rainier's shoulders. Slate pushed off Rainier as Rainier straightened upwards, catapulting Slate into the air. His forward momentum carried him over the six-foot fence with room to spare. He landed on the lawn of the Regallo estate, rolling once before springing to his feet.

Slate straightened up as quickly as possible, and walked with the dutiful boredom of a delivery man. At the back of the cart, loaves of bread and other assorted baked goods were lined up in crates, having been set aside in a single group for this delivery. Slate picked up a crate with some pastries in it.

A man with a white apron hurried toward him. Slate spoke before he could be questioned. "The kitchen wanted these right away, so I got sent for 'em." The questioning turned into a lecture from the baker. "This is good honest work. Straighten your back, and carry those with pride. You could do worse in life than earning an honest living."

Slate straightened his back and headed for the service entrance. Inside the door, a clerk catalogued the incoming order. Slate applied the same strategy a second time. "I'm the baker's help. He wanted me to bring these in, but he didn't tell me where to go." Ignorance was a valuable tool when properly applied.

"Then you should have thought to ask him. I don't have time for incompetence. I see you have three orders of pastries. Bring them to the kitchen. Take the first right, and the kitchen is at the end of the hall." Perfect…directions and dismissal. Slate gained information and would be forgotten nearly before he left. Slate left the pointy nosed clerk to his ledger and turned the corner of the hallway.

At the end of the hallway, a large door opened into a bustling kitchen. In here he'd be discovered immediately. Thankfully, there was a small service stairwell along the hallway for the servants' use. Slate started up the stairwell, but some potted flowers on a small table in the landing caught his eye. There was a decorative plate beneath the pot to catch any excess water that drained through. Slate grabbed it along with the white cloth covering the table. At the top of the stairs he spotted a lavatory and ducked into it. He wrapped the cloth around his waist like a busboy's apron, wiped off the decorative plate using the monogrammed hand towel, arranged a few pastries on the plate and hid the crate in a cabinet, walking out the door carrying the plate in one hand at shoulder level.

While pretending to serve the pastries, Slate used his peripheral vision to get the layout of the second floor. The hallway formed an H, with rooms lining the sides of the hallways. The great room of the main floor opened to the ceiling, with the hallway turning into a catwalk that looked down upon the great room and beyond that, the back lawn. The last room drew Slate's attention because someone stood guard outside the door. If there was a trunk of great importance, it would probably be in there. Slate made for the door. He would simply convince the guard that he was supposed to lay out the pastries for Brannon's arrival and gain access.

Halfway down the hall, a female voice called from an open doorway. "There you are, you lazy oaf of a servant. I called for those to be brought up ages ago. You took so long you forgot which room I was in."

Slate stopped in his tracks. Was he caught? The voice was loud enough that the guard could hear it, so Slate had little choice but to respond, "My apologies, Madame."

He turned around and an urgent whisper commanded as he entered the room, "Close the door". In the room, a well-dressed lady lay heaped unceremoniously on a cushioned bench. An elaborate looking trunk sat in the center of the room, and the Sicarius headmaster rested upon it.

The headmaster dressed in a series of black wraps that concealed every inch of skin and the folds of which hid innumerable weapons. The design was impressive in its practicality and the freedom of movement built into its construction. Slate wondered if it was enchanted but only momentarily because his attention was drawn to the face, or rather the mask, of the headmaster. It was a dark grey, or perhaps a dull black and Slate could not make out any defining features, including a mouth or eyes. It made his head hurt to look at it too long.

The headmaster obviously didn't have any trouble seeing him or reading his expression. "Your eyes see the reflection of light. The mask is enchanted to attract light, making its features difficult to discern. Without the benefit of light, people tend to fill in the blanks with surrounding information, predominantly the clothes one is wearing." The headmaster revealed an object hidden under a fold in a leg wrap.

"This is a shock stick, which I believe you are familiar with…"

Slate subconsciously rubbed his neck, remembering his first encounter with the headmaster.

"The lady of the estate was just introduced to it. I then mimicked her voice to call you into the room so as not to alert the guard." The headmaster then continued in a decidedly more masculine voice. "She'll be rejoining us in a few minutes, so let's be brief. I am unsure what to do with you, Slate Severance." The confession gave the headmaster rare pause. "You progressed quite rapidly through the missions I provided, faster than any recruit I've ever trainied. Your rapid success indicated you were ready for a test, which you are currently undergoing. The note I sent to you described an Ispirtu-inspired mansion on this street. You must have realized that *every* house on this street could be described as Ispirtu-inspired. Students choose a mansion with higher security to show their abilities, but they use the vague description as an excuse to choose a mansion in which they are sure to succeed. As a result, I am able to get a realistic assessment of skill level. Once a house is chosen, I break in before the student, set up the trunk, and observe. This is where you have caused me a problem."

The headmaster stood up from the trunk and walked over to the unconscious woman, checking her pulse. "Two minutes…" The headmaster moved silkily toward Slate until hot breath angrily tickled the side of his neck.

"You, Slate Severance, chose to break into the home of Brannon Regallo, the most powerful wizard in this fractal-forsaken kingdom." The headmaster nearly spat with the forcefulness of the whispered condemnation. "The fact that you made it this far into his estate required an immense amount of talent and luck. The fact that you attempted to do so shows an even more obvious lack of judgment and flaw in your character. If I had let you continue into Brannon's office as you were planning, you would have set off his alarms and would be lucky to survive long enough to grovel for forgiveness."

The headmaster walked toward the trunk and kicked the lid open. "The contents are yours. Claim your prize while I figure out what to do with you."

Slate peered inside the trunk and found a sealed letter, which he tucked away. Then Slate noticed it was difficult to look into one corner of the trunk. He placed his hands around a Sicarius mask identical to the one the headmaster was wearing. His hands were still quivering when the heap on the couch began to stir.

"Time to go, Slate." The venom in the headmaster's voice had disappeared and Slate was ushered toward an open second-story window. The headmaster threw a round object and shoved Slate through the window after it. Panic swept over Slate, but as he fell he saw the round object hit the ground. There was a hissing sound as the object grew in size until it was roughly twice as large as his body. He landed on his back expecting a crunch, but instead the object absorbed his fall and catapulted him back into the air. The fence to Brannon's estate passed beneath his airborne body and he landed with a thud in the neighbor's hedges. Rainier appeared at his side a moment later, pulling him to his feet. The two sprinted as fast as their feet would take them until the sounds of raised alarms faded far into the distance.

CHAPTER TEN

PEACE, IN VARIOUS FORMS

The apartment building was indistinguishable from other complexes. Four apartments rose above a small merchant shop in a blue-collar district of Ravinai. Slate and Rainier chose this particular spot to reside because the apartment had a separate entrance to the street, solid locks, and access to the rooftops via a balcony.

Slate appreciated the comfort of his new home by propping himself against lounging pillows arranged in the manner of the Tallow tribe. "What happened in the Regallo estate and why did you fly over the fence like a drunken squirrel?" Rainier tired of waiting for Slate to explain their afternoon's adventure.

"I was about to walk into Brannon's guarded office, and presumably imminent danger, when the Sicarius headmaster intervened. I was given a note and this mask, before being shoved out a window, which is when you witnessed my graceful flight over the neighbor's fence. Why would you waste liquor on squirrels? In Pillar, we left the squirrels alone and saved the liquor for pretty girls."

"Does that mean you completed the mission? Squirrels take less liquor to provide entertainment and if you need help from liquor to meet a pretty girl, maybe I should be the teacher." Rainier responded.

"The mission was a sham. It gauged my capabilities based upon which house I entered on Rue Street. The headmaster would sneak into the house and hide the trunk somewhere on the second floor." Slate enjoyed bantering with Rainier. "I don't need liquor to meet girls. I just say the words tournament champion, and they forget their dignity. It works great, but you wouldn't know about that."

"Why did the headmaster stop you when you broke into the Regallo estate? Even a nomadic tribesman knows that is an adventure wrapped in folly, and yet you partook." The student chided his teacher. "The words 'tournament champion' will just as likely get you stabbed in a back alley as they will get you the girl. I'll take Tallow charm and charisma any day."

"Apparently I'm an innovator. No one has ever chosen to break into the Regallo estate and the Sicarius headmaster needed to intervene due to the uniqueness of the situation. Regardless, the headmaster prized me with the contents of the chest, so I would say the mission was a success, although it probably relies on the contents of the letter. Judging by the quietness of our apartment on most nights, I would say the mission was more successful than the Tallow charm."

"Before making any claims against the Tallow charm, you better make sure you know what that letter says."

Slate pulled the unopened envelope from his pocket and read it aloud.

Dear Slate,

You club-footed son of a ballerina – I did not think it possible to make such a royal mess of things. You must temper your anger at the death of your parents with a thread of self-preservation. Even I can only help you so much. If you continue down this path, my help will not be enough.

Your achievement in breaking into the Regallo estate has nonetheless passed the test. The mask in the trunk marks you as a full member of Sicarius. Welcome to the Crimson Guard. The only orders you will respond to are mine or orders directly from King Darik. The mask is only to be used on official Sicarius business, upon penalty of death.

As a member of Sicarius, you will be required to attend guild meetings. The next meeting will be tomorrow. Please wear your mask to preserve your identity. More details will follow.

Regards,

"I would say that becoming a full member of the Crimson Guard qualifies as a successful mission, wouldn't you?" Slate couldn't help but let a smile creep onto his lips.

"Even I won't diminish this moment. Congratulations, Teacher. Should I break out the liquor?" Rainier offered.

"Let's save that for later. I still have a visit with Master Primean tonight, along with attending Brannon. The liquor might help with Primean, but I'd pay two-fold showing up at Brannon's office inebriated. Besides, I've heard Tribesmen can't handle their liquor."

"Fine…if you won't drink with me, why don't you practice your *attending* and bring me a drink? I might not be visiting Primean tonight, but I need to numb the pain of conversing with you." Slate laughed and poured Rainier a drink before fixing a small dinner that he ate on the way to Primean's laboratory.

Primean's office was located in the basement of Ispirtu so Slate went to the side of Ispirtu where a storage closet was located. He unceremoniously smashed the window and dropped to the basement floor. That was one nice thing about Ispirtu…with all the recreated battles in the hallways, no one thought twice about a broken window or two. Besides, by tomorrow morning, the broken window would be magically repaired along with the collateral damage of the day's recreated battles.

The basement of Ispirtu didn't encourage guests. If the main floor of Ispirtu had been designed as a monument to the great wizards and battles of lore, the basement was the battleground of wizards hoping to one day become immortalized as a statue above. The basement housed the research laboratories for Ispirtu, along with the incredibly driven and anti-social wizards housed within them. It was Slate's favorite place in the building, despite being home to Primean's laboratory, because everyone was so preoccupied with their own discoveries they paid no attention to him. The sounds of failed or successful experiments arose from the closed doors of basement laboratories. Slate knocked at the double doors with the sign "Pain Tolerance Laboratory" scribbled above the door. Master Primean was always in need of test subjects, so he served as both Ispirtu's disciplinarian and one of their most commended inventors. Slate was a regular test subject.

"Yes, yes, come in," the familiar old voice came from within the room.

Slate opened the doors to see Master Primean bending over a particularly cruel looking chair. It sat next to a pool of water with a sponge in it and contained various forms of blades and other sharp objects. "Good evening, Master Primean. How is your research progressing today?"

"Slate! Good to see you!" The old wizard met him with an embrace. "I'm working on a most exciting discovery." Exciting usually meant painful. "By using the pattern of a sponge soaking up water and linking it to a Bellator Guardsmen's armor, the armor will collect the pain caused by injury!"

"That's great, Master Primean...that could save a lot of guardsmen in battle. How will you know if it works?" Slate praised Primean while trying to mask his doubts. "...I just hope I'm not the first one to test it?"

The old wizard's exuberance couldn't be slowed. "Nonsense, young warlock. Now put on this armor, sit down in the chair and prepare to make history!" Slate did as he was told but was beginning to question whether his embarrassment of Lattimer was worth an evening with Primean. The wizard continued, "You will be perfect for this experiment. Since you are a frequent test subject, I have very good baseline data to see at which point you pass out. If you can withstand more pain than that, then my experiment will be a success!"

"...so today's experiment will be on acute pain?" Acute pain was always preferable to chronic pain because the experiment would be short.

"Yes, these are just feasibility trials. Now let's get the apparatus ready. Please place your arms on the armrests with your forearms facing upwards." Slate obliged. Master Primean tightened leather bands across his wrist and upper forearm, holding it in place. Then a moveable arm with a collection of blades was positioned above his forearm. If Slate hadn't been cut and healed so many times previously by Master Primean, he would have been worried.

"Ok, I've set the controls to be just above your baseline pain threshold. If this works as intended, you should feel nothing more than a pinprick." *If? Dammit.* Slate knew this was the first time Primean had tested this contraption. Primean began to countdown, "3...2...1..."

Slate flexed his forearm instinctually before he heard a large explosion from across the room. A two-foot wide medicine ball shot toward his chest, crushing him against the solidly built chair. He vaguely remembered Primean staring at him with his laboratory notebook out before his eyes rolled into the back of his head.

A pungent aroma brought Slate back to his senses. Primean had already healed any damage inflicted by the medicine ball and unstrapped his arms from the chair. Other than fatigue from the healing process and the memory of the medicine ball hurdling at him from across the room, he was no worse for wear. "Thanks for fixing me up, Master Primean." Master Primean always healed his subjects after experiments, but no one checked to see if he healed you completely, so it was best to stay on his good side. "How did the experiment turn out?"

"I was pleased with my test setup. The knives successfully diverted your attention and prevented any preemptive physiologic response to the medicine ball. Unfortunately, the armor didn't absorb your pain as I had hoped. The armor soaked up your sweat like a sponge when your body went into shock, but the pain remained...I guess it is back to the drawing board. Thanks for coming in...see you tomorrow?"

By fractal's grace, Slate hoped he wouldn't see Primean anytime soon. Slate flashed his best smile toward Primean. "Your discoveries are so exciting I can hardly stay away. Brannon requested that I serve as his attendant tonight, but I confess I don't know where his office is located. Could you tell me?"

"Ahh...that is very good or very bad, young warlock. I hope you haven't found yourself outside the good graces of the Head of our Order..." Slate relayed the story of the lecture hall duel, culminating in the launching of his body toward Lattimer. "Ha! Excellent, excellent. Brannon respects decisiveness, even in the face of orders, if it is the only way to succeed. I wouldn't make a habit of embarrassing the Regallo name though." Slate hid a grimace. "During the day, Brannon keeps his office at the top of the highest tower, but this time of day he will be at his home office. It is located on Rue Street. Do you think you'll be able to find it?"

Finding the house wouldn't be a problem. "I'll figure it out. Thank you Master Primean. Have a good night." Slate left the laboratory before Primean could dream up any corollary experiments and tried to push aside his anxiety at returning to the scene of his afternoon break-in.

As he exited Ispirtu and made his way through Ravinai, Slate considered the approaching dangers. Would the same guardsman be on duty? Surely the baker wouldn't make two deliveries in one day. What about the clerk? Any decent clerk had a sharp eye for detail. Returning to the Regallo estate was a recipe for disaster, but he could see no way out of it. Before he had the opportunity to devise a proper plan, he had arrived at the guardhouse of the Regallo estate.

"I'm Slate Severance. Brannon requested that I attend him this evening." A different guardsman was on duty. He looked down at a list of names and opened the gate without giving Slate a second thought.

Slate headed for the front door with his head held high, despite his sense of foreboding. Slinking toward the door would incriminate him before he ever opened his mouth. A fatherly looking butler opened the massive oaken door before Slate had the chance to knock. "Welcome to the Regallo estate. Brannon is expecting you, but he is currently occupied with other business. I will show you to the sitting room until he is ready to meet you."

"Thank you." The butler showed him to a room with several uncomfortable looking chairs. They were undoubtedly expensive, but welcoming they were not. Slate sat on the overstuffed cushion and leaned against a chair-back that reminded him of Master Primean's contraption. He missed his lounging pillows.

After a few minutes of shifting his weight on the chair, footsteps approached and Brannon's voice carried into the room. "Thank you for your time, officer. A daylight break-in unsettled my wife greatly. I doubt she will take her mid-afternoon nap in peace for quite some time."

"We will work diligently to resolve this matter. You can trust the soldiers of King Darik's army to keep the streets of Ravinai safe." The footsteps reached the front door and Brannon concluded the conversation. "I'm sure your team of crack investigators will find the culprit. Have a good evening." Brannon's comments were laced in sarcasm, which was lost on the poor officer. The door closed before a reply could be made.

Brannon bellowed for the butler. "Tell the guardhouse to double the security for the next two weeks. If anyone looks even remotely suspicious, I want them held for questioning. Is that understood?"

"Yes sir, and may I remind you that a Mr. Slate Severance is waiting in the sitting room."

"Ah…thank you. You are dismissed."

The headmaster of Ispirtu walked into the sitting room. Slate decided directness would best mask his trepidation at being associated with the afternoon's events. "Is everything ok? I didn't mean to eavesdrop, but…"

"Then Sicarius has taught you nothing. Some fool broke into my estate today. I've since reassigned the guardsmen on duty to the Pillar outpost. I've heard there is little left there to guard, so they shouldn't have trouble fulfilling their duty." Despite Slate's best efforts, the anger showed on his face. Brannon continued, "I heard rumors that you witnessed Pillar's destruction and now I know for certain. Control your anger. Follow me and we'll discuss in my office."

Slate bit his tongue and wiped the anger from his face, standing obediently and following the headmaster upstairs. They took the main stairwell, overlooking the great room with the view of the back of the estate. At the top of the stairs, Brannon turned on the catwalk toward the guarded room.

The office was everything you would expect from a wealthy, privileged egomaniac. Awards and gifts from other noble families, even King Darik himself, filled the walls. Brannon sat behind a gigantic desk, which served to protect him from interacting too closely with anyone seated in the small uncomfortable chair across from him. "Close the door." Slate obliged and sat in the chair.

"When I first met you, I tested you for the spark and…finding you lacking a shred of magical ability, I assumed you would be as inconsequential to me as the rest of the Malethya masses. You are no longer inconsequential. You embarrassed the Regallo name at the tournament by spitting on the family crest, signed up for Ispirtu when you have no business there, and now you have attacked my son openly within a classroom. Your efforts have turned you into an annoyance but a mysterious one. Why did you attack Lattimer today?"

"It was the only way I could defend myself…" Slate responded.

"Horse shit. You weren't in any danger. The fireball would have dissipated before it reached you."

"I couldn't be sure he would shoot a fireball at me. The shield would have only protected me from fire."

"True…but still horse shit. You are a terrible liar. Add it to the things you need to work on." Brannon's comment quieted Slate for a second.

"Pride…I wanted to beat Lattimer." Slate finally responded.

"Partially true…those are the best kinds of lies. You are learning. Why did you join Ispirtu? Why not just join Bellator and become a mindless weapon?"

Slate was already tiring of this line of questioning. "Before the tournament, my knowledge of magic could be summed up in a campfire story. Since then, someone has turned my hand to stone and nearly killed me in the process. I find out that there are enchanted weapons, armor, and scepters that turn a fair fight into something far from it. I was attacked by bandits as I left town only to find my hometown, peaceful Pillar, wiped out by someone. Magic seems to have played a hand in all of it. Joining Ispirtu seems to be the only way to make some sense of it all." Slate couldn't believe he had just said all of that to Brannon, of all people.

"There it is…and with a reason like that, it makes sense that you haven't dropped out of Ispirtu yet. I would tell you that I had nothing to do with the events you just mentioned, but if you took me at my word you'd be an even bigger fool than I already believe." Brannon leaned backwards in his chair, thinking. He idly formed a fireball in his hands and juggled it back and forth. "Ok, you can stay in Ispirtu. If you ever attack my son again, though, I'll have you thrown out of the guild faster than I can throw a fireball." As demonstration, the fireball rocketed toward a picture hanging on the wall but dissipated before it hit.

Brannon continued. "Now that we've settled that, what am I going to do with you? I don't want you as a personal attendant because without the spark you are worthless to me in that capacity. It seems the best use of your time is to keep me up-to-date on the actions of my counterpart Villifor. You will continue to serve as my attendant and report to me once a week. Meanwhile, you will find out why Villifor has been traveling so regularly. Villifor was on one of these excursions when your parents were killed, so it would seem to serve both of our purposes."

Slate sat quietly, slightly shocked at the turn of events and trying to process Brannon's comments.

"You don't trust me." Brannon's words were a comment, not a question.

"No." Slate stated simply while looking the wizard in the eye.

"Good. Trust is given too freely to those with warm words and a nice smile. Real trust can only be earned through actions. Make me trust you, Slate, and someday you might find that you trust me as well. Now get out of my house. I think you have been here one too many times today…" Brannon turned his back to look out his office window, leaving Slate to find his own way out.

Slate ambled slowly on his way home, finding peace in the knowledge that the day's activities were coming to an end. As he entered into the more tightly packed buildings of the city, he decided to take to the rooftops. The sun sat low in the sky and the solitude of the rooftops fit his mood. He could see why the Sicarius headmaster recommended their use. He passed overhead of an eatery, watching people dine and couples stare into each other's eyes. He continued on, but the scene at the eatery made him think of Sana. Where was that girl? Their travels from Pillar had drawn them together, but Lucus' orders for his apprentice coupled with his own hectic training left little time for romance.

The answer to his question came as Slate swung onto the balcony of his apartment. Sana enjoyed a drink with Rainier to end the evening. Even more pleasantly, Sana rose from her chair and greeted him with a kiss before he could say hello.

"I see you didn't miss me enough to track me down." Sana baited Slate, but Slate turned the subject in a safe direction. "Where have you been?"

"Lucus sent me on a mission after we returned to Ravinai. I'm meeting him tomorrow over lunch to report my findings, so tonight I thought I'd make sure you two weren't getting into too much trouble without me."

Rainier jumped in. "We wouldn't dream of causing trouble. Take today for instance…After a morning of getting beaten to a pulp in Bellator and an encounter involving fireballs at Ispirtu, the Sicarius headmaster sent us on a mission. Our infallible leader chose to fulfill that mission by breaking into Brannon Regallo's estate. Needless to say, the ill-fated misadventure required a well-timed rescue from a certain nomadic tribesman…and we haven't even asked him how his night went yet." Sana cast a stern look toward Slate, making her affectionate greeting vanish from memory.

Slate felt a lecture from Sana coming on and tried to cut it off before it began. "That about sums it up. I'm sure it was nothing compared to your adventures." Slate's father had deflected questions about their training by asking his mother the simple question "How was your day?" The question always brought an onslaught of activities and gossip from the town and by the time she had finished, she had forgotten all about her original question.

"I was digging through lost manuscripts in the Wizard Council's library trying to research your ability to sense magic cast upon you. Now you put yourself in danger before we know what we're up against? Sometimes you are the most fractal-forsaken fool I have ever met!"

Did that qualify as a lecture or a tirade? Maybe it was a combination of the two. Rainier took the opportunity to leave before Sana took the exhibition up a level or two. "Slate has me digging for information all over town in the morning, so I'm heading to bed. Sana, it's great to see you again."

He ducked into the apartment, and Sana's diatribe continued without acknowledgment. "If you expect my help in your schemes, you better start coming up with better plans! I can't be expected to save your neck every time you do something stupid enough to..." The door to Rainier's room closed. Sana's voice calmed immediately. "I enjoy Rainier's company, but I wanted to talk with you alone. There is a very important question you forgot to ask. Did I miss you?"

As always, the abrupt change in Sana's demeanor took him off-guard. Hopefully it was part of his charm. Slate managed to stammer, "Well...did you miss me?"

Sana stood up from her chair, walked inside and reappeared with an armful of lounge pillows. She laid them on the balcony floor, and then grabbed Slate's hand. Sana knelt on the pillows, pulling him downwards and onto his back. She laid her head on his shoulder and whispered "Yes, Slate, I did miss you. Now tell me what happened today. I want this neck to stay attached awhile, and I wasn't lying when I said your sense of strategy is terrible."

Slate recounted his day of training at Bellator, focusing mainly on the competition the following morning. Sana summarized, "If you win this competition tomorrow, you get to be a personal attendant to Villifor? The man is pompous, but we need information on him, so you need to win."

"That sounds easy." Slate laced sarcasm into his reply. "Unfortunately, Jak, Cirata, and ...everyone else are better trained than I am."

"You don't need to be the best fighter. You just need to win. Tell me the rules again."

"Villifor will choose two fighters to attack the contestant. Hedok will choose the weaponry. The person that stays off his back the longest is the winner. It's not too complicated."

The sun was setting, providing a perfect backdrop for a few moments of contemplation. Slate's thoughts got sidetracked and he pulled Sana closer, stealing a kiss in the process. Sana pushed upward halfway through the moment of intimacy. "I've got it...here's what you are going to do." She then whispered her plan in Slate's ear, and it brought a smile to his face.

"Will they allow that?" Slate asked.

"They didn't disallow it in the stated rules." She had a point. It was hard to argue with Sana. "Now what happened at Ispirtu, and what did that crackpot wizard Primean do to you?"

"Brannon decided to have a duel between students by having them shoot fireballs at each other. A shield was in place to dissipate the fireball before hitting the student. I disrupted Lattimer's concentration before he was able to complete his spell." This was not a time to overemphasize his heroics.

"You mean you *attacked* Lattimer...in front of Brannon?"

"As a result, I paid a visit to Primean. He's developing a spell to absorb pain during battle, so Bellator Guardsmen can fight through minor injuries. He was using the pattern of a sponge soaking up water as his link..."

Sana was quiet for a while. "That's not a bad idea, but pain is the wrong application for that link. The sponge is soaking up a liquid, not a feeling. If it were applied to blood, it may be possible to limit the amount of blood loss during a battle. The wizards at Ispirtu can't even recognize a discovery when it occurs in front of them...idiots!" Slate tried not to smile at her quick temper, less its attention be directed at him next.

Slate decided to bring up his Sicarius mission. Despite Sana's affiliation with Lucus and the Wizard Council, she always seemed intrigued by Sicarius. It must have been the mystery with which they operated. Sana couldn't leave a question unanswered. "Bellator and Ispirtu weren't the only guilds to provide training today. Sicarius sent me on a mission."

Sana was immediately distracted. "Ah yes, Rainier described it as an 'ill-fated misadventure' to the Regallo estate. How did you end up there?"

"I was instructed to copy down the contents of a trunk from within an Ispirtu-inspired home on Rue Street. I quickly realized *all* of the estates on Rue Street were decorated with Ispirtu references. I chose the Regallo estate because of the orbs in the front lawn. When I think of Ispirtu, the most unique feature is the orbs."

"Didn't you stop to question whether the Sicarius headmaster's orders should be followed? What has the headmaster done to earn your respect?"

"I still don't know what to think of the Sicarius headmaster. The headmaster has saved me from a number of precarious situations, but I've also been incapacitated for no reason...and I'll admit the shroud of secrecy doesn't exactly inspire trust. For right now though, I need the Sicarius headmaster. The skills I'm learning in Sicarius will help me to investigate my parents' deaths, even if the investigation leads me right back to the Sicarius headmaster." Sana remained quiet following Slate's explanation. "But I'll need to follow orders for the time being. After today, I'm officially a Crimson Guardsmen within Sicarius. I have a meeting with Sicarius and its members tomorrow."

Sana appeared dismayed at the news. "Be careful, Slate. We know so little about Sicarius..."

"I don't know much about Bellator or Ispirtu either..."

Sana said, "We at least know something of their nature. Your only contact with Sicarius has been through cryptic notes."

"I'll be careful, Sana." The simple statement seemed to placate Sana. Her body relaxed against his. "Besides, now that I'm Brannon's personal attendant whose job it is to spy on Villifor, I'm sure I'll be learning more about both Ispirtu and Bellator as well."

Sana's relaxed muscles tightened against him reflexively at the news. He quickly stated, "Let's forget about all that. Tell me about your mission. What did you find out?"

For a second, Slate thought Sana was going to begin a thorough tongue-lashing, but she decided against it. Her jaw unclenched and she stated, "I'm meeting Lucus at the infirmary tomorrow for lunch with Ibson. Join us there, and we can discuss in more detail. Besides, there are other ways I want to spend my evening." She looked up at Slate, and he kissed her while it still suited her mood.

The kiss led to Slate rolling on top of Sana, and it gave him pause. "The last time I was in this position, you pulled a knife on me."

Sana's eyes sparkled in the setting sun. "...and I will again if you get too bold." Slate interpreted her words as a threat, but the sparkle in her eye suggested an invitation. The rest of the night he had a wondrous time exploring how bold was *too bold*. By the time sleep arrived, Sana lay on his shoulder, and the pitch black sky covered them both like a peaceful blanket.

CHAPTER ELEVEN

MAY THE WORST MAN WIN

Jak found Slate after he entered Bellator's locker room. "Hey, Slate, are you ready? I stayed up all night practicing defensive techniques and searching variations in forms that will give me an extra edge today. I know I should have rested up, but I had too much energy. How was your night?"

"I didn't get much sleep either," Slate answered truthfully. Sana had left before Slate awoke, but she didn't leave him empty-handed. They had talked through the competition's rules in detail and formulated a scheme to win.

"Did you think of a plan of attack?" Jak finished putting on his armor.

"I don't necessarily have a plan of attack, but I do have a strategy of sorts."

Jak laughed. "I knew you would. See you out there, Slate." He left the locker room to warm up in the courtyard.

Slate put on his armor and looked at his right hand as he stepped onto the sandy courtyard. Everyone saw him punch through Lattimer's shield. Hopefully the memory was fresh enough to still inspire intrigue among his competitors.

Cirata walked by and saw him examining his hand. "You're too slow to land a punch against me, Slate. You'll be on your back in seconds."

She was probably right, but his strategy didn't depend on him actually landing a punch. "This hand is good for more than punching through shields." Slate flashed a knowing look and was rewarded by a pause in Cirata's bravado. He finished the conversation by saying, "I hope you get the opportunity to find out what else it can do," loudly enough for the other contestants to hear.

The conversation in the courtyard died down after that, but the energy continued to grow until the sun's rays touched the sand of the courtyard. Members of Bellator interested in the day's competition filled the overlooking balconies. Slate recognized a few of them as Bellator instructors, including Halford Patton, a general from the Twice-Broken Wars who taught battlefield tactics.

Hedok entered the courtyard and addressed them. "Line up and look presentable before Villifor arrives. I know none of you are worth two fractals with a sword, but you might as well look like you know how to fight. There is no sense in embarrassing yourself prematurely, although I'm guessing some of you have already done that! Ha!" Hedok laughed at his own cleverness, but the contestants were too preoccupied to indulge the old soldier's sense of humor.

Villifor and his attendants appeared at one of the second-floor balconies where he addressed the assembled observers and contestants. "Today, our lowest members will showcase the skills they've learned from your excellent tutelage. The contest is simple, and yet will require the application of knowledge from weapons training, strength training, conditioning, and of course the venerable Halford's battlefield tactics." Villifor acknowledged the esteemed faculty member. "Each contestant will be attacked by two opponents. The contestant that remains standing the longest will advance to the second courtyard. Additionally, I have taken it upon myself to train some of our more promising members of Bellator personally." Magnus stood at the right shoulder of Villifor and his back straightened at the indirect compliment.

"Let's not delay...Jak, start the competition with a good showing, will you?" Jak stepped into the center of the courtyard. "His opponents will be Cirata and our own tournament champion, Slate Severance!" Villifor continued his showmanship as a light round of applause died down. "Hedok, please distribute the weapons." He then released an orb from a pocket. "Our friends at Ispirtu have spirited the blades in today's competition to prevent any mortal damage and have graciously created this orb to be our official timekeeper. It will float over the head of the contestant currently winning the competition."

Hedok approached the three contestants carrying short swords, a staff, and a broadsword. "The preferred weapons of the competitors are chosen...but given to their opponents. Slate will yield the broadsword, Cirata the staff, and Jak the short swords." Hedok handed the broadsword to Slate with a smirk. Slate hefted it into a ready position, feeling clumsy and weak. Cirata and Jak dropped comfortably into their stances. Their proficiency with other weapons was much higher than

Slate's skill level.

"Fight!" Villifor commanded from above. Cirata and Slate engaged Jak, moving in opposite directions to flank the fighter. They had a decided tactical advantage, but Slate's inexperience with the broadsword allowed Jak to focus his defenses on Cirata. Slate modified his attack to coincide with the blows of Cirata's staff, but Jak was able to fend off the blows. Slate let the battle establish a rhythm and then swung forcefully a half beat early. The unexpected timing of the attack required Jak to shift his weight as he deflected Slate's sword. In that moment, Cirata had an opening and landed a blow under Jak's arm. Cirata's blow prevented Jak from properly defending that side of his body and he was knocked to the ground a moment later. The orb floated toward Jak and remained a few feet above his head.

"Excellent, excellent! Get up and take a bow, Jak! That was a brilliant display of defensive forms and a great start to our competition." Villifor then addressed the crowd and remaining combatants. "Will any of you best Jak's showing? Let's find out…"

Contestant after contestant was called and Slate was forced to attack several other students during their tests, but the orb remained above Jak's head. Even Cirata, despite an impressive performance, rose from the sand after her battle to see the orb remain near Jak. Slate was the only contestant left untested.

"Now, ladies and gentlemen, let's discover whether our most well-known champion can rise to the occasion. Jak's performance has stood the duration of the morning's bouts. Slate 'Stonehands' Severance, please enter the courtyard." Slate stepped forward to meet Hedok while Villifor continued. "Jak, if you wish to advance past the first courtyard you will need to earn it by defeating Slate. Please step forward." Slate tried to appear confident despite his dismay. If he faced Jak, his only chance for victory lay with Sana's schemes and the appearance of fear would ruin his chances. "I have had a special request from Magnus to avenge his tournament loss by facing Slate today. Although I feel no incentive to honor this request, I do think it would be entertaining…and that is reason enough for me. Magnus, join Jak in the courtyard."

Magnus jumped from the second floor balcony and his landing shook the entire courtyard and caused a cloud of dust to rise from his crouched form. When the dust cleared, Magnus stared at Slate and announced, "I should have won the tournament and will prove it today." Slate maintained his confident posture, which bordered upon arrogance. Magnus looked for more than victory. He wanted to send Slate to the infirmary. Slate hoped Sana's battle plans worked more smoothly than some of her testing plans. *Trust... no one said it would be easy.*

Hedok performed his part in the show. "For the last battle of the day, I will allow the competitors to choose their own weapons. Jak and Magnus, please choose first." The two men hefted weapons that appeared undersized for their large physiques. Jak chose the broadsword while Magnus chose a large two-handed battle axe. Apparently he had found the brutal weapon more to his liking than a broadsword.

"Slate Severance, choose your weapon." Slate scanned the weapon racks, drifting his hand over short swords and stopping at a staff. Everyone expected him to pick it up, but his plan relied on some intrigue and choosing a weapon his opponents didn't expect would help build it. Trust. His hand continued down the weapons rack to an audible gasp from the audience. A mace, various swords, and the large two-handed weapons favored by Jak and Magnus were all available, but he passed them by and continued toward a table with weapons laid upon it. Sai, kunai, knives, and other weapons too small to fit on the weapons rack remained untouched since the start of the competition. Even Hedok, with his unique sense of humor, had found it unfair to assign one of these offensive weapons to someone defending against two armored attackers. Slate picked up a packet of throwing knives. Slate spoke to Magnus but carried his voice for all to hear. "How long did it take for me to beat you, Magnus? 7 seconds? Your embarrassment will last a lot longer today."

Jak and Magnus faced Slate in the courtyard, spaced evenly apart about ten paces from him. Magnus said, "I wouldn't be so quick to claim victory. Let's see how you do against a real blade."

It was time to play his cards. Everyone knew about his hand, but they didn't know what it could do. "I won't pretend to fear you this time, Magnus. I have everything I need right here." Slate raised his hand in front of his face and flexed his fingers into a fist. "And it's far more dangerous than that meat cleaver in your hands. Don't come near me. The ground you walk on may be the very thing that sends you to the infirmary."

"There is a better way to settle this argument!" Villifor exclaimed. "Combatants ready…fight!!!"

The two heavily armed, massive men closed the distance on Slate. As they approached, Slate started an uppercut from somewhere around his ankles. His fist flew up and then he windmilled his arm, changing the direction of the punch to be pointed back toward the ground. Jak and Magnus were closing the distance fast. Trust. Slate let out a guttural scream and drove his hand into the sand. Nothing happened, as Slate expected.

Jak, having heard Slate's warning prior to the fight, rolled clear of the impending unknown attack. That was the opening Slate was looking for…but he had hoped for a similar response from Magnus. Instead, Magnus continued his charge and Slate barely had enough time to grasp his throwing knife. He aimed for Magnus' chest, but in his haste he jerked it downward. The blade flew end-over-end toward the sand in front of Magnus' foot. His eyes went wide with the memory of Pillar fresh in his mind. Magnus tried to sidestep the throw and in the process stumbled to his right as the throwing knife hit the sand harmlessly behind him.

Slate located a second-floor balcony without any onlookers and sprinted toward it, leaving Jak and Magnus at his back. This wasn't tactical positioning but a full-out, run for your life sprint. Jak recovered from his roll and gave chase, but with his bulky broadsword, he couldn't keep up with Slate.

Slate estimated the height of the balcony railing; it would be close. Slate stole a quick glance over his shoulder and saw that Magnus had overtaken Jak and was closing fast. Slate reached the edge of the courtyard and launched himself off the wall and slightly backward in order to slow his momentum. He planted his second foot higher up the wall and pushed away from the wall, directing his body toward the empty balcony. His momentum swung his legs up over his head and he landed on the concrete railing of the balcony, doubling himself over and leaving his torso hanging precariously in the air. Slate hooked his feet under the railing to gain leverage and lifted himself just before Magnus released his battle axe while in an all-out sprint. It flew through the air and passed where Slate's overhanging head had been just a moment before. Slate stood with the safety of the balcony floor beneath his feet and the battle axe buried in the courtyard wall. The orb floated from Jak's head toward Slate. Jak touched two fingers to his chin before extending them toward Slate, a gesture of respect that wasn't shared throughout the courtyard.

"Coward!" Magnus shouted. "You are a disgrace to Bellator! Anyone displaying your lack of courage should be removed from the guild!" Similar, if less passionate murmurings could be heard around the courtyard.

During the commotion, Villifor remained uncharacteristically quiet and Slate understood that he was being given the chance to explain his antics. "Magnus calls me a coward, but I have used my training in Bellator to win this contest. It seems everyone has forgotten Professor Patton's lessons in battlefield tactics. I haven't even had the privilege of his lessons, but I know choosing the location of a battle is of tactical advantage. I was outnumbered and outmatched, so I used the tools at my disposal to improve my odds of success. By ascending to the balcony I claimed the high ground, a position I could successfully defend and hold. If this were a real battle, I would have survived and held my ground until reinforcements arrived. No other contestant can make that claim."

Professor Halford Patton stood up from his balcony chair and clapped. "Well said, Slate. A death in battle is only as honorable as its necessity. I hope to have the honor of teaching you soon."

Villifor heard enough. "Slate advances to the second courtyard and will receive personal training from me. Slate, I will come have a word with you. Everyone else is dismissed."

Slate silently thanked Sana for her suggestion to use the balcony during the contest. He had to improvise once Magnus charged through his bluff, but the plan had worked. A moment later, Villifor joined him on the balcony. "I asked for an entertaining bout and you certainly provided that."

"I couldn't pass up the opportunity to train with you."

"It seems to have worked out for you then, because I will train you. Your first lesson is that you put me in a difficult position by pitting Halford's reputation against Magnus' objections. In your situation, I would have played my cards the same way, but there will be consequences to your actions. You are now in my debt for the trouble you caused me."

"And what does that entail?" Slate asked while trying to keep the apprehension out of his voice.

Villifor gazed across the courtyard for a while before answering. "You are in a unique position by being in all three guilds. All the headmasters have allegiance to King Darik, but the guilds are only linked through opportunity, whether that is political, tactical, or some other tenuous collaboration. In times of peace, this is enough, but I saw what happened at Pillar, Slate. Not the official explanation of an explosion in the mine but the aftermath of what really happened. Someone is attacking the innocent people of Malethya and the attacks are becoming more frequent. I've been searching for an explanation, but my sources of information are not as extensive as Sicarius. I need you to look for information within Sicarius and particularly from the Sicarius headmaster. If anyone knows who is behind these attacks, it's the Sicarius headmaster."

Brannon had mentioned the best lies were partial truths. Slate wasn't sure if this was a moment of honesty or a carefully crafted half-truth, so he responded in kind. "I never believed the official explanation. The miners of Pillar were too careful and too experienced to cause an explosion of that magnitude. If there was a battle as you say, the townspeople didn't own weapons or train in combat and would have been overrun. I will search for information in Sicarius that describes the destruction of Pillar and the responsible parties. Train me, find the attackers, and let's put an end to this."

Villifor looked him in the eye and extended his forearm to shake. "It's a deal. Report to the second courtyard and I will supplement their teachings." Slate left to change from his Bellator armor into his Ispirtu robes before walking across Ravinai.

The architecture of Ispirtu morphed while Slate waited at the security gate. Tommy stepped out to greet him. "Ho, Slate! How did things go at Bellator today? Learn any new tricks you can share with me?"

Slate saw Annarelle waiting in the front lawn and decided to forego any small talk. "Tricks? I have something more important…come with me."

Tommy responded to this shift from their daily communication by following obediently. "Annarelle meet Tommy. Tommy…Annarelle." Tommy looked rather uncomfortable in front of the fairer sex, but he held out his hand and managed to keep the social awkwardness to a minimum.

"Both of you view yourselves as weak wizards. Am I wrong?" Silence answered his question sufficiently. "In Ispirtu that relegates you to a life of subservience to the stronger wizards. No one will challenge this truth if you do not. Ispirtu places so much emphasis on magic that the more natural skillsets are neglected. This morning I saw a Bellator fighter run straight into an impending attack with complete disregard for his own safety. I have seen the Sicarius headmaster break into Brannon's own home and leave unscathed. These people lack the spark but are as powerful as the wizards of Ispirtu. You can't let these walls define you or who you can become. Are you up for the challenge?"

Annarelle didn't hesitate. "I asked for your help, Slate, and I meant it." Tommy nodded with steel in his eyes.

"Good. Here is your first task as a student of Sicarius, Annarelle." Slate took a coin from his pocket. "Stratego is a simple game that is complex in application. It will teach you to be aware of your surroundings and of people at all times." Slate explained the game of Stratego but didn't mention that he still treaded lightly in the hallways of Ispirtu despite his own training. There was no point in shattering their fragile confidence in him. "Tommy, you are interested in Bellator. Many wizards are trained to depend on magic and that is their weakness. Your task is to incorporate magic with physical attacks. You may be weak in magic, but you will be the strongest fighter with magic at his disposal. Do you understand?"

Annarelle hugged Slate and snatched the coin. "Thank you. We'll train every chance we get." Tommy grabbed his forearm and then began discussing training schedules with Annarelle. Hopefully some training would help them survive this place.

Slate left for Brannon's lesson, scaling the wall and climbing through the second-story window. Brannon began talking before he was three steps past the doorway. "Yesterday we had our first practical exercise in the use of magic. Lattimer, tell me what the class learned."

Lattimer answered in a respectful and deferential tone that gave no hint of their family ties. "The best defense against magic is a quick offense. We cannot anticipate which spell will be cast against us, so it is important to strike before being struck." He glanced toward Slate. "We also learned not to underestimate our opponents and that concentration must be maintained while casting a spell regardless of the situation."

"These lessons can only be learned through practice. They must become innate responses before you are ready for battle. Line up and we'll do it again." The students formed lines too slowly for Brannon's liking. "For fractal's sake, do *something* quickly. You can't cast a spell in a timely manner, but at least line up with some speed." Brannon had the candles positioned and lit. The first person in line behind Lattimer was still arriving to the combatant's position when Brannon ordered, "Begin!" The student wasted two precious seconds running to position and was rewarded with a fireball that dissipated inches from his face. "Too slow! Next combatants, begin!" Neither student was in position, but the student in Slate's line managed to run and concentrate on the spell at the same time, sending a fireball toward the student in Lattimer's line and winning the bout. Brannon continued the rapid rate of the bouts and lectured while they were ongoing. "You need to be able to do more than stand in one place casting spells while an arrow finds you during battle."

Slate stole a glance at Lattimer, who was positioned across from him. The new method of starting the bouts meant more distance between himself and Lattimer, so he had no chance of repeating his strategy from yesterday. He wasn't about to stand behind a shield and wait for a fireball to find him. "Begin!" Brannon commanded.

Slate raced forward knowing he couldn't cover the distance to Lattimer quickly enough. ...*1* Lattimer sprinted toward the shield and maintained a look of concentration. ...*2* Slate rushed past his shield and dove in the air. He wasn't even close to striking distance from Lattimer. His outstretched hands came down on the open flames of the candles. ...*3* No fireballs shot at him. Instead a rush of air hit him in the face, causing momentary disoriention.

"Stop!" Brannon ordered. "I ordered a fireball to be cast, not an air wave. Lattimer, you are disqualified from the competition and will report to Master Primean this evening." He then rounded on Slate. "This may not have been a direct assault, but you still disobeyed a direct order from your headmaster. You will join Lattimer for a session with Primean." Brannon then managed a smile. "Your approach was original, though, and within the spirit of the competition. You can leave via the window if you'd prefer."

Slate climbed out the window to avoid the hallways as Brannon continued lecturing. "A worthy opponent will not act predictably. You must read your opponent and anticipate the need to react." Slate dropped to the Ispirtu lawn and could no longer hear Brannon's lecture that Slate took as indirect praise. Today was shaping up to be a good day and it was still before lunch.

Slate had forgotten to mention the lunchtime meeting with Sana, Lucus and Ibson to Rainier. Thankfully, his early exit from class at Ispirtu provided enough time to catch Rainier at the apartment. Slate switched out of his Ispirtu robes and took to the rooftops, traversing the city and jumping onto the apartment balcony where he found Rainier preparing his disguise for their daily game of Stratego. He was dressed as a little old lady, complete with handbag and spectacles.

Slate laughed. "I'm afraid you wasted one of your better costumes today, Rainier. We'll be heading to the infirmary to catch up with Lucus. Stratego will have to wait for another day...oh, and I gave away the medallion today. We've progressed past the point of needing a symbolic token to drive the competition."

Rainier sighed at the waste of a good costume. "I'll go change out of this disguise, and then we can go to the infirmary. I must admit, it will be nice to see Lucus again."

"I'm afraid we don't have time for you to change. See if you can fool Lucus!" Slate laughed and Rainier groaned. Wearing a disguise in a public place was one thing, but dressing like a woman while having lunch with a friend was something quite different.

After walking through Ravinai at a hurried pace that belied Rainier's disguise, the infirmary came into view. The massive, sprawling complex was surrounded by immaculate grounds. Marble pillars framed the entryways and walking paths connected gardens for the use of the infirmed. Slate realized the scale of the complex would create an unanticipated problem. "How are we going to find Ibson?"

"Ibson was quite famous and well-respected. I don't think we'll have a problem."

Inside the infirmary, they were greeted by a helpful wizard wearing white. "Welcome to the King's Infirmary. We provide care for all of his majesty's subjects through both herbal and magical techniques. How can I help you?"

"We are joining Ibson for lunch. He has been a patient for the last few months..."

"Of course, we all know Ibson well. If it weren't for Brannon's quick work in the arena, he wouldn't still be with us. I'll walk you to his room."

Slate walked what seemed like an endless distance through a maze of shining tunnels and other wizards dressed in white. "Has Ibson's condition improved?"

"It has stabilized. But I fear he won't be the same person you remember."

That response quieted Slate for the rest of the walk. Their guide pushed through doors labeled PSYCHIATRIC WARD and knocked on a door. Lucus answered and thanked the infirmary wizard for his time before hugging Slate. Ibson smiled coyly at Slate's companion. Evidently, Rainier made for a fine looking elderly woman.

The inside of the room looked like one of the nicer inns of Ravinai, but closer inspection revealed padded walls, rounded corners, and furniture bolted to the floor. Lucus sat at a small square table and Ibson gazed through his window with garden view. Physically, he looked like the same man, but his gaze wandered and he made senseless rhymes while tapping his foot to some internal rhythm.

The sky is blue,
The flowers are pink,
People have joined me,
For food and drink.

Lucus gestured for Slate and Rainier to join them at the small table. "For a while after the accident, there was hope he would regain all of his faculties, but after some early improvements, his condition has stabilized. I continue to visit him, and as long as he appears happy to have my company, I shall continue to make the trip."

"Ibson showed me great kindness and is still paying the price," Slate said. "I don't know how to repay him."

"Ibson knew what he was doing. He saw something in you he considered worth the risk. You can repay him by reaching the potential he saw in you." Lucus always had a way of easing Slate's worries and challenging him at the same time. Before he could continue the conversation, Sana joined them.

"I apologize for my tardiness, Master Lucus. I was suffering through a morning with the nobility and they confuse conversation with sport." Slate had never seen her dressed for a high society gathering. She was absolutely radiant, but apparently didn't suit Ibson's tastes.

Beautiful girls still will age,
Until they do I'll remain at bay,
Your taste is yours so please allow,
If I wait until they are colored grey.

Ibson winked at Rainier and reached to massage his shoulders before Rainier swatted his hand away with his purse. Ibson managed to retrieve his hand before it could be smashed and produced a decidedly childlike giggle from the old man and widespread laughter around the table, with the exception of Rainier.

Lucus brought the group back on topic as an infirmary attendant served lunch. "Ibson, in the past few months, I have investigated your attack, assuming it was linked to the events of the tournament. We learned Slate can feel magic directed toward him, but he has no spark. Due to the complexity of this investigation, I divided the efforts of our group. Sana researched literature in the archives, and Slate and Rainier gathered information from within the guilds. It is the purpose of this lunch to update you on the progress and formulate a plan. Slate and Rainier, would you go first?"

Slate thought his accomplishments seemed minor when asked to summarize them. "I have no solid evidence regarding the culprit from the tournament incident, Ibson's assailant, or the Pillar attack. My contact with Brannon has been limited, but he recently enlisted me as his personal attendant and directed me to gather information on Villifor's activities. Villifor has been travelling in secret and accelerating his advancement of students through the ranks of Bellator. No one knows where Villifor goes during his travels, but Rainier has been listening to reports from travelers as they enter Ravinai."

Rainier picked up his cue to continue with the summary. "Travelers report that small villages are disappearing in the north, but I've found nothing similar to the carnage of Pillar. Merchants report having traveled to these villages to trade and upon arrival have found no signs of inhabitation. It is our estimation that Villifor's travels are linked to the disappearance of these towns, but we do not know the manner in which he is linked."

Slate picked up the story. "As of this morning, I won a contest in Bellator to advance to the second courtyard and will be training directly with Villifor. He directed me to gather information from Sicarius concerning the attacks. His implied expectation was that I would befriend the Sicarius headmaster, but my relationship with the Sicarius headmaster is far from intimate. My most recent conversation was duplicitous and confusing. I was chided for my judgment and thrown from a second story window while being praised for the advancement of my skills and rewarded with a Sicarius mask, a symbol and tool used by the Sicarius members of the Crimson Guard. In short, I believe any of the headmasters have the skill and tools at their disposal to coordinate these attacks, but I do not have the information necessary to implicate any of them. I'm hoping your investigation has proven more fruitful."

So many fruit

Which one is ripe?

A bad apple you seek

Oranges, grapes, and tripe.

"Your knowledge is not tripe, Master Ibson, and I hope you don't consider our investigations to be tripe either." Lucus nodded respectfully toward Ibson and continued. "My efforts have centered on Ibson's findings from the tournament investigation and the events leading up to his injury. Ibson reached a point in his investigation that caused concern for his personal safety. Few things would inspire such a strong reaction in Ibson. He was a master of defensive magic and held more shields in place than any wizard save for Brannon."

Slate interrupted with a question. "Defensive magic? Brannon teaches the wizards in Ispirtu that a quick attack is the best defense against magic."

Lucus grimaced. "Defensive magic is a lost art. A wizard holds spells as shields that dissipate the effects of offensive spells. Ibson was one of the few masters of defensive magic left. He could hold multiple shields at any given time and they were flexible enough to defend against a number of offensive spells. This makes his attack even more troubling. If Ibson feared for his safety, he would hold his shields in place, but there were no signs of battle in the arena where Brannon found Ibson. The lack of struggle also makes me suspect the use of Blood Magic."

The quiet room grew even quieter at the mention of the taboo subject. "I had difficulty finding reliable sources of information on the topic, but what I found is quite troubling. Blood Mages favored spells that affect an enemy's internal components, like the iron in one's blood. The spell couldn't be detected by other wizards and the small changes produced profound effects, like the extreme fatigue experienced by Slate in his final tournament bout. Unfortunately, the changes to Slate's hand and the stratego medallion tied to his arm couldn't be explained by my findings. I am still searching for a clear piece of evidence." Slate, sensing the story was still unfolding, remained quiet. "Upon receiving word of the attacks in Pillar, I investigated types of mental subjugation commonly employed by Blood Mages. These spells are more complex than moving iron around in someone's veins, but they could be used to drive common villagers to attack with the frenzy observed in Pillar. I'm afraid I don't have concrete evidence to implicate anyone, but Ibson's fears of Blood Magic within the kingdom are gaining merit." Lucus paused before offering a final fear. "If there is a Blood Mage with the capability of subjugating minds, it becomes even more paramount to gather information on the headmasters. The Blood Mage would undoubtedly target someone of influence and give orders through their subjugated minion rather than risk direct exposure."

"You are suggesting that anyone could be behind these attacks?" Sana asked incredulously.

"No, we are looking for someone with the spark, since Blood Magic is dependent upon its use. We are also looking for someone with access to one of the headmasters. They, save for the King himself, would be the only people with enough power, authority and cunning to hide an evil of this magnitude."

Rainier spoke for the first time, and when he did, he spoke with authority that rarely entered his voice. "The Tallow Tribe remains uninterested observers in most of the politicking of Malethya. However, Blood Magic threatens our most sacred beliefs and we will stop at nothing to end the threat." Slate knew little of the Tallow tribe's beliefs despite his time with Rainier, but this wasn't the setting to inquire further. Ibson found the pronouncement of importance though.

> Ink flows like blood,
> Blood flows like ink,
> If the two should collide,
> With whom shall he link?

Other than the word blood, the rhyme made little sense and Slate considered them to be the ramblings of a confused man. Lucus directed the conversation toward Sana. "What have you found in the archives?"

"The only reference I could find was that Cantor, the founder of Blood Magic, had the same ability to feel magic directed at him. He credited the ability for his most profound discoveries, claiming that feeling magic provided him insight into both the pattern and the spark. Later wizards claimed the ability and labeled themselves Perceptors, but all were exposed as frauds. It appears Slate is a true Perceptor but without the ability to cast spells like Cantor." Sana held a mixture of wonder and empathy on her face that made Slate feel like a test subject. He preferred the look in her eyes from the night before...although that look could be equally confusing. "Nothing I found implicates a likely suspect. What will we do next?" Sana let her frustration at failing to find more solid answers show during her final comment.

Slate looked to Lucus but found the wizard staring back at him. "Slate, it appears you have a sense of intuition that is unnaturally adept. Given the lack of evidence to point us in any single direction, I suggest we follow your intuition." Slate almost laughed out loud until he saw Sana, Rainier, and even Ibson nodding and looking toward him. "Well, we need more information on the headmasters and I am in the best position to obtain it. I will continue to gather information from Ispirtu, Bellator, and Sicarius. It also strikes me that if we are up against a Blood Mage, they would need training of some sort and they would be unlikely to get that training within Ispirtu or the Wizard Council. Lucus, could you look for any wizards that have recently left the Council or a position within Ispirtu?"

Lucus responded, "Renegade wizards are not spoken of amongst the Council, but I have ways of inquiring..."

"Good. Rainier, you have been taught all the skills that I have as a member of Sicarius. Use them to investigate the liaisons of Villifor.

The Sicarius headmaster is beyond either of our abilities at the moment, but we already know Villifor is interested in the comings and goings of the enigmatic headmaster. He undoubtedly has other sources looking for information besides me. We may gain more information about the Sicarius headmaster through your efforts to watch Villifor. Additionally, the information you gain may help me to win favor with Brannon."

Rainier smiled the same dangerously confident smile he flashed Slate during their tournament match. "The best teachers aren't afraid to trust their students." Lucus nodded in agreement.

"Sana, my biggest fear is that King Darik is subjugated by the Blood Mage. If that were the case, the headmasters could be operating with complete integrity and carrying out the orders of a corrupted King. We need someone close enough to the King to determine if this is the case. Seeing that you are already capable of intermingling with the nobility..." Slate referenced her current attire. Sana stared back coldly at the prospect of spending more time with nobility. "...you are best positioned to determine if someone in Darik's inner circle is feeding him direction behind the scenes." Slate's directness in asserting the presence of a Blood Mage was met with mild surprise, so he explained. "Until we prove otherwise, we must assume that a Blood Mage not only exists but that he is behind all of the activities we've been investigating."

Sana answered. "Your logic, for once, is sound. I will do what I can to gather information within the King's court...even if it means conversing with pompous, entitled nobility."

Up and up and up,
Down and down and down,
The king that long has reigned,
Soon will lose his crown.

Lucus finished the meeting by addressing Ibson. "We shall meet occasionally to update you on our progress. We will not let your sacrifice, even if we are still figuring out its significance, be forgotten." With that, the group left Ibson to his own internal poetry.

Slate timed his exit to coincide with Sana in an attempt to placate her mood. "I didn't mean to place you in a setting where you felt uncomfortable…"

"You did what you thought was best and shouldn't feel guilty for it. If you are going to be a leader, you will face much more difficult decisions than that."

Slate could see that Sana's mood wouldn't be easily turned, and questioned Rainier about his tribe instead. "Why are the Tallows so concerned about Blood Mages? They haven't been seen in years…and how does that tie into your tribe's beliefs? You never speak about them."

"It is not the tribe's way to discuss our beliefs. They must be lived to be understood."

A little girl ran up to Slate, interrupting the question he wanted to ask Rainier. "Can I help you?" Slate asked the girl.

"I was given a lollipop and two ribbons for my hair. Aren't they pretty? All I had to do was give you this note." She handed Slate a sealed envelope with the very familiar seal of Sicarius upon it.

Slate smiled down at her. "Yes, your ribbons are very pretty and I hope you enjoy your lollipop." The group gathered around while Slate opened the letter.

Good afternoon Slate –

Your first meeting with Sicarius will occur in precisely 30 minutes. Please retrieve your mask. Another note will be delivered to tell you the location of the meeting. Arrive unseen and you will gain respect amongst the members.

"I need to leave to prepare for a Sicarius meeting." Lucus was gracious, as expected. "Have no worries, Slate. Each new task is one less mystery." Slate gave a smile to Lucus and sprinted to retrieve his mask.

Slate took to the rooftops to avoid the crowded city streets and entered his apartment from the balcony. He contemplated a disguise, but without knowing the location of the meeting, choosing an appropriate disguise was difficult. Instead, he did his best to mimic the look of the Sicarius headmaster by tying his Ispirtu robes so they wouldn't restrict his motion. Finally he put on the Sicarius mask for the first time.

The enchanted mask formed to his face but didn't block his peripheral vision or his breathing. Slate tested his newly identified perceptor abilities and sensed the enchanted mask was...grey. It wasn't light or dark, encouraging or ominous. After having experienced the range of emotions and feelings from previous encounters with wizards, the neutrality of the mask felt strange. Slate interpreted the feeling to mean the mask was not intended for good or evil. It was simply a tool of Sicarius. Perhaps this meant it could be used in any way the wearer intended or that the previous owner had committed acts on all spans of the spectrum.

Slate found the Sicarius headmaster waiting for him on the balcony. "Follow me." The headmaster commanded before climbing to the roof and bounding across a few buildings. The headmaster stopped a few rooftops away and said, "Nice outfit."

"Next time you should send a dress code."

"I couldn't risk telling you the location of the meeting. I still don't trust your judgment after your antics at the Regallo estate. To protect the members of the guild, I decided to personally escort you to our meetings until I feel you are trustworthy. Do you accept these terms?"

"I don't believe I have a choice."

"There is always a choice. Accept my terms or turn in your mask and never hear from me again."

Slate stood by his original comment but didn't feel the urge to say so. "Your terms are accepted."

"Excellent." The headmaster retrieved a shock stick and signaled with a whistle. Two shadows in Sicarius masks jumped onto the rooftop. "Sicarius Guardsmen are adept at handling and disposing of incapacitated targets. Perform your duties with honor so that you don't become a target for disposal." The headmaster reached for Slate's neck and a jolt preceded a wave of blackness as he fell into the waiting arms of the guardsman behind him.

Slate awoke in a haze and shook his head to clear the cobwebs. His memory came back in short order and he gathered his bearings. Slate sat in a chair within a small four foot by four foot room with a door and a full length window. A quick check of the door proved it to be locked.

As his senses cleared, his circle of awareness broadened. Outside the full length window was a small stage with the Sicarius symbol inlaid upon it. The lions of King Darik were set on either side of the stage, although the symbolism was unclear. Were Darik's lions protecting Sicarius or were they shoved to the sides of the stage as an afterthought? No other members of Sicarius were visible from his vantage point.

The headmaster strode onto the stage and pronounced in fluctuating intonations, "We are the eyes and ears of the kingdom. We go where others fear and carry out our mission with speed, silence, and absolute finality. We do this to protect the people of Malethya from those that plot in the night. We are Sicarius." An orb near Slate's feet illuminated and the light reflected off a huge, multi-faceted mirror that made up the wall behind the stage. Slate could make out the reflections of the other members of Sicarius, but he found it impossible to number them or even identify which reflections were duplicates due to the Sicarius masks. The headmaster had arranged for a meeting of the entire guild without risking the identities of any members...it was brilliant and paranoia-inducing all at the same time.

"Two of our Sicarius brethren have fallen in service to the King since our last gathering." A moment of silence passed. "I will recount their missions, so that our brethren can teach us even in their passing. One member was sent to a northern village where reports surfaced of animals acting with uncharacteristic aggression. House cats turned on their owners and birds dove at villagers when they fled outside. The guardsman underestimated the widespread affliction within this village and didn't bring enough darts, his preferred modus operandi, to dispatch the rabid animals. A second guardsman was dispatched to the village and found the body of the first guardsman devoured by rats in an alleyway. After her initial report, she was not heard from again. I went to the village myself, only to find that it had disappeared." The headmaster reflected for a second. "Recently, similarly aggressive attacks by animals and people have been reported through the Northern villages. I have reported these findings to King Darik, and he has chosen to address you directly."

King Darik stepped from a recessed doorway in formal dress bearing his characteristic lions and stood beside the Sicarius headmaster. He spoke with a predatory snarl worthy of his crest. "Since the Twice-Broken Wars ended decades ago, I have held this kingdom at peace. Now a cowardly enemy lurks in the shadows and threatens the peace I work so diligently to maintain. I implore each of you to provide information on these attacks using whatever means necessary. As the eyes and ears of my Kingdom, I expect you to uncover the truth. If you are unable to do so, I will seriously question the usefulness of this guild. I have complete faith in your training and abilities, but now is the time to prove your worth. Report to the headmaster immediately with any findings related to this topic. I now conclude this meeting." King Darik swirled around and left the meeting room. His demeanor was in opposition to the public persona displayed at the tournament. This was a man every bit as dangerous as the headmasters he employed.

The orb at his feet grew dim with the departure of the king and Slate sat patiently in his room since the door was still locked. A few minutes later, the Sicarius headmaster opened the door. "What did you think of your first guild meeting?"

Slate didn't feel like exchanging pleasantries. "The mirrored wall was a nice touch. It really made me feel connected to the other members of the guild. I almost forgot that I was sitting in a locked cage."

The headmaster sighed. "The king requests the doors remain locked when he attends our meetings. Our training makes him feel uncomfortable, but his logic is flawed because there are better places to carry out an assassination than here. My arguments didn't assuage the king's discomfort."

"The Crimson Guard serves the king. Does he have reason to mistrust Sicarius?"

"The king is a battle proven war hero accustomed to meeting his enemies head on. Without a war to fight, he fears the potential enemy at his side. The occurrences of late have increased his paranoia, and the secrecy surrounding the attacks has a distinctly Sicarius flare. The fact that we are unable to find information on the subject reeks of incestual plotting. We have battled our own internal demons within Sicarius in the past, but in this instance I believe the enemy to be elsewhere. Do you have information on the topic?"

"A wise person once told me that information is power, even going to unprecedented lengths to preserve anonymity amongst allies. The same person told me I wasn't to be trusted. So why should I trust you with information, and power, when you already hold more of each?"

"Trust is not one of my strong suits. I could formally request the information as the headmaster of Sicarius, but then I would worry about misinformation. I would spend endless hours verifying the accuracy of your information and the entire exercise would be a waste of time. How about a trade instead? I have information of interest concerning Pillar and its inhabitants. I will provide it to you under two conditions. The first is that you provide information of equal value that is specific to the attacks. The second condition is that I judge the value of your information relative to mine."

"…and if it is not?" asked Slate.

"You, Rainier, Lucus, and Sana have spent considerable time in the wake of the Pillar attacks investigating potential causes. If you haven't found anything by now, you don't deserve to be a guardsman."

Slate thought they had managed to find surprisingly little information in the past few months, but the enticement of learning about Pillar was too great. "Agreed, you have a deal."

"The attack on Pillar intrigued me because of its connection to our new tournament champion and because of the town's size. Pillar is not large, but most of the villages attacked in the north didn't even have names, so the attack on Pillar was of a much grander scale. The connection between Pillar and you is obvious, but why wouldn't they wait until you were in the village or attack you directly? I suspected some link between the instigator of this attack and Pillar itself, so I looked into its history. I discovered that Pillar did not exist before or during the Twice-Broken Wars. It was established as part of the treaty that ended the war, but its inhabitants and their past lives could not be discerned."

Slate's mind reeled. Pillar didn't exist until after the war? The townspeople never spoke of the Twice-Broken Wars with the exception of his father when confiding that he had been a soldier. "My father served in the King's Army and Villifor knew him on sight. Do you know anything of Villifor's past?"

"Books proclaim his deeds in the Twice-Broken Wars. Against the Disenites, he was the champion of the people for defending them against the invasion while Darik struggled to unite the nobility under his banner. During the Civil War, he pretended to side with the revolutionaries and won some preliminary battles against Darik's forces. Then he combined his forces for an assault on Ravinai, only to lead the revolutionaries into the awaiting defenses of Darik's army, causing their unconditional surrender. Villifor was hailed by Darik and by soldiers of the King's Army for delivering them victory. The people of Malethya, tired of the bloodshed from two wars, chanted Villifor's name in the streets for bringing peace to the land. However, everyone was surprised when he was appointed headmaster of Bellator at the end of the war. Halford Patton was the general of the King's Armies and most people presumed he would head the guild...I will look into it. Now, I believe it is your turn."

Slate was still processing the information about Pillar while choosing the information he would share with the headmaster. "I saw Pillar before the mine exploded and witnessed the aftermath of the attack. People, armed only with farm implements and rudimentary tools, attacked my parents. My childhood home was built into the side of a mountain and was heavily fortified. My father defended against the attackers, but he was overwhelmed by the sheer number of people." The memory brought back the images from that night, but Slate held his emotions in check. "Common villagers would not have attacked with that ferocity, especially against a more skilled and heavily fortified opponent. It was unnatural."

The Sicarius headmaster considered the value of the information shared. "I realize that was a difficult story to tell, but I need more information. You have only just confirmed what I summarized at the guild meeting. Please continue."

Slate bit his lip and then said the statement he was afraid to say. "I believe the events of the past few months are the works of a Blood Mage who is subjugating minds and forcing them to attack upon command." He didn't mention that his other fear was that one of the headmasters, and quite possibly the one standing in front of him, could be orchestrating the entire ordeal.

The headmaster didn't laugh. "Blood Magic is a serious accusation and one that has occurred only rarely since Cantor's time...don't be surprised that I know the name. It is my job to have information of all sorts and with people like Brannon around, it pays to have a healthy understanding of magic." The headmaster thought for a while before continuing. "That makes us even in terms of our trade. I trust your concerns are merited considering the company you keep. Lucus and

Ibson have good reputations for honesty even taking into account their status as wizards."

"Why do you assume Brannon was involved?" Slate inquired.

"I don't assume his involvement, but he was present at the tournament bout, was the person to find Ibson after his fall, and has the ability and power to coordinate an attack on Pillar from across the kingdom without anyone finding out." *Didn't that mean the Headmaster was assuming Brannon's involvement then?* The headmaster abruptly changed the direction of the conversation. "You positioned yourself to have personal interaction with both Brannon and Villifor. I'm assuming they have need of your Sicarius skills to obtain information regarding me or the other headmasters." Slate's eyes widened just enough to confirm the statement, which was the intent of the headmaster's abrupt questioning. "This is good. You will report to the other headmasters the updates I provide and share any information that arises from conversations with the headmasters to me." Before Slate could argue, the headmaster held out the shock stick and touched his neck.

When he awoke, Slate sat on a grassy hill under the shade of a large oak tree with a rather pleasant view of Ravinai. By the position of the sun, he estimated that it was around dinner time. He would have to hurry home in order to make it back to Ispirtu in time for his session with Primean.

Slate picked himself up and tried to work out the sluggishness with a light jog into the city. On his way back to the city he contemplated the day's events. He was now searching for more than the murderer of his parents but also a Blood Mage. The headmasters were still the main suspects, but they could be acting at the command of the Blood Mage or King Darik, if he had been subjugated. He was now in personal contact and under direction to spy on the headmasters by the opposing guilds. Slate found it rather surprising that the guilds knew so little about each other, but in retrospect, it was a brilliant move by King Darik. He had set up the guilds relatively autonomously from each other but under his direct control. It created parity between the guilds that resulted in stiff inter-guild competition and if any one guild challenged his authority, the other two guilds would be enough to counteract the threat to his reign. After hearing King Darik at the Sicarius meeting today, Slate no longer thought this setup was an accident. It also brought on the realization of the unique position he was in, and the reasons why he could be seen as a threat. Threats to the guilds were taken care of quietly, but Slate didn't think quietly corresponded to painlessly. He had visited Master Primean on too many occasions to assume that. Slate headed for Ispirtu to find what the old wizard had in store for him tonight.

CHAPTER TWELVE

PAIN TOLERATED

Inside the walls of Ispirtu, Slate slipped into the catacombs occupied by the guild's army of researchers. The orb patrols were infrequent in the deep parts of Ispirtu because simulated battles distracted them from their research. This allowed Slate to reach Master Primean's Pain Tolerance Laboratory with relative ease.

Master Primean looked up from his work when Slate pushed through the double doors of the laboratory. The congenial wizard's demeanor differed this evening, looking too serious and single-minded for the researcher that Slate had come to know over the last few months of punishment. "You are late."

Lattimer waited in the laboratory and addressed Master Primean formally to contrast Slate's late arrival. "Master Primean, my father has told me of your great discoveries and the honor you bring to Ispirtu. If I must serve as a test subject this evening, I am grateful it is within your laboratory."

Master Primean rose from his desk and pointedly ignored Lattimer's attempts at flattery. "Master Brannon told me the two of you have developed a rivalry in your time at Ispirtu. It will end tonight. I will set aside my research to perform pain tolerance testing of the simplest sort. One of you will withstand the pain for longer than the other and get the pleasure of seeing your rival reduced to a sobbing pile of robes. Please join me in the back of the laboratory."

Slate ignored the stare that Lattimer directed his way. Lattimer hadn't been sent to Primean before and didn't know what was coming. In this lab, Slate had been cut, punched, and had objects shot at him, all with some unproven and unpredictable magic involved. Whatever Primean had in store for him, the look on his face was enough to know it would be a long evening. He followed Primean toward the back of the lab, an area he had never been before.

Primean stopped at an open area of the laboratory. Wood chips covered the floor and two large hooks hung from the ceiling. Slate couldn't help but ask, "What are the wood chips for?" Primean was first and foremost an academic, and couldn't resist a question. "I have found they are excellent at soaking up liquids. It makes clean-up easier." Slate didn't see any water around, so he assumed Primean was referring to blood. Primean then ordered, "Please disrobe and remove your shirts. When you are done, stand under one of the hooks."

Slate began to question whether his position in Ispirtu was worth subjecting himself to torture. His positions in Sicarius and Bellator would still provide valuable information, but then Slate clenched his fist and remembered the iron inside. Someone had done this to him. That same person had hurt Ibson, killed his parents, and was now responsible for attacks on defenseless villages. If a little bit of pain helped him find and stop that person, then it was worth it. He looked at Lattimer and saw a look of false confidence on his face that Slate didn't bother to comment on. He just took his robes and his shirt off and stood underneath one of the hooks.

Primean stepped toward him holding a rope. Slate wanted to prepare himself for what was to come, so he continued to ask Primean questions. "What is the rope for?"

"I will bind your hands and hang you from the hook above using the rope."

"Thank you for not hanging me directly by the hook." That got a chuckle from the too-serious wizard. Slate asked the main question on his mind. "What will happen next?"

Primean bound Slate's hands and looped the rope over the hook. "It is an inelegant experiment. The two of you will hang from these hooks. I will whip you in alternating blows. The first to scream for mercy will lose. At that point, the winner can choose to end the experiment."

"Why wouldn't the winner choose to end the experiment?" Slate had to ask.

"Each person will receive equal blows, but only the winner can end the experiment. If the winner chooses, he can continue and watch his enemy receive more blows as he screams for mercy. As I said…it is rather inelegant." Slate looked over to Lattimer as Primean hoisted him into the air. Would he be so cruel as to continue past the point of winning? Slate didn't want to give him the opportunity.

Primean bound Lattimer's hands. Slate tried to remain calm and looked around the room for a way to distract Primean. For some reason, his gaze kept gravitating toward the area of the lab he was in last night. The chair sat next to a sponge in a bucket of water. What had Sana said about the sponge? It didn't seem relevant to his current situation, but his mind couldn't let it go.

Primean hoisted Lattimer into the air. Lattimer was offering up some verbal abuse prior to the whipping. "Try not to cry for mercy too early, Slate…when you say the words I want you to know you have been bettered." Slate ignored him. The sponge…why was he still thinking about the sponge? Sana said Primean shouldn't have used the sponge to soak up pain but rather to staunch the flow of blood.

"Master Primean, I have seen the genius of your research and it pains me to see your talents wasted on such an inelegant experiment. I believe I have a way to continue tonight's experiment and fulfill your obligation to Master Brannon while still advancing your research." The words *genius* and *advancing your research* to an academic are like the words *free* and *collector's edition* to a hoarder. They were too good to pass up.

Sure enough, Primean's eyes twinkled with curiosity. "What do you propose?"

"I have been thinking of our study from last night. I don't pretend to have your knowledge of magic, but what if the spell was used to staunch the flow of blood from open wounds?"

The twinkle dimmed slightly. "A spell of that sort would have no effect on a person's ability to withstand pain." Sana was right. Primean couldn't see the healing benefits of the spell because he was so focused on his own area of research. Slate modified his approach.

"That's true, but it would limit the severity of the injuries to the test subject. By applying the spell, it would allow you to test someone's true pain tolerance, because they would still feel the pain of the injury but wouldn't have their senses dimmed by blood loss."

"So physically, they would be able to withstand more pain…it would just be a matter of how much they could deal with…" The twinkle returned and magnified. "You may be onto something Slate. I'll set it up!" Primean ran back to collect the sponge and bucket of water.

Lattimer whispered feverishly, "What have you done?"

Slate answered honestly. "I don't know…"

Primean came back mumbling to himself. Slate was able to catch only snippets. "...apply with the sponge...direct contact should...stand in the bucket...link, and yes...it should work!" The old wizard soaked the sponge in the bucket and then came over to Slate. He rubbed the sponge vigorously over Slate's torso, soaking him in water. He repeated the procedure with Lattimer and then positioned the bucket of water to be halfway between them. Primean grabbed a whip from a nearby table and stuck one foot in the bucket of water.

"We are ready to begin." Primean said excitedly. "I apologize for soaking you in water, but it will make the spell easier for me to cast. Are we ready?" Lattimer just grunted and Slate didn't respond, but Primean was unfazed. Slate knew he had cast the spell because he felt it. Primean's magic couldn't be described as comforting like Sana's or a thunderhead like Brannon's. It felt almost indifferent and well used. It reminded Slate of a rusty knife, an implement that was still useful but for which there were some tasks it shouldn't be used. Slate hoped this didn't fall into that category.

Primean then explained, "I will maintain the spell for the duration of this experiment. Let us begin the inelegant portions of the study." The whip lashed out and struck Slate in the shoulder, and he managed to stifle a cry. The whip stung on contact, opening up his skin and creating a burning sensation that lingered far after the whip was gone. Despite the pain and the open wound, only a small trickle of blood flowed from the wound. Primean was ecstatic, "It works! It works! They are probably casting a statue of me for the hallways upstairs as we speak!"

Crack! Lattimer was struck in a similar location to Slate and the effect was the same, except Slate was pleased to hear Lattimer release a small grunt on impact.

Crack! Crack! Crack! The lashes continued and the impact drew increasingly loud exclamations from Slate and Lattimer. The spell continued to work though. Slate's chest and back were dripping with blood from all of the wounds, but it was an unsettlingly small amount. Through it all, Slate could feel the constant presence of Primean's spell. It felt as though he was being held tightly...like a good set of leather armor on his skin, except the feeling permeated throughout his body, drawing everything toward his core.

Crack! Crack! Lattimer cried out in anguish. He wouldn't last much longer. Crack! Slate exhaled and felt the burning sensations across his back and chest. He forced himself to relive the sights of Pillar. He would withstand this if it prevented that from ever happening again. He didn't bother opening his eyes anymore. He just waited for the next blow and steeled himself with his memories.

Crack! "Mercy!" Lattimer cried out. Slate breathed a sigh of relief and opened his eyes. Crack! A blow from Primean struck him in the side. Slate cried out in surprise and stared at Primean with eyes bulging. "Slate is declared the winner." Master Primean declared officially. He then continued to hit Slate and the twinkle in his eyes turned into a crazed stare. "Unfortunately, the results of this test are too promising to end prematurely." Crack! Slate accidently bit his tongue. "I will need to see the limits of its potential." Crack! Crack! "Don't worry, Slate...you will be perfectly safe." Crack!

Slate's mind was burning even more than the wounds from the whip. What had he done? Crack! He closed his eyes and suffered through the blows. Crack! Crack! "Stop!" Lattimer cried. Crack! "Mercy..." Slate said, although no sound came out. Primean's excitement couldn't be stopped. "This is the highest pain tolerance ever exhibited in my testing. It is ten times the level previously recorded!" Crack! Crack! The feeling of the spell had changed. The indifference had gone and it was replaced by something utterly frightening. Crack! "Stop...you are going to kill him!" Lattimer begged of Primean. Crack! Slate was starting to feel light-headed. Crack! He was losing too much blood, despite the spell's effects. He felt the spell acting on him and he clung to the "tightness" he felt. Crack! Slate was losing consciousness. He pulled as tightly as he could on the spell, drawing everything toward his core, trying with all his might to stop the blood loss. He pulled tighter and tighter and somewhere in the back of his mind he realized the whip had stopped. Slate was too tired to concentrate on anything but that feeling of tightness. That was keeping him alive. He held it in a vice grip and then he felt the spell stop, but the tightness remained and the world went black.

Slate opened his eyes...a simple act but one he didn't take for granted. He could remember what had happened in Primean's laboratory, but what he really remembered was the pain. It was blinding. It was excruciating. It was blissfully gone. He was too disoriented to even lift his head, but he could see enough from his position to realize he was in the infirmary.

A white-robed wizard was in his room and she noticed that Slate was awake. "Welcome back to the living, Slate. You have been healed to the extent possible. You also have several visitors anxiously awaiting news. I will send them in." Slate was excited. In contrast to his experience with healing from Ibson, Slate found he had most of his energy back. That told him he'd be recovered much sooner than he originally thought and hopefully he wasn't under investigation again.

Slate was getting ready to welcome Rainier, Lucus, and Sana when Brannon and Lattimer Regallo entered his room. They were the last people Slate expected to see. Upon looking at him, Lattimer flinched slightly, and the wizard's words "to the extent possible" crept back into his mind.

Brannon addressed him. "Slate, I am in your debt. I requested Primean to settle the dispute between you and Lattimer using his…unique…talents, but this was not my intent. No wizard should put his research ahead of another's well-being."

"So I won't be under investigation this time?"

"No, Slate. Lattimer witnessed the entire event. His testimony is sufficient to implicate Primean."

A wave of relief went through Slate. He had no desire to have his memories ripped from him again. "What will happen to Primean then?"

Brannon looked to Lattimer and back to Slate. "Slate, Primean didn't survive the encounter." Slate was shocked. "Lattimer was worried you had died as well, and if it weren't for his actions, you probably would have. I will leave the two of you to talk. If nothing else, I hope today's events will end the dispute between the two of you. Slate, you should be well rested and able to attend classes tomorrow. I will see you then." The headmaster of Ispirtu, having displayed more compassion in a two minute conversation than Slate believed him capable, turned quietly to leave.

Lattimer sat on the edge of Slate's bed. "Let me say a few things before you speak…" That was fine with Slate because he didn't really have much to say to Lattimer. "I thought you schemed your way to tournament victory by having the iron suddenly appear in your hand. The timing was too convenient, but tonight changed my mind. I know how much that whip hurt and I had to hang helplessly from that hook while I watched what Primean did to you. Through it all, I saw you fight on and never give in. You have the heart of a Champion, Slate. I can't explain what happened at the tournament, but now I know that you deserved to win."

Slate was dumbfounded. His nemesis, a Regallo nonetheless, was apologizing to him? Did he have a concussion? Was he still dreaming? "Thank you, Lattimer. Can you tell me what happened in Primean's lab? Toward the end there, things were getting a bit hazy."

"After I called for mercy and you requested an end to the competition, Primean...went crazy. He whipped you repeatedly despite my cries to stop. I could see you were losing a lot of blood and your skin drained of color. Primean must have been increasing the power of the spell as he continued to lash you because your wounds bled more slowly and then ceased to bleed altogether. At some point, Primean attempted to stop the spell. He stepped out of the bucket and started stumbling toward you, but he collapsed before he made it. I tried to get myself off the hook, but I couldn't. Eventually, the student responsible for collecting the blood-soaked woodchips arrived and let me off the hook. That was when I discovered that Primean didn't have a pulse...and much to my surprise...you did."

"How did Primean die?"

"He used ALL his spark. His fatigue was so great that he collapsed and his muscles stopped working, including his heart."

"How did I end up here?"

"Upon feeling a faint heartbeat, I performed a transfusion for you from the student who discovered us. I would have used my own blood, but I had lost a great deal myself. After that, I called for help and we transferred you to the care of the infirmary. They did a great job, but there are a few things you should know..."

"Like what?"

"Your injuries were severe because of their quantity. There was very little skin left for the infirmary wizards to work with...they were able to close the wounds, but they aren't very cosmetic."

"I can live with that...what else?"

"Do you remember me saying that the color in your skin had drained?" Slate nodded. "I assumed it was due to the loss of blood, but even after the transfusions it hasn't come back."

Slate slowly lifted the bed sheet and looked at his torso. Thick, rope-like scars covered every inch of his chest and shoulders. They should have been red and enflamed, but they weren't...they were the palest shade of white he had ever seen. He lifted the sheet a little more and saw that it wasn't limited to his chest. His skin was ghost white. "I look like Death."

Lattimer gave an uneasy chuckle. "...only because you have recently cheated it..." The uneasy chuckle gave way to an even more awkward silence and then Lattimer continued. "When I told my father on the way over here that you had earned my respect, he shared with me that Pillar was destroyed. I would like to help you catch the person responsible for the tournament and Pillar."

Slate had experienced more shocking things since he first arrived in Ravinai, but this definitely counted as one of the most unexpected. Lattimer wanted to help him investigate his parents' attack? Maybe it was the fact that Lattimer had just saved his life, but Slate decided to accept the invitation. "I need all the help I can get." Slate grasped Lattimer's extended forearm and the two shook.

Despite the show of solidarity, Slate decided to give his new ally a test. "Could you investigate a lead for me? I found an interesting weapon buried in the rubble of Pillar. It was a throwing knife with catalpa trees on the hilt and of exquisite workmanship...much too fine for someone in Pillar. Could you find out who the owner of the knife is?"

"There are a lot of knives, but the one you describe sounds rare enough that it might be possible. I'll look into it." Lattimer then rose and left Slate to rest, something he had no intention of doing.

After waiting several minutes, Slate rose and tested his strength. The famed infirmary wizards did work worthy of their reputation. He felt the same strength as he had when he got out of bed this morning. He found his clothes folded neatly in a corner, dressed, and slipped out of the infirmary using skills honed in the hallways of Ispirtu.

Slate took to the rooftops of Ravinai and jumped onto the balcony of his apartment. Rainier was gone, but Sana rested on the lounge pillows. Rainier must have given her a key. "Good evening, Sana."

"Slate! What happened to you? Are you all right? You look like you've seen a ghost!"

"It might be more accurate to say I've turned into one. I'll explain everything later, but for now, I need your help. Do you remember the testing you did on my hand?" Sana nodded slowly. "Please take out one of your knives. I have a new test for you and it will require your skills in healing afterwards."

"What are you planning?" Sana sounded afraid for the first time in Slate's memory, but she complied with his request and one of her knives appeared from a fold in her robe.

"I hope this doesn't frighten you." Slate took off his shirt, exposing his wounds.

"Fractal's pattern..." was all Sana managed to say. Slate didn't blame her.

"Cut me in the chest...anywhere you see a scar will do." He spoke with authority and confidence to discourage questions from the shell-shocked apprentice. Sana hesitated, but then she made a small, shallow cut near his sternum.

It stung and the pain lingered, but no blood exited the wound. It was as he had thought. When Slate awoke in the infirmary, he still felt the same feeling of *tightness* as he had in Primean's laboratory. It seemed that the effects would be permanent. Slate smiled at Sana, but she was too shocked to smile back. "Try my arm."

Sana complied, this time cutting a bit deeper. Again, no blood flowed from the wound despite the pain. This time Sana had recovered enough to ask a question. "Slate, what is going on?"

"First, please heal me. They still hurt as much as a regular cut." Seconds later, Slate felt the warmth of Sana's magical touch permeating and repairing his wounds.

When she was finished, Sana demanded the whole story. "Let's lie down...it's been a long day."

Slate then proceeded to tell Sana about the Sicarius meeting and the fateful trip to Primean's laboratory. He described the whipping in as much detail as he could remember, but Sana was mainly interested in the spell and his description of tightness drawing toward his core and how he clung to it, pulling it as hard as he could. Finally, he described waking up in the infirmary and the turn of events regarding the Regallos. Sana appeared openly skeptical until Slate said that Lattimer saved his life. Then Sana had one final question. "Why did you lose the color from your skin?"

Slate was amazed that he had forgotten to tell her. "I don't know. It happened during my time in Primean's laboratory, but I can only assume it's related to my lack of bleeding."

Sana then answered for him. "That makes sense based on your

description. I think the spell draws blood toward your key internal organs, like your heart and brain, and away from your peripheral organs, such as your skin. With the loss of blood flow, you would lose color. I will have more tests for you to understand how you are able to retain your strength with decreased blood flow to your periphery...starting tomorrow."

Slate groaned but only in jest. Her excitement was enough to bring a smile back to his face. When she returned a smile, he rolled over and kissed her. She flinched for a second and Slate drew back. "I forgot, I must look completely different to you..."

Sana stopped him before he could finish his sentence. She kissed him on the lips before slowly working her way to each of his new scars across his chest and back. The act was better than any words of assurance she could have said. Slate took some initiative and sat up to kiss her, but she pushed him back down.

"You already took my knife from me tonight, Slate. I am completely defenseless and I don't trust you without it." She smirked mischievously. "The only solution I can see is if you let me be in control and you stop me when you feel uncomfortable."

Slate leaned back and relaxed. "Who am I to argue with logic like that?" He smiled up at her. He had already been probed by a half dozen wizards in the past few months and he had little left in the way of humility. Sana failed to find something that could make Slate uncomfortable, despite multiple inventive attempts...

REFLECTION OF REGRET

The clacking of the practice swords ceased, the silence drawing Slate's gaze from his revelry, where the innkeeper and his son stared into the distance. Slate heard the distinct, and yet still far off sound of hoof beats. Dust rose against the horizon, failing to hide the riders approaching with the inevitability of an imminent thunderhead.

The guardsmen found him. The king had labeled Slate a threat to Malethya and the decades of peace. Slate admitted he looked the part…but if he died, no one would know the truth. Was it worth fighting for? The people in the kingdom seemed happy enough living under the control of a Blood Mage.

Deep inside though, Slate knew the Blood Mage would seek more and more power, just as the followers of Cantor had done. Even if peace was kept for now, it was only a matter of time before oppression was a way of life within Malethya.

He looked down at the innkeeper as he put an arm around his shaking son, uncertain of who approached but certain of their inability to defend against such a force. Slate knew the riders would bear the shining armor of the Bellator Guardsmen and carry the crest of King Darik. Upon sight of it, the townspeople would stop shaking and cheer.

Then the guardsmen would get closer, and the townspeople would see their eyes turn red. By the time they were done, this town would be as empty as Pillar. The people would be killed and the buildings burned to the ground. Slate didn't know if he could stop it from happening…he certainly hadn't stopped any of the Blood Mage's other plans. But he couldn't give up. Somehow he'd find a way to protect people like this innkeeper and his son.

Slate dressed, but not in the traveling clothes he used to hide his identity. His pants had a series of black ties and folds that allowed freedom of movement and plenty of hiding places for darts and knives. Slate didn't wear a shirt. He wanted people to see the scars on his body and the bloodless wounds if someone were lucky enough to land a blow. He hung the Stratego medallion around his neck as a reminder that nothing appears as it seems. Slate decided not to wear the Sicarius mask. He wanted people to know who saved their village and see his red, fractal-forsaken eyes. Finally, Slate put on his glove and thought of Lucus as he always did when wearing the gift.

Slate jumped out the window, flipped once and landed on one knee, an old habit from his tournament days. The innkeeper and his son were startled and then terrified at the sight of the Blight-Bringer. Slate didn't bother to console them. "You should go inside now. This will all be over soon..."

CHAPTER THIRTEEN

HOUSE OF CARDS

"Pick up your things. We are heading to the courtyard." Brannon pronounced to the class. "Don't waste your spark on simulated battles in the hallway. You'll need it for today's testing." Brannon's scepter glowed and the sounds of battle ceased outside the lecture hall.

Slate walked through the hallways with Annarelle and Tommy. Brannon may have stopped the battle, but Slate preferred to walk between his two friends for protection. Annarelle and Tommy had begun joining Magical Defense late to get quiet lessons from Slate when the opportunities arose. They had also worked out a technique for surviving the halls of Ispirtu. Annarelle scouted the hallways, and Tommy would dispatch any alerted patrols. Tommy wasn't big by Bellator standards, but in Ispirtu, he looked like Jak. If any Ispirtu wizards witnessed their bending of Ispirtu rules, Tommy used physical means to encourage their silence. The prideful Ispirtu wizards refused to admit defeat by such lowly means as a physical beating, so Tommy and Annarelle eluded punishment. Pride filled Slate to know they now walked the Ispirtu hallways in confidence.

"What do you think Brannon has in store for us today?" Annarelle asked.

"Whatever it is, he won't be happy in our performance." Tommy snickered. Over the course of the last few weeks, the temperamental Brannon had turned downright irritable, spending his time locked in his office.

"He can't be angrier than the other day. When you couldn't shake the ground beneath your feet, I thought he would make a hole for you and bury you in it." Slate was only half joking.

Tommy stopped snickering. "Let's hope today's lessons don't involve moving the ground."

Brannon led the class into a beautifully manicured courtyard with ornamental trees clinging to the last leaves of autumn, denying the inevitability of the oncoming winter. A series of concentric rings lined the grounds and Brannon stood at the epicenter.

"The first ring simulates the strike of a swordsman. The second corresponds with the thrust of a pikeman. Any wizard hoping to survive the battlefield must be able to defend himself from these distances." Brannon let out a pressure waves in all directions that reached to the second circle. "This, of course, is only the minimum defense needed in battle. Powerful wizards can take out any archers within range as well." A massive firewall emanated from Brannon toward a distant line in the courtyard. Despite his distance from Brannon, the heat passed over Slate's face and forced him to turn away. When he looked back, the ornamental trees were left barren and charred, their remaining leaves incinerated from the heat.

"Speed is important in battle, but power is a great equalizer. With a powerful spell, you kill your opponent before they are in range to attack. Unfortunately for some of you, power is related to the strength of your spark. Lattimer, you will be tested first."

Lattimer walked to the center of the circles and unleashed a powerful spell that shook the ground around him, almost reaching the archery line.

"That was an impressive display, but the strength of your spark indicates you are capable of more. Continue practicing." Brannon then tested some wizards from Lattimer's ever increasing group of admirers. The strongest wizards sought Lattimer's attention in the hopes of increased access to Brannon and prestige within Ispirtu. With each wizard tested, their power decreased and Brannon's interest waned. "You there...what's your name?" Brannon asked.

"Annarelle."

"Try to do better than that sorry excuse for a wizard that went before you." Tommy hung his head since he had preceded Annarelle's testing.

Annarelle entered the center circle and concentrated, producing a small pressure wall that didn't quite reach the line indicating a pike thrust. Brannon had seen enough. "I can't watch this anymore...get out of my sight."

Slate, Annarelle, and Tommy scampered for the courtyard entrance. They were still catching their breath when Lattimer and his entourage exited the courtyard with a verbal barrage. "Out of breath and out of spark...a dangerous combination." Maintaining an abusive discourse helped to hide Slate and Lattimer's newfound alliance.

"It must be difficult having so many fractal-fanning ass-kissers following you around all the time." Tommy offered up.

"Tough words from a wizard who could be killed by a hand-held weapon," Lattimer countered.

"A sword is all I need." Slate flexed his fist. "Sometimes I don't even need the sword."

"Let's go. I don't want to hear any more threats from Death Incarnate. The sight of him causes me much pain. I couldn't tolerate it for another five seconds."

Lattimer walked off and Slate needed to leave. "I gotta run...there's a Sicarius mission I have to fulfill." Awe filled Annarelle's eyes. No one knew what Sicarius really did or when, so it was an excellent alibi.

"Do you want us to escort you to the entrance?" Annarelle offered.

Slate wasn't about to pass that up. "That would be much appreciated, Annarelle. Thank you."

At the door, Slate thanked them again and asked who had the Stratego medallion. "I do," said Annarelle with a smirk.

"How did she get it from you?" Slate asked Tommy.

Tommy turned red and Annarelle answered for him. "I kissed him and slipped it from his pocket." She smiled, Tommy looked at his feet and Slate laughed.

"It must have been a good kiss then." Slate left his friends and ran to the side of Ispirtu. Lattimer included the words "pain" and "tolerance" in his final volley of verbal abuse. That meant he wanted to meet him in the abandoned Pain Tolerance Laboratory in five minutes.

Slate ducked into the storeroom window and hurried down the hall. He opened the doors into the now dark lab and waited inside the door. Ispirtu didn't bother using orbs to light the room anymore, so Slate didn't have much choice.

A few minutes later, Lattimer walked in with an orb floating a few feet above his head, illuminating enough of the laboratory to avoid any painful mistakes traversing the room. Out of habit, they met in the back of the lab where two hooks still hung from the ceiling. They sat at opposite ends of the table that used to hold a whip.

"Sorry I was late. It really is difficult to escape when I want to." Lattimer apologized.

"Ahh...the price of fame. Why did you want to meet?" Meetings were difficult to arrange and Slate wanted to maximize their time.

"You asked about a weapon rumored to be in the Pillar wreckage...a throwing knife with catalpa trees engraved on the hilt. I gathered information about the blade and retrieved it for you." Lattimer smiled and placed the throwing knife on the table between them.

"How did you get it?"

"I learned that a Bellator squadron visited the wreckage shortly after the explosion, and Magnus informed me of the details. He said they examined the wreckage for signs of foul play when the Sicarius headmaster threw the blade and hit him in the foot." Lattimer laughed. "The headmaster must not be as good of a shot as the rumors say...Magnus is a pretty big target. Anyway, Magnus called the headmaster a toothpick throwing coward and blamed the headmaster for the whole Pillar incident. I don't know if I believed that part of his story, but the knife clearly belongs to the Sicarius headmaster."

The information was mostly correct, except for the parts that Magnus wouldn't have wanted to divulge. "Did you find out anything else?"

"With the knife in hand, I had the engraving on the hilt researched. Catalpa trees have long been revered as a symbol of wisdom, but this specific engraving is a near replicate of an etching from the days of Cantor and the Blood Mages."

"What do you know about Cantor and Blood Mages?"

"I am the son of the Ispirtu headmaster. He taught me the history of magic before I could walk and told the fantastical tales of the Blood Mages as bedtime stories."

Slate tried to keep his face impassive. "What did the etching depict?"

"There was a man rising in a grove of catalpa trees...if there was anything else to the story, I'm afraid I don't know it." Lattimer shrugged like it was inconsequential, but the description reminded Slate of Lucus.

"You've done good work." Slate hid his incomplete trust in Lattimer with a compliment. Before he questioned Lattimer further, fluctuating intonations came from the shadows.

"Thank you for finding my knife." A figure slid just outside of view from Lattimer's orb, but the alternating speech left little doubt about the identity of the observer. "Don't do anything as foolish as attacking me with a spell, Lattimer." A bright blue light flashed briefly near the figure. "My shock stick has a way of disrupting a wizard's concentration. I can reach you before you cast."

"How can we help you today, headmaster?" Slate responded formally to prevent the conversation from degrading too quickly.

"Return my knife to me." Slate obliged and the headmaster whispered in his ear. "The winds are shifting and a storm is coming. Prepare yourself."

Lattimer couldn't hold his curiosity. "How did you know I had your knife…and how to find me?"

"Did you think your inquiries within Bellator would escape my attention?" The headmaster didn't wait for a response. "As for knowing that you'd be here…call it an educated guess. You've been frequenting this abandoned lab the last few weeks. What have you been doing down here in the dark? I trust it was something to help our Champion and his investigation…"

Slate faced Lattimer, curiosity piqued. Lattimer seemed at a loss of words, but then they rushed out. "Primean's experiment intrigued me. I've been trying to recreate it…safely…for the past few weeks, but without success. If I succeed, it could save many guardsmen's lives if the Disenites come back. I didn't want to tell you until I had some measure of success."

Lattimer's inability to recreate the experiment probably related to Slate's mysterious Perceptor abilities, but he wasn't willing to give up that information yet. "Has your father told you anything about the attacks on the northern villages?" Slate asked.

"What attacks? The kingdom is at peace."

"That isn't quite true, Lattimer." The headmaster jumped into the conversation. "Small villages are being attacked without any trace of survivors. The attacks are carried out with extreme aggression, but we do not know by whom, or what. I have seen the aftermath of encounters with our new enemy. They are relentless. Can you think of a way to increase someone's speed or strength? It would be more useful against this enemy than blood staunching. Guardsmen will need speed to keep their distance and strength to stop these enemies in a single blow."

"The blood staunching experiment used a sponge to link the spell. I'd have to find something else suitable…"

"Give it some thought. We might need a surprise or two when our true enemy surfaces." The silhouette of the Sicarius headmaster disappeared into the deeper darkness of the lab. Lattimer stood up to investigate, but Slate just shook his head. "It won't do any good. The headmaster is gone...or at least out of sight. You might as well sit back down."

"Do you deal with the headmaster often? That was..."

Slate finished his thought for him. "...uncomfortable? Yes, most encounters with the Sicarius headmaster are quite uncomfortable." Slate unconsciously rubbed his neck.

"What did the headmaster mean by 'our true enemy'? Was that related to the attacks?"

Slate temporarily ignored the question, giving himself a chance to feel out Lattimer without revealing too much. "Someone powerful is behind the attacks. I think it's the same person responsible for the attack on Pillar. There are very few people in the kingdom powerful enough to keep something of this magnitude a secret. It would take someone like the Sicarius headmaster or..."

"...my father." Lattimer finished and nodded in understanding. After a moment of silence, Lattimer asked a question of Slate. "Have you ever wondered why I fought in the tournament?"

Slate hadn't given it a second thought. "Fame? Honor? ...to uphold the Regallo name?"

Lattimer shook his head. "My father has enough fame and honor to make the Regallo name prominent for generations." Lattimer confessed, "The tournament champion has the right to choose guilds. I have the spark and knew I'd be forced to attend Ispirtu if I didn't win."

"Why wouldn't you want to attend Ispirtu? You obviously enjoy it if you take the time to experiment in this lab."

"I do enjoy casting spells and experimenting...on my own terms. My father is the most famous wizard in Malethya. He is the headmaster of the Ispirtu and leader of the Ispirtu Guardsmen. He was also more concerned with matters of the crown than with being bothered by small matters...like his family." Slate stayed quiet, waiting for Lattimer to continue this story. "I know more of my father through stories and history lessons than personal interaction. He tested me for the spark and when he saw my potential, sent me away to study...he was too busy to teach me himself. By the time I came home, my mother slept in a different bedroom and my sister Rose had disappeared from Ispirtu to escape his control. My parents haven't spoken of her since. I don't know what happened when I was away, but my father was responsible even if it was responsibility through neglect."

Slate empathized with Lattimer's story after losing his own family. Lattimer continued, "I started looking for a way to distance myself from my father and the tournament seemed like my best chance. I started training on my own, but I soon found I needed some live competition to hone my skills. I discovered an underground fighting ring in Ravinai and Magnus was the leader of the ring. I offered the use of the grounds on my estate to train legitimately and he took me up on it. We trained relentlessly and my skills, especially my defensive skills, grew. He beat me most times, so you impressed me by beating him in the tournament."

"I wouldn't like to face Magnus directly again." Slate replied modestly.

"Now I find myself in Ispirtu under my father's control once again. I can't offer insight into whether my father is involved with these attacks, but if he is, I would not withhold information to protect him."

Slate came away convinced. Lattimer had saved his life by bringing him to the infirmary and Slate needed all the help he could get. "You mentioned Cantor and the Blood Mages...we've been looking for information from that time period. It's been a difficult search."

Lattimer jumped in. "Then I guess you haven't looked in my father's personal library. I spent most of my time training for the tournament so I'm not too familiar with it, but if there are manuscripts related to Cantor, I'm sure my father has them. I can start requesting books to search for information, but I'll have to do it slowly so that my newfound interest in his library doesn't raise suspicions."

That wouldn't do. Slate needed the information soon and wanted to see it for himself. "Your father requested the assistance of his attendant in his office. I don't want to be late." Lattimer shook his forearm and stayed in the laboratory to think about the Sicarius headmaster's suggested experiments.

Slate ascended from the basement laboratories of Ipirtu toward the opulent offices of the towers, careful to avoid any patrolling orbs. The pathway to Brannon's office required him to navigate the entire Ispirtu complex, including complex twists and turns through a warren of orb-created pitfalls if he misstepped. Slate gingerly put a foot down at each intersection to ensure the ground was solid. After what seemed like an eternity, Slate reached two large wooden doors, created from the trunk of a massive catalpa tree.

The doors swung open upon his approach to reveal the elder Regallo overlooking the Ispirtu grounds. He turned and regarded Slate with sunken eyes and sagging shoulders. The fire he displayed in class was absent and in its place was a shell of the man Slate knew as the Ispirtu headmaster. He must not have slept for days.

"Report the activities of our friend Villifor to me."

Slate stood in the middle of the room, not feeling comfortable enough in Brannon's presence to sit while the wizard stood. "Villifor has taken guardsmen with him to investigate attacks on the northern villages. They have been occurring more frequently as of late. Since I have not been assigned to accompany Villifor on any of these missions, my interaction with him has been limited." Slate tried to lower the expectations of his report.

"Have any of these *investigations* been corroborated by someone other than Villifor? He makes it to the villages before word of the attack can reach anyone else. It makes me wonder if the Bellator Guardsmen don't have more to do with the attacks than simply cleaning up the mess. Get invited on one of these missions. This is information I need."

Slate had no idea how to make that happen. "I don't know if the attacks have been corroborated by anyone other than Villifor." Slate couldn't possibly tell Brannon about the Sicarius headmaster visiting one of the villages. That would simply lead to more questions he couldn't answer. "However, he has been ordered to investigate the attacks personally by King Darik. They meet regularly and privately when Villifor is in town." Rainier had proven to be quite successful at shadowing the headmaster.

"Darik has asked me to investigate the attacks as well, but I did not know he met Villifor regularly. You have done well."

Slate ventured a question after the rare praise from Brannon. "What have you found regarding the attacks on the villages?"

The question raised the fire within Brannon to the surface. "There is no point in investigating an attack on some tiny village in the middle of nowhere. Do you think I should waste my time traversing the countryside chasing pawns? I'll leave that to Villifor. Me, I'm going to find where the king is hiding and put him in check. Then I just have to make sure we are prepared for what we find."

Slate knew just enough about chess to understand the analogy. It made sense to look for the Blood Mage behind the attacks. Was Brannon hinting that he knew there was a Blood Mage? Slate played innocent to keep him talking. "What do you think we'll find?"

Slate thought Brannon was going to throw him out of his office, but after a brief flare of his temper, Brannon's shoulders sagged and the air of invincibility was removed. "I think a Blood Mage is responsible for these attacks and your parents' deaths. I am preparing Ispirtu for the battle to come, but I'm afraid our guardsmen won't be enough, so I've pushed the students hard this year...they will be needed."

"One Blood Mage could challenge all of Ispirtu?"

"The tales of Blood Mages described unlimited power, but those are tales from a different time. All of us get fatigued as our spark wanes, but I don't know if it is the same for a Blood Mage. We know so little about Blood Magic." Brannon actually seemed to relax a bit telling Slate everything. "And then there is the other problem..."

"What is that?"

"Over the past few years, the number of wizards that are strong in the spark has reduced dramatically. That is why we now require anyone with the spark to join Ispirtu. There aren't many wizards left, and the ones who remain aren't very powerful. The statues you see in the main hallway are a testament to powers long passed."

"What about the arena during the tournament? That must have taken an enormous amount of power."

"It did. In fact, it took the combined efforts of Ispirtu and the Wizard Council to move the ground and create the effects of the arena during the Championship bout. After that, we used a trick with the orbs to create the invisible ground. The orbs were placed on two sides of a surface. An orb on one side looked upwards and sent the image to the orb facing downwards, which projected the image. An opposite set of orbs did the same thing for the downwards direction and the end result was an "invisible" ground."

Slate couldn't believe what he was hearing. "Well what about the orbs? Who created those?"

"They've been around far longer than Ispirtu. We don't know how to create them any longer." Brannon paused with the admission. "I need to figure out why the magic in Malethya is decreasing before this Blood Mage surfaces or, fractal forbid, the Disenites return. We barely defended against the Disenites during the Twice-Broken Wars. In our current state, I'm not sure we can withstand a Blood Mage or the Disenites."

Slate processed the information quickly while keeping in mind Brannon had told him the best lies were half-truths. Slate had no way of verifying the magic in Malethya was decreasing and it gave Brannon an excellent excuse for his recent solitude. If it wasn't true, Brannon could bide his time gaining power while others investigated the isolated attacks of the outlying villages. Slate tried a different tack. "Do you have any information on Blood Mages or the Disenites? I could look into it for you. I may not be a wizard, but I can dig through manuscripts."

"Thank you, Slate, but very little information still exists on either subject. Cantor destroyed documents that described his discoveries in the hopes they wouldn't be rediscovered. The Disenites showed up unexpectedly and told us little of their homeland. We have sent ships to investigate, but they don't return. It is assumed that the Disenites have sunk the ships before they reach their shores.. I'll think about your offer, but in the meantime, I ask for your silence. If the Blood Mage discovers that Ispirtu is a house of cards, he may resurface before I have time to prepare a defense."

"For all of our sakes, I hope the kingdom is ready." Slate said politely and left. He had learned all he needed to know. Lattimer had already told him that Brannon had books on Blood Magic in his personal library. Slate had given Brannon the chance to admit it, but the wizard had played ignorant. Now Slate needed to see the books. If there were books on Blood Magic at the Regallo estate, it would be the first clear lead since the tournament ended. It was time to find Rainier and make a plan.

The tribesman proved adept at following Villifor and was rarely around the apartment. To find Rainier, Slate needed to find Villifor, and while the Bellator headmaster typically stood out in a crowd, he had been traveling a lot lately. Slate hoped he was at Bellator.

Slate ran through the day's information and let his feet pick his route, winding up on a side street with a crowd of people centered on a small, upscale restaurant called The Royal Boar. Slate started to slide around the periphery of the crowd when he heard rumblings. "Did you hear? Villifor is here!" an excited citizen of Ravinai proclaimed. "A true war hero!" another citizen yelled above the crowd. Slate couldn't believe his luck, but maybe his innate intuition associated with being a Perceptor was finally coming to fruition.

Slate stood on a crate, hoping to pick out Rainier while he remained inconspicuous, but his pale complexion was immediately noticed by Villifor. The headmaster stood up from his table and addressed his adoring fans. "Ladies and gentlemen, your kind words are too much. And now I must burden you with a humbly requested favor. A friend of mine is here to dine with me, but he has been relegated to a crate on the street." Heads swiveled as the crowd looked for Villifor's friend. "He is a student I privately teach, a colleague, and most importantly a friend, but you all know him as the Malethya's tournament champion, Slate 'Stonehands' Severance! Slate, please come join me!"

Slate approached Villifor's table as urgent whispers regarding the sickly state of the tournament champion circulated through the crowd. Villifor ate alone, but then again, he couldn't imagine anyone that knew him would want to accompany him either.

Slate embraced the smiling headmaster and mimicked his false exuberance. He then sat across from him and the headmaster spoke quietly with his smile never faltering. "You either have news for me or you are spying on me. For your sake, I hope it is the former."

Rainier had been spying on Villifor for weeks and hadn't been caught. Slate managed that feat in a manner of seconds. "Villifor, it was so gracious of you to invite me to lunch. I know your duties to the crown have kept you traveling recently and our personal sessions have understandably been reduced." Slate thought about Brannon's suggestion he find a way to accompany the next missions to the northern villages and decided this was the perfect opportunity. He spoke loudly enough to be overheard by the crowd. "In the best interests of Malethya, I would like to offer my talents as the tournament champion to aid you in your selfless travels to preserve our kingdom's peace."

A large murmur went up in the crowd and Villifor's fake smile almost faltered. He spoke through his teeth loud enough for only Slate to hear. "You aren't ready yet."

Again, Slate spoke to Villifor loudly enough for his voice to carry through the crowd. "Your legend was forged on the battlefield, and there is no better way for me to learn than from joining you in action. Will you teach me, headmaster?" The murmur within the crowd grew with anticipation of Villifor's acceptance of their tournament champion.

"You don't know what you are asking." Villifor gritted through a smile. Then he spoke to the crowd. "A true hero must prepare the next generation of heroes. I take this responsibility gladly and welcome you on the battlefield with me, Slate." The crowd erupted. During the commotion, Villifor addressed Slate privately. "Be at the Bellator complex tomorrow morning. We leave at sunrise. Now get out of here." The look in his eyes was intense, so Slate hurriedly snuck away.

As he left the restaurant, a young busboy ran up to him. "Excuse me, sir, but you have to pay your tab." Slate hadn't even eaten yet, so he looked questioningly at the busboy before recognizing Rainier. Rainier added, "...or should I just put it on the Bellator tab?"

Slate picked up the piece of paper and read "apartment in 30 minutes." Slate put the paper back down and said, "Villifor said he would pay for his good friend's meal."

CHAPTER FOURTEEN

AN UNSANCTIONED MISSION

Rainier joined Slate at the apartment. "I take it you have some exciting news to discuss?"

"Lattimer told me that Brannon has manuscripts describing Blood Magic in his personal library. Brannon then denied that he had access to information regarding the Blood Mages, so we have some investigating to do."

"Haven't we tried this once already?" Rainier replied, referencing their earlier Sicarius mission.

"Yes, but now I've been inside and know what to expect."

"If you are planning on breaking into the Regallo estate again, we need a better plan than hopping the fence and improvising." Slate knew he was right, but he didn't have a better plan. Then Rainier smiled at him. "Thankfully, I assumed you'd need to go back there at some point. I've been scouting the Regallo estate when Villifor leaves town."

"Fractal's fortune!" Slate slapped the tribesman on the back. "So what's the plan?"

"Mrs. Regallo hosts her socialite friends every evening at eight o'clock. The discussions can go late into the evening and involve copious amount of wine."

"You create realistic disguises, Rainier, but no one will mistake us for Mrs. Regallo's friends. We'd be recognized immediately."

"No one notices the servants handling the carriages. They drive onto the estate, drop off their employers for an evening of entertainment, and remain in the stable until called upon."

"So that gets us into the estate...but then what?"

"I hope you aren't too attached to that Sicarius mask..."

Rainier filled Slate in on the rest of his plan and the two made preparations for their evening. They dressed as servants and Rainier applied makeup to hide Slate's ghostly complexion. Their supplies for the night's events were packed into a trunk that was loaded onto a two-wheeled cart appropriated from the merchant downstairs. Slate finished their preparation by piling on a few packages of produce to hide the trunk.

Rainier identified one of Mrs. Regallo's friends, Ms. Babblerone, as their mark. She lived nearby and was light on security. Slate pulled the cart through Ravinai and approached the Babblerone estate from the service road adjacent to Rue Street. Rainier headed for the stable. "Let me do the talking. When it comes to striking a deal, the Tallow clan always gets what they want."

Slate was actually excited to see the famed negotiating skills of the Tribesman. "Ok, but if things go sideways, I'm doing things my way."

"You won't need to do that." Rainier thought for a minute and then added, "...but if you do, make sure to use your LEFT hand."

Slate laughed and the sound brought the attention of the stable hand. "Can I help you?"

Rainier gave a desperate look. "I sure hope so...we came to make a trade for some hay."

The stable boy looked toward the main house. "I should get the clerk. I just take care of the horses and drive around Ms. Babblerone."

"I was actually hoping to trade with you. You see, I didn't make it to the market in time to buy hay and the only shop left open was the produce stand. I used the money for the hay on this fruit with the hopes that I could trade it with one of the other estates. If you call the clerk, that will make it an official trade between estates and my employer will find out. I can't have that...one small mistake and I could be kicked out and jobless. Help me out!"

The stable hand remained skeptical, but he begrudgingly said, "We've all been there before. I'll help you out, but it won't come cheap. I'm going to need to explain why I have all this fruit."

"We normally order fruit tomorrow, so if you could just hold it for a day, I can bring hay tomorrow and no one will ever know the difference..."

"What's in it for me?" I'd be in a heap of trouble if I got caught."

"You're right...and I don't have much to offer..." Rainier hung his head.

The stable hand shrugged his shoulders and started to turn around. Rainier gave Slate a quick wink. "Wait...there is one more thing I could do for you..."

The stable hand turned around and waited for the offer. "How would you like a night without work? I know how to handle horses and could drive Ms. Babblerone around tonight…"

That gave the stable boy pause. "All I have to do is hold onto this cart for a day and give you some hay tonight? And you know how to care for horses?"

Rainier exhaled in exaggerated relief. "Absolutely, I can prove it to you." Rainier headed into the stable before his unwitting trade partner changed his mind. He yelled over his shoulder in Slate's direction, "Go check on the carriage and load up the hay into our cart."

The stable hand followed Rainier toward the horses and Slate brought the cart into the carriage house. He unloaded the fruit onto a crate and loaded their supply trunk into the travel compartment of the carriage. He was throwing hay into the two-wheeled cart when Rainier and the stable boy returned.

"We'll need some spare clothes with the Babblerone crest on it to make sure we don't get you in trouble by being out of uniform." Rainier had gone from desperately in need of a favor to complete control of the conversation without the stable hand noticing.

"I'll grab two of them from my quarters…" The stable hand, excited to get a night off work and impressed enough with Rainier's ability to care for the horses, ran off.

Slate said to Rainier, "Remind me never to barter with you."

"Usually I'm the one that ends up with a night off work." Rainier grinned and the stable hand ran back to meet them.

"Put these on." The stable hand was now fully committed to the ruse. "Pick up Ms. Babblerone at the main entrance of the estate in a few minutes. The butler believes I've fallen ill and my two cousins are filling in for me tonight. Now I'm going to see if Sheila is available on my night off. She works mornings in the kitchen. I want to see if I can make her late for work!"

"Thanks for helping me out…and good luck to you tonight!" Rainier bid the stable hand farewell. He then hooked the horse to the carriage and Slate sat next to him on the carriage seat. Rainier easily handled the reins and a smile of contentment filled his face. "It's been too long since I've driven a horse. My nomadic blood has been stirring these last few months."

"I'll use my own two feet. There wasn't much use for horses in Pillar. Goats are more sure footed and oxen are better at hauling stone."

"Until you ride a horse in an open field with the wind rushing past your face and angry villagers at your back, I'll just pretend you didn't say that." Rainier smiled at the memory as he pulled the horse and carriage to the front entrance of the Babblerone estate where the butler waited.

"You were nearly late." The anxious butler admonished Rainier for being on time. "At the Regallo estate, announce her arrival at the gatehouse, escort her to the main entrance, and drive the carriage in back. Wait there with the other drivers until you are summoned to pick up Ms. Babblerone."

Rainier responded simply, "Yessir."

The doting butler held the door for Ms. Babblerone and accompanied her toward the carriage. Slate could see she was accustomed to such treatment from her dress and the way she walked. She looked rather like a chicken on the farm, with her chest puffed out and tiny little steps due to ridiculously uncomfortable shoes. She also tattered on and on about nonsense. Slate was bored with her before she made it onto her seat.

When they arrived at the Regallo estate, Rainier pulled up to the guardhouse. "Ms. Babblerone is here to join Mrs. Regallo for a social hour," he announced formally to the Crimson Guardsman.

"She is expected." Rainier dropped Ms. Babblerone at the main entrance with the butler. They then drove around back and joined the other drivers in the stable. Slate and Rainier relaxed on a crate with a view of patrolling guardsmen while the drivers bided their time playing dice. The guardsman on duty walked along the perimeter of the estate but occasionally stopped and remained motionless for long periods of time. Sometimes she double-backed in the direction she had just come. The patrol route took the guardsmen out of view of the stable for a brief period, giving Slate the window he needed to reach the main house undetected.

"It's dark enough now. Let's get our supplies." Slate discreetly caught Rainier's ear.

They walked casually into the carriage house. Slate adjusted the rigging of the carriage while Rainier engaged a Regallo servant in conversation. "I was just admiring the Regallo crest painted onto the side of the carriage. Can you tell me what it means?"

"Of course. The Regallo crest has a long and storied tradition. The raven is shown in profile, its gaze scanning the purple expanse beyond it. It symbolizes the Regallos looking over the kingdom..." *Thwack.* Slate brought the side of his hand down against the base of the proud servant's neck and he crumbled instantly.

Rainier asked, "Did you really need to do that? With a little persuasion, he would have given us a tour of the estate."

"I couldn't listen to the story of the Regallo crest for one second longer. Besides, I used my left hand..." That received a quiet chuckle from Rainier before he returned to the task at hand.

"Ok, let's go to plan B then. Break out the trunk. I'll strip the servant."

"I like plan B better than plan A anyways," Slate followed with a smirk as he opened their supply trunk and pulled out layer upon layer of grey wraps and bandages, setting them in a pile by Rainier. He then extricated two lengths of rope, setting one in a pile with the wraps and setting one aside for himself. Next was a set of plain black clothing and Slate tossed them to Rainier. Near the bottom of the trunk was a pack of smelling salts that Slate put in a pocket. That only left one object in the trunk and it filled Slate with trepidation. The Sicarius mask stared up at him from the bottom of the emptied trunk. The words 'upon penalty of death' kept ringing through his head.

In the other corner of the room, Rainier stripped the servant of his Regallo robes and handed them to Slate. He then dressed the unconscious servant in the black clothing from the trunk. Slate switched his Babblerone attire for the Regallo set, hiding a length of rope beneath the robes.

"It's time to turn you into the most infamous figure in Malethya." Slate saw the excitement on Rainier's face at his words and knew the tribesman was ready for the night's challenge. Slate took wrap upon wrap of clothing and tied it in a way that created folds within the fabric. Within a few minutes, Rainier transformed from a servant into a close approximation of the Sicarius headmaster. There was only one part of the costume left. Slate lifted the Sicarius mask from the trunk and handed it to Rainier.

"Are you sure this is smart?" Rainier asked.

Slate was wondering the same thing. "We need the effect to be real. This is the only way...try it on." Rainier did and Slate had a hard time looking directly at him. "Besides, the headmaster told me I couldn't use it for Sicarius missions. Borrowing it to someone else isn't against the rules…"

"I'm not sure I'd want to argue semantics with the headmaster, but you're right. This is the only way it will work." Rainier took off the mask and handed it back to Slate. "…but you have some work to do first."

Slate took the mask and put it on. "If I get caught with this, we don't deserve our Sicarius training. You'll have it when the real danger starts." Rainier looked at Slate's feet as he spoke to him.

"How does the mask work again?"

"It doesn't make someone invisible, it makes them completely unmemorable. People can see me, but I'm not worth a second thought unless I do something that calls attention to me. So in my current attire…"

Rainier continued his thought, "…you should appear as a Regallo servant…"

"…and able to walk directly into a well-lit mansion with guardsmen protecting it." A mischievous smile crossed Slate's face as he prepared to leave. "I'll walk ahead to where I have a view of the patrolling guardsmen. When I signal you, sprint toward the location I jumped the fence last time." Rainier nodded his understanding and Slate slipped into the night.

He walked across the back lawn of the estate, trying to look the part of a servant counting the hours until the end of his shift. Through the Sicarius mask, he watched the patrolling guardsmen walk around the edge of servant's quarters, making Rainier's path clear. Slate signaled toward the stable.

Rainier slung the unconscious servant over his shoulder and moved as quickly as he could toward Slate, forming a strange silhouette in the light from the stable. After a few excruciating seconds, Rainier crossed the lawn and regained cover in the bushes without attracting notice of the patrolling guardsmen.

"Next time, if you decide to knock someone out, you are carrying the body." Rainier whispered to Slate while trying to catch his breath.

"Sorry, it wouldn't have worked with the costume." Rainier grunted to indicate concession of the point even if he didn't like the circumstances. Slate gave him a minute or two to catch his breath, not wanting to push his luck. "Do you see that window on the first floor? It has its light out and it will be your best entry point. I'll see you inside in a few minutes. Don't forget to tie the rope to the top of the fence. We might need a quick exit."

Slate left the bushes and walked straight to the servant's entrance. He opened the door and saw the clerk at the entryway. Slate nearly froze in fear but forced himself to keep walking. The clerk looked up from his books briefly but then returned to his work without a second thought. Slate could get used to this Sicarius mask. He turned into the hallway and started counting doors. At the third door, he entered a dark room.

Slate waited and allowed his eyes to adjust to the surroundings. Even in the darkness, he could make out that he was in a girl's room, and that it hadn't been touched in years. He noticed the bedposts twisted upwards with sharp spikes sticking out of it. Atop the bedpost was a rose in partial bloom. This must have been Rose Regallo's room. All pictures and signs of Rose had been removed. The bedposts must have been an oversight in the family's haste to lock the door and forget the existence of their estranged daughter. He crept across the room and opened the window, thankful the infrequent use didn't result in creaks and groans to alert the patrols. Through the open window, Slate motioned toward Rainier's position.

Rainier hauled the unconscious servant from the bushes and Slate helped bring the body through the window. Rainier jumped into the room, leaving the window open because he would need it later. "Just to the right of this room is a servant's stairwell. The kitchen is closed for the night, so there shouldn't be much traffic. I'll check to make sure no one is around and then follow me upstairs to Mrs. Regallo's room. It's the third door on the left. We know it will be empty since she is entertaining guests."

The awakening servant stirred on the ground and released a soft groan. Rainier bent down and gave a light chop to the base of his neck, sending him back into a deep sleep. "Then I get rid of this dead weight...let's get it over with."

Slate listened through the doorway, but the giggling of women from the adjacent great room were the only sounds. Slate walked over to the stairs, and not hearing footsteps above, signaled Rainier to carry the servant into the stairwell. Slate saw the tribesman's exhaustion, but it couldn't be helped. A door closed on the second floor, so Slate ascended the remaining stairs, ready to take out any unfortunate observers. The footsteps belonged to Lattimer. He strode down the hallway with his head buried in a book, mumbling to himself. The only bits Slate picked up were "...boring family histories..." and "...I'd rather read a clerk's ledger..." Most importantly, he wasn't bothered by the sight of a servant in the hallway and he didn't go down the service stairwell. Slate pretended to dust some of the decorative touches adorning the Regallo estate, which left him in close enough proximity to hear Lattimer address the guardsmen outside his father's office. "Return this book to my father's library. It was even less interesting than a conversation with Ms. Babblerone." Slate had just located Brannon's personal library.

When Lattimer left the hallway, Slate helped Rainier bring the servant into Mrs. Regallo's room. They were completely exposed for this section of the mission if anyone were to happen upon them. His heart raced as they passed the second door and the third door opened silently into blessed blackness and safety. It was amazing how small parts of a mission like a thirty foot walk down a hallway could bring such stress, but that was life in Sicarius.

In Mrs. Regallo's room, lit only by the night sky from a window he knew very well, Slate took off the Sicarius mask and handed it to Rainier. "It's your time...be careful first and convincing second."

"I'll do both." Rainier answered using two different octaves in his voice. Rainier's looped a length of rope through the leg of a heavy dresser and opened the window.

"I'll see you shortly. Fractal's blessings, Slate..." Rainier climbed through the window and rapelled down the mansion's wall.

Slate pictured Rainier dropping to the ground, squeezing through the window to Rose's room and sneaking into the closed kitchen, which had direct access to the great room. Shortly after, an imitation of the headmaster's voice shouted loudly throughout the estate. "The secrets of the Regallos shall be revealed. No place is safe from the Sicarius headmaster!"

The guardsman outside of Brannon's office hurdled the catwalk bannister and landed on the floor of the great room in pursuit of Rainier. This was his chance.

Slate slipped into Brannon's unguarded office carrying the unconscious servant on his shoulder. He stole a quick look down at the great room to see women clutching each other in fear and guardsmen emerging from their posts to join the hunt for the headmaster. Rainier's diversion had worked, buying Slate a few minutes.

Slate scattered objects in Brannon's office around the room, making it look disheveled, and stuffing a few of the more expensive items into the servant's pockets. Outside the room, the commotion was dying down, so Slate's time was running out. Slate broke the smelling salts from his pocket and wafted them beneath the servant's nose. Then he crawled beneath Brannon's imposing desk and waited.

The groggy servant groaned as he started to rouse. The servant made it to his feet and stumbled toward one of the walls, trying to make sense of his current situation. Slate thought he had awoken him too soon when the door opened. "Intruder!" yelled the guardsman. The servant didn't even manage a rebuttal before being brutally tackled to the ground. The guardsmen hauled the servant to his feet, found the stolen property stashed in his pockets, and marched him out of the room. Slate heard the guardsman addressing the other patrols. "I've got one, boys. This one was snitching objects from Brannon's office. Take him to the guardhouse for questioning and call Brannon."

Slate didn't want to think of the methods they would use for questioning and felt sorry for the servant, but the only way to keep the guardsmen from performing a detailed search of Brannon's office was to give them what they were looking for. The Guardsmen searched for an intruder and upon finding the servant, discontinued his search. It was a basic tenet of Sicarius. People were blinded by what they sought.

Alone in the heavily guarded office of the Ispirtu headmaster, Slate prepared his escape route by tying a length of rope to the heavy desk and coiling it by the window. His time was limited before the guardsmen discovered the servant's innocence, so Slate searched the bookcases lining the walls feverishly. He recognized several books from his Ispirtu studies as classic literature on magic, but none of the titles referenced Blood Magic. Of course, Blood Mages were named after the atrocities they committed, so it was unlikely that a title describing their practice would include such a name. With a quick look failing to reveal any obvious books, Slate looked more closely at the titles, with the clock ticking slowly in his head.

A History of Wizards sounded promising, but after skimming through several sections and using precious time, Slate couldn't find anything. He found Cantor listed in the back of the book, but when he turned to the section, the pages were missing. Frustrated, Slate silently put the book back on the shelf and looked for the next relevant title. *A Compendium of Spells* looked to be a very useful book for an actual wizard, but it was of little use to Slate. All the spells listed a qualitative amount of spark required and a recommended object, animal, or motion to use as a link. From the little Slate knew of Blood Magic, a link wouldn't be required.

Slate returned the *Compendium* to the shelf and slowly looked around the office. If Brannon did have such rare and forbidden texts in his possession, he would probably keep them hidden. There weren't many places to hide objects, with the exception of an ornate box stuffed innocuously into the corner. It was smaller than a trunk but definitely large enough to fit a few books inside. Slate's internal clock was winding down. If there wasn't evidence in this trunk he'd have to leave empty-handed. Slate gently removed a statue of a golden raven adorning the lid

Slate, expecting the box to be sealed, was surprised when the lid rose gently on its hinges. Before Slate could see what was inside, a security orb flew out of the box. It took a quick lap around the office before looking at Slate's shocked, upturned head. Slate sprinted for the window at the same instant the security orb activated and released a high-pitched alarm. Slate threw open the office window as a guardsman came barreling inside Brannon's office. They made eye contact for one brief moment before Slate hurled himself out the window, holding onto the rope.

The rope went taut and Slate's hands slid the remaining length of the rope, burning as he plummeted. He dropped the final few feet into some bushes in a tremendous crash.

Through the perilous dive, the security orb tracked his movements, releasing a loud siren to alert the guardsmen and floating several feet above his head. The guardsmen in Brannon's office started to repel down from the window above and figures were emerging from the guardhouse. He got up and sprinted toward the side of the house, hoping he could clear the fence before getting caught by the guardsmen. Slate pumped his legs until they hurt more than his burning hands.

Slate rounded the corner of the estate and saw the rope that Rainier left for him. It was halfway down the fence and Slate thought he'd make it until the guardsman patrolling the rear of the estate sprinted around the opposite corner of the house, alerted by the security orb. Slate pushed his legs even harder, trying to gain the advantage on the advancing guardsman.

Slate reached the rope with a three-stride lead on the guardsman, gripped the rope with his burning hands, planted his feet against the fence, and swung backwards with all his might. The guardsman had committed to tackling Slate off the rope and his momentum brought him between Slate and the fence. Slate delivered a two-footed kick to the back of the guardsman as he swung back down, crumpling him against the fence.

He then used the limp guardsman's body to reach higher up the fence, fearing to look at the approaching footsteps. Slate climbed hand-over-hand and started to pull himself over when the force of a tackling guardsman ripped him from the fence. Within seconds he was piled upon, beaten, and dragged away by guardsmen who had experienced a very frustrating evening. All their frustration was released in the form of capturing and securing Slate. The mission had failed.

Slate awaited his fate silently within the guardhouse despite the advanced questioning techniques of the guardsmen. He had been a regular at Primean's Pain Tolerance Laboratory, and these guardsmen, despite their skill, didn't have nearly as many tools at their disposal as Primean. Besides, he knew the real questions would start once Brannon arrived. He might as well save his breath for then.

Slate looked up when the punches stopped to see Lattimer at the door. He had been expecting Brannon. "Slate Severance...I should have known it was you. You've been a thorn in my family's side ever since you publicly mocked the Regallo name at the tournament. We've taken the high road until now, but you crossed a line by breaking into our home." Lattimer spit in his face. "You deserve whatever punishment my father has in store for you. You'll receive no pity from me." Lattimer stood him up from his chair by grabbing the front of his robes in his fist. He punched Slate as hard as he could in the stomach, doubling him over. Then Lattimer leaned close and whispered in his ear, "Clutch your stomach...there's a note in my fist." Slate groaned, causing laughter amongst the guardsmen, and reached for his stomach. Lattimer relaxed his fist and Slate grabbed the note. When Lattimer pushed him back into the chair, Slate snuck the note into his pocket. Lattimer turned back around and addressed the guardsmen, who nodded approvingly toward him. "Do what you want with him. I have nothing left to say to this fractal-forsaken refuse. Just make sure he's in good enough shape to see my father."

The guardsmen laid into him with renewed vigor, but Brannon arrived quickly. He questioned a guardsman with fire in his eyes. "What happened here?"

Dutifully, the guardsman gave a succinct report of the night's events to Brannon. "There was a disturbance during Mrs. Regallo's dinner party. The Sicarius headmaster appeared but escaped us." Slate had thought Rainier escaped, and hearing the news relieved him. "We checked the premises, and a burglar was found in your office. Upon questioning, we learned the burglar was actually a servant at the estate who claimed not to have any memory of the night's events between working in the stable and being discovered in your office. We were still questioning the servant when one of your hidden security orbs was triggered. We caught this one trying to jump the fence into the neighboring estate."

During the story, Brannon's jaw started to clench, and even more concerning, his scepter had a faint glow to it. "Thank you, guardsman. Now, if I could ask all of you to leave me with the intruder. Please go attend to my wife in the estate." The guardhouse emptied and Brannon stared silently at Slate until they were out of earshot. As he waited, the faint glow increased to a soft light emanating from the scepter.

Brannon's silence ended abruptly. "You sat in my office this afternoon and listened as I confided in you, while scheming to break into my home this evening? I was just beginning to trust you and then you pull this Sicarius crap on me!" The volume of Brannon's voice increased with the light from his scepter. "I don't even care what you were looking for...I never want to see your traitorous face again. You are stripped of all honor associated with your name and are expelled from Ispirtu."

Slate didn't have time to comprehend the news. The fire in Brannon's eyes peaked and the scepter's light swirled angrily. "This world is changing, Slate. When big changes start to happen, sometimes it's best to simplify the situation." A wicked smile crept onto the lips of Brannon. He held open his hand and a ball of air swirled like a storm.

More and more air forced itself into the swirling mass held in front of Brannon as he talked. It reminded Slate of the explosive orb that Magnus used to blow up the mine in Pillar. "You are an unknown in a world with too many unknowns. I can't have you causing problems for me because I have too many others to deal with…goodbye, Slate."

The ball swirling in Brannon's hand was released and Slate shut his eyes. He felt the pressure wave of expanding gasses hit him, toppling his chair. A deafening explosion soon followed, although Slate couldn't pinpoint the origin. The noise was all around him.

Slate, lying flat on the ground against the back of his chair opened his eyes to see the sky above him. He didn't know whether to be more surprised at the sight of the night sky, where the ceiling of the guardhouse should have been, or the fact that he was still alive and capable of opening his eyes at all. Brannon stepped into view, looking down upon Slate. "Since you are no longer associated with Ispirtu, I see no reason for us to meet again. If I see you at Ispirtu, or catch you playing your Sicarius games at my estate, I won't be as careful casting my spell. Take a look around you and think hard about the consequences of your little games here tonight."

Brannon disappeared into the night and Slate waited for the ringing in his ears to stop before he got up and looked around. The guardhouse was demolished from the explosion, but the blast was definitely directed away from Slate. The stone walls on either side of him were pulverized to rubble and the ceiling had been lifted and scattered across the front lawn. There were only two sections of the wall remaining, the one behind Brannon was left entirely intact and the one behind Slate was leaning precariously.

Slate stumbled through the broken guardhouse and into the street. He had gotten a block away from the estate, when Rainier sprinted to him.

"Slate! Are you ok? What did you do to the guardhouse?" Rainier blurted out a string of questions before realizing that Slate wasn't in the state of mind to answer them at the moment. Rainier ducked his head under Slate's arm and steered his dazed friend back to the apartment. Slate slowly returned to his senses and Rainier ran out of patience. "Tell me what happened." Slate, not anxious to describe his encounter with Brannon, started his tale in Brannon's office. "I woke the servant up in time to be discovered by the guardsmen searching the premises.

After finding him with valuables in his pocket, they stopped searching the room. I was free to peruse the books for several minutes."

"Did you find evidence linking Brannon to Blood Magic?" Rainier pushed the story forward.

"If he is, he didn't keep any manuscripts on his bookshelf. All the books I found with references to Cantor had the relevant pages removed. I spotted a trunk that appeared to be about the right size to hide a few books in and I went to check its contents. A security orb popped out to announce my presence. I almost made it over the fence, but I got grabbed by the guardsmen before I could clear it..."

"And what about the explosion...I don't recall packing exploding orbs."

"Brannon came from Ispirtu and needed an outlet for his anger. He destroyed the guardhouse but restrained himself enough to only expel me from the Ispirtu Guild...I thought I was a dead man."

"You were expelled from Ispirtu?"

The direness of the situation began to sink in for Slate, and he didn't reiterate his failure. Having failed to find evidence and being expelled from Ispirtu left him no means to further investigate his most promising lead. Disgust with being caught at the Regallo estate leaked into his conversation. "At least I won't have to wear this fractal-forsaken Regallo robe ever again..."

Slate took the robe off and absently threw it into the corner. In the process, the note from Lattimer fell out and caught Rainier's attention. "What's that?"

Slate looked back and saw the note on the ground. "Oh, I forgot about that. Lattimer punched me in the stomach and slipped me that note before his father arrived."

Rainier picked it up and read it aloud.

Dear Trusted Friend,

When I heard the commotion in the estate tonight regarding the Sicarius headmaster, I instantly recalled telling you about my father's personal library and had no doubt that you were the cause behind the disturbance. I hope you escape tonight, although I have my doubts. In the event of your capture, I am penning this letter and deliver the note in a closed fist to your stomach. You deserve it for not trusting me.

I could throw the guardsmen off your trail, but that would only serve to implicate both of us. I don't know what my father will do to you as punishment, but I can say I don't want any part of it. At least this way there will be one person left with access to my father' personal library.

How do I know you didn't find it? ...Because you broke into my father's estate without asking me where it was. You are undoubtedly searching his office or some other trivial location that a common burglar would expect. Do you think my father is the type of man to leave objects of that nature in easy to find places? Someone smarter than you would have trusted me enough to ask where my father's personal library was located. Someone smarter than you would have asked for my help to give your ill-fated mission a slight chance of success. Someone smarter than you would have known the trick that my father used to conceal an entire room.

Do you remember the Championship bout in the arena? The dueling courtyard appeared invisible when in fact it was fully supported. Orbs attached to either side of the surface created the appearance of invisibility. The entire time you were sneaking through the estate, my father's personal library floated above the great room, accessible from the catwalk past the guardsman posted at my father's office. I had even started asking for books from the hidden library as early as this evening, since my trusted friend was interested in the information.

Oh! There's the sound of a security orb, so I'm sure you've been found. I know the locations of several hidden security orbs, if you would have asked me. I'll start making my way to the guardhouse now. At least I'll get a chance to punch you in the stomach. If you survive your encounter with my father, I'll meet you tomorrow at noon in Ravinai square.

Fractal's fortune,

Lattimer B. Regallo

Rainier quietly refolded the letter and handed it to Slate, whose disgust at being caught turned into disgust in his actions for the evening. Lattimer was right. The whole mess could have been avoided if he had just trusted Lattimer enough to help him. He wouldn't make that mistake again.

"Rainier, meet Lattimer tomorrow and convince him I'm sorry. I should be back from my Bellator mission tomorrow evening. Can you coordinate a meeting at the infirmary with everyone the morning after…including Lattimer? He's our only eyes on Brannon now."

"I'll do what I can, Teacher. In the meanwhile, why don't you rest? From the beating those guardsmen gave you, you're going to need all the recovery time you can get."

"I wish Sana were here to heal me."

"I'm sure you wish Sana were here…but if she were, she'd be leaving you more fatigued than you are now. Get some sleep." Rainier returned the Sicarius mask and left Slate to collapse on the lounge pillows in exhaustion, thankful that Rainier hadn't gotten caught.

CHAPTER FIFTEEN

A FURIOUS BATTLE

A grim determination to redeem the previous day's failures forced his swollen musles into action as he packed his travel sack for the day's Bellator mission. This was not Sicarius business, so the choice to leave the mask was an easy one. He brought the glove from Lucus, however, to hide under his Bellator armor, and dashed from his apartment.

On his way to the Bellator complex, the hairs on his head moved and a throwing knife embedded in a wooden beam of a merchant's storefront, missing him by inches. Slate jerked away from the sound a split second later, but it would have been way too late to avoid the first knife thrown. He stalled his instinctive roll when he saw the hilt bore a catalpa tree with a note pinned to the wood beam. The method of the note's delivery hinted that the contents would not be pleasant.

Dearest Slate,

My sources alerted me oft an imposter dressed in my likeness during a failed attempt to infiltrate the Regallo estate. Due to the location of the robbery, I naturally assumed you to be the culprit. Upon further examination of the estate this morning, the rubble formerly known as a guardhouse evidenced your capture and overall failure.

I hope the information obtained from Brannon is worth the trouble your stunt has caused me. Word will undoubtedly reach King Darik, who is already suspicious of Sicarius, as you observed at our last guild meeting. I do not take kindly to people who cause me trouble. I find enough of it on my own.

The Bellator mission is ready to begin, or I would talk to you right now. As it is, this is an excellent opportunity for you to prove your worth to me and to Sicarius. When you return, we can trade information regarding Villifor for information of greater value that will partially compensate me for the trouble you caused last night.

§

Slate glanced around the rooftops, but the headmaster was already gone. Everyone was getting desperate for some answers, and he wanted to remain in the Sicarius headmaster's good graces. Considering he made an enemy of Brannon, he hoped the Bellator mission would be as fruitful as the Sicarius headmaster suggested.

At the Bellator complex, the rising sun cast an eerie light on the Bellator Guardsmen preparing for the day's mission. Villifor took a brief second away from his conversation with Magnus to address Slate.

"Slate, you'll be driving the supply cart. Make it to camp by lunch or the troops could kill you before you see your first battle." Villifor pointed to a horse-drawn cart filled to the brim with food and supplies. Slate bit his tongue. He couldn't afford to offend another headmaster.

Instead, Slate climbed atop the cart and Villifor spoke to the assembled guardsmen before departure. "Today we travel to the village of Minot. It's a small collection of houses gathered in the woods a 3-hour ride from here. I plan to make it there in two and be home by dinner. Any questions?" *Why are we going to Minot? Are all the attacks so close to Ravinai or were they getting closer? How do I drive this fractal-forsaken cart?* All of these questions came to mind for Slate, but they didn't seem appropriate. "Good, let's ride!"

The Bellator Guardsmen kicked the flanks of their mounts and left Slate behind. Slate tried to remember the commands Rainier used to steer the carriage from Ms. Babblerone's house to the Regallo estate, but his inexperience with horses prevented him from keeping pace with the seasoned Bellator Guardsmen. He drove the cart out of the northern exit of Ravinai and was able to glimpse the guardsmen disappear into a wooded path in the distance. Slate spent the next two hours progressing from a road through the woods, to smaller paths, and finally a trail so small his cart barely fit. With each fork in the road he passed, Slate's confidence in his direction decreased. Just when he questioned his ability to return to Ravinai, much less find Minot, he heard a familiar voice. "This is a quiet path and yet it has seen much activity today. Perhaps you can tell me whether I should expect more travelers?"

Lucus released his camouflage spell and appeared with Sana in the path ahead. The woodcutter made a habit of appearing when Slate needed him most. "Lucus! What are you doing here?"

"Rainier found me last night and told me you planned to accompany Villifor on a Bellator mission. I thought you could use some friends to keep an eye on you." Sana pointed out Slate's obvious disorientation. "We followed Villifor's troops out of Ravinai. You must be using some of your Sicarius training to ride in circles and disorient any potential enemy?"

"Do you know where Minot is located?" Slate didn't bother to explain the food cart.

"Yes, I know Minot well. They are a simple people that welcome wandering woodcutters into their homes and tell tales by the fire. It pains me to think they could have been harmed." Lucus continued with a solemn expression. "I don't think Villifor will set up camp in the town, though. This path empties into a large meadow that would serve as a more suitable army camp. You should come across them in a short while."

"What do you plan to do?" Slate asked Lucus, who thought for some time before answering.

"Villifor has too many people for us to investigate Minot undetected. Sana and I will help where we can but must remain hidden in the woods. I trust that you will investigate thoroughly and we can meet soon to discuss our findings."

The ease with which Lucus trusted him contrasted sharply with his own mistrust of Lattimer. "I'll be sure to investigate thoroughly. Will you join me for breakfast with Ibson tomorrow?"

"Of course... Fractal's blessing to you." Lucus left through the woods, guided by signs that only a master woodsman could decipher.

Slate followed the small path until it opened into a large meadow, just as Lucus described. The guardsmen spread out to form a perimeter while Villifor stood in a command tent erected in the center of the meadow. Slate tied his horse and cart to a tree and headed for Villifor. "The tournament champion joins us." Villifor announced as he approached. "If he starts now, he may have lunch ready for Magnus and his men upon the scouting party's return from Minot."

Slate couldn't swallow his pride completely and said, "I'll serve Bellator in the manner in which I am needed, but why invite me on the mission if all I do is drive the food cart?"

"You used a public gathering, an admitted weakness of mine, to force your invitation. I conceded to your inclusion in this mission, and to that end, I have fulfilled my obligations. Perhaps you can use this as an opportunity to learn horseback riding." Villifor answered Slate, but his mind was somewhere distant.

Slate wanted to get his attention. "What about your obligation to personally teach me? I have hardly seen you since the Bellator competition. Surely a war hero such as you would have at least a few words of wisdom for someone who can't even ride a horse..." Slate added a little bit of derision in the words war hero, and it wasn't lost on Villifor.

"You ungrateful bastard! I have kept you away from these missions because you aren't ready to fight with guardsmen."

"I'm a tournament champion and a survivor, the last from Pillar."

"You are a liability. I don't expect you to understand since you haven't taken a single Bellator course beyond individual combat, so I might as well just show you. Hop onto my horse and I'll carry you like the dead weight you are to learn from Magnus and the reconnaissance party." Villifor offered his arm to Slate with a sneer.

"I'll run. No one from Pillar needs a horse to carry them anywhere." Slate's wounded pride played a role in that last comment.

"Suit yourself. Hya!" Villifor kicked the flanks of his horse and took off, leaving Slate to run in full armor and track the hoof prints through the woods. He churned his legs at a steady clip, not wanting to burn all of his energy at once and the physical exertion helped him to clear his head. He may have gone about it poorly, but he had managed to get Villifor alone. Slate intended to take advantage of the opportunity. The run worked up a good sweat by the time he came upon Villifor atop a rocky ledge. "You wouldn't make a good horse, Slate. You are too slow and sweat too much."

"What is it you wanted to show me?" Slate asked respectfully, biting his tongue for once.

"So you can hold back when you want to...maybe you aren't a lost cause after all. Come here and look." Slate stood beside Villifor and looked down upon a tiny, empty village situated against the rocky bluff upon which they stood. Magnus and his troops searched building after building. "Do you see how they work together? One person scouts ahead while another watches the rear. No one is trying to be a hero. This is the strength of Bellator. We don't have magic and we don't slink around in the night. We fight the battles that need to be fought...you would know this if you had proper training. By only taking the individual combat courses, you have made yourself into a liability. We fight together, but no one can trust you to know your role on the team. That makes you dangerous."

Slate kept quiet and watched Magnus and his teams methodically move throughout the village. The Bellator headmaster was right. "I understand your point. Why are you taking the time to teach me this? If I can't be trusted to fight, than I'm of no use to Bellator."

"Magnus' technique is perfect. His execution is superb. He would be a formidable commander to face in any battle, but he lacks one thing. Do you know what it is?" Slate watched Magnus more closely. He moved precisely and with absolute confidence, but it was almost too regimented. After a long period of observation, Slate had his answer.

"Creativity..."

"Correct. We don't know who or what we will be facing. We haven't had a direct encounter with our enemy in any of these missions. There have been signs of battle, including bodies, but we don't know who sent them and we don't know how to fight them..." That explained Villifor's distant gaze earlier. The man had a lot on his mind.

"Do you think it's a Blood Mage responsible for the attacks?"

"Blood Mage is a meaningless name. What does that tell us? We'll be fighting an enemy with limitless power who can rain fire upon us and turn the man standing next to us into an enemy?" Villifor snorted. "These are childhood stories. In reality, no one knows the capabilities of a Blood Mage because we've lost all knowledge of them. That is the most troubling piece out of everything. We don't know anything about Blood Mages. We don't know anything about whatever is attacking these villages. When the real fighting begins we will need to learn, and learn quickly. If we don't, it will be too late."

Villifor turned his gaze from the village below to Slate. "You won the tournament by tricking Magnus and beguiling Lattimer into attacking when he should have maintained his defensive tactics. You adapted to your opponents, finding their weaknesses and exploiting them." The look on Villifor's face was more intense and focused than he had ever seen from the headmaster. In that moment, he knew for certain that the peacocking, crowd-pleasing act he put on for the public was a disguise every bit as effective as a Sicarius mask. "Malethya will need you. It won't need you for your fighting skills. It will need you to adapt and lead us against our hidden enemies once they expose themselves. Do you understand me?"

Slate had never thought of himself in that way before, but from the intensity of Villifor's expression, he found himself nodding. "I understand."

Villifor turned back toward Minot again. "The search is wrapping up. I'm sure we have found the same thing we find at every other empty village...nothing. Let's walk back to camp to get the report. I think you've run enough today."

Slate walked beside Villifor through the woods as he led his horse by the reins. The headmaster continued talking to Slate as he went. "Despite your directness back at camp, I believe you are right. I haven't spent enough time teaching you, because I've been caught up in these investigations. Your final lesson for the day is adaptability. You might think this means the same thing as creativity or ingenuity, but it doesn't. I have survived by being adaptable and there may come a time when you understand what I mean..."

That didn't make any sense to Slate, so he changed the direction of the conversation. "Are these attacks on tiny villages worth investigating? Brannon believes they only serve as a distraction from preparation for the true battle with the Blood Mage."

"Brannon has been spending too much time in his tower lately. I should go over there and beat him in a game or two of chess again to remind him of the importance of pawns. He is very clever, but he spends all his time positioning the kings, queens, and knights. Whatever is attacking these villagers may be a pawn in the eyes of Brannon, but he forgets that the tide of a chess match is usually established by the pawns. Pawns are like Bellator...individually we may not be as powerful as Ispirtu or Sicarius, but few can withstand us when we attack in numbers. Do you know my favorite piece on the chessboard?"

Slate shook his head no.

"The pawn that is left standing at the end of the game. I'm sure Brannon doesn't even notice them, but they remind me of myself. If a Blood Mage surfaces, try to be the pawn left standing in the end..."

Slate was beginning to understand Bellator and maybe even Villifor. He had viewed the guild simply as a collection of the kingdom's best fighters. Now he knew better. Of all the guilds, Bellator was the most cohesive unit. Ispirtu fought incestuously and Sicarius didn't even have knowledge of the other members, but Bellator Guardsmen depended on each other. Slate's thoughts were interrupted by Villifor. "So what has your friend the Sicarius headmaster been up to?"

"This morning, it involved throwing a knife a few inches from my head. If that is friendship, you can keep it..." Slate was happy to hear Villifor chuckle. He had managed to put the headmaster at ease for once. Wanting to stay in his good graces, Slate offered up some information.

"The King has charged Sicarius with identifying the person behind these attacks. I'm sure this doesn't come as a surprise, since he admitted giving similar objectives to Ispirtu and Bellator. What may surprise you is that the headmaster hasn't found anything yet."

"If the Sicarius headmaster can't find something, it is either because our enemy can outwit the headmaster or the headmaster is hiding something." Villifor sighed, "I don't know which outcome is more concerning..."

The two of them re-entered camp to find it abuzz with excitement. Magnus awaited Villifor's return with pride and arrogance smeared across his face.

"Report," Villifor commanded.

"Minot was deserted, headmaster. We discovered signs of a struggle at multiple locations, including blood mixed with the dirt floors of the houses. Like recent missions, there were no bodies left behind."

"Then tell me why the excitement in the camp is so high, and why the guardsmen were privy to information that hasn't yet reached my ears."

"Because we found this..." Magnus produced a small patch of fabric. On the fabric was the familiar symbol of King Darik. It was embroidered onto fabric bearing the familial colors of House Regallo. "It was hanging from the corner of a broken window. It must have gotten torn as the attacker entered the house."

"...and what does it mean? What are we to learn from a piece of fabric bearing the colors and crest of the two most powerful figures in

Malethya?" Villifor looked to Magnus for a suggestion, but Magnus hid his ignorance with silence. Villifor studied the fabric for a second before understanding reached his eyes. He handed the fabric to Slate. "Let's see if the cook can figure it out."

Slate studied the piece of purple fabric. It was unremarkable in every way, with the exception of a seam below the embroidered lion. Slate tried to picture the part of a shirt or uniform it would have belonged to, and he couldn't pinpoint the location. If it was on the chest or the shoulder, the seam would be above the lion. He flipped it over, and the seam was a perfect match for a shoulder. "It's not an emblem of a lion...it's an emblem of an upside-down lion."

"Correct, Slate. Just for that, I'll have someone else do the cooking today." Villifor smiled and Magnus glared discreetly at Slate. "This is a cheap way for revolutionaries to get their point across. The lion is a prevalent symbol throughout Malethya and would be readily accessible to anyone. By sewing it upside-down, it signifies overturning the reign of King Darik."

"What about the Regallo fabric?" Magnus asked, attempting to make up for his initial ignorance. "That would seem to indicate Brannon, but he would never use his own colors on uniforms during an attack that he's worked so hard to keep secret."

"You are right...and that's what makes this piece of evidence even more damning. Brannon would not have purchased uniforms, but soldiers want to display their allegiances and tell everyone who and why they are fighting. Some passionate peasant purchased a lion patch and sewed it upside-down on purple fabric as a proclamation of their intent. We will need to show this to King Darik." Villifor carefully tucked the fabric away. "Magnus, Slate, you have both done good work here today. Let's see if you can combine your talents. I want you both to lead the clean-up crew. Magnus, you will be in charge of defense and Slate will be responsible for clearing the village."

"Why do we need to clear the village?" Slate inquired.

"What was your first reaction when you heard the words 'Blood Mage'?" Villifor knew the answer without a response. "If you thought that, how do you think the general population would react? They would board up their homes and cry themselves to sleep over bogeymen, blood mages, and every other campfire story. We need to keep this quiet until we know what we are dealing with..." The distant look reappeared on Villifor's face, and Slate held any further questions. The headmaster was lost in his thoughts, probably trying to figure out how to combat an enemy he didn't know.

Magnus brushed past Slate and headed for his horse. "I'll grab my men and meet you at the village. Try not to make them wait for you." As much as he hated to take advice from Magnus, Slate wanted to impress the Bellator Guardsmen he hoped to one day lead. Slate took off running while Magnus gathered the troops. It may have been embarrassing to run, but not as embarrassing as if the guardsmen saw him trying to ride a horse again.

Slate arrived in Minot with just enough time to catch his breath before Magnus rode in with the guardsmen. Magnus ordered, "At ease soldiers. Slate, you'd better get to work."

"What do you typically use to clear the village?"

"Oh, I thought a leader would know what to bring. I would have brought men to help and pitch to pour on the houses, but I didn't want to interfere. What do you plan to do?" The guardsmen laughed with their commanding officer.

"Which guardsmen do I get to help me?"

"These men are needed for defense. I can't spare one because you failed to plan ahead. Maybe you should run back to camp and ask for help...or tell Villifor you weren't up for the task and let me handle it for you." The guardsmen laughed again.

"It doesn't appear that you need all of these men for defense..." Slate gestured toward a few men lounging on a crate.

"To the untrained eye, I can see why you would think that, but these men are perfectly ready and capable to defend themselves from the many hidden dangers this deserted village has to offer. Now, I suggest you complete the task assigned to you."

Without help from the guardsmen, Slate looked around the village and found someone's stash of alcohol. If this was anything like the alcohol in Pillar, he wouldn't have any trouble starting a fire. Slate tied some straw from the thatched roofs into a torch and soaked the end of it in alcohol. He used the flint from his traveling sack to spark and ignite the makeshift torch.

The flames caught quickly on the alcohol-soaked straw, but it burned too quickly to ignite the thick, rain-dampened thatch roofs. From somewhere in the southern woods, Slate heard the cry of a meadowlark. He walked around the edge of town, out of sight of Magnus and imitated the call of a dove. Lucus stepped out of hiding in the woods. "It looks like you could use some help..."

"Villifor ordered me to burn the village, but I can't get the fire to catch."

"Nothing burns hotter than wizard's fire..." Lucus walked over to the nearest house and held his hands beneath the thatch. A ball of fire formed in his cupped hands and instantly spread to the thatched roof. "It's just like starting a campfire. Use your torch to transfer it to the other houses."

Slate did as advised and made fairly quick work of igniting the town. He headed away from Magnus' men until he had a couple homes left nestled between the woods and the rocky bluff overlooking the town.

Slate lifted the torch when he thought he heard a noise in the woods to his right. He scanned the woods for a minute or two and wondered if the master woodsman had stumbled on a tree root. Chuckling at the thought, Slate lit the thatched roof of the last house. He turned to leave but stopped in his tracks, dropping his torch.

A little girl and her dog stood before one of the burning houses. She knelt beside her dog and cried softly into his fur. *Did this girl somehow survive the attacks? Maybe she had been away gathering berries or doing another chore. Had Slate just burned down her house?* He approached her slowly, not wanting to frighten her. If this girl had really survived the attack and seen the attackers, she could provide more information than a simple piece of fabric.

"Excuse me, little girl..." Slate gently placed his hand on her shoulder and turned her around.

She turned toward him with eyes closed, still crying and whimpering.

"It's ok, you're safe now..." Slate opened his arms to embrace the frightened girl, but the alarmed cry of a raven came from within the woods. Slate drew back at the sound of Lucus' alarm and the little girl opened her eyes. They were blood-red.

She launched herself at Slate's throat, trying to bite him. He threw her small frame away, but the dog attacked a second later. Slate used his forearm to prevent the dog's teeth from locking on his neck. The dog's powerful jaws crushed Slate's forearm, but he wrapped his free arm around the rabid dog and snapped its neck. He saw the red eyes of the dog close as he pried its locked jaws off his forearm.

The little girl jumped onto his back and bit. Slate grabbed her and heaved forward, throwing her in front of him. The force of the impact didn't slow her down. She stood up and came at him again, red eyes piercing.

Slate reached his staff and hit her with light, defensive blows, just keeping her a safe distance away. Somewhere in the woods, the cries of a Raven could be heard again. How could he stop this crazy girl? Fire would fend her off, right? Slate picked up the torch with his left hand, pain shooting through his forearm where the dog had bitten.

"Stay back! I'm warning you!" Slate stopped hitting the girl with his staff and waved the torch in front of him. She ran into him without hesitation, her hair and dress catching fire in the dry air next to the burning houses. Her little blows into his stomach didn't really hurt, but her burning hair caught his shirtsleeve on fire as he held her away. The fire seared the open wound on his forearm, riddling him in pain. Pain gave way to instinct and training. Slate punched the little girl…with his right hand. He felt her bones crush beneath his stonehand and she fell to the ground in a flaming pile.

Slate snuffed out his burning forearm and bent down to check on the demon child. He had just killed a little girl. *Should he feel bad about it? What was that red-eyed witch?* Slate felt fatigued from the fight and wanted to contemplate the morality of his actions, but more raven cries warned of impending danger.

Dozens of people and animals emerged from the woods. Most were adults and some carried rudimentary weapons, predominantly axes and kitchen knives. Their red eyes trained on him and they attacked.

Slate had time to yell, "Magnus!" Then they were upon him, kicking, punching, cutting, and swinging axes. Slate kept them away with his staff but was forced to give ground because of their numbers. The mob backed him into a corner between a rock wall and a burning house. Slate switched tactics and started thinning the herd.

Slate transferred his staff to his injured left hand, sacrificing defense in favor of his stonehand. Slate gave an uppercut to an untrained farmer swinging an axe, dropping him to the ground. He gave more ground and punched a red-eyed woman in the chest. Her heart stopped and so did her attack. Slate backed up again and felt his heel hit solid wall. He had run out of room.

Slate swung one last time, connecting his fist to a dog in mid-air. It fell to the ground in a thump, but the attackers overwhelmed him. An unarmed villager broke his guard and clung to his arms, further lowering his defenses. Slate was about to lose out completely when some of the attackers turned the other way at the sight of incoming guardsmen.

Magnus took a giant swing with his battle axe and decapitated three villagers at once. Then the guardsmen lunged beneath his swing to stab other villagers through the chest in precise blows. Slate took a superficial knife wound to the shoulder. The villagers dropped quickly now, but Slate wasn't sure the guardsmen could keep up with the ferocious attack. Another dog bit into his leg, tearing flesh as its teeth sunk deeper and deeper. In front of him, someone with a knife swung at his head.

Slate reached up with his right hand and caught the blade before it reached his face. He didn't feel any pain and silently thanked Lucus for his glove. The spike of Magnus' battle axe flashed inches from his face and the head of the red-eyed attacker accosting him rolled to the ground. Seconds later, guardsmen dealt fatal blows to the villagers closest to him. Slate leaned back against the rock wall behind him, resting while the carnage was pulled away. He closed his eyes and reopened them to find Magnus had pinned his neck to the wall between the spike and blade of his battle axe.

"If I picked up one of those kitchen knives and killed you, no one would know differently. I would say we got here too late and the best we could do to honor your memory was to avenge your death. These are MY men and they follow me anywhere." A crooked, crazy smile was etched on Magnus' lips. It contradicted starkly with the mixture of remorse and relief Slate felt after battle. Magnus scared him. "You can live because battle action always puts me in a good mood. The next time you cause me trouble, I wouldn't expect the same fortune. In fact, I still owe you from our previous encounter." Magnus pressed his chest against the rock wall, keeping him pinned while removing his battle axe. He casually flipped the axe downwards and drove the spike into his foot, sending shots of pain radiating up his leg. "I doubt I'll ever have the chance to repay the Sicarius headmaster for that stunt in Pillar, so send along my regards." Magnus pulled the spike from his foot and laughed. "It looks like a battle axe works just as good as my old broadsword."

Slate knelt to inspect the damage. A slow trickle of blood oozed from his foot, as it did from his arm and leg where the dogs had bitten him, but it was far from life-threatening. He stood up and kept his weight on his good foot.

Magnus had one last laugh in store for Slate. "Let's go, men. We'll tell the story of our heroic defense of the village when we get back. Slate is thankful for our rescue, but his wounded pride won't let him accept any first aid from us. And his fear of horses won't let him accept a ride back to camp with one of us either. Our only option is to succumb to his stubborn wish of walking back to camp on his own. Isn't that right, Slate?"

Slate mouth dropped open. They were going to leave him here by himself? What if more red-eyes showed up? He'd be nearly defenseless.

"The fun of this infested town is over and I'm ready for some lunch. Let's ride." Magnus skirted the edge of the burning village and disappeared down the trail back to camp.

As Magnus and the men disappeared out of sight, Lucus and Sana emerged from the woods. Sana cradled a broken arm and blood flowed from several fresh wounds. Slate would have run to help her, but running was out of the question and Lucus was already healing her wounds. "What happened to you?"

"A group of villagers came from the north," Sana said slowly. "When I noticed the torn clothes and red eyes, I raised the raven's cry, but my attention was diverted from the group."

"Is that how you got injured?" Slate asked. Lucus offered healing to Slate, but the guardsmen were expecting him to return injured. Instead, he allowed Lucus to support him as they began the walk back to camp.

"An even larger group approached from near the bluffs," Sana continued. "I barred their way by stringing grapevines across the rocky, narrow path. Unfortunately, the strategy left me within arm's reach while the coiled grapevines unraveled from my arm. I'm sorry for letting the first wave into the village…"

"You saved my life. I couldn't have defended against any more of them. What were they?"

Whatever the answer was, Sana was uncomfortable with it. She diverted her eyes at the question and Lucus answered for her. "Blood Mages preferred magic that affected the body's function, since small changes in a person's body can produce profound effects. The brain, in particular, was a favorite target of Blood Mages and mental subjugation was commonplace. A skilled Blood Mage could push an idea or a desire onto a person without any visible signs. Less skilled Blood Mages lacked the tact to hide the implanted ideas, so they simply overran the desires of the subjugated mind, leaving them with a single purpose to fulfill. The subjugate's mind would fight back when this happened, but they would inevitably lose out. During the process, the blood pressure to the head would increase and rupture small blood vessels, including the capillaries in their eyes, giving them the defining red-eyed look you observed in the villagers."

"So these possessed villagers were under the control of the Blood Mage. I think we knew that, but how does that change anything?"

Slate's skills of deduction didn't impress Sana. "Try to think two steps ahead for once. Though we've heard rumors, this is the first direct evidence of Blood Magic and it indicates a level of proficiency high enough to burn out some villagers' brains and turn them into mindless soldiers. That brings up a very dangerous possibility—the Blood Mage may be capable of more advanced forms of subjugation and anyone could be affected."

They approached camp and Slate promised to meet them at Ibson's in the morning to continue the conversation. Slate contemplated the ramifications of Sana's concern as a way of distracting from the crippling pain in his foot. *Could Villifor be subjugated? Could he have sent Slate into Minot knowing the red-eyed attackers would be coming?* Even Magnus and his troops might not have been enough to withstand the larger attack of red-eyes, which Sana had prevented.

A patrolling guardsman found him and propped him up next to a tree in camp. "Villifor will want a report. In the meantime, I'll sew you up. The Ispirtu healers stopped accompanying us on our missions, so you'll have to tough it out the old-fashioned way." The guardsman held up a bottle of unknown content, but it didn't take a genius to understand the offer. That stuff was probably just as potent as the alcohol he had used to soak his torch in the village. Slate shook his head, declining the offer. "Suit yourself." The guardsman started on his arm. "I can't do much for the burns. This will probably hurt worse than

202 J. Lloren Quill

the others because of them." She held down Slate's arm and poured the contents of the jug into the dog bite. Slate didn't have to worry about screaming in pain...his jaw clenched instantly and he was thankful to have missed his tongue. The guardsman then pulled out needle and thread that she soaked in the contents of the jar and started closing up his arm. It was painful and ugly, but it was nice to see the wound closed, even if it had released only a trickle of blood. The guardsman repeated the procedure for the wound in his leg, and then Villifor arrived.

"Magnus gave his report but I don't believe it. Tell me what happened." Villifor knelt beside him and carefully removed his boot. Slate attempted to tell the story while the guardsman starting stitching the puncture wound in his foot, having to sew several layers of the underlying tissue to properly close the wound.

"I was clearing the village when a little girl and her dog came out of the woods. I thought she had survived the attacks and when I got closer, they attacked me. By the time I had finished with them, over a dozen more had come from the woods. I found myself trapped and Magnus and his team saved me."

"It couldn't have taken too long to dispose of a little girl and a dog. How did a dozen people corner you?"

Slate thought about his early conversation with Villifor. Someone had to fight these things...they might as well know what they were. "The little girl wasn't just a little girl. She kept her back to me until I got close, and when she turned to look at me, it was with blood red eyes. Then she attacked. Since she was unarmed, I was able to keep her away from me. The dog attacked me too, and I snapped its neck after getting one of these bites. The most worrying thing to me though, was that this girl kept attacking at all costs. Hits that should have wounded her didn't even faze her. She ran straight through fire and didn't stop her attack to put out the flames consuming her. It took a lethal blow to her head to stop her." Slate grimaced as the needle went into his foot.

Villifor grimaced too, although Slate couldn't tell if it was from watching his surgery or the news he had just delivered. "Magnus says these attackers are simple peasants. His men went through them without injury."

"They were peasants. They fought without skill or armor and only rudimentary weapons. Magnus couldn't see what I saw because they arrived late and only dealt lethal blows."

"Magnus had another suggestion. He thought the peasants you described were survivors of the attack. Maybe they saw your...complexion...and it reminded them of the real attackers. He thought they attacked you because you looked like...I don't know what. Why do you look the way you do? I've heard rumors, but I want the truth."

The guardsman tied off the last stitch and Slate sighed. "That was a mishap in Ispirtu. Master Primean was conducting a pain tolerance experiment with me as the test subject. The experiment reduced blood loss to superficial wounds so that I could experience higher levels of pain without passing out due to blood loss. His experiment worked and he became overeager, pouring himself into the experiment and eventually dying from using too much spark. I survived, but it left me looking very pale. Fortunately, the blood staunching abilities have remained with me."

"I did notice there was very little blood in your boot for that type of wound. I don't necessarily understand what happened to you...but I do believe you."

"I don't understand it either."

Villifor looked to the guardsman who had sewn up Slate. "Please leave us." After a minute, Villifor continued. "It seems you have more tricks up your sleeve than I've given you credit for, Slate. Let me ask you this. Do these red-eyed attackers scare you?"

"Yes. Now that I know what they are capable of, I won't be holding back the next time I encounter one."

"I'm inclined to believe you," Villifor said, "because the hole in your foot looks remarkably like the spike of a battle axe, and your story reminds me of a campfire story handed down in my family since the days of the Blood Mages." Villifor moved over to prop himself against the tree beside Slate and began his tale. "A farmer and his wife lived a quiet life. They minded their own business, subsisting on what they grew or raised. Then one day, their crops began to wilt and no amount of sun or rain brought them back to health. Autumn came and the farmer hadn't harvested enough crops to survive the winter. He went to the nearest village, several hours away, and asked if anyone had a bumper crop they could share or barter, but the entire region suffered the same fate. He found out a Blood Mage had created a blight in the region, causing the crops not to grow properly. The farmer was desperate and entered the local tavern to drown his fears when someone joined him at the table. After hearing his story, the stranger said he could help. 'How?' asked the farmer. 'Blood Mages aren't the only wizards left in the land.' The wizard then pulled a seed from his jacket pocket, dropped it into a crack in the wooden tavern table and the farmer watched as the seed grew into a little flower right before his eyes. The wizard winked at him and said, 'Let's go to your farm.' Along the way they chatted amicably and the farmer asked why the wizard was helping him. 'Well, to be honest, I'm hoping you will help me in return.' The farmer asked how he could possibly help a wizard. 'Everyone needs help once in a while. Let's fix your field and then decide on the payment.' They traveled the rest of the way to the farm and the farmer's wife met them in relief. The wizard spread his arms outwards and walked the rows of the field. Everywhere he went, the crops grew instantly, leaving the farmer and his wife stunned at the sight of the miracle. By the time the wizard returned, the farmer would have agreed to anything, but the wizard's price wasn't that extravagant. The wizard asked the farmer to keep his eyes open for other signs of the Blood Mage and to report back to him every week at the tavern where they met. The farmer gratefully made the weekly trip to the village and it was the farmer's wife who first noticed disturbing behaviors. First, rabid animals started showing up around the farm. Then, neighbors started reporting that something had broken into barns and killed all the livestock. Soon, the entire area was overflowing with tales of brutal attacks that had spread from the barn to the neighbors. Even more disturbing to the wife was that her husband began leaving in the middle of the night and showing up with small scratches on his arms in the morning, except he didn't have any memories of leaving his bed or recollection of where the marks came from. Finally, she stayed awake one night and heard her husband get out of bed. She called out to him and he didn't answer, but continued to walk out of the house, so she ran out to confront him. He was sleep-walking and she couldn't get him to stop, so she slapped him in the face. He opened his eyes and returned a blood-red stare. He pushed past her and returned in the morning with blood on his arms. Word spread from their neighbors of a brutal murder in the middle of the night. The farmer's wife didn't know what had happened, but she knew her husband was to blame. The next night she cut his throat and then kissed his forehead."

"So she never learned what happened to her husband?"

"No, but we know who was responsible. The wizard in the story was the Blood Mage. He did a good deed to earn the farmer's trust and then used him for some fractal-forsaken purpose, turning him into the red-eyed monster in the story. That, Slate, is why I believe your story. It's also why I don't trust wizards." Slate knew a wizard who could probably help plants grow, but he refused to believe that Lucus, the pacifist, was capable of creating the destruction in Pillar and Minot. "So what do we do about the red-eyes?"

"We? I think we're starting to turn you into a Bellator man."

"I just want to stop the red-eyes and anything else the Blood Mage sends after us." More importantly, he had to pay back the bastard who had killed his parents. Now that he saw what his father was up against, a sense of pride swelled up in him. A pile of bodies lay at the feet of his father's corpse. Given the tenacity of the attackers, his father had fought well.

"Me too. That's why I'm reporting immediately to King Darik. We'll force this Blood Mage from hiding." Villifor patted his pocket where the scrap of fabric was held. "I'll have someone drive the lunch cart and you can ride along."

After the Bellator camp had packed up and returned to Ravinai, Slate was happily surprised to see Sana awaiting him. "The wounded warrior returns home..." Sana opened with a smile.

"I guess the trick to having you around is to keep getting injured." Slate limped over and gave her a hug.

"Guys always want what they can't have...if I was hanging around all the time, you'd be bored within a week."

"Modesty doesn't suit you, Sana."

"You're right. It doesn't. You should be damn thankful to see me. If that ever changes, you'll regret it."

"That's my girl. Now help me home."

"I thought tonight we could try something different. Let's get out of the city, if you can make it that far." The last part was spoken as a challenge, just to make sure Slate obliged.

"I know just the spot. The Sicarius headmaster dropped me off on a hill overlooking the city. I imagine it'd be a pretty nice place to visit if you're not shaking off the effects of a shock stick."

"Toughen up. The next thing you know you'll be asking me to heal you too." Sana gestured toward his burned and bitten arm.

"Well, they were pretty crude with the stitches. I wouldn't want an unsightly scar." Slate referenced his recent scar invoking lacerations.

"Scars I can deal with…but I'll heal you later. I don't want you to be too fatigued…during the walk, I mean." Her smile hinted that she was looking forward to wearing him out in ways other than healing. Slate leaned in for a kiss but was dismissed. "Don't get warmed up too quickly. I won't be able to make it to the infirmary tomorrow and wanted to discuss something with you."

"Why won't you make it to the meeting at Ibson's?" Slate and Sana reached the hill overlooking the city.

"King Darik has been increasingly paranoid lately and I want to be in the King's court when Villifor reports on Minot. I haven't been able to figure out his plans, but I think he's tired of waiting. Darik has always been a man of action and my source thinks he's looking for an excuse to force his opponent out of hiding.

"Your source?"

"I've been hanging around one of the members of the court." Slate let his feelings on the subject unintentionally show up on his face. "Relax, he has a hooked nose, terrible breath, and the sense of humor of someone sentenced to the gallows. What happened when you got back to camp?"

"I got sewn up by someone who won't be opening a tailor's shop anytime soon and spoke with Villifor."

"Let's get the healing over with…anything to stop your self-pitying. I mean, it's just a spike through the foot." Sana teased him, but there was concern in her eyes and she was very cautious in removing his boots. Slate thought it might be worth waiting a little longer, but the walk to the hill had done him in. Slate was relieved when Sana began probing his foot. "You're right. These stitches are atrocious. Wasn't there an Ispirtu Guardsmen there to fix you up?" Slate relaxed at the comforting probing of Sana. He just wouldn't tell her that.

"Brannon ordered his wizards to stay in Ispirtu because he doesn't see the value in chasing after inconsequential battles. He's conserving his forces for when the Blood Mage surfaces…or he's combining his forces for when he surfaces." Sana frowned a bit at that last comment, but she continued her healing probe, moving from his foot to his leg and now toward his burned and bitten arm. She finished up, leaving Slate without pain but extremely tired.

"What did Villifor say to you?"

"Well...I know what he'll be reporting tomorrow to Darik, so you can probably sleep in a little in the morning."

Sana sat up from the hill to face him. "...and you didn't tell me until now?"

Slate enjoyed having a leg up on Sana for once, so he strung it out a bit. "It makes me more mysterious...I wouldn't want to get boring." Slate sat up for a kiss and was promptly pushed backward.

"I'm less interested in any of your mysteries and more interested in information. Tell me."

"Magnus discovered a piece of purple fabric bearing an upside-down lion. Villifor took it as a symbol that Regallo supporters were trying to overturn King Darik's rule."

"Darik has been looking for an excuse to act and Villifor could have given Magnus the piece of fabric to 'discover.' I will need to be at court tomorrow to judge Darik's reaction. Is there anything else you've forgotten to tell me?"

Properly admonished, Slate continued his report. "Actually yes, Villifor knows about the red-eyes and is intent on forcing the hand of the Blood Mage."

"That fool. What if this is part of some larger plan? The Blood Mage subjugated some simple villagers in Minot. What would happen if one of the headmasters was the Blood Mage? Can you imagine red-eyed wizards, Bellator fighters, or Sicarius shadows that are driven beyond the point of sanity?" Sana hung her head. "There is more to the story than Lucus told. He accurately described what happened to the villagers, but he described it in terms of magic. That doesn't properly convey the atrocities that red-eyes committed. When I was searching libraries for information on your Perceptor abilities, I came across a commoner's chronicle of his days during the reign of the Blood Mages. Friends and neighbors were subjugated and forced to serve in the Blood Mage armies. Red-eyes were the foot soldiers in the battles fought between Blood Mages. Their effectiveness and brutality in battle gave them their own name. What you fought today was known as a Fury. Fractal's fortune we can stop this mess before we see guardsmen turned into them."

CHAPTER SIXTEEN

A NECESSARY CHOICE

A brisk wind slapped Slate in the face and reminded him of the approaching winter, but the sun peaked over the horizon and fought to stave off the inevitable freeze. Its rays gave a colorful show to anyone ambitious enough to wake up and watch. Slate enjoyed the few moments of peace and wondered at the world around him before it awoke for the day and all its activities.

Slate walked from the hilltop overlooking the city toward the infirmary, amazed at the changes from yesterday. The body remembers pain long after it is gone, and each step on his newly healed foot was precluded by an internal cringe and followed with a sigh of blissful relief. Sana had done a wonderful job of healing him. Her studies with Lucus must be paying off.

The sprawling infirmary was complicated enough that he didn't try to find Ibson's room on his own. He inquired with one of the white-robed wizards and was graciously led to his room. Lucus and Rainier were already seated at the table. Sana was absent as expected, but Lattimer's absence concerned him. Had Rainier failed to make amends?

> Another arrives,
> Who could it be?
> I hope it's my lady,
> Come to see me.

"I'm sorry, Ibson, but the lady present at our last conversation won't be available today. We did bring Rainier though…" Slate's joke produced a scowl from Rainier, a grin from Lucus, and caused Ibson to pout rather dramatically. The door opened behind him and Lattimer entered, alleviating Slate's concerns.

Slate walked to meet him. "I failed to trust you the other night. You saved my life and deserve better. I won't make the same mistake twice." Slate extended his hand.

After a moment, Lattimer shook it. "Malethya is dangerous in the best of times. It has become so volatile lately that allegiances can change quickly. My father thrives in that environment. I yearn for more…stability. Don't mistrust me because of the deeds of my father." Slate took the rebuke and gestured toward a chair.

"Do you know everyone here?"

"By reputation only…"

Lucus, ever the gentleman, introduced the group and brought everyone back to the topic at hand. "Our search for a Blood Mage in Malethya gained credence yesterday when Slate was attacked in the village of Minot. By visiting my contacts on the Wizard Council, I have concluded that the recently excommunicated wizards in Malethya do not possess the ability or the ambition to be the person we are after. Either the Blood Mage has been in hiding for a long period of time and escaped my search or the Blood Mage hasn't been excommunicated from the Wizard Council or Ispirtu."

> He looks and looks,
> But cannot find,
> What is in front,
> Or just behind.

Slate ignored Ibson's babble. "Rainier, do you have any news for the group?"

"I tracked Villifor this morning until he entered the palace to meet King Darik. Sana is inside and may find out more information. Other than that, I think most of the news involving Villifor comes from your adventure yesterday."

"I suppose I might as well start from the beginning and my failed attempt to break into the Regallo estate. Lattimer had given me information regarding manuscripts in Brannon's personal library. I wanted to see them for myself, so I broke into the estate, didn't find the manuscripts and got caught. My actions drew the ire of the Sicarius headmaster, got me expelled from Ispirtu, and nearly killed by an enraged Brannon. I failed on all fronts. Now Lattimer is our only eyes in Ispirtu. Would you be willing to tell us any significant events there before I continue with my Bellator mission?"

Lattimer responded, "Yes, actually, something strange did happen yesterday. Two students from Ispirtu went missing. No one has seen them since yesterday morning. I checked with your friend Tommy at the gate and he looked back at the security orb footage. They were seen arriving at Ispirtu the night before, but they never left. I don't know any more than that."

Slate recalled the story of Villifor. The farmer began disappearing in the middle of the night and not remembering what he had done. Then an even more disturbing thought came to him. The Blood Mage in the story had been a wizard very in tune with nature, both causing a blight and fixing it. Lucus was present in Minot when the Furies attacked and his return to Ravinai coincided with the disappearance of wizards in Ispirtu.

"Lucus, I was thinking about Brannon's scepter. You said it was enchanted like your axe. If Brannon's scepter is a Regallo heirloom, is your axe also an heirloom?"

> Things pass down,
> Their meanings lost,
> Use them only,
> At great cost.

"Yes, it is." Lucus lifted his axe from his belt and looked at it with the affection of something more than a prized possession. "I wish I knew the history of it, but my family is not storied as are the Regallos." He nodded in acknowledgment to Lattimer. "The spark—and solitude—runs in my family. My relatives have an affinity for nature that leads to reclusivity and large holes in the family history. An ancient wizard sought me out to hand down this axe to his closest kin with the spark. He claimed to be my uncle, but I had never met him and I never saw him again."

Lucus looked intently at his wood axe and Slate was sure he didn't see the look of concern temporarily cross Slate's face. The Blood Mage in Villifor's story could have been a relative of Lucus' and reclusivity provided a convenient excuse for scheming outside the public eye. Despite these concerns, Slate had made the mistake of not trusting Lattimer and he wouldn't repeat that mistake with Lucus, who had done more than enough to deserve Slate's trust. He would need the help of his friends to confront the Blood Mage. They needed to fight together like a Bellator squadron and have complete trust in each other. Trying to push doubt from his mind, Slate continued his report.

"I hope I never see a villager from Minot again." Slate described the trip to Minot and his observation of the Bellator squadrons that searched the village. "Magnus found a piece of fabric with Regallo colors and an upside-down lion embroidered onto it, seemingly implicating Brannon in the Minot attack."

"That is a small piece of evidence that is hardly irrefutable," Rainier added in.

"Even so, Darik is a man of action and will likely view a small piece of evidence as damning when he considers his opponent's ability to hide their identity up until this point. That piece of fabric could be the spark that ignites this conflict. Wars have begun over smaller matters than this," Lucus spoke ominously.

Tensions build,
Sparks fly,
Soldiers fight,
People die.

"What happened with the villagers of Minot? If the village was empty, why did you say you never want to see them again?" Lattimer asked.

"...because they were turned into Furies by the Blood Mage." His friends grimaced at Slate's description of the red-eyed attackers' savagery. "I reported the attacks to Villifor and I think he believed me, although most of the guardsmen believed I was responsible for the attack in one way or another. I returned to Ravinai and Sana told me the red-eyes were called Furies and were the foot soldiers of Blood Mages. Their minds are wiped out and replaced with a single desire to attack and kill. I can personally attest that nothing short of a lethal blow will stop them."

"What are their weaknesses? How do we fight them?" Rainier asked.

"These villagers lacked combat training, so we have the advantage in battle unless we are outnumbered. However, if the Blood Mage turns Bellator Guardsmen into Furies, they would be formidable opponents.

With skilled Furies attacking, I couldn't stand against them, even with your help. Magnus could deal lethal blows, but I lack his strength and would need to be much quicker to keep my distance from their relentless pursuit."

Slate's admission of fear sobered his companions to their situation. Finally, Lattimer said in frustration. "I wish my experiments were going better. Then maybe you could be both…"

"What do you mean?" Slate asked.

"What experiments?" Rainier asked.

"The Sicarius headmaster visited me and Slate at Ispirtu and suggested I focus my research on ways of increasing someone's speed and strength. The headmaster must have guessed that we'd be up against Furies. I haven't succeeded in increasing someone's strength or speed, but I may be able to maximize the strength and speed that someone already has. I just haven't gotten the effects to persist."

Slate thought that if an objection arose it would come from Lucus, but instead it was Rainier. "Magic should never be used to alter the pattern of the body!" It was the most adamant and emotional statement that he had heard Rainier give.

"What do you think wizards do every time we use healing?"

"Healing returns the pattern of the body to its natural state. You're talking about disrupting the body's pattern in an unnatural way. It is only one small step below Blood Magic to a tribesman." Rainier stood and Lattimer rose to meet him. Lucus put a hand on each of their shoulders and quieted the room.

"Rainier, you know I respect the tribe's beliefs even if the rest of the Malethya doesn't take the time to understand them. Lattimer is not beholden to your beliefs and you should give him the benefit of the doubt because he shares our cause. We are facing a terrible enemy, the like of which hasn't been known for generations. The important thing is that we defeat this enemy, or arguments about our methods will be moot."

> Singular focus on,
> Things of import,
> Can make priorities,
> Get out of sort.

Slate remained seated while the others argued. He had fought the Furies and knew how dangerous it would be to face a trained Fury without some advantage. More importantly, if he had trouble with a foot soldier, he needed a few more tricks for the Blood Mage. It was time to tell Lattimer another secret.

"I know why you haven't been able to replicate Primean's experiment or sustain the effects of your own experiments. Have you heard of anyone called a Perceptor?"

"I've heard of a lot of false Perceptors. They are a bunch of lying conmen. What does it have to do with Primean's experiments?"

"I am a Perceptor, although I'm still learning what it means to be one. I can't cast spells, but I can feel them. Cantor was the last known Perceptor and he credited the abilities with some of his greatest discoveries. I think I know why. When Primean was conducting his experiment on me, I felt his spell slowing the blood flow out of my wounds. As he continued to injure me, I knew that feeling was helping keep me alive, so I...pulled...on it. My last memory before passing out was to cling to that feeling and hold it. I think that is why I've been able to retain the blood staunching capability."

"What do you mean you can feel magic? And if you can feel magic, why don't you know who cast the spell that caused your stonehand in the tournament?" Lattimer questioned.

"I didn't know I was a Perceptor during the tournament. Even though I could feel the spell that was cast on me, I wasn't really concentrating on the spell at the time. I had my hands full fighting you," Slate smiled. "Besides, if it was a Blood Mage that cast that spell, who knows how that changes things. If they can wipe somebody's mind, they can probably mask what a spell feels like too."

"I don't believe the Blood Mage would think to mask what the spell felt like. If you truly are the first Perceptor since Cantor, then why would someone expect that you would feel the spell and be able to identify them?"

"Good point, but I think Sana, Ibson, Lucus, and Brannon are the only wizards that have cast enough spells on me that I could truly identify them."

"Do you think it was Brannon?" Rainier asked.

Slate thought back to the times Brannon had cast spells on him. The spell during the tournament had felt similar, but Slate couldn't say for certain. "The spell didn't feel like Sana, Ibson, or Lucus…but that's as much as I can tell." That realization alleviated some of Slate's earlier concerns about Lucus. Slate pushed them even further from his mind.

"So you can't identify the Blood Mage, but these Perceptor abilities will somehow make my experiments work?" Lattimer refocused the conversation.

"I visited Primean many times in the Pain Tolerance Laboratory. Despite his sadistic side, he was always quite kind to me. He took his experiments seriously but healed me promptly afterward."

"That's one way of looking at someone who was trying to inflict as much pain as possible onto you…" Lucus frowned.

"I know, I know. It doesn't really make sense, but I can't imagine Primean losing control of an experiment the way he did that night. He never deviated from his protocols or got carried away." Slate finally said what he had feared ever since that night. "I think when I *pulled* during the experiment, it prevented him from stopping. I think I pulled his spark right out of him and killed him."

Silence permeated the room and the resident poet filled the void.

Pull me up
Push me down
Pull, pull, pull,
He fell down

"Slate…you don't have the spark. Why do you think you can *pull* on it? We know as little about Perceptors as we do about Blood Mages, but I do know you. You didn't kill Primean." Rainier spoke with the same quiet confidence he had seen in the nomad when he'd first entered the arena during the tournament. It gave Slate some reassurance.

"Even if I didn't kill Primean directly, I think I influenced the spell in some way. When I pulled, I retained the effects of the spell. I might be able to do it again. I just worry about whoever is casting the spell."

"That would be me," Lattimer said, "and I agree with Rainier. You couldn't have forced Primean to continue. He got overzealous in the results and lost track of how much energy he had left. If you want to try the experiment, I'm willing to try it on you." Lattimer stood up and prepared to leave. "If things are going to happen as quickly as Lucus believes, I better set up the experiment in the lab. I'll have Tommy keep an eye out for you and sneak you into Primean's old lab. If you decide to do it, just look for him."

"Thank you, Lattimer," Slate said as Lattimer departed.

"No matter what we are up against, you can't volunteer for this experiment, Teacher." Rainier pleaded his case. "My tribe values the pattern, and specifically the pattern of the body, above all things. You are not one of us, but I chose you as my teacher because of the way you fought in the tournament. Tribesmen fight within the pattern instead of relying on strict forms like King Darik's men. You hit me because you saw the natural variation within the pattern and used it to predict my movements. It is the only way you could have won."

"I won because I landed a lucky blow."

"Do not be so simple, Slate Severance. You accomplished highly improbable things since becoming my teacher. When you have faltered, you didn't rely on your instincts. This experiment Lattimer speaks of intentionally changes your own pattern. Amongst my tribe, you would be exiled for such a thing. As it stands, I will not claim you as my teacher if you participate in this experiment."

Slate was dumbfounded. Ever since he had come to Ravinai, he had been mingling with wizards and experimented on with spells. Why was this so different? "You are a true friend, Rainier, but you weren't there when the Furies attacked. I am not skilled enough to beat one if someone from Bellator is turned. That is what my instincts are telling me. I am going to Lattimer's lab."

"I do understand, but I can't approve. My studies under you have come to an end, and I will need to return to the tribe."

"You are leaving?"

"The tribal laws require my return…but they fail to specify the time span in which I rejoin." He smiled and Slate again hoped he never had to barter with a tribesman. "I will face the Blood Mage with you and rid the land of this abomination."

Lucus asked Slate, "So what now?"

"I need to go to Ispirtu. With Lattimer's help, I might be able to surprise the Blood Mage. People know about the stonehand from the tournament and the blood staunching from the Bellator mission. No one knows about the glove you made for me and no one will know about the experiment with Lattimer. Hopefully that will be enough to give us the element of surprise."

"You think Brannon is the Blood Mage, don't you?" Rainier prodded.

"Brannon was overseeing the tournament. He was present when Ibson was hurt. He is the most powerful wizard in the kingdom and he has been hiding information. Before my exile from Ispirtu, Brannon told me that magic was decreasing in Malethya. If that is true, his entire way of life is nearing an end. He may do anything to prevent that..."

Lucus added his opinion. "Brannon and I both studied under Ibson, and for a long time we were friends. Ibson taught spells that were dependent upon strong links and thorough understanding. With my small spark, I gravitated toward Ibson's teaching. Brannon, on the other hand, had less need for strong links. He left his studies for King Darik's army and Ispirtu to teach his methods to others. I have been hoping that my former friend was not behind these attacks." Sadness filtered into his last words.

Slate thought about Lucus' words and how they may affect Lattimer, but it couldn't be helped. He would do anything necessary to stop the Blood Mage, but he could at least soften the blow a bit by withholding any final judgments. "Hopefully there will still be time to gather more evidence. I don't know if Brannon is the Blood Mage, but we'll need to adapt once the Blood Mage surfaces. Until then, we must maintain contact and stay flexible. Prepare in any way you can, Lucus, and wait for my word. We are about to put an end to your investigation. Let's make sure we get the right guy."

CHAPTER SEVENTEEN

SIMPLIFYING THE EQUATION

Slate left the infirmary compound and walked through the side-streets toward Ispirtu; a figure dressed in black flipped from a rooftop and landed in front of him. Slate dropped into a defensive stance until his mind had time to process that the hard-to-see mask in front of him belonged to the Sicarius headmaster.

"Good morning, Headmaster."

"Hardly. You are needed immediately. King Darik requested an emergency meeting of Ispirtu. If we hurry, you can still gather your things from your apartment. We will be taking the rooftops and I won't slow down for you. Your training has ended. Now it's time to prove it." The headmaster jumped off the side of a building to reach an overhang and swung up to the rooftop. Slate was impressed, but quickly recovered his senses as he realized the urgency of his mission.

Slate scaled the building wall, but it took more than the single fluid motion the headmaster had just demonstrated. He reached the rooftop in time to see the Sicarius headmaster bounding onto a rooftop two buildings away. Slate sprinted ahead and watched the maneuvers of the headmaster to guide his path through the city. Even with that help, he fell further behind. Luckily, he knew the destination and jumped onto his balcony. The balcony door hung open and Slate realized that the Sicarius headmaster had easily side-stepped his rudimentary security features. Damn, the headmaster was good.

"It seems you've been spending your time on the rooftops stargazing with that liability you call a girlfriend instead of training. Get your stuff and catch your breath. You sound like a dog panting."

Biting his tongue had served him well on the Bellator mission with Villifor, but in reality he was too out-of-breath to say much of anything. Instead he went to his room and pulled out the grey outfit he had made for Rainier when they'd broken into the Regallo estate.

Finally, Slate pulled out his trunk and grabbed the Sicarius mask and the glove from Lucus. He wrapped the glove to hide it from the headmaster when he heard the headmaster behind him.

"This isn't the royal ball...let's go." The alternating voice of the headmaster still gave Slate chills. "And bring that glove you've been hiding. I don't have time to come back here later." Slate was thankful for his Sicarius mask; it prevented the headmaster from seeing his mouth open in surprise.

"How did you know about my glove?"

"Don't fool yourself, Slate. I broke into your apartment the first night you were in town. I'm glad you have a surprise or two up your sleeve. We'll need them. I just didn't want to be caught off-guard in case you decided to use them on me."

Slate couldn't argue with that. The headmaster had perfectly paranoid logic, as always. "I'm ready."

"I hope so. King Darik might mobilize Sicarius and Bellator against Ispirtu. I can't think of an enemy I'd want to face less than Brannon...if he is the Blood Mage."

"I take it you've heard about the evidence found against Brannon on the Bellator mission then? And you also aren't certain it was Brannon?"

"I promised I'd look into Villifor's past and the famous war hero has some skeletons hidden. Before the final battle of the Civil War, Villifor provided key information to Darik about the revolutionary's plan of attack. Darik and Brannon mounted the perfect defense, ending the war. Common knowledge is that Darik placed Villifor as an agent within the revolutionary troops and that Villifor acted at the command of Darik."

"But you don't believe this is true?"

"Even before Sicarius was formed, certain members of Darik's army coordinated and controlled sensitive information. These records passed into Sicarius possession upon its formation, and I never found a single communication from Villifor. Either Villifor reported only to King Darik or he truly was a revolutionary and struck a deal with Darik while betraying his friends." The disgust in the Sicarius headmaster's voice was apparent even as it rose and fell throughout the story. Villifor's advice concerning adaptability and survival suddenly took on new meaning to Slate. "So, no, I am not convinced Brannon is the person behind all of this. If Villifor betrayed his own cause in the Civil War, then I think he is entirely capable of siding with an all-powerful Blood Mage to wipe out the kingdom's most powerful wizard. Now let's go. Keep your eyes and ears open during the meeting. We need every clue we can get from here on out."

The headmaster signaled that the conversation was ending and Slate asked, "What, no shock-stick?"

"Why would I need to use it? You know I trust you." Slate heard the Sicarius headmaster laugh for the first time. He had become accustomed to the headmaster's alternating speech, but the vacillating laugh disturbed him. This was the headmaster he placed his trust in? He couldn't even place a name to the enigma.

The headmaster jumped to the rooftops and Slate gave chase at perilous speeds. They were meeting at Sicarius, but Slate didn't know where Sicarius was located. If he fell behind, he might not get the chance to find out. The two figures raced across the rooftops in broad daylight, high above the citizens of Ravinai who were going about their everyday activities, oblivious to the living shadows flying overhead.

The arena came closer into view and Slate wondered if the Sicarius headmaster would be so brazen as to locate Sicarius in such close proximity to the Bellator and Ispirtu landmark. The Sicarius headmaster jumped from a low roof onto the grassy area outside the arena that had been situated with tents for the fighters during the tournament. No structures could hide the size of room that Sicarius had met in, Slate thought, and then a realization settled in. "You meet in the arena?"

"The arena was built to hide the Sicarius Guild. King Darik conscripted an architect to build the guild, but I persuaded the architect to add a few of my own modifications. The arena sits empty when the tournament is completed, making it perfect for clandestine meetings. The best way to hide is in plain sight. If you saw people walking into an underground tunnel, you'd wonder what was in the tunnel. That's not a problem here."

"What about the meeting room? Don't people notice a large section of the arena is off limits?"

"This is Ravinai, where factions compete and secrets abound. I simply put the insignia of King Darik's lions on a locked door to discourage unintentional exploration. A few strategically placed guardsmen discourage anyone who fails to take the hint."

As with all magic tricks, the mystery and excitement vanished with the explanation, but the scheme's simplicity impressed Slate. "Are we going in?"

"Not yet..." The Sicarius headmaster gestured to three cloaked figures walking toward them. "Act as my attendant and try not to say anything foolish in front of the king." Darik was flanked by two cloaked figures, one who was enormous. The cloak couldn't hide the bulk of Magnus or the battle axe slung across his back.

The Sicarius headmaster knelt before Darik, so Slate followed suit. The headmaster spoke, "We are honored to serve you, King Darik."

"Rise, rise...I don't have time for formalities." Darik removed his hood and the two figures behind him did the same, revealing Villifor as the third companion.

"Would you enlighten me regarding the purpose of this meeting?" the Sicarius headmaster said. "And why you decided to bring our Bellator brethren to Sicarius?"

"A Bellator mission identified the source of the attacks on the northern villages. Villifor and Magnus, who discovered the evidence, will present it to *my* guardsmen." The king's intonation made it clear that the secrecy of Sicarius was bestowed at his discretion.

"Sicarius welcomes you and your invited guests, your majesty. I am excited to hear this new information and to learn how your Sicarius Guardsmen can act on your behalf." The headmaster led the group into the arena and down an unmarked staircase into the Sicarius Guild. At the bottom of the stairs was a small door with faded lions painted on it. Solid hinges, a sturdy lock, and the appearance of disuse discouraged further exploration, but the eyes and ears of the lions were more pronounced than other visages of the King's crest. The effect was minor, but to Slate, the meaning was crystal clear. Sicarius meetings began with the motto, "We are Sicarius. We are the eyes and ear of the Kingdom. We go where others fear and carry out our mission with speed, silence, and absolute finality. We do this so that the people of Malethya can carry out their lives without fear of people that plot in the night. We are Sicarius." To a trained Sicarius Guardsmen, the sign was as clear as the orbs dancing around Brannon's citadel announcing the location of Ispirtu.

The Sicarius headmaster said, "My Bellator brethren, would you please turn around? You are invited guests in Sicarius, but we want to make sure you only come to visit when you have an invitation."

Villifor answered the Sicarius headmaster, "I prefer a squadron of

Bellator Guardsmen for protection instead of relying on secrets and shadows in the recesses of the arena, but these are the methods applied by your kind." Slate didn't think it was wise to insult someone capable of sneaking up on you while you slept, but he never understood the politics of Ravinai. The games between the headmasters were still beyond him.

Villifor and Magnus turned away, and the Sicarius headmaster opened the door, but without turning the lock. A nasty surprise surely awaited anyone who attempted to enter using conventional means. Instead, the headmaster pulled upwards on the door's hinges, which activated a mechanism that slid the door into its frame. The hinges were the lock and the lock was a decoy. As the door disappeared into the frame a fake door from inside the room took its place to maintain the appearance of a conventional door. The whole ruse moved smoothly along a track in the stone floor, which was promptly covered with a rug bearing the symbol of Sicarius. The Sicarius headmaster had more tricks than Slate cared to count.

"Welcome to the shadows, Villifor." The Sicarius headmaster held the fake door for his guests. Slate followed King Darik, Villifor, and Magnus into a small anteroom adorned with beautiful tapestries and shelves filled with riches. The Sicarius headmaster closed the fake door, leaving it essentially unlocked but maintaining the secret of the entrance.

"I like your style." Villifor reached for a bejeweled shield that caught his eye. "Who did you steal this from?"

"I wouldn't touch that if I were you," the Sicarius headmaster warned soon enough for the Bellator headmaster to snap his hand back. "It wasn't stolen from anyone. We are not common burglars and thieves."

"I have lent the Sicarius Guild these items from my personal treasury. The headmaster thought it would be a good security precaution to have some high valued items in the entryway. If any of these items were removed improperly, the thief would be in for a very unpleasant surprise." King Darik's explanation of the riches reminded Slate of his first encounter with the Sicarius headmaster when he had been shockingly introduced to the value of information. This room was the physical confirmation of that ideal. King Darik had willingly parted with items from his treasury to protect the information held within

Sicarius.

"This security measure is particularly effective against thieves seeking monetary gain and others blinded with vanity." The Sicarius headmaster hinted toward Villifor's oversized public persona.

Villifor countered, "Notoriety is a form of vanity. You simply hide yours behind a mask."

King Darik ended the banter. "Headmaster, are all the members of Sicarius assembled?"

"All Sicarius Guardsmen will be present."

"Good... let's begin."

The Sicarius headmaster led the group toward the assembly of guardsmen and used the moment to instruct Slate on his duties as personal attendant. "Please hold the door for our esteemed guests and stand guard during the meeting to maintain the safety of the King."

Slate nodded in acknowledgment so that Villifor or Magnus wouldn't recognize his voice and identify him. The headmaster intended for him to stand guard, but was it for the protection of the king or the headmaster? The headmaster's plan eluded Slate.

The Sicarius headmaster stepped onto the stage, standing atop the Sicarius symbol laid into the floor. The King waited patiently against the back wall, which consisted of angled mirrors, with Villifor and Magnus positioned on either side of him. Statues of Darik's lions framed the Sicarius headmaster, gazing outwards to the far walls of the large room.

Large, multi-faceted mirrors segmented the small rooms set against the far wall at various heights and distances from the stage. The Sicarius headmaster positioned the collection of mirrors to reflect images from within each small room into every other room. The complexity of the design astounded Slate.

"We are Sicarius. We are the eyes and ear of the Kingdom. We go where others fear and carry out our mission with speed, silence, and absolute finality. We do this so that the people of Malethya can carry out their lives without fear of people that plot in the night. We are Sicarius." The orbs within the small rooms lit, revealing another Sicarius secret. No more than a dozen guardsmen made up Sicarius.

The purpose of the room became apparent. The reflected images served to protect the identities of the Sicarius Guardsmen, but it also prevented the guardsmen from knowing the size of the Sicarius Guild.

The other guilds assumed that Sicarius was of comparable size to Ispirtu and Bellator. The reflected images gave the illusions to the Sicarius Guardsmen that their number was much larger. If any information from within the guild did filter to Bellator or Ispirtu, their assumptions would be maintained, allowing the Sicarius headmaster to maintain equal footing in negotiations or arguments. By bringing Villifor here, King Darik had significantly reduced the power of the Sicarius headmaster.

"Fractal's blessing that none of our Sicarius brethren have left us since we last met." The Sicarius headmaster gave a respectful pause anyway and then continued. "This emergency meeting of Sicarius was called by King Darik, who will address you directly."

King Darik took center stage as the headmaster receded toward one of the lion statues. "The disturbances in the northern villages have been resolved by the Bellator Guild, completing your mission on your behalf. As a reward for their service, they will present the evidence in person. Villifor and Magnus, please give your report to the Sicarius Guardsmen."

Villifor and Magnus stepped forward, with Magnus reporting his findings in an overstated voice of command. "No bodies were found in the search of Minot. I did, however, notice a piece of fabric that had torn on a shard of glass in a broken windowsill. The color immediately caught my eye." Magnus produced the fabric from his pocket and held it out for all to see. "You will notice the shape of the fabric as well as the lions embroidered onto it. This obviously came from the shoulder section of a sleeve, meaning that someone had sewn the lion on upside down." What Magnus lacked in deductive reasoning he made up for with inaccurate recollection. "Since it is common for peasants to support a rebellion by displaying overturned insignias of a king, I brought this important evidence to Villifor at once."

If Villifor was perturbed by the exaggerated role Magnus painted for himself while retelling the story, he didn't acknowledge it. Instead he continued on like any good showman would do. "The purple fabric is clearly a reference to House Regallo, but I had difficulty acknowledging that one of my fellow headmasters and sworn protectors of the King could be responsible for these attacks. With such circumstantial evidence, I sent the team back to Minot to search for any other connections."

Magnus picked up where Villifor left off. It was too smooth to not be practiced. "We returned to Minot and one of our more junior members got separated from us. The attackers besieged the village, pinning the untrained soldier near the base of the rock wall. They lit fires to the village huts, separating us further, but Bellator Guardsmen protect their own. We circled around the blazing village, slicing through attackers and hoping beyond hope that we could get to the soldier in time. We made one final push and found the overmatched soldier fighting with a stick, having dropped anything resembling a real weapon. Our valiant efforts saved his life, but he was not the same. He had killed a defenseless girl, watching her burn and likely provoking the original attack. Upon questioning, he referenced unfathomable enemies despite multiple conflicting accounts of the event."

Villifor finished the rehearsed speech. "The untrained soldier's account of the attack indicated magical intervention. I presented this evidence to King Darik, who will proclaim his conclusions."

Villifor and Magnus split to either side of the stage, giving room for King Darik to announce the fate of Malethya on the basis of circumstantial evidence and a skewed report. "The citizens of Malethya are under my protection, and as such I have failed in my duties as their king. Even more troubling are the continuing but unsubstantiated rumors of forbidden magic having played a role in these attacks. I set up the guilds to ensure parity beneath my rule, but the current evidence suggests Ispirtu has disrupted that balance of power." Darik paused before continuing loudly and with the authority of a king. "If Brannon has been using or teaching Blood Magic, he must be stopped before his power grows. I will not stand by as Brannon attempts to place a raven on the lion's throne. Tonight we will take the battle to him. At dusk, we will attack Ispirtu."

The Sicarius headmaster knelt before King Darik. "Sicarius will aid you in your task. Command us."

"Your devotion will truly be tested, Sicarius." King Darik rested his hand on the Sicarius headmaster's shoulder. "During the Twice-Broken Wars, I learned the value of teamwork on the battlefield, so I established Bellator and tasked Villifor with teaching battlefield tactics. The wars also taught me the value of information, so I established Sicarius. To defeat an army of trained wizards, I need Sicarius and Bellator to work together."

The King motioned for Villifor and Magnus to join him and the Sicarius headmaster. A slight nod by the King toward Villifor and Magnus was noticed by the Sicarius headmaster, who twisted the King's arm off his shoulder. But the headmaster's move was too late to prevent Villifor and Magnus from pinning the Sicarius headmaster's arms and preventing escape.

Darik continued. "Unfortunately, I don't believe that is possible. You have been my eyes and ears in times of peace, gathering information and ending threats to Malethya on my behalf. Despite your networks and methods of extracting information, it fell to Bellator to uncover the truth. How is that possible?" Silence filled the room. "Am I expected to believe that our opponent was so cunning that he hid his plans and schemes from all of you? I am left with only one reasonable explanation. My loyal servants of Sicarius have been compromised by Brannon."

A roar of objection filled the room, muffled slightly by the glass the guardsmen spoke through. Some rose to leave but found the rooms locked. Had the King asked for locks on the doors knowing this day would come? Was this his plan all along? The King spoke over the din with an absolute authority and self-assurance born of years on the throne. "I appreciate the years of loyal service you have provided. I now ask one more thing. If you are truly loyal to me, prove it by offering the ultimate sacrifice."

Slate watched in horror as many of the guardsmen produced knives and fell upon them. "Nooooo....!" The guttural scream of the Sicarius headmaster filled the enclosed room, its pain bouncing off the mirrored walls and echoing indefinitely.

The King surveyed the rooms and addressed Villifor and Magnus. "The guardsmen that remain have proven their loyalty to Brannon through disobedience. Dispose of the remaining Sicarius Guardsmen..."

Slate had to free the headmaster. He rushed forward. Villifor and King Darik turned, but Slate flew by them before they could draw their swords. Magnus positioned the Sicarius headmaster between himself and Slate, wrapping one arm around the headmaster to maintain control of the gyrating spy. Slate threw a punch with his stonehand, and connected with Magnus' forearm, shattering the bones constraining the Sicarius headmaster.

With her arm freed, the headmaster produced a dart from one of the numerous folds and jammed it into Magnus' leg, causing him to collapse. The headmaster held the king and the Bellator headmaster at bay with the threat of throwing knives.

"You just killed people who devoted their lives to serving you." The Sicarius headmaster spat the venom-laced words to the king. Darik positioned himself between them and the only exit. Villifor circled to flank the headmaster.

"They killed themselves. No one should trust someone implicitly. I see you didn't…"

"Someone needs to atone for the terrible mistake you just made."

Bellator Guardsmen streamed into the previously secret home of Sicarius. They were trapped. "You are not in a position to threaten anyone." Darik and Villifor, now protected by a full squadron of Bellator Guardsmen, ordered the advancement of the troops.

"You're right. There are too many of you to fight." The Sicarius headmaster kicked the head of the closest lion statue, toppling it over. A noise emanated from beneath the floor and the Sicarius symbol emblazoned on the stage dropped away. The Sicarius headmaster grabbed Slate and jumped into the darkness below before the Bellator Guardsmen could react. A second noise sounded as the moving plate covered their escape route, blocking pursuit from above.

Frantic shouts of the Bellator Guardsmen trying to find an entrance to the subfloor filtered through the floor and into the darkness surrounding Slate. As they tried various doors and switches, their shouts turned to screams of unbridled pain. The Sicarius headmaster had left plenty of surprises for unwanted guests. "I had the builder install the trapdoor, but I never thought I'd have to use it." Remorse carried along the alternating tones of the headmaster's speech. Slate reeled from the events above and didn't speak.

Slate made a split-second decision to free the Sicarius headmaster, using his stonehand in the process which revealed his identity. He acted in direct opposition to the King. Slate was an enemy of the crown.

"I left a lantern down here. This should help." A soft light reached into the darkness of the room, spreading upward to reveal the method of their escape. The Sicarius symbol and a wooden support beam lay beneath them and a second section of flooring covered their escape route, supported by a series of steel tracks. The Sicarius headmaster saw him examining it. "I hid a lever arm inside the statue of Darik's lion. When I kicked it, it released the support beam, opening the trapdoor. When the support beam fell, it triggered a second mechanism that lowered rails beneath the opening. The second set of flooring slid down the rails and covered our escape."

The slight decline of the rail system created a small gap between the stage and the second section of flooring. Darik could be heard above. "You, guardsman with the battle axe, get over here. Turn this floor into kindling and be quick about it."

The Sicarius headmaster chuckled joylessly, "I had the wood floor laid on top of a metal frame. They won't be getting in here anytime soon. Regardless, we should be on our way. Follow me."

They traveled a short distance to a ladder and climbed into a long, narrow room that made Slate's jaw drop. He was inside the mirrored wall overlooking the Bellator Guardsmen, hidden from his pursuers. Darik silently asked Villifor very pointed questions, undoubtedly involving their escape. Villifor in turn barked orders at any guardsmen who appeared to be milling around without a purpose. Magnus reawakened and held his arm while trying to control his rage.

Above the Bellator chaos raged a different battle. Three Sicarius Guardsmen frantically attempted to escape their locked cells. One kicked at the glass without success. Another worked on the hinges of the door, and the last guardsman tried to break into the ceiling. "Can we save them?" Slate asked without hope.

"The trapdoor was an exit." The Sicarius headmaster stepped up to the window. "I cannot save them. I have failed the Sicarius Guardsmen. I have failed the Sicarius Guild. I have failed Malethya."

Slate did something he never thought he would do. He put an arm around the shoulders of the Sicarius headmaster and didn't find a shock stick in his neck or a dart in his leg for the trouble. He said, "The King made a mistake. Let's make sure he doesn't continue the pattern."

"What do you suggest?"

"They are marching on Ispirtu. We need to uncover the truth before they do."

The headmaster removed his arm. "A shadow is used to plotting and avoiding traps. It isn't often that someone comes to our aid, even amongst other members of Sicarius." Bellator Guardsmen broke down the door of a Sicarius cell. The Sicarius Guardsmen threw a flurry of kunai and incapacitated several Bellator Guardsmen before becoming overwhelmed. Similar fates awaited the remaining members of Sicarius. Finally, the headmaster spoke. "They fought bravely and served Sicarius honorably. I owe it to them to uncover the cause of tonight's tragedy. Let's get to work, Slate."

"Lead the way…" From within the mirrored walls, the headmaster traversed a series of ladders, crawl spaces, and tunnels. After what seemed like an eternity, the lantern's light shined on a tiny room filled with nondescript trunks.

"It dawned on me that if I ever needed the trapdoor, I would probably need supplies as well. Provided that no one has found this room, there are some items that may help us." Slate didn't know how anyone could ever find this room. The Sicarius headmaster opened the first trunk to reveal a collection of exploding orbs. "In the early days of Sicarius, King Darik sent me on missions to track down and terminate rogue wizards. The mission never specified what to do with any artifacts or items in the wizards' possession, so I collected them for my personal use."

"There are enough exploding orbs here to outfit an entire army."

"Yes, but they aren't the only things I collected." The next trunk was opened, displaying a wide variety of weaponry. Another contained robes bearing the crests of every noble family in Malethya. Trunk after trunk contained countless items of importance to a member of Sicarius. It couldn't be called an armory because that wouldn't have done it justice. With the items in this room, the Sicarius headmaster could become anyone and go anywhere. The headmaster was truly a master of the environment and Slate was glad to be on the same side.

"Will it be safe to leave the items here?" Slate asked the headmaster while picking out a few darts and kunai and fitting them into the folds of his robes. Slate reluctantly donned an Ispirtu robe, rationalizing he would need one to visit Lattimer.

"Eventually those Bellator Guardsmen will break through the floor and Darik will send men through every tunnel in the arena. We can't assume they won't find my storeroom."

"Depending upon how things go this evening, we may need to disappear for a while. If I'm not mistaken, we are both fugitives now. Can you think of somewhere that would be safe to temporarily store all of this?"

"Somewhere outside of Ravinai would be smart," the headmaster said. "If things go badly, it will be easier to retrieve later. We should also choose somewhere familiar to your friends. Lucus favors a catalpa grove outside the city, correct?"

"That would be a good spot, but it's just a grove of trees. There is nowhere to hide your supplies."

"There is always a hiding place if you know where to look." Slate thought there was a smile behind the Sicarius mask. The Sicarius headmaster hid various weapons and orbs while talking to Slate. "...and what were the plans for the rest of your group? I'm assuming that you met this morning in anticipation of larger upcoming events and formulated some plans."

"I summarized the Bellator mission, which sounded quite different from the version Villifor and Magnus told Darik. The Furies are formidable opponents. Lattimer has been researching in the areas you suggested with some initial progress. I plan to go to Primean's lab and see if my Perceptor abilities make any difference. Rainier reacted strongly to that decision and denounced me as his teacher. Lucus will meet up with us when we send word to him, Sana was at the palace, and Ibson's state hasn't changed."

"You were expelled from Ispirtu and people aren't known for breaking into the guild. I hope you formulated plans with more care than you did at the Regallo estate..." Slate offered only silence because he shared the headmaster's concerns. The headmaster finished rearming. "I will show you out and then relocate my supplies to the catalpa grove. When I am finished, I will wait for you to leave the Ispirtu grounds."

Slate knew what the next part of the plan would be. "Then we'll get the answers we are seeking. We'll sneak into the Regallo estate one last time to find out if it's Brannon we should be fighting."

"Exactly. Although, I think I've been in the shadows too long. I no longer have a guild to protect and owe allegiance only to myself. I won't be sneaking anywhere. I plan to walk in the front door and get the information I need...one way or another." The headmaster left the storeroom without waiting for a response, guiding Slate down another small tunnel and giving Slate time to contemplate the full meaning of the headmaster's words.

On the one hand, Slate was relieved to hear the command and confidence return to the Sicarius headmaster's voice. The moment of vulnerability he witnessed after the death of the guardsmen seemed to disappear with the formulation of a plan. On the other hand, the loss of Sicarius seemed to release a reckless side of the headmaster that Slate hadn't previously seen. He didn't care to predict the carnage a reckless Sicarius headmaster could create.

Slate's thoughts were broken by light that filtered in around the edges of the tunnel, forming a halo around some indiscriminate shape. That must be the exit. As they approached, the lantern's light reached the silhouette, giving shape to a large rock blocking the entrance. Slate noticed another track mechanism on the floor of similar construction to the trapdoor in Sicarius.

The headmaster stopped short of the rock and pointed upwards. Slate looked up and saw two handholds recessed in the ceiling. The headmaster reached up, grabbed hold, and gave a quarter turn. The handholds, now released, dropped down to eye level in the tunnel via a telescoping tube. "Take a look." Slate peered into a clear viewport on the side of the mechanism, revealing a grassy knoll a few hundred feet from the arena. It might even be the same grassy area where his tent had stood during the tournament; the memory of that day seemed to be from a distant age.

Slate pulled away, questioningly, so the headmaster explained. "There are two mirrors inside the view piece. One is near the viewer and the other is atop this hill. The light from the grassy knoll bounces off the two mirrors and into the viewport, which lets me check for any citizens who might be strolling into this area at the precise moment I want to exit. I have found this configuration of mirrors to be very useful, both for avoiding chance encounters and for observing people without attracting notice." The headmaster returned the mechanism to its original configuration.

Slate thought this was every bit as impressive as any magic he had seen Brannon summon. "It's brilliant. Did you come up with all of this on your own?"

"The previous headmasters wrote down their thoughts for various mechanisms that might be of use to future Sicarius members. I was the first to put it to practice."

"You aren't the original Sicarius headmaster?"

"Our line of work has a high mortality rate. It's one of the reasons we stop using our names when we take the position. I may die, but the Sicarius headmaster will live on. I tell you this now because we are the final two members of Sicarius. If I die and you do not, it will be your responsibility to take my place." The finality of the statement was not spoken as a question. Before Slate could argue, the headmaster changed the subject. "Now let's get out of here."

The headmaster walked up to the boulder and Slate noticed two more handholds carved into the rock. A locking mechanism was released on the track and the headmaster pulled the handholds, sliding the stone quietly along the track into the larger tunnel. There was just enough room for Slate to slide by the side of the stone to exit the tunnel. "I will need you to hold the rock in this position. There is a slight downhill slope which will slide the rock back into the locked position. If you allow it to lock, I won't be able to access my storeroom."

"You didn't plan a way for you to get back in?" With the complexity of the plans put together up until this point by the headmaster, it seemed like a major oversight to not have a method of entry.

"This was designed as an exit, not an entrance. If there was a way to enter, then I would need to worry about someone discovering it and finding their way into Sicarius." The logic made sense but sounded slightly defensive. "Just hold the rock."

Slate did and was relieved that the decline wasn't too great. The headmaster found a collection of small stones and sprinkled them into the rail until they went past the locking mechanism. "Ok, release it." The rock slid down the track but stopped when it butted up against the rocks in the rail mechanism. It left a small gap around the edge of the stone, but it wasn't noticeable unless someone was looking for it.

"Now we part ways. I will see you at Ispirtu. Fractal's fortune, Slate." The headmaster shook hands with Slate as friends, fugitives, and the last remaining members of Sicarius.

Slate navigated the streets of Ravinai in his Ispirtu robes and Sicarius mask. People didn't want to be involved with Ispirtu business to begin with and the effects of the Sicarius mask compounded the effect. People parted for him to pass on the busy city streets and closed in around him. Bellator Guardsmen stopped citizens and searched houses looking for the escaped Sicarius fugitives. He walked right past them and they averted their eyes at his approach. He felt like a ghost, no more interesting than the city walls around him. He was a master of his environment. He was a Sicarius Guardsmen.

SLIDING FILAMENTS ALIGN

The Ispirtu walls rose above Slate in magnificently shifting splendor. Rather than soak in their beauty, Slate soaked in sweat. Not long ago, he had been chased out of the Regallo estate by a security orb, expelled, and nearly killed. Brannon told him in no uncertain terms that if he saw him again, he would consider him an enemy. Now he stood at the front gate of Ispirtu, relying upon friends to sneak him in and get him out without alerting the wizard.

Relief overran trepidation when Tommy and Annarelle stepped out of the guardhouse. "Slate, it's great to see you!" Annarelle and Tommy greeted him in excited whispers.

"I wish it were under different circumstances."

Tommy filled him in on the plan. "We'll get you into the basement storeroom that Lattimer described as your preferred point of entry. Forgive me if I was skeptical of Lattimer when he approached me to help you. You hide your allegiances well."

"He saved my life. What do I need to do?"

"I'll accidently open the security gate from the guardhouse. It happens from time to time when someone isn't attentive at their job. I've done it often enough that it won't be questioned too closely. When the gate opens without the security orbs scanning someone first, the alarm will be raised. Security orbs will then attach to the person who first crosses into or out of Ispirtu."

"I've been tracked by security orbs before and I can't shake them."

"That's where I come in." Annarelle's confidence made Slate's heart sink. He didn't want to endanger any more of his friends. "I'll run out of Ispirtu, drawing the orbs with me. Then I'll run back inside and act like it was an accident."

"I'll tackle her to make a good show of it, but she should get out of the incident with just a slap on the wrist."

Slate still didn't like the plan. Annarelle read the look on his face and her demeanor became more forceful. "Quit worrying about us and do what you need to do!"

Slate knew she was right, but hated the circumstances that required it. "Let's get this over with then. Fractal's grace to both of you."

Tommy ran into the guardhouse and opened the gate. Annarelle ran through and gave Slate a hug. She whispered, "Thank you for helping me survive in Ispirtu. I'm glad I have the opportunity to help you now." She pushed away from him as security orbs blared and rushed toward her. She put a confused look on her face and ran into the Ispirtu grounds with her hands flapping in mock apology, drawing the security orbs away from Slate and his entrance route. Tommy emerged from the guardhouse and tackled her on the grass.

Slate slipped into the grounds of Ispirtu and sprinted toward the storeroom window with his heart in his throat, fearful of the consequences of capture. He rounded the corner of Ispirtu and saw the storeroom window had already been broken for him. Hoping everything was ok with Tommy and Annarelle, he slid through the window with a tremendous crash when a shelf full of cleaning supplies fell on top of him. He brushed himself off quickly and listened. He thought he was safe, but then the doorknob turned and he froze. He hadn't heard anyone coming. How had he been caught?

Lattimer looked into the room with a scowl. "If I knew you would announce your arrival like a circus act coming to town, I wouldn't have bothered with all the secrecy. You might as well have been carrying cymbals and banging on a drum. Now get over here...quickly."

Lattimer and Slate slipped through the hallway and into Primean's laboratory. The lights were off except for a single orb floating in the far reaches of the lab. "Don't tell me you're the nostalgic type."

"No one knows that I've been using Primean's old laboratory and I'd like to keep it that way. If anyone looks in the windows of the double doors, it'll just look like a dark room." That made sense, but then Lattimer admitted to some superstition in his nature. "Plus, I wasn't sure if there was anything else that made Primean's experiment successful that night. I wanted to duplicate everything as precisely as possible." They walked to the back of the room and suppressed memories came back to him. Sawdust covered the floor, hooks hung from the ceiling, and all that was missing was his blood pouring onto the floor.

Slate rescued himself from his memories by asking about the most obvious change to the room. A large tank of water sat prominently atop the sawdust. Behind it was a black curtain, held taut. "You require a larger bucket of water than Primean needed?"

"You would find it difficult to swim in Primean's bucket."

Slate groaned, thinking of Sana's experiments during their trip to Pillar. "Is there any other way?"

"I'm afraid not. What do you know about muscles and how they work?"

"I don't want to face Magnus in a feats-of-strength competition...otherwise, nothing."

"After the Sicarius headmaster suggested I try to improve the strength or speed of our warriors, I looked into manuscripts from the infirmary. Muscles consist of overlapping fibers or filaments that slide over each other. Stored energy momentarily binds these filaments to each other and pulls, or contracts. To create more force, your muscles use more stored energy and optimize the amount of overlap. I want to train your muscles to know where that optimal overlap is and to access it instantly."

"But how would that make me stronger or faster?"

"Think about when you are running. To reach your top speed, you need to accelerate over a long distance. As your body adjusts to what you are asking, it recruits more muscles and makes the contractions more efficient. If this experiment works, you will be able to reach your top speed, or your maximum jump, or throw your strongest punch every time, right away..."

Slate was beginning to understand the benefit. "Essentially making me stronger and faster... How does swimming play a role?"

"I needed a link, and the best analogy I could think of was people rowing a boat. Their paddles enter the water simultaneously and during the rowing motion it propels the boat forward. This synchronized effort is similar to how muscles work. Unfortunately, our discretionary needs prohibit me from bringing an entire boat and rowing crew into the lab. You need to do the job yourself."

"How do I serve as both the link and the subject of the experiment?"

"I am hoping a Perceptor has the capability to figure it out. In essence, the better you perform in the water, the better link you will become and the easier it will be on me. This will be the difference between Primean's experiment and mine."

Slate understood enough to know his role in the experiment. He stripped down and entered the tank of water, flinching as it reached his waist. "You couldn't have made it a little warmer?"

"You are going to save us from a Blood Mage and you are afraid of a little cold water? We're all doomed," Lattimer deadpanned.

Slate started treading water to warm up his muscles. For the first time, he noticed small ribbons attached to the walls of the tank. As he moved his arms and legs, the ribbons swirled. "What's with the ribbons?"

"I'll need to control the water to match your speed. The ribbons help me to visualize the water flow in the tank. I hung the curtain behind to see the ribbons better."

Slate had warmed up his muscles in the cold water. "Let's do this before the stone in my hand makes me too fatigued."

The water began to flow in a circular pattern, with the water in the top of the tank running headlong into Slate to apply resistance to his swimming strokes.

When he settled into a rhythmic breathing pattern, a spell was cast upon him by someone powerful but tentative in its application. Lattimer was a powerful wizard, but the tentativeness was unexpected. Slate couldn't pinpoint exactly what the spell was doing. He could feel it all over his body, but he couldn't pull on it in the manner he had before. Then he remembered Lattimer saying the harder he swam, the better the link would become. As confirmation, he heard Lattimer shout in between strokes. "Harder, Slate! Swim harder!"

Slate pushed himself and the current sped up accordingly. The feeling in his muscles caused by the spell became more pronounced. He concentrated on it and sensed the spell trying to *shift* his muscles with each contraction. He tried to pull on the feeling but couldn't quite grab hold. Slate swam faster.

Slate felt the spell's effect increase with his effort and Lattimer shouted encouragement, "Go, Slate! Go faster!" The problem was that Slate's stonehand started to lag behind the rhythm established by his arms. He struggled to maintain his pace, but then Lattimer increased the speed of the current, pushing Slate to his breaking point. Gasping for air between strokes, he focused on the spell affecting his body. He could feel it prominently now, ebbing and flowing with the contractions of his muscular strokes. He had tried *pulling* on it as he had done with Primean but without benefit. Exhaustion clouded his thoughts, leaving only the cyclic motions of a swim stroke. They coincided with the ebbs and flows of the spell. Without thinking, he slowly started to *pull and relax* with the ebbs and flows of the spell. His speed increased immediately. "That's it! Keep going!" Lattimer increased the current's speed and Slate kept up by pulling harder during the ebbs of each stroke, relying on the spell to maintain his speed more than physical exertion. The spell felt stronger, but worry crept into Slate. Was he pulling too hard on Lattimer? Would he meet Primean's fate? Slate couldn't think clearly. The current kept increasing and Slate's empty mind could only focus on the pulsating spell urging his muscles forward. *Pull, relax, pull, relax…*faster, stronger, faster, stronger—the current kept increasing and Slate kept pulling harder, right up until his empty mind slipped into unconsciousness.

Whack! "Slate! Are you ok?" *Whack!* Someone hit Slate repeatedly on the chest. *Whack!* Slate wretched all over, projecting water in the general direction of the voice. "Bastard!" Slate recognized Lattimer's voice and other conscious thoughts followed quickly behind.

He opened his eyes to see that Lattimer was soaking wet, having jumped in the tank to rescue him after he passed out. Then Slate realized that Lattimer had received a second bath for his troubles. Despite his exhaustion, he had to laugh.

"You think this is funny? You almost died, you fractal-forsaken fuck!"

"…but I didn't…and neither did you…" Slate laughed in joy and relief. Lattimer hadn't met the same fate as Primean.

Finally, Lattimer's anger at having been vomited on gave way to relief and laughter of his own. "You think you can take my spark? The Regallos are the strongest wizards in the kingdom. The only people with stronger sparks were my sister Rose and my father." The mention of his sister sobered Lattimer. He stood up and extended his hand to help Slate to his feet.

Slate grabbed it, but Lattimer flew face-first into the sawdust covering the laboratory floor instead of Slate rising. When he tried on his own, his body launched into the air. He rotated in midair to land on his feet, consciously trying not to push off the floor when he landed.

"Woah…I guess it worked." Lattimer said from the ground.

Slate looked down at himself, moving his arms and legs slowly. He jumped from a standstill and flew into the air as if he'd had a running start. "This is awesome…" He tried to run, but his first step was at the speed of a full sprint, covering more ground than he anticipated and sending himself into the laboratory wall in a thud. "…but it might take some getting used to."

That brought laughter from Lattimer again. "Try a punch."

Slate walked slowly and carefully over to where his clothes lie, getting redressed. With the glove from Lucus in place, Slate eyed the small table that once contained Primean's whip. If anything deserved to be demolished in this laboratory, the table would do. He held his fist an inch above the surface of the desk and punched. The desk exploded in a shower of splinters. Slate smiled. "That should work against a Fury…"

"I'd say so." Lattimer rubbed his jaw with a smile. "I'm just glad you punched me a few months ago. I wouldn't want to get one on the jaw from you again."

"The Blood Mage will have a surprise in store now…"

"I just hope it isn't my father. What are your plans?"

"I'm not convinced that Brannon is the Blood Mage, because Villifor and Magnus presented Darik with a modified account of the Minot attack. The king will attack Ispirtu this evening with the aid of Bellator. I plan to visit your father's estate one last time with the Sicarius headmaster. We will find out once and for all if there is evidence of Blood Magic manuscripts in your father's personal library. If a battle is imminent, I want to be on the right side. Would you like to join me?"

"I need to stay in Ispirtu and prepare a few tricks of my own. If you find out my father is to blame, place an exploding orb at the southwest corner of Ispirtu's walls. I am assigned as the commander of those forces and will make sure the defenses are down at that location."

"Won't everyone be suspicious?"

"Not if I figure out a clever way of doing it…so get out of here and give me time to plan."

"How do I leave unnoticed?"

"You are a Sicarius Guardsman. It shouldn't be a problem with the combination of your training and newfound abilities." Lattimer said with a smile but an air of finality. Lattimer had obviously inherited Brannon's sense of authority.

"Thank you, Lattimer." Slate clasped hands with his former rival.

"We make a good team, Slate. Malethya is changing and recent events have made that only more clear. If we stick together, maybe we can do more than survive. Maybe we can steer things in the right direction…"

Slate had trouble thinking past the survival part. For now, that was enough for him. He left Lattimer and snuck down the hallway, darting from corner to corner in seemingly impossible spurts of speed. Then he put on his Sicarius mask and jumped through the storeroom window onto the Ispirtu grounds, forcing his muscles to walk at a casual pace. Slate felt exposed amongst all the Ispirtu wizards, but with the mask and his Ispirtu robes, he was able to walk directly into the guardhouse without notice. Tommy and Annarelle were not present.

The Ispirtu wizard on duty watched citizens pass by the Ispirtu gates alertly, but his eyes passed over Slate in disinterest. Slate looked around for a button or switch for the gate and couldn't find it. Finally, he decided to wait for someone to enter the Ispirtu grounds. After a few moments of anxious waiting a nobleman approached the gates claiming to have a meeting with Brannon. The wizard concentrated and then shot a spell into a recessed location in the guardhouse wall. Slate felt like an idiot…of course Ispirtu would have a magical gate. That meant Tommy couldn't have opened the gates unless he did it intentionally. He lied to Slate and was probably in a heap of trouble because of his actions. Blast! There could have been another way. The doors swung open and Slate sprinted through the opening gates. Since he was the first person through, the security orbs registered that someone was leaving and the security orbs activated when the nobleman entered. The surprised nobleman fell to the ground in fear as the security orbs deafened his ears.

Slate took to the rooftops, looking for the Sicarius headmaster. With his new abilities, he jumped easily from building to building and circled the entire Ispirtu grounds. He stopped to look around and felt a shock stick pressed against the back of his neck. "I see the experiment worked, at least so far as to speed up your ridiculous attempt at stealth. It sure didn't make you any more observant either. I've been tracking you across the last three buildings."

Slate shrugged. "It's tough to beat the best." A huge boom interrupted Slate's act of nonchalance and he looked up to see a spell cast in the sky. The spell formed the symbol of Ispirtu high above Brannon's tower. "Brannon must have just received word of the pending attack. That signals all Ispirtu wizards stationed within sight of that symbol to return and defend the guild."

"Let's leave before they decide we're a threat. Did you hide the supplies?"

"They are safely stowed away. Let's get to Brannon's estate. My anger at the events in Sicarius is rising and I need to direct it before it boils over." The thought of the eminently dangerous Sicarius headmaster losing control scared Slate to his core. Finding the identity of the Blood Mage and pointing the Sicarius headmaster in that direction seemed like a great option.

"See if you can keep up." Slate jumped from rooftop to rooftop, gaining ground on the headmaster but less ground than he had imagined. The city flew beneath their feet and soon the rooftops gave way to the large estates and manors of Rue Street. Slate stopped on a rooftop with an overlooking view. The Sicarius headmaster was there momentarily. "What's the plan?"

"I walk in and take what I want." The headmaster dropped to a terrace below and then to the ground, walking directly to Brannon's estate. Slate shook his head in amazement, jumped to the ground, and took up a position at the headmaster's side. The headmaster looked over at him. "Take off those robes. We aren't in Ispirtu and I'm not hiding. We are Sicarius and the guardsmen will know who defeated them today."

Slate removed his robes and the two last remaining Sicarius Guardsmen walked down the center of Rue Street. The Sicarius mask, normally an instrument of disguise, served as a beacon of warning to surrounding onlookers. Dressed in nearly identical strips and folds of fabric, Slate and the Sicarius headmaster would not have fit in on Rue Street or any other street in Malethya. Estates that had security guardsmen identified the figures as Sicarius Guardsmen and turned into a frenzied mess of activity at their passing. The headmaster paid the guardsmen no attention.

By the time they reached the remains of the Regallo estate's guardhouse, the commotion had announced their arrival and they were greeted in the form of six Bellator Guardsmen in a defensive formation. The guardsman in front spoke, sword drawn. "You have no business here. Leave now or suffer the consequences."

The eerily alternating voice of the headmaster sent shivers down Slate's spine. "I do have business here and if you stand in my way, you will be the one to suffer. Step aside while you still can." Slate grasped his staff and prepared for the coming onslaught.

"We are trained Bellator Guardsmen. You are outnumbered and armed with sticks." The guardsman referred to the staff in Slate's hands.

"You are dogs trained to protect Brannon without the intelligence to question whether he deserves your protection. Nonetheless, every dog knows when to run from a fight. I hope you have enough intelligence to do the same." The headmaster looked to Slate. "Give this dog a demonstration of what you can do with your stick."

Slate whirled his staff around a few times and flipped the end of it into his palm, pointing it at the guardsman. He inched the staff closer and closer to the bridge of the guardsman's nose, antagonizing the Bellator Guardsmen into action. The guardsman swung his sword arm to deflect the staff, but Slate reacted with uncanny speed, flicking his wrist so that the tip of his staff connected with the inner, unarmored portion of the man's elbow. A blow of this nature wouldn't normally have enough force to slow the guardsman's swing, but this one ruined the man's arm, leaving the sword to clatter to the ground and his arm to hang lifelessly below his elbow.

Slate hoped the demonstration would break the group, but he wasn't surprised when the Bellator Guardsmen attacked as a unit, with practiced discipline. The Sicarius headmaster threw darts into the necks of two men in the front of the formation, finding the soft spots between their armor perfectly. Slate simply flashed around the outside of the group, immediately flanking them and exposing their unprotected backsides. He swiped two knees in succession, causing the men to crumble beneath their own weight. That left only one armed guardsman.

The headmaster addressed the woman with the shocked look on her face. "Answer my questions and it will save you a trip to the infirmary. How many guardsmen are inside and are any of them Ispirtu wizards?"

The remaining guardsman answered quickly. "There are ten more inside and we are all Bellator Guardsmen." She started to run off, but the headmaster buried a catalpa knife into her heel, tearing the Achilles tendon of the retreating woman.

Slate looked questioningly at the headmaster who said, "She lied. Sixteen guardsmen await us and three are Ispirtu wizards. Brannon added security after your latest failed break-in. Let's go say hello."

Despite the guardsmen writhing in pain on the front lawn, the estate looked quiet and peaceful. Slate scanned the grounds for signs of any new surprises, but not seeing any made him certain they would find a few along the way. Slate's eye caught a slight movement from a figure in the shadows of a second floor window. Slate could barely make out a look of concentration on his face in the poor lighting when a throwing knife shattered the glass and the Ispirtu wizard fell through the open window. "The other two wizards will be more careful. Get us to cover." Slate grabbed the headmaster by the waist and flashed, using his newfound abilities to cover a previously impossible distance. A fireball scorched the earth where they stood, encouraging Slate to continue his escape. He changed directions and speeds in a dash to the guest house, trying to present an unpredictable path for the wizards reigning fire from above. They sheltered behind the guest house as a fireball slammed into the wall, alighting the vacant building in flames.

The Sicarius headmaster let out a low growl. "I hate wizards. It's easier to kill them in their sleep." A pressure wave from one of the wizards hit the far wall of the guest house and it crumbled.

The headmaster readied an arsenal of throwing knives and darts. "I located the two remaining wizards and can pin them down. You break for the estate and take them out. Go."

The Sicarius headmaster leaned from cover and unleashed a flurry of knives at two second-floor windows. With his targets located, Slate flashed into the front lawn. He kept counting in his head, timing his flashes to come in two second intervals, dodging in anticipation of any spells that might come his way. Seven Bellator Guardsmen poured from the front door, taking up an offensive formation, but Slate focused on getting to the wizards. At this range, they were the largest threat.

Slate took the most direct route to his first target. He flashed beneath the second story window and jumped. At the peak of his jump he punched the wall with his stonehand, sending his fist a good eight inches into the stone block. Having gained purchase on the wall, he pulled upwards, going high enough to get his foot in the handhold he had created. The flurry of knives around the window frame stopped and the wizard inside looked out to aim his next spell. He didn't have the chance because Slate jumped upward again, reached the windowsill with his left hand and drove his staff through the open window. The force of the stab entered the wizard, causing Slate to recoil slightly at his act and pull backwards. The wizard fell two stories to the ground below in a motionless thud. Slate pulled himself into the window and tried not think about the blood on the end of his staff. Now wasn't the time.

Slate entered a room adjacent to Brannon's office, but the door burst open before he could gather his bearings. In this confined room, the Bellator Guardsmen would have the advantage because he couldn't flank the group as he had done on the estate lawn. Instead he met them head-on at the doorway, trying to prevent their entry.

The guardsmen didn't strike with sparring blows and Slate didn't either. The staff found one guardsman below the chin, collapsing his airway. The next guardsman tried to ram him with a shield. Slate flashed to his right, sidestepping the blow, and delivered a punch with his stonehand that crumpled the guardsman's helmet. In the hallway, a guardsman reached into a sack of exploding orbs. Slate dove headfirst over the guardsman blocking the doorway and landed in the hallway surrounded by guardsmen. Their surprise didn't outweigh their training and attacking blows were swung just as the exploding orb Slate had been worrying about was removed from the sack. Slate stabbed his staff into the forearm of the guardsman, causing him to drop the exploding orb. Before it hit the ground, Slate flashed into the railing overlooking the great room, crashing through it and falling into the room below. In his wake, a flurry of swords and axes attacked the spot he had stood before a deafening explosion transformed the weapons into shrapnel. The guardsmen didn't hold together as well as their weapons.

A pressure wave hit Slate and sent him flying into a great room wall. He had forgotten about the second wizard. ...*1* Get up. ...*2* Slate pushed against the floor, propelling himself through the air as a fireball singed the flooring. ...*1* He needed to locate the wizard before one of those fireballs found its mark. ...*2* Slate flashed again and stopped just short of a fireball that raced past him. ...*1* Slate thought it came from Brannon's office on the second floor. ...*2* Slate flashed toward the stairs, covering three quarters of the distance in a single bound. No fireball came. Slate looked up and saw a fireball form in the palm of the wizard's hand. He had waited for Slate to flash before releasing his spell. Slate was a dead man.

A catalpa hilt burrowed into the wizard's chest, halting the fireball just as it was being released. The fireball had formed but stayed where it was, lighting the wizard's robes and falling to the ground along with the dead wizard.

In the quiet after the wizard fell, Slate realized that the stately manor was ablaze all around him. The Sicarius headmaster emerged from Brannon's office. "Hurry. Up here. We'll only have a few minutes before we get smoked out."

Slate bounded up the stairs and jumped across the hole in the hallway created by the exploding orb. "Lattimer said the hidden library is at the end of the catwalk." Slate flashed down there but couldn't find any clues as to the location of the room…the orbs did their job remarkably well. Slate hoped they hadn't stormed the estate just to burn the library down and destroy their only evidence.

The Sicarius headmaster joined him and, reaching into the folded robes, produced a fist full of powder. The headmaster threw it in the air and the small particles floated down and accumulated on a hidden path. "Powder is great for getting past orbs." The headmaster jumped over the railing onto the hidden path. One more throw of powder revealed the door handle and the headmaster turned it.

Brannon's hidden library was immaculately maintained and ornately decorated. Shelves of books dominated the wall space and contrasted with a single table and chair for reading on the floor. Various trunks completed the room, but Slate didn't open them and risk triggering any traps left by Brannon.

"Look for documents that refer to 'spark-dependent spells,' 'innovation through weak linkages' or the like. You won't find a direct reference to Blood Magic because that name was given to the Blood Mages after their passing." Slate scanned one section of bookshelves while the Sicarius headmaster found the evidence they sought in a different section. "This describes the creation of orbs. Wizards created them from pure spark and were able to store energy within them." The headmaster got more excited with each text, or perhaps the rising heat in the room contributed to the effect. "This describes methods of enhancing soldier's abilities in combat by altering the soldier's perception of pain. Do you think Brannon tasked Primean with discovering how to accomplish this?"

"I didn't get that impression, but it sure looks that way." Slate was having trouble finding anything of note. All the texts in his section were on history.

"Here is a biography on Cantor!" Smoke seeped into the room and the heat stifled their efforts. "Have you found anything? Grab what you can and let's go!" The Sicarius headmaster left hurriedly with an armful of books.

Slate scanned the bookshelf furiously, seeing nothing he deemed important. The smoke caused his eyes to water, but he continued searching titles, confident there was more to find. Amid the beautiful bindings of the other rare books, the plainness of an unbound manuscript stood out to Slate. He read the title, "An Unrevised History of the Twice-Broken Wars" by Brannon Regallo. Slate grabbed it and turned to leave, but a wall of flame on the catwalk barred Slate's exit. Beneath him, fire covered the walls of the great room. He was trapped. Panicking, he looked around for any object that hadn't caught fire yet. In the middle of the room hung a large chandelier, and beyond that the far side of the catwalk wasn't aflame. Slate jumped, and with his newfound abilities was able to land with his feet near the center of the chandelier. As soon as he landed, he jumped again, but the chandelier's mount gave way from the rapidly deteriorating ceiling. Slate landed awkwardly on the railing but recovered in time to haul himself over the railing. He coughed and stumbled through the service entrance and into the cool evening air.

The headmaster was waiting for him. "I warned you to leave. Why didn't you listen?" Despite the harsh tone, the headmaster hit Slate in the back to help clear the smoke from his lungs.

After he stopped coughing, Slate said, "I had plenty of time..."

"Yeah, and I'm sure you had that last wizard right where you wanted him too." They walked toward Rue Street, where a crowd of onlookers gathered. Upon seeing the two emerge from the burning building, they dispersed immediately, pretending not to have seen anything.

"It all worked out. How did things turn out with other Guardsmen?" They rounded the corner of the estate and the grounds, riddled with Bellator bodies, came into view. "I held my own," the Sicarius headmaster said. "Now, we need to find any useful information in these texts, and there is no place safer than right here." The headmaster propped a large stone of strewn rubble against a nearby corpse, using it as a doorjamb. "Brannon will not waste Ispirtu resources to investigate this incident when Darik is gathering his forces for the assault."

Another corpse and stone later and Slate sat beside the Sicarius headmaster. He pulled the manuscript written by Brannon from his sleeve to find it partially damaged from the fire. Nonetheless, Slate needed every piece of information he could get from the document. The flames of the burning estate lit the pages to replace the failing light of day.

I led a division of King Darik's army today against a band of revolutionaries. Without wizards in their company I assumed the day would be quick. We positioned our conventional soldiers in the front lines to shield our wizards from the heathen's attack. The wizards rained fire amongst the oncoming soldiers, but the soldiers fought with tremendous vigor, slicing through Darik's army so quickly that I had to call a retreat for fear of losing my wizards in direct combat.

Later that evening, I called the most senior surviving member of the common foot soldiers to my command tent. I questioned how his trained soldiers were routed so quickly against presumably common fighters. He said, "A single man led the charge against us, yielding a prowess with the sword that would be envied by any member of the king's army. I believe you are familiar with the name of this master swordsman, since he just saved us from the Disenites. Villifor is fighting for the revolutionaries." I must learn more of this former hero turned enemy of the king.

The Sicarius headmaster interrupted Slate's reading. "Well, I think we know that Brannon possessed books that the Wizard Council wouldn't condone. This one describes the rise to power of Cantor and the glories of his discoveries. It describes him almost as a savior to the people… it must have been written before the later atrocities began."

Slate acknowledged the headmaster and then went back to the next section, burning with a need to learn more about Villifor. Brannon's text did not disappoint.

We regrouped our forces today and prepared a defense against Villifor's band. Reinforcements arrived from Ravinai, so I put the soldiers in position to get the most battlefield experience. The wizards were prepared for the onslaught of the virgin soldiers and cast fireballs immediately into the enemy without regard for collateral damage. Unfortunately, Villifor learned from his previous encounter and grouped his men into tight formations, with a large shield held overhead in anticipation of fireballs from above. With a defense prepared, our own men burned while Villifor's men waited under protection until it was clear to charge the offending wizards. I barely had time to cast a spell that moved the earth beneath the feet of Villifor's men. At the distance from which I was observing, it was only enough to scare the soldiers and give my wizards time to retreat. I was haunted by the chants of Villifor as we departed. The image of that man carving through the remaining soldiers of the king's army will haunt my dreams.

Slate commented to the Sicarius headmaster. "I am reading Brannon's memoirs from the Twice-Broken Wars. So far, it appears that Villifor was every bit the hero the stories made him out to be." This time it was the Sicarius headmaster's turn to give Slate a complimentary acknowledgment. Slate jumped ahead in the story, sensing their time was running short.

After several battles, the revolutionaries have advanced to the outskirts of Ravinai, in large part due to the cleverness of Villifor. I fear this leader of men has more tricks left for us, but we are running out of common soldiers to face him. I have resorted to trickery myself by placing orbs that mimic soldiers along the watchtowers. To the enemy it will appear that our numbers are insurmountable. I only hope that the ruse is sufficiently effective to force surrender. After facing Villifor and his men I fear Ravinai may be lost if they continue their assault.

Slate skipped ahead again.

My trickery has finally paid off. Several days of inactivity amongst Villifor's men was followed by a midnight visitor. He claimed to be Villifor's second in command and that Villifor planned to attack the following evening at dusk. I questioned the authenticity of the information and the informant agreed to allow me to share his memories in return for three things. I summoned King Darik who foolishly agreed to the man's terms in writing. I investigated the authenticity of the man and found that he indeed had fought alongside Villifor and had helped draw up the plans. The informant whimpered following my investigation and told the king every detail I already knew. Villifor would attack tomorrow and he would find King Darik's army in perfect position to wipe out the rebellion once and for all. I looked down at the pathetic excuse of a man in front of me in disgust. In return for the information, this man had arranged for any members of the revolution who surrendered in battle to retain their lives. He also requested to assume the identity of Villifor with all the exploits and victories of the master swordsman attributed to him. Finally, he demanded to be the headmaster of the newly formed Bellator. I was disgusted with this man, but perhaps even more so with King Darik. For agreeing to terms with such a man, Darik does not deserve to be king…

An explosion filled the air somewhere in the distance and Slate was pulled from Brannon's memoirs before he finished. Slate had heard enough exploding orbs to know the sound and it didn't take much imagination to know the location was Ispirtu. "It is time," the Sicarius headmaster said. "We've found numerous documents in Brannon's personal library linking him to blood magic. Do you think Brannon is behind all of this?"

"I just read Brannon's personal memoirs from the end of the Twice-Broken Wars. He describes the man posing to be Villifor as a pathetic and weak man who betrayed his own people. The Villifor that we know is not the war hero of stories, but a pompous impersonation living vicariously through someone he betrayed. He may be treacherous, but he is no blood mage."

Distant explosions rocked through the evening sky, making silhouettes of Ravinai's skyline. "We know that Brannon was present at the tournament and that he was in charge of monitoring spells during the championship match. He is the most powerful wizard in the kingdom and the one person who has the power, influence, and spark necessary to keep the attacks on Pillar, Minot, and the other northern villagers quiet. He knows that magic is dying in Malethya and that he was desperate to restore that power. The more I think about it, I've always known Brannon was responsible for my parents' death and everything else. Now I have read his own admission that he believes Darik is unfit to be King. Coupled with the evidence from Minot and the books we found tonight, I can come to no other conclusion. It has always been Brannon. Brannon is the Blood Mage."

"I was hoping it wouldn't be him..." Slate thought he sensed melancholy enter the voice of the Sicarius headmaster. "Now let's go kill a Blood Mage."

CHAPTER NINETEEN

THE CARDS CRUMBLE

Slate walked beside the Sicarius headmaster toward Ispirtu, leaving the ruins of the Regallo estate in their wake. The two of them must have struck quite an image to the neighbors peering cautiously from the safety of their windows. The stronghold of Brannon Regallo was immersed in flames and dozens of the kingdom's best fighters mixed evenly with the strewn rubble adorning the front lawn, while from the wreckage emerged two figures in dark clothing and masks. The incident at Sicarius had made him a fugitive, but the Regallo estate would have the more profound effect to the citizens of Ravinai.

Slate Severance was now infamous.

When the stories of this night spread, he would become a ghost...someone who could enter your home and destroy everything that you held dear. The witnesses of this wreckage would never know his intentions. He was trying to preserve the lives they knew. A creature from the stories of their youth, a Blood Mage, was loose in Malethya, and Slate would succeed in stopping the Blood Mage before these people knew it existed, even if the cost was invoking the looks of fear he saw in the eyes peering at him from around corners.

His determination returned his tangential thinking toward the task at hand. "We need to meet up with Lucus."

"I've already arranged it. Lucus sought the solitude of the catalpa grove before the storm. I enlisted his help to camouflage my supplies within the trunk of a hollow tree. Like I said...there is always a place to hide." The Sicarius headmaster smirked beneath the mask. The more Slate became accustomed to wearing the mask, the more he was able to read the expressions of the Sicarius headmaster. "He will assemble your friends and meet us on a rooftop near Ispirtu." After reentering the confines of the city, they took to the rooftops out of silent familiarity. Large, ominous clouds closed in on the city, bringing with them the death of winter. The silence of the foreboding clouds and fading light of day mixed with deafening explosions and fireballs in the sky ahead.

The headmaster paused atop a rooftop overlooking the battle for Ispirtu. Ranks of Bellator Guardsmen led the larger King's Army. They punished Ispirtu's walls with large battering rams protected by stone canopies. Wizards sent pressure waves at the canopies and roiled the ground beneath the feet of the soldiers. If they faltered and lost formation, fireballs found the cracks of the unsupported canopies and the soldiers beneath. So far, the walls shook, but Ispirtu stood strong.

Ispirtu's main gate remained free of attackers. That would have been the first place to send the battering rams, but a large contingent of wizards kept the area clear. After watching for a minute or two, Slate saw how they managed. A lone figure raced toward the gate, shooting a fireball straight into the air as a signal of his allegiance to Ispirtu. The defending wizards protected the figure as he ran to the gate and answered Brannon's call for aid.

Lucus and Rainier emerged from a stairwell with rooftop access to rendezvous with the Sicarius Guardsmen.

"Where is Sana?" Slate asked before offering a greeting to Lucus.

"I sent her away from the battle. She is my apprentice and must learn the principles of my teaching. She was too eager to fight." Great, the pacifist wizard chose now to get philosophical. "Besides, if none of us survive, we need someone to know the truth." Four would have to do then.

"Our time is short. The battle at Ispirtu has begun." The Sicarius headmaster interrupted the reunion of friends with the rather blunt assessment of the situation. "We raided the personal library of Brannon Regallo and it contained a multitude of documents regarding Blood Magic. In addition to the findings at Minot, the evidence points to Brannon. How do we reach the Ispirtu headmaster, and what's the plan when we do?"

"We need to trigger an exploding orb at the southwest corner of Ispirtu's walls. Lattimer will direct the Ispirtu forces in that area and coordinate our entry. From there we will locate Brannon and question him."

The Sicarius headmaster was unimpressed. "That is a rather vague and uninspired plan. Whose idea was it that won the Bellator competition? What about the failed break-in at the Regallo estate? Those plans at least had creativity."

Slate happily acknowledged the cleverness of his colleagues but couldn't prevent a defensive tone. "Sana is the most strategic amongst us and Rainier orchestrated the raid of the Regallo estate. Sana is not with us, so maybe you have a suggestion? Should we walk up to the front gate and knock? I believe that summarizes your most recent plan."

"Against inferior opponents the simplest plan is often the best." The headmaster's definition of inferior was a little too close for comfort. "...but you are right. I will walk up to the front gate of Ispirtu and be let in. My concern was for the three of you. If you can't infiltrate the Ispirtu defenses, I will reach Brannon without you. Lucus, did you bring the items I requested?" Lucus opened a trunk containing several Ispirtu robes and packed one into a travel sack, motioning for Slate and the others to do the same. It made sense...once they infiltrated Ispirtu's walls, it would help to look the part.

"...so you are leaving us?" Rainier objected.

"It's the Sicarius way. I only know how to work alone, but I will aid you where I can. Use all of your skill to find a way in, as I will use all of mine to do the same. We are out of time. Slate, I suggest we leave while there is still a battle to be won."

Slate found it difficult to argue with the Sicarius headmaster. "We are in this together, headmaster, but if we fail then it falls to you to kill the Blood Mage. Malethya is depending on us." They all shook hands, realizing there might not be time for another conversation until this was ended.

Then the headmaster turned toward Slate and got strangely sentimental, "You saved my life and have earned my trust. I have saved your life as well, but I fear your trust in me will be tested. Please remember, I am on your side. Fractal's truth, Slate." The headmaster descended from the rooftops into the alleyways of the city. A minute later, a figure emerged cloaked in Ispirtu robes. What was the headmaster doing? Without a fireball to signal the defenders within Ispirtu, the headmaster wouldn't stand a chance.

A ball of electricity formed in the hand of the cloaked figure and shot into the air.

Slate felt more confused than at any point since he had come to Ravinai. The Sicarius headmaster was a wizard? The headmaster ran to the gate within the protection of the Ispirtu wizards. The Sicarius mask had been removed, but the cowl prevented Slate from identifying the figure. A security orb scanned the Sicarius headmaster's face, the gates swung open, and the headmaster entered the Ispirtu grounds with disturbing ease.

Slate's confusion faded as he remembered the headmaster's words. The Sicarius headmaster was an Ispirtu wizard, so the relationship between Brannon and the Sicarius headmaster was even closer than Slate imagined. The headmaster's words were meant to calm Slate's reaction to the news. His brain tried to process the information, but his stomach clenched in betrayal. He hadn't actually seen any books describing Brannon as a Blood Mage. The Sicarius headmaster had found them. What if he had been lied to?

Slate thought most clearly with physical exertion, so it was time to enter the battle. Maybe his head would clear and maybe it wouldn't. He would just have to adjust as the circumstances changed. He had gotten quite used to that since coming to Ravinai.

He scanned the southwest corner as he looked for Lattimer, but couldn't make him out amongst the Ispirtu defenders. That was worrisome but not entirely unexpected in the given chaos. Then Slate saw Jak Warder leading a small squadron of Bellator Guardsmen and soldiers from the King's army. Given his current standing as a fugitive, Jak might be the only person to risk helping him. Slate signaled to Rainier and Lucus to join him. "Jak Warder commands the Bellator Guardsmen at the southwest corner. He might be willing to aid us...or at least look the other way long enough for us to slip past. Are you ready?" Slate didn't want to cloud their minds by adding his concerns regarding the identity of the Sicarius headmaster. Confusion led to distraction and distraction led to mistakes. Mistakes in battle were deadly. It was best to keep them focused on the task at hand.

"We are ready." Rainier spoke first and Lucus confirmed the sentiments. "Let your staff be swift, our feet be fast, and our fortunes be filled with fractal's grace."

That was more eloquent than Slate could articulate, so he simply nodded his gratitude for their help and made his way to the southwest corner of Ispirtu. He helped Lucus descend into one of the alleyways nearby and asked him to wait while he and Rainier scouted the surrounding area.

"Would you prefer to be camouflaged?" Lucus offered. It would certainly make it easier to navigate through the warring armies, but then Lucus would need to be carried due to his fatigue. All things considered, Slate didn't want to exhaust Lucus quite yet.

"Conserve your spark for the Blood Mage. We'll get there without camouflage." Lucus nodded and Slate hoped he was right.

Rainier and Slate peered from the edge of the alleyway to see Bellator Guardsmen positioning members of the King's army in rows. When the soldiers manning the battery ram were injured, they signaled the next row of soldiers to run into place and continue the efforts. The strategy sent the least skilled soldiers into harm's way and saved the best warriors for when the battle was on more equal grounds.

Apparently some of the soldiers in the King's army didn't appreciate the strategy. While the guardsmen's attention was diverted toward the action at the Ispirtu walls, the back row of soldier's quickly and quietly slunk away. Some sprinted toward the city proper and others sought quarter in a nearby residence. Unfortunately for them, Rainier, the master of disguises, spotted a new mark.

"Keep your eyes out for Jak. I'll be right back." A twinkle lit up his eyes and Slate was once again thankful the tribesman was on his side. Anyone crafty enough to use the skills of Sicarius and persuasive enough to be a member of the Tallow clan was dangerous indeed.

Rainier reappeared in a matter of minutes, stripped to his underwear and holding a bundle of armor. "How did you lose your shirt?"

"I didn't lose it…I traded it. It was much faster than fighting." Slate would have just knocked them out. "I convinced them their chances of escape from the King's service would improve if they rid themselves of their uniforms. They saw reason but asked for my clothes in return to aid their escape." Rainier paused, seemingly ashamed. "It was a high price to pay, but it was quick. Have you found Jak?"

"I spotted a tent that has too much bustling to be anything other than a command center. He will be there."

"Do you have a plan?"

"Get dressed and start running in place. I need you to be winded." Rainier donned the uniform of a low ranking soldier. Slate stopped him before he put on the armor. "You won't need that."

Slate dressed in armor while Rainier ran in place. By the time he finished, Rainier had worked up a healthy sweat.

"Run to the command tent. If anyone asks, you hold an urgent encrypted message for Jak Warder from Villifor. Bellator Guardsmen don't question orders from superiors. At Villifor's name, you should be allowed access to Jak."

"What do I say when I get there?"

It needed to be unique enough to imply a connection with Slate and general enough to maintain secrecy. "Battlefield tactics have won many wars. The one who applied them to greatest effect in Bellator did not have the benefit of Professor Halford's tutelage. He is in need of Halford's most attentive student during this most important of times."

Hopefully that message would grant a private audience to Rainier…unless he didn't want to help a fugitive. Slate put on the Sicarius mask. "I'll enter the command tent once I see people streaming out of it. This armor along with the Sicarius mask should be sufficient to avert the eyes of the other soldiers. I'm sorry to put you in the dangerous position for this mission. My ghostly face is too recognizable without the mask, and I'm a wanted man."

"It's about time you let me in on the fun." Rainier clapped Slate on the back and sprinted toward the command tent. Slate followed behind at an inconspicuous pace, fast enough to show purpose but slow enough to exhibit calmness in the surrounding chaos. Soldiers and Bellator Guardsmen alike let their gazes pass over him in favor of other priorities. Rainier arrived breathlessly to the command center where a guardsman stopped him and heard his request.

A moment later, Jak emerged and filled the entryway to the tent with his massive frame. He must have gained thirty pounds of muscle since Slate last saw him. Rainier spoke to him, carrying on with the ruse of being a simple messenger for Villifor. Recognition flashed across Jak's face and Slate was close enough to hear his response. "Everybody out! I need a moment to plan and send a response back to Villifor. Clear the command tent!"

Guardsmen left the large tent in droves. Jak grabbed Rainier by the arm and nearly tossed him inside. Slate passed into the tent, unnoticed by the exiting guardsmen with the aid of the Sicarius mask.

Inside, Rainier picked himself up from the ground. "What's the meaning of this?" Jak tersely whispered.

Slate took off his Sicarius mask before things got out of hand. "If you are going to blame somebody, blame me." Jak was startled, and he instinctively turned and swung. Slate anticipated the dangers of startling a trained Bellator Guardsman and ducked beneath the powerful blow. "We need to get to Brannon and we need your help to do it."

Jak stared at Slate and took weight of the situation. Slate thought of his pale complexion...it was good for inspiring fear, but it didn't encourage trust. Finally, a smile broke across Jak's face. "First, explain why everyone in the kingdom is trying to capture or kill you. You've always found your way into the spotlight, but this is a bit much even for you." Slate hoped Jak didn't see him in the same light as he saw Villifor. "After you've done that, explain what you need from me."

Slate tried to summarize as succinctly as possible. "Villifor and Magnus told a slightly modified version of the events at Minot to King Darik. That caused Darik to call for the sacking of Ispirtu to get to Brannon, but before he came here he called an emergency meeting of Sicarius. The Sicarius headmaster believed Darik was there to enlist Sicarius' help in the battle tonight. Instead, Darik questioned the loyalty of Sicarius and ordered their deaths. The Sicarius headmaster and I escaped with our lives, but we are now the most wanted people in Malethya...besides Brannon of course."

"Are you saying Brannon isn't responsible for the attacks?"

Slate didn't want doubt to creep into his answer, even if it was there. "No, I believe Brannon is not only responsible for the attacks, but that he is also a Blood Mage. I also think there is more going on between the headmasters and the King than I've been able to figure out."

"Where do I fit in?"

"I need two things. Firstly, Lattimer told me to set off an exploding orb on the southwest wall and he would arrange for us to sneak into Ispirtu..."

Jak interrupted, "That will be difficult. Have you seen the large battering rams outside? Those weren't our first options. The trebuchets and siege weapons are on their way from Darik's palace, but they will take until morning to work their way through the narrow streets...if they can make it through the snow that is..." Jak motioned to the clouds overhead threatening to bury the city at any moment. "The archers are out of range and we tried setting off exploding orbs, but none of them worked. Being magical in nature, they were created for us by Ispirtu wizards. They must have created them in a manner in which they deactivated in proximity to Ispirtu's walls. Maybe a wizard could make one work, but we don't have any at our disposal."

Rainier gave Jak some good news. "We have one with us. He may be able to help…"

Jak grunted noncommittally. "And what is the second impossible task you ask of me?"

"Villifor." Slate stated simply. "He isn't the war hero he claims to be. His loyalties to King Darik are suspect at best."

"…and I'm supposed to do what with that knowledge?"

"The Sicarius headmaster is already inside Ispirtu. Can you deliver Villifor and Darik to where we confront Brannon? People have been playing their cards pretty close to the chest. If we can get them all in one place, we might discover the truth."

Jak thought for a moment. "If we can blow a hole in Ispirtu's walls, I won't be able to keep those two away. I'll send a runner as soon as your wizard triggers the explosion. Once inside, you'll need to be quick to stay ahead of them."

Slate, with the clock ticking in his head, asked Jak the question he came to get answered. "Will you help us?"

Jak clasped Slate on the shoulder and smiled. "Villifor has yet to earn my trust or my respect. We will be entering a very volatile situation and you've managed to bend in the changing winds of all three guilds ever since you came to Ravinai. I respect you and choose to fight at your side, Slate Severance." Sufficient words of gratitude escaped Slate, but Jak spared him the awkwardness of a reply. "Here's how we'll get your wizard to the wall…"

Rainier retrieved Lucus from his hiding spot and changed into Ispirtu robes in preparation for success. Slate wore the Sicarius mask so that soldiers wouldn't question helping a fugitive or try to claim the reward on his head.

Jak issued orders for his men to lift the stone canopies from all four battering rams aloft so they joined in the center, creating one massive canopy. "You three will be positioned at the center to protect yourselves from any fireballs that might splatter in your direction. It should keep you safe for a few minutes, but the Ispirtu wizards will likely concentrate their spells as you approach."

Slate looked to Lucus. "Do you know why the exploding orbs fail to activate?"

"There are too many possibilities to speculate upon." That sounded like a fancy way of saying no.

"Rainier, do you have the orbs?"

"I have them." They took their positions and Jak ordered the advance. The soldiers marched in perfect synchrony, closing the gaps between the canopies. After a few dozen paces, the most powerful wizards on the wall sent spells crashing into the stone canopies. Thankfully, the stone canopies worked to shelter them even if some of the soldiers near the edges were not as fortunate.

The ground beneath their feet began to roil, signaling their proximity to the Ispirtu walls and causing the soldiers to lose balance. In some ways, the massive stone overhead helped them to maintain their footing. While the ground below them moved, the weight above was a steady reminder of the direction of gravity. Despite wobbly legs, the strong arms of the soldiers held the weight overhead and the canopies reached the Ispirtu wall.

Rainier stacked exploding orbs while Lucus sat next to the wall as calmly as if he were relaxing in a catalpa grove, thinking quietly amid the chaos surrounding him. He extended his hand to touch the wall, a gesture Slate recognized as a probing spell from the times Lucus healed him.

Around him, soldiers fell at an alarming rate because the wizards above had a stationary target. Jak sent reserves to take their places, but men fell as fast as they arrived. Rainier finished stacking the orbs, and Lucus touched one of them instead of the wall, serenity upon his face. The man would be calm in a tornado.

The canopy above their heads wavered, signaling their time ran short, but Lucus took a single orb from the pile and pointed to a location a dozen paces to the right. Slate understood his meaning, but he wasn't sure the soldiers had the strength left to carry out the order.

"Right! Right!" Slate screamed to the soldiers, trying to get his voice above the deafening explosions. The well-trained soldiers tried to move the large canopies, but the task was too great. The stones wavered and one of them would have fallen, but Slate flashed to the inside corner in time to keep it overhead. The canopy in front of him was about to fall when Jak intervened with a group of Bellator Guardsmen. Their added strength moved the canopy swiftly to where Lucus indicated. The wizard placed the dim exploding orb in the prescribed location and it began to flash.

"Back! Back! Double Time!" Jak bellowed at the soldiers. Slate understood the urgency in Jak's voice when the frequency of the orb's flashing increased steadily. The exploding orb Lucus had randomly chosen had an extremely short fuse. "Prepare to drop canopies on the Ispirtu side...on my mark..." The canopies had only cleared a few dozen paces from the wall when Jak yelled, "Mark!"

The canopies dropped on the side facing the Ispirtu walls, forming a lean-to of sorts. A split second later, an explosion rocked the stones overhead. Before the dust cloud had passed, the men jumped from beyond their makeshift shelters. A hole opened in the Ispirtu wall, cracking all the way up to where the wizards above rained spells down on the men. The earthquake-like event threw the wizards off balance and the air remained temporarily free of fireballs.

"Guardsmen... Secure the entryway at all costs!" Archers sprinted into range and unleashed a volley of arrows into the reeling wizards. Guardsmen scaled the cracked Ispirtu walls before the wizards could recover. Up close, the wizards were no match for the Bellator Guardsmen. A few managed to let out compression waves to stun the attackers, but that merely bought them a few seconds before they were overrun. Jak spared a second to communicate with Slate. "I've already sent a runner to Villifor. I'm going with you."

After Jak had just risked his life and saved his own in the process, Slate didn't feel the urge to argue. "Bring some of those men with you too." Slate smiled and clasped his friend on the arm.

"You three, you and you...you're with me. We enter Ispirtu to reach Brannon. Protect these three dressed in Ispirtu robes at all costs."

Jak led the formation of five Bellator Guardsmen who accompanied Lucus, Rainier, and Slate into the Ispirtu grounds. Slate's eyes searched frantically for the unknown dangers ahead while his mind wrestled with the questions he already faced. *Would there be red-eyes combing the halls?* Slate saw no signs of the Sicarius headmaster. *Had the headmaster gone ahead to find Brannon? Where was Lattimer? Had Brannon discovered he was helping Slate?*

Brannon appeared from his tower, scepter glowing. He delivered a massive fireball that encompassed the entire wall they had just passed through, leaving nothing but blackened stone and destruction behind. Wizards mobilized within Ispirtu to retake the blackened wall from Bellator control. Slate simply pointed and ran toward a basement level window. The guardsmen slid through the window, shattering glass and landing in a ready position within a research laboratory that was abandoned due to the call-to-arms. Slate moved the team before they were pursued, slipping into Primean's darkened laboratory.

"This lab isn't in official use. Let's stay quiet and hope those wizards that streamed out of Ispirtu's main entrance don't find us." Bellator Guardsmen were a proud group, but even they saw the benefit of letting things quiet down for a minute or two before pressing onward.

Jak took the opportunity to ask Lucus a question. "How did you activate the exploding orb?"

"I didn't...I simply knew where to put it. There was a net cast over the walls of Ispirtu that prevented the orbs from activating within their blast radius. I never would have had time to understand the pattern sufficiently to counteract it, but part of the net had been lifted. It was only in one very small section of the wall, but by placing the security orb there, it activated."

"So they just made a mistake and left a hole in the net?"

"I don't think so...someone was trying to help us out. The net had been lifted. I could tell that the pattern had changed there recently."

Lattimer's earlier words made more sense to Slate now. "That must have been Lattimer. He said he would arrange for the defenses to be down. I assumed he meant the wizards..."

The conversation was interrupted by a sound in the hallway...footsteps, and a lot of them. Did Slate trap his party in the laboratory without planning an exit?

The noise grew louder in the empty hallway and headed straight for them. How many people were there? Five? Ten? "Prepare yourselves." Jak's men took up a defensive formation. Slate planned to flash into the doorway when it opened. Rainier found a recess to hide in so that he could attack unseen. Lucus hid in a dark corner.

Shadows of Ispirtu robes cast upon the laboratory floor from the light in the hallway. The door opened and Slate flashed into the opening with his staff extended to strike a fatal blow. It took all his effort to keep from striking Lattimer. Lattimer flinched and shoved Slate backwards, causing him to tumble into the darkened lab.

"For fractal's sake, Slate...I thought you wanted my help." Slate stood back up and brushed himself off.

"I wasn't expecting you to bring friends."

"You expected me to take on the most powerful wizard in the kingdom by myself? When the wall was breached and a small group entered Ispirtu, I volunteered to lead the search party. I figured this would be the most logical place for you to go."

"This is one of the few times it pays to be predictable, I guess. I'm happy you recruited some help. Come inside...you need to meet some people."

Lattimer formed a blue orb of light that floated into the room for the introductions.

"You've met Lucus and Rainier. This is Jak Warder and his guardsmen." Lattimer was polite enough to shake hands, but he maintained his father's brashness.

"I don't want to waste time on pleasantries. I've rounded up a few Ispirtu students I trust...and a few that you do too..." Two cowls fell to reveal Tommy and Annarelle.

Tommy answered the question on Slate's mind before he could ask it. "We were taken for questioning when the call-to-arms went up. Our small mistake didn't warrant further investigation in light of the upcoming battle."

"I had them placed under my command so that I could keep an eye on them." The other wizards Slate recognized to be part of Lattimer's sycophants. The group was smaller than Slate remembered, but maybe Lattimer didn't trust them as much as they idolized him. "What's the plan from here?"

"Brannon is in his office and the Sicarius headmaster is in Ispirtu. If we reach Brannon's tower quickly, we will have the Sicarius headmaster's aid when we confront Brannon. If we arrive too late, one of the two may already be dead."

Jak spoke up. "I didn't risk my life storming in here to miss out on the fun."

"I agree. Jak, can you coordinate the Bellator Guardsmen and work with Lattimer to position the wizards?"

Lattimer interrupted. "Wizards aren't pawns to be ordered around."

"You're right, but Jak has studied past battles and battlefield tactics and how to work as a team. Would you be willing to take his advice?"

His ego as a wizard properly assuaged, Lattimer relented. "What do you recommend?"

"I *advise* that when we encounter Ispirtu wizards, you cast weak spells as quickly as possible, just powerful enough to break the concentration of the wizards attacking us. That will buy us time to close and attack."

"Why wouldn't I just shoot a fireball at them and kill them myself?"

"I have no doubt that a wizard of your pedigree could do just that. Considering a Blood Mage waits for us, you need to maintain as much spark as possible through these initial skirmishes."

Lattimer agreed with Jak as only a Regallo could. "It's good to see they are teaching you something over at Bellator."

Slate changed the subject quickly. "Also, I'd like to ask you to protect Lucus. He is a pacifist, but we will need his help if we reach Brannon." Jak nodded and surrounded Lucus with guardsmen. "I will scout ahead and Rainier will guard the rear."

Slate left the laboratory and ascended two flights of a side stairwell. On the second floor, wizards used the elevated positions of the classrooms as battlements to attack the Bellator Guardsmen in the Ispirtu grounds below. That left the hallways as a strategic thoroughfare. Wizards moved from classroom to classroom to obtain the best vantage point.

Bellator Guardsmen weren't known for stealth, so Slate didn't consider slipping by the wizards unnoticed. The prospect of moving from room to room wasn't very attractive either. It would take too long and force them to clear out every wizard on this floor. Slate was still assessing his options when the scene changed dramatically.

Wizards emerged from the main stairwell halfway down the hallway. They wore Ispirtu robes but moved without the regality that Ispirtu wizards embodied, replaced with an unmistakable fierceness. The rogue wizards entered the classroom nearest the stairwell and the sounds of trained wizards in battle ensued. The flurry of activity ended as quickly as it began, but the commotion drew the attention of the other Ispirtu wizards defending the adjacent classrooms. Ispirtu defenders rallied to the unexpected danger, rushing the classroom door.

With the attention of the Ispirtu wizards drawn by the rogue wizards, Slate ordered, "Stick to the near wall and run as fast as you can." Slate flashed ahead of his team. Explosions emanated from the classroom and Slate silently urged his team to run faster. With that much noise, it would draw every wizard in Ispirtu to this location.

At the main stairwell, footsteps signaled the impending arrival of reinforcements. Slate pushed a statue of some long deceased Ispirtu wizard. With his newfound strength, the stone statue crashed through the stairwell railing and the footsteps below ceased.

Slate looked back to see the Bellator Guardsmen running in formation, surrounding the wizards protectively. Lucus was unable to keep up with the younger legs of his companions, so Jak picked him up and threw him over his shoulder without breaking stride. Rainier kept pace with ease and maintained eyesight on the group's rear.

Happy with the teamwork of the newly formed group, Slate flashed ahead again, sparing a second to look into the classroom where the action took place. Smoke, fireballs, and flying rubble clouded his view, but within the carnage he saw one thing clearly. Beneath the cowls of Ispirtu robes, the blood-red eyes of Furies were unmistakable. They cast spells as quickly as they could form them. One Fury was knocked to the ground by a fireball but managed to unleash a concussion spell before succumbing to the flames. The Ispirtu wizards were unprepared for the attack from the near-death Fury and the spell stunned them. Unable to defend themselves momentarily, the Ispirtu wizards were engulfed in flames a second later.

Furies infested Ispirtu and waged war against Ispirtu wizards. *What did that mean? Had Brannon become aware of the Sicarius headmaster's presence and released the Furies? If the Sicarius headmaster was an Ispirtu wizard, could he be the Blood Mage? The Sicarius headmaster could have released the Furies to create a distraction and an opportunity to reach Brannon. If that was the case, Brannon was the one who was in danger. Either way, they needed to reach his tower to sort through the pieces.*

His team had advanced ahead of his position when three Ispirtu wizards rounded the corner ahead of them, responding to the battle within the classroom. In watching the Furies, Slate left his team without a scout, confirming Villifor's criticism. He couldn't be counted on as part of a team. His stomach clenched in knots, but as it did so, the training of the Bellator Guardsmen came through. Lattimer's wizards launched a series of small, disorienting pressure waves to keep the approaching wizards off-balance. Jak ordered his guardsmen forward and their work was beautiful in its efficiency. With disoriented targets, they closed quickly and struck lethally, taking longer to wipe their blades than they did to kill.

Slate wanted to make amends for his lack of attention to his duties. The hallway ended ahead, giving way to a catwalk that ran between the classrooms and Brannon's tower. Slate had taken it many times as a student, so he flashed ahead. As he did so, he heard Annarelle's voice yell, "No! Look out!"

Slate had time to turn his staff sideways, catching it on the pillars framing the catwalk entrance. Stopping his momentum at that speed jarred his shoulders, but it was worth it as his feet fell through the catwalk surface and he hung above the ground. The orbs danced around his body, making it appear to the whole world that he had been poured into the concrete of the catwalk, with his legs dangling in the air. He stared down at the battle raging below him. Soldiers and guardsmen threw themselves into battle to retake the broken Ispirtu wall while absorbing massive damage from the wizards. Beyond the scrum, Slate identified the King's standard. Villifor and Magnus accompanied Darik, waiting for the soldiers to fulfill their duty and capture the Ispirtu wall. The distraction caused by the Furies inside Ispirtu was just enough to turn the tide in the King's favor. Soldiers overran the Ispirtu defenses and stone canopies were hoisted above the heads of Darik, Villifor, Magnus and the rest of the King's honor guard as they entered the Ispirtu grounds. Brannon stopped casting fireballs from his tower as the King walked through, either conserving his energy or acknowledging that the battle for Ispirtu's walls was lost. The King and Villifor would be right on Slate's heels. That was perfect, as long as he managed to stay ahead of them.

Annarelle and Tommy sprinted over to help him up. "Brannon switched the pathways when he heard that Ispirtu would be attacked. The paths you used to know don't work anymore."

Slate looked up and counted dozens of potential pathways to Brannon's tower. It was a very clever tactic. Brannon could sit in his tower and defend the few entry points that only his men knew. Slate was starting to hate clever people. The look on his face must have given away his thoughts because it made Tommy and Annarelle smile.

"Don't worry, Slate. I've been taught to always know my surroundings. The second I learned that the orbs had shifted and the pathways changed, I searched through them to find the new ones."

Pride crept into Annarelle's voice, and deservedly so. "Of course, I would have been caught if it weren't for Tommy."

"There were a couple first-years that saw Annarelle snooping around. I caught them before they left and made sure they didn't feel the need to tell anyone about it."

"You've both done well…thank you. Annarelle, will you join me in front and point us in the right direction."

"I was going to offer earlier, but I thought there would be time for me to tell you about the orbs. Your speed surprised me…"

The explosions from the classroom stopped, meaning their distraction had also ended. There wasn't time for an explanation to Tommy and Annarelle. Annarelle pointed toward a bridge one floor up from their current location. "That's the one we need to traverse." The wooden bridge looked unsteady compared to the ornately carved stone bridges surrounding it. It would also catch fire much easier if Brannon decided to terminate the entrance. They couldn't be seen walking on that bridge.

"Find a window beneath the bridge on this floor." They sprinted ahead with the team following them. Just as the last group of guardsmen rounded the corner, four wizards emerged from the remains of the classroom. Rainier, checking the group's rear, met the Fury's red-eyes and his face went white. Slate and Rainier rushed to rejoin their friends before the Furies could attack, with the full knowledge that they would give chase. Slate also heard the heavier footsteps of Villifor's men in the main hallway beneath them. If he could evade the Furies' attention long enough, they would soon be occupied.

Annarelle found that the window beneath the wooden bridge belonged to a small bathroom. Slate urged the group inside and shut the door. The Furies couldn't have seen where they hid, but their safety was tenuous.

Slate pushed his way toward the window, pressing flesh against everyone packed into the tiny bathroom. He opened the window and looked up to examine the trusses supporting the wooden bridge beneath its walkway. The crossbeams of the trusses were close enough together to swing across, but Slate doubted if the Ispirtu wizards could accomplish the task. This was the type of thing children in Pillar did for fun, but never three stories in the air with someone threatening to shoot a fireball from above if you were seen. Across the bridge was another window, but it was a full five feet below the trusses. That wouldn't do. He called to Jak and Lattimer and filled them in on his plan.

"I need to cross first, and we were spotted in the main hallway. If anything comes through that door, I need the two of you to organize a defense." Slate paused, trying to figure out the best way of telling them what they'd be fighting. In the end he settled on, "Whoever comes through that door, use killing blows. Do not hold anything back until they are decapitated or your sword goes through their heart. Do you understand?"

Their grave nods convinced Slate that he had sufficiently communicated the gravity of the situation. Jak spoke next. "My guardsmen will help those across that can't make it on their own. Lattimer, will you stay with me on this side until everyone else makes it across. You are the strongest wizard and it sounds like we'll need it."

Lattimer showed the fortitude that often remained hidden beneath the entitlement he wore as a cloak. "I'll stay here...let's get these people across this bridge."

Slate slid through the window and grabbed the truss above him. He quickly swung from one crossbeam to the next, spanning the distance with ease. Upon reaching the other side, he held onto one rung with his left hand and punched the wall with his right, breaking into the smooth stone wall. Creating handholds was a purpose in which his stonehand excelled. He then dropped down to the handhold and punched a new one, sculpting a rough ladder into the wall. Slate kicked through the closed window and looked around the empty room. Two wizards mistakenly came to investigate the sound of the broken glass. Slate flashed and extended his staff through the opening door to find the throat of one wizard. The second wizard started concentrating, but Slate used his stonehand for the other purpose in which it excelled. Neither wizard had the chance to make a sound. He dragged the bodies into the room and returned to the window.

His team slowly worked their way across the network of trusses, with the Ispirtu wizards clung to the backs of the Bellator Guardsmen. Slate wished he could capture the looks of embarrassment written on the faces of the proud group of wizards.

The shattering of glass coincided with a particularly large guardsman squeezing through the small bathroom window. The noise was loud enough to draw the attention of the Furies and Tommy,

Annarelle, Rainier, Jak, and Lattimer were still stuck in the bathroom.

He watched helplessly as the group took up defensive positions, with Lattimer in the lead. The door opened and Lattimer unleashed a well-timed concussion wave, sending four Furies flying backwards. ...*1* Jak was the first one through the door, his broadsword severing red-eyes from body. Rainier was just as quick and plunged his short swords into the chest and neck of a second Fury. Tommy had enough experience patrolling the halls of Ispirtu to know where to stick a knife, and he did so without hesitation. Annarelle rushed forward to get the last Fury, but her forte was not battle and the Fury threw her to the ground. ...*2* A fireball started to form in the Fury's hand as he stood over Annarelle. Jak and Rainier were too far away to help. Tommy dove toward the Fury, but he wouldn't make it in time. He would miss her by a swords length. Slate's heart dropped. He knew what the outcome would be and he felt responsibility for it. ...*3* Tommy erupted in flames that emitted in all directions from his body. It was a weak spell by wizard's standards, with the flames only reaching a sword's length, but the intensity was sufficient to char the Fury where he stood. Tommy prepared the spell in anticipation of the battle and released it at the perfect distance to engulf the Fury while leaving Annarelle untouched. Slate dropped to his knees in relief. Tommy and Annarelle embraced, but it was cut short by more approaching footsteps...Villifor and Darik had arrived.

Jak, Lattimer, Rainier, Tommy, and Annarelle crossed the network of trusses with urgency, joining Slate and the rest of the team in Brannon's tower. "Brannon's office is at the top of this tower with a guild's worth of Ispirtu wizards stationed between here and there. We can either fight our way through or let someone else do it for us..." Slate smiled and the rest of the team caught on to his next plan. "Jak, leave one of your guardsman behind and show Villifor and Darik how to cross the bridge when they investigate the dead Furies?"

"Of course, Slate."

"Annarelle, can you lead the group up one flight of stairs and wait for me? Stay hidden and I'll meet up with you after I check on something..."

Concern crept across Rainier's face at the ambiguous nature of Slate's request, but he held his questions. Annarelle didn't know him well enough to decipher when he was up to trouble. "We'll meet you in the alcove next to the back stairwell in five minutes."

Slate ascended the nearest stairs, counting on his Ispirtu robes and Sicarius mask to let him pass by any Ispirtu wizards. He second-guessed that decision when he found a host of wizards attentively watching the wooden bridge and lying in wait for any intruders. Slate's pulse rose, but no one paid attention to him as he filtered through the wizards and headed for the uncovered bridge, waiting for someone to shout or send a pressure wave at his back. Slate forced a deep breath and walked onto the bridge when snow began to fall from the clouds overhead. Beneath his feet, a faint rhythmic sound indicated Villifor and Darik's men were following his plan, unnoticed by Brannon and the wizards watching the bridge. Finally, Slate reached the end of the bridge and knelt down, which is where he saw what he needed to see. Slate's luck was with him, had he arrived even a few minutes later, the descending snow would have hidden what he had come to find. A fine powder coated the bridge indicating the Sicarius headmaster had passed this point, so the headmaster wasn't informed of the new pathway to Brannon's tower and needed to find it. At least he knew Brannon hadn't met the Sicarius headmaster as a co-conspirator and that the two headmasters lay in wait together. He thought he could still trust the Sicarius headmaster...at least as much as he could trust anyone.

Slate stood to re-cross the bridge knowing that Brannon's tower was filling with Bellator Guardsmen and Darik's soldiers with every passing second. Halfway across the bridge, a Bellator Guardsman saw his Ispirtu robes and rushed after battlefield glory in the form of a lifeless wizard. Knowing the number of wizards guarding the bridge, Slate dropped to his stomach. A wave of spells passed over his head, slamming the guardsman backward and throwing his burning body from the bridge. Slate stood back up, thankful to still be alive, when he noticed the wave of spells had blown several planks off the wooden bridge, exposing the once hidden soldiers hanging from the trusses below. Slate gave up his cover and dove at the exposed gap, swinging from the truss below and launching himself into the broken window of Brannon's tower just as a massive fireball from Brannon decimated the wooden structure.

Slate didn't look back to assess the damage. He rolled as he hit the ground and flashed in the direction of the door before anyone knew what was happening. He was out of the room and ascending the back stairwell before the assembling soldiers could give chase. Even if they had given chase, they would be engaging the wizards descending from the floor above in short order. Slate found his team hidden in the vacant alcove chosen by Annarelle.

"It is good to see you, Slate. When that many wizards cast spells at once it usually means disaster for someone. I'm glad it wasn't you." Lucus remained calm and collected despite the day's activities.

"I always said you had a knack for surviving…" Jak smiled widely.

"You've alerted the wizards within the tower to our presence. I hope you found information that was worth it…" Rainier was less forgiving than Jak.

"The Sicarius headmaster is still ahead of us somewhere within Brannon's tower. An unfortunate set of circumstances led to the bridge's demise and only a small group of soldiers and guardsmen made it across." Thankfully, he did see Villifor and Darik as he flashed through the room. Magnus was also present, strategizing with Hedok and Cirata. Slate felt fortunate Magnus was preoccupied upon his arrival. Even if his arm had been healed, he didn't think Magnus would forget their previous encounter. "A large contingent of wizards will engage them soon. Jak, do you think we should aid the guardsmen?"

Lattimer spoke up first. "Why would we help them? We should head for my father's office while the path is clear."

Jak understood that Slate needed Villifor and Darik to force Brannon's hand and learn the truth. "Those are the best fighters Bellator has to offer, but they'll be pinned down in that room. I'd give even odds on the outcome. We should attack and retreat so they are forced to defend their rear guard. That should open things up for the guardsmen."

"Rainier, we are especially suited for this job. Let's go down the back stairwell and silently take out a few wizards. Lattimer, can you and your men arrange a diversion when the cries go up?"

"We'll launch a volley from the main staircase. A concussion wave or two aimed at the railing should cause it to crash below and slow any wizards who give chase."

Jak liked the strategy. "Guardsmen, find any statues or other objects that can be pushed down the stairwell. Whoever grabs the smallest one has to buy the first round of beer after this is done."

Rainier and Slate slipped down the back stairwell and Slate

entrusted him with the Sicarius mask. "Kill silently. I'll do my best to remain hidden, but if I get discovered, it will be easier for me to flee."

"A good student wouldn't let his teacher put himself in harm's way for his own sake...but you're not my teacher anymore, so I'm ok with saving my own skin." Rainier winked at him and put on the mask. He then slipped into the battle, killing any wizard that made the mistake of disengaging too far from the others. Slate was once again happy that he could call Rainier a friend. He was disturbingly good at what he did.

Slate borrowed Jak's strategy to create a distraction. Using his newfound strength and speed, he hurled statues amongst the wizards and then flashed away. He caused an impressive amount of damage before the wizards caught on and began defending their rear.

The shouts signaled Lattimer and his wizards to launch a volley. Fireballs and concussion waves landed amongst the wizards as they tried to form a defense against Slate and Rainier. Half the wizards, having identified an opponent, began to cast spells up toward the main stairs. Some rushed to get better tactical position, only to be met by a series of statues raining down on them from above. The remaining Ispirtu wizards were already engaged with the Bellator Guardsmen inside the room, but Slate could see it was only a matter of time before the guardsmen pushed through.

He signaled Rainier and they ascended the main stairs to rejoin the group.

"What now?" Tommy asked.

"Everyone except for Rainier, Lucus, and me will finish off the wizards down there and join the ranks of Villifor's men. Jak, it is up to you to convince Darik and Villifor of Lattimer's allegiance to them. "

"After what we just did for Villifor's men, it shouldn't be a problem. What will you do?"

"Villifor will not trust me after I've freed the Sicarius headmaster during the guild's termination. We'll follow from a safe distance and stay out of sight. Once you get to Brannon's office, we have one final trick up our sleeves. Just stay flexible and bend where the wind takes you." Slate didn't have any more inspiring words or answers to give the group. He didn't know what to expect when they encountered Brannon.

"I've always preferred strength to flexibility, but we'll do our best." Jak's light-hearted reference to his own physique was a good sign. People performed better when they were loose. The guardsmen chuckled and left with Lattimer's wizards to finish the battle below.

Slate addressed Lucus and Rainier. "Ravinai forced us to flee in fear on my first visit. Now we face the dangers of Ravinai head on. Lucus, how long can you hold that spell that makes us invisible?"

"That spell doesn't make you invisible. It just camouflages you amidst your surroundings." Slate acknowledged his poor description of the spell and Lucus skipped the lecture. "Ten minutes, less if I cast the spell on myself, and I'll be incapacitated while I hold the spell."

"That will have to do. We'll stay out of sight and allow Villifor and Darik to pass us and then follow closely. When we get within sight of Brannon's office, cast the spell. We need to make it into his office unseen, so prepare to sneak in when the guardsmen break down the door."

Rainier added, "In Pillar, Sana cast a spell that made our feet silent by growing moss on our boots. Could we do that now to mask the noise from our footsteps?"

Lucus answered with obvious pride in his apprentice. "Sana cast that spell? That is one of my favorites. I use it in the woods to get closer to the animals I am studying. I know it well and it would take little effort to maintain the effects due to my familiarity with it."

The woodsman held his axe and concentrated. ...*1*...*2* Lucus opened his eyes and Slate took a few trial steps, producing no sound. Slate was thankful Rainier remembered it. "Let's hide in Annarelle's alcove."

The sounds of battle diminished below and a scout team ascended the stairs. Darik and Villifor followed shortly behind in a group that contained Magnus, Hedok, Cirata Lorassa, and now Jak. Lattimer led his group of wizards, but they had been spread out amongst the guardsmen to employ the same strategy Jak had previously utilized. Slate, Lucus, and Rainier followed up the main staircase to Brannon's office after the rear scout had passed by.

Along the way, one or two small skirmishes broke out, but they were over quickly. This was a group very skilled in their profession and they ascended the remaining floors of Brannon's tower with expedience. Slate expected a battle to begin, so the silence upon their arrival concerned him. Unable to see what was transpiring, Slate made his play. "If you would be so kind, Lucus…"

The wizard knelt and concentrated. ...*1*...*2*...*3*...*4* Lucus and Rainier disappeared. Slate looked down at his arm and saw the floor beneath it. Reaching out and feeling with his hands, Slate located the incapacitated woodsman crumpled on the stairs. He picked Lucus up and slung him over his shoulder. "I have Lucus. Let's get inside Brannon's office unnoticed."

Slate ran up the stairs with silent feet, bumping into Rainier occasionally since neither really knew where the other was at any given time. They passed the rear scout and reached the top floor of Brannon's tower, where an unexpected scene lay before them. The massive catalpa doors to Brannon's office opened invitingly. The soldiers and Bellator Guardsmen spread out along the walls of the office. Inside Brannon waited with smug confidence, scepter in hand, glowing brightly. At his side was the Sicarius headmaster. Slate's stomach knotted in disgust at the betrayal of someone he had fully trusted.

"Brannon Regallo, you are accused of being a traitor to the crown and orchestrating the attacks plaguing Malethya. There can be only one resolution for such maleficence." King Darik spoke with all the authority of his position.

Brannon responded with the confidence of the most powerful wizard in the kingdom. "Don't speak to me as if I am a child. I have proven my loyalty to you in the Twice-Broken Wars and in all my actions since. Tell me, who is my accuser?" Brannon didn't wait for a response. "Is it Villifor? He is admittedly a traitor, having fought against you in the Civil War and then doubling his sins by sacrificing his fellow rebels to save his own neck. He has perpetuated the lie ever since the day he assumed the identity of Villifor."

Slate snuck into the office and hid Lucus beneath Brannon's monstrosity of a desk. Rainier's location was lost to Slate.

King Darik responded, "Villifor prevented widespread panic amongst my citizens by concealing the attacks in the north until evidence was obtained. You hid in your tower. Now the evidence points toward you and you stand next to someone who defied my direct orders earlier today."

The Sicarius headmaster spoke, having an unsettling effect on everyone present. "Your direct orders resulted in the deaths of loyal servants who had given their very identities to serve you, so yes, I defied you. You are acting irrationally. Let us get to the bottom of this."

Villifor continued the accusations. "Then let's start with the Regallo estate. You and your co-conspirator, Slate Severance, killed or wounded a number of my Bellator Guardsmen to enter and burn the estate to the ground. What evidence were you hiding from me?" Slate didn't think the headmaster would honor Villifor's request, but Darik waited for an answer.

"I broke into Brannon's personal library and found texts and manuscripts on Blood Magic. I came and talked to Brannon as you are doing now and am convinced he was set up to appear to be the Blood Mage."

Slate's head was spinning, but he knew this would happen. He just needed to bide his time and gather information. Hopefully everything would come to a head while Lucus' spell was still in effect. Thankfully, King Darik's notoriously short patience worked to Slate's advantage in this instance.

Darik addressed Brannon. "I broke down Ispirtu's walls because of a piece of fabric. Now I learn that your personal library contains Blood Magic documents and your only ally spent enough time alone with you to have been subjugated. I have also received testimony from your own son confirming your association with the Blood Magic documents in your library." Brannon registered Lattimer's presence with a mixture of confusion and anger. Darik didn't wait for the Regallo family to settle their differences. He pointed to the Sicarius headmaster and Brannon. "Kill them and their loyalists."

"Wait!" Brannon pleaded, but the bloodbath began when Magnus carried out the King's orders with eager anticipation, sending his battle axe through the midsections of two nearby wizards. Their deaths ignited a full battle within the confines of Brannon's office.

The Sicarius headmaster launched darts at the necks of the attacking guardsmen, never leaving Brannon's side. That was the safest place in the entire office, as Brannon launched concussive waves that cleared the entire area around him and prevented anyone from coming within striking distance. The Ispirtu wizards outside of Brannon's care fought fiercely but were overwhelmed by the Bellator Guardsmen. Jak carved through wizards with a cold efficiency bred from training while Magnus, Hedok and Cirata displayed a deadly joy for the task at hand. Lattimer's wizards launched volleys of fireballs and concussive waves at Brannon, but they dissipated before reaching him or the Sicarius headmaster. Despite Brannon's teaching that denied the usefulness of defensive magic, he was an expert at its usage. No spells reached him as his scepter grew brighter and flashed with each spell he cast.

Slate still hadn't joined the fray. He was torn between his distrust of Villifor and his former trust of the Sicarius headmaster. Watching the battle unfold from within Brannon's sphere of safety, he started to believe Brannon had told the truth. He was using non-lethal spells to keep the soldiers away from him and he hadn't attacked Darik.

The eyes of the wizards surrounding the office turned red. Any constraint they had displayed in battle left immediately. Wizards who were about to be overwhelmed used every last bit of their energy and converted it to spark. The effects were devastating. One of the wizards turned into the equivalent of an exploding orb, blasting the guardsmen around him at the expense of his life. Brannon cast a concussive wave just as the wizard exploded, funneling the expanding explosion upwards and ripping the roof away in the process. Brannon remained safely in the middle of the room, protected from everything but the snow that descended upon them. He appeared unfazed by the death of one of his wizards or the carnage the wizard had caused in his passing.

Brannon's lack of emotion at the carnage disturbed Slate. Brannon was too powerful to be taken by the guardsmen, but he didn't attack the Ispirtu Furies either. Slate knew one thing for certain. Furies had killed his parents. Furies were under the control of the Blood Mage. If Brannon wasn't attacking the Furies, then he controlled them.

Suddenly Slate saw Rainier appear across the room, his short swords buried in a Fury. He looked down and saw his hand appear before his eyes. He was out of time! Having made up his mind regarding Brannon he jumped toward him while reaching for his staff. The Sicarius headmaster saw Slate appear and launched into the air to intercept him. The headmaster collided with Slate, deflecting his killing blow from Brannon. Slate changed targets to the arm that held the scepter. Slate barely touched Brannon's outstretched wrist, but with the strength provided by Lattimer's experiment, the force was enough to shatter the bones. The scepter crashed to the ground.

Slate landed and moved with uncanny speed to pin the Sicarius headmaster's arms and prevent the headmaster from reaching any hidden darts or knives. Without the scepter, Brannon's spells formed more slowly and grew defensive, casting only weak concussive waves toward Lattimer's wizards to disorient them long enough to retrieve the scepter. Brannon bent down with his good hand to grab the fallen scepter. In that moment, Lattimer stepped forward and formed a fireball twice his size. The heat radiated in Slate's face like a blast furnace.

Slate, still holding the Sicarius headmaster, jumped to safety behind Brannon's desk. Lattimer released the fireball, but instead of dissipating like all the others, it found its mark. The strength of Brannon's defensive spells had come from his scepter, and without it he was overwhelmed. The most powerful wizard in the kingdom and the first Blood Mage in centuries, was immolated where he stood, killed by his own son.

ORDER IS RESTORED

With the death of Brannon, the red eyes disappeared from the Ispirtu wizards and their relentless casting of spells ceased. Guardsmen detained the fatigued wizards without further bloodshed, aided by their disorientation as the spell ceased and their minds reeled from the return of their senses. The Sicarius headmaster slumped in Slate's arms, but he knew enough of the dangers regarding the headmaster to relax his grip. Villifor pointed toward him. "Detain the Sicarius headmaster and Slate Severance."

Darik trumped Villifor's command. "Detain the headmaster. Slate, come here."

Magnus took the headmaster from Slate rather forcefully. He was eager to make amends for the headmaster's earlier escape. Cirata Lorassa encouraged compliance by holding a knife against the headmaster's throat.

Slate followed the King's orders but took time to help Lucus rise from beneath Brannon's desk. Through tired eyes, Lucus scanned the room and took in all the information he missed while incapacitated. His eyes lingered longest on the detained Sicarius headmaster, Lattimer, and curiously, Brannon's scepter.

Slate approached the King and knelt before him as the Sicarius headmaster had earlier that day, hoping the show of respect would inspire leniency for his crimes. "King Darik, I am at your service."

"I know you are, Slate. Stand up." The King let his hand fall on Slate's shoulder. "Your actions here today absolve you of the misdeeds you naively participated in at Sicarius. Brannon is brought to justice because of your intervention. Your crimes are pardoned if you pledge to serve the crown and the people of Malethya." Slate sighed in relief. He preferred a lifetime of serving the King to a lifetime in prison or a life cut short.

As Slate pledged his service to the king, Lucus bent near Brannon's body and touched his axe to the still-glowing scepter. The axe grew brighter and brighter, rejuvenating Lucus in the process. The color returned to the kindly woodcutter's face and he rose, glowing axe and scepter in hand.

Darik turned to Lattimer. "Lattimer Regallo. No son should be forced to face his father in battle. By doing so, you proved your loyalty to me. Your father served me faithfully for many years. Will you continue your training in Ispirtu and do the same?"

Lattimer answered with the innate authority of a Regallo. "I am humbled and honored to serve Malethya."

Lucus joined the group, despite his lack of invitation from Darik. He held the scepter outward. "Lattimer, this scepter should pass to you. Brannon was once my dear friend, and he spoke of the responsibility required to wield such an enchanted scepter. Regallos have wielded the weapon for generations, with the admirable goal of protecting and serving the citizens of Malethya. I hope you will carry on these missions."

Lattimer turned toward Lucus and bowed his head in reverence. "Thank you, Lucus. I'm only sorry that my father didn't use the scepter properly." He reached out and took hold of the scepter, the glow flickering back and forth as Lattimer learned how to use it. Afterward he turned toward Darik.

"My father had the responsibility of keeping your kingdom safe. Instead he obsessed over the fact that magic is fading in Malethya. You saw the evidence that magic is fading as you broke through Ispirtu's walls and reached my father in his tallest tower. That wouldn't have been possible even a generation ago." Lattimer walked amongst the dead soldiers and Ispirtu defenders as he talked. He reached the group of guardsmen who fought with Magnus. "While credit should be given to the level of training and skill of the Bellator Guardsmen"—Lattimer clasped Hedok on the shoulder and greeted the members of his team— "it should also be seen as a failure of my father to provide the defense that the kingdom needs. Brannon tried to hide this failure by shrouding Ispirtu in secrecy. King Darik, I promise to protect the people of Malethya."

Lattimer lifted the scepter and the orb swirled with blood.

The soldiers under Hedok's command fanned out to protect Lattimer. All of Lattimer's sycophants, the people Slate led into Brannon's office, joined their Blood Mage at his side. Slate grabbed the

King and flashed toward Jak, whose soldiers surrounded Slate and the King. Lucus, Rainier, Tommy, Annarelle, and surprisingly, Villifor, took up positions around Darik. The Sicarius headmaster struggled against Magnus despite the placement of Cirata's knife but without success.

Lattimer's voice rose. "I will protect the people of Malethya and bring power back to Ispirtu. The Disenites will come back to Malethya even stronger than when they left. We must be prepared. There is a near limitless source of power that can defend the kingdom upon their return. Without my father to stand in the way, I will defend our shores and bring back the Golden Ages of Cantor."

Rainier spoke with condemnation. "Blood Magic corrupted the most righteous of men of Cantor's day. Your twisted intentions will bring nothing but destruction."

"Malethya is no place for someone to hold ideals. We do what must be done and leave it to the past. I don't expect a tribesman to understand." Lattimer cast a concussive wave that threw Rainier into an office wall and left him unconscious in a crumpled heap on the floor. Slate tensed in anger but held his position. Lattimer was protected by too many wizards and Bellator Guardsmen.

"Slate, you should understand the necessity of what I've done. You have experienced the power of spark-based magic." Slate's mind reeled. *What was he talking about?* "I cast the spell that created your stonehand." *Why would Lattimer cast a spell that would lead to his defeat in the tournament?* "Spark-based magic saved your life in Primean's laboratory and lets you dart around a room almost as fast as a ball of wizard's fire can fly. People like Rainier believe spark-based magic is inherently evil, but do you feel different now that you have these abilities?"

"You didn't want to help me in the tournament…something went wrong…"

"That is true. I trained to be the tournament champion since the day I fully understood the failures of my father. He blindfolded me and sent me to Ibson for teaching in some fractal-forsaken corner of the kingdom. Ibson forced me to sleep outside some tiny shanty in the woods. The only good thing about that fractal-forsaken place was the old texts that mentioned spark-based magic, or as you so crudely call it Blood Magic. When Ibson discovered my interest in the subject, he dismissed me from training. He put me to sleep and I awoke in my bed in Ravinai with all my possessions...and a few of Ibson's. He didn't find the texts on spark-based magic I had stowed away in my travel bag. After studying the texts intently, I hid them in my father's private library. He never noticed because he locked himself in this tower to determine why magic was fading in Malethya. His neglect of our family alienated my mother and drove my sister Rose away. For me to correct his failures to my family and Malethya, I needed to escape his oversight and my inevitable training in Ispirtu. The tournament granted me that opportunity because the tournament champion chooses his guild. It was my only chance to gain independence. In the tournament, I cast a spark-based spell to push the iron in your blood toward your extremities. Without the needed mineral circulating in your blood, you experienced extreme fatigue. Your Perceptor abilities altered the spell to draw the iron from your blood and the medallion on your arm into your hand where it fused with your bones. Your alteration of the spell drew more spark from me than I anticipated and I was left defenseless to your punch."

Slate finally understood how his stonehand had formed, but that didn't reverse the damage caused by Lattimer's plans. "What about the people you turned into mindless Furies? What about the people of Pillar, Primean, and all the soldiers and wizards who died here today? I would gladly give up the abilities I have gained to bring back those people."

"Those are the costs necessary to bring forth a new Golden Age to the kingdom. With my father deposed, spark-based spells will usher in a new era of powerful magic where all citizens are cared for and don't need to fear ships coming to port. You just pledged your life to the service of Malethya. Will you protect them from our enemies? Will you help me rid its people of poverty, hunger, and need? With my father's scepter, I can accomplish all of that and more..."

"Sacrifices for the greater good need to be given freely...they are not to be taken, young Regallo." Lucus spoke respectfully, but anger flashed on Lattimer's face.

Slate didn't have to think too hard to find an answer. "I will not perpetuate your schemes. I will stop you, Lattimer, even if I have to kill you."

Lattimer grimaced. "I wanted your services to be employed of your own free will as Lucus suggested, but I will have it either way. Do you remember Primean's laboratory? I arrived early for our punishment and *compelled* Primean with the desire to inflict extra pain on you for attacking me in class. Then you suggested the blood staunching experiment and the effects were profound. I hung from the hook next to you and watched your body get cut open in ways a butcher couldn't imagine, and yet you lived. The more wounds you received, the more spark you drew from Primean. The old wizard drained of life as you saved your own. Even after his desire to end the spell was greater than the compulsion I provided, he couldn't stop. You wouldn't let him— you drew the spark from him and held it inside. It was the most beautiful thing I have ever witnessed. That was when I knew there was something special about you, Slate. I could have killed you, but instead I gathered some blood from your lacerated body."

Lattimer retrieved a small vial of blood hidden in his robes and poured a drop onto the glowing orb of the scepter. Slate instantly felt attacked and dropped to his knees, clutching his head. "I hate the term Blood Magic, but there is some truth to the term. The mind is very complex and even spark-based magic has difficulty subjugating the strong-minded. People think the term Blood Mages came from the destruction caused by the warring of the spark-based mages. That isn't entirely true. Blood can serve as a medium to subjugate the uncooperative and control minds without consent. It maintains the integrity of the mind without burning it out like the mindless Furies."

"You will never get away with this, Lattimer!" King Darik broke through the monologue. "My troops surround Ispirtu. Our numbers will overcome your treasonous plans."

"Am I the one who is outnumbered?" The scepter flashed and the eyes of the Bellator Guardsmen and Ispirtu wizards in the room turned red, with the exception of the small group protecting the King. The eyes returned to normal at Lattimer's command. "My father placed too great an importance on the strength of spells. Ispirtu wizards were willing to try anything to gain strength and improve their standing within the house. Once a few wizards saw the benefit, more wizards sought my services. The Bellator Guardsmen were more difficult to convince, but after Magnus became my first willing subjugate, recruitment rose dramatically. I met Magnus while training for the tournament. He fought in underground duels for the amusement of the rich. I freed him from captivity and he trained me as a fighter. Magnus has been instrumental in gaining the support of other guardsmen unhappy to serve a pompous blowhard like Villifor. These individuals are the first to join what will become the most powerful military force ever seen. Magnus will be one of my generals. Slate will be the other. His unique Perceptor abilities have allowed him to hold on to the effects of spark-based spells, although it drains the life of the spellcaster in the process. I sacrificed several loyal subjugates from Ispirtu during testing and another in the most recent round of experiments on Slate. He came away with the ability to run fast and jump high, but the subjugate hidden in Primean's lab was not so fortunate. I controlled the flow of water in the tank while the subjugate was drained of life behind the curtain, never seeing the benefits of his work."

Slate heard the conversations going on around him, but the words floated into his head without meaning. *Something* was attacking his mind. It slowly seeped into his head and took hold of his thoughts, his fears, his being. Slate pushed back…

"Furies are useful, but once created their usefulness is rather singular since the brain needs to be burned out. I solved that problem by creating warriors who can think for themselves and strategize, but maintain the benefits of Furies during battle." Lattimer smiled to Darik. "You have been very helpful in coordinating the formation of my army. By eliminating Sicarius and bringing the Bellator Guardsmen into Ispirtu, you have gathered everyone in one place. By the morning, all of your soldiers will be converted."

At the mention of the events at Sicarius, the headmaster struggled again, but was unable to free himself from Magnus' grasp. Lattimer turned toward the headmaster. "Don't worry, I haven't forgotten about you either. You will be subjugated just as Slate is, tasked with the creation of a new Sicarius…"

Lattimer was interrupted again by Darik, who had heard enough. "I will not stand idly by and watch you take my kingdom from me. Attack!" Lattimer raised his scepter and said casually, "Protect me. Do not kill them…yet." Red eyes reappeared and guardsmen threw themselves in harm's way to protect Lattimer. Darik's men were unable to push through the defense.

Slate stood despite the war waging in his head. An intense pressure threatened to burst within his skull, but Slate felt the urge to sieze King Darik and bring him to Hedok. It wouldn't be difficult. Darik engaged Lattimer's forces ahead of him. He knew if he did this, the pressure in his head would decrease, but he couldn't remember why. Slate flashed forward and grabbed the King. Before anyone could react, he jumped over Lattimer's men with Darik in his arms and delivered the king to Hedok. "No!" Lucus shouted. The pressure in Slate's head decreased dramatically when he complied with the command to capture the king, and it was replaced by a soothing feeling. *Maybe if he listened to what the voice said, the pressure would stop?* He knelt and held his head.

Hedok captured King Darik, and with the help of a few guardsmen, disarmed and constrained him. "It appears Slate is starting to see the error of his ways. Thank you, Slate." Lattimer passed a hand over Slate and a gratifying wave of calmness washed over him. When he left, the pressure began to build again. *Why was he fighting it?* "In a few more moments, he will do anything I ask of him...and so will the King." Hedok cut Darik's forearm and Lattimer touched the orb of his scepter to the bleeding wound.

Darik knelt to the ground and stood up again after only a few seconds. "I do as you command, Lattimer."

"You will continue as King but will accept any future commands I give you. You will listen to my counsel absolutely and defer large decisions to me. Finally, you will proclaim my father was the Blood Mage. Tell the citizens of Malethya that the assault on Ispirtu is successful and that my efforts were paramount in the elimination of the threat. My heroics warranted that you entrust to me command of the Ispirtu forces. Do you understand?"

"I understand. Why would I tell them anything else?" The question was asked without sarcasm. It was the only truth he knew.

Jak yelled to his troops. "Darik is lost. Push through to save Slate." Slate knew he needed help, but he wasn't sure how his friend was going to relieve this pressure inside his head. Even his eyes began to hurt. *Why did his eyes hurt so badly?* That seemed like a bad sign, but Slate couldn't comprehend why...

Lattimer looked down toward Slate, kneeling next to Hedok. "Slate's Perceptor abilities are helping him to delay the Blood Magic's effects. That's ok...it's just a matter of time before he gives up fighting."

Finally, he turned his attention back to the Sicarius headmaster. "I don't expect to obtain your help, headmaster. You have already proven that by siding with my father. Instead, I intend to offer you a trade. If you voluntarily offer your services to me and allow me to subjugate you, I won't kill your friends."

The alternating voice of the headmaster came out with extra venom. "You know nothing of leadership and you know nothing of me if you think threats will sway me."

"We shall see. Cirata, please restrain the headmaster." Magnus transferred the Sicarius headmaster into the control of Cirata and awaited orders from Lattimer. "Magnus, you have been a very loyal friend. You taught me to fight and have carried out my orders perfectly, if a little aggressively. Since you voluntarily subjugated yourself to me, I will ask you first. Would you like to attack Slate's companions as a Fury?"

An evil and joyful smile spread across Magnus lips. "Slate was the first person to ever defeat me in battle, and he humiliated me in the process. I am thankful you allowed me to lead a group of Furies into that fractal-forsaken town of Pillar to gain retribution for my defeat. My broadsword felt the warmth of his father's stomach and I finally felt vindicated. The notches on that broadsword symbolized my survival in the fighting clubs of Ravinai. Slate created an enemy for life when he destroyed it. I would have killed him in Minot if you hadn't given me strict orders to the contrary. If I can't kill Slate, I will gladly kill his friends." The words floated into Slate's head, but he couldn't understand why Lattimer would send anyone to hurt his parents. *Lattimer was the person who eased his pain, the one who sent soothing waves to relieve the pressure. Could Lattimer relieve the pain behind his eyes?* Everything started to look red…

Lattimer held aloft his father's scepter and Magnus turned into a Fury. He raised his battle axe in a roar and rushed forward. Jak positioned his guardsmen perfectly to sustain a charge, but Magnus was too strong. His huge battle axe reached past the defenses of the guardsmen and kept Jak's men at a distance too great to counterattack. They slowly retreated with each swing of Magnus' axe.

"Resolve is one of my favorite traits, headmaster…I always enjoy watching it wither away." He walked over to the Sicarius headmaster, who stood motionless. Even with the Sicarius mask on, Slate could read the expression beneath the mask. The headmaster was concentrating. That seemed like an odd thing to be doing. *Did the headmaster's head hurt like his?*

Cirata held the knife against the headmaster's throat as Lattimer reached up and peeled off the Sicarius mask. His face froze in disbelief. "Rose," he whispered. Slate beheld the woman he'd known as Sana. Immediately, Sana released her spell, casting a small electrical spark that reached into the bodies of Cirata and Lattimer. They fell to the ground as she yelled, "Now, Lucus!!!"

The subjugated guardsmen and wizards tasked with protecting Lattimer rushed to his defense. The guardsmen took up position between Lattimer and Sana, preventing her from finishing the job of killing Lattimer or grabbing the scepter. The wizards prepared spells, but Sana incapacitated them with a flurry of darts from her robes. She ran to Slate, grabbing him from his knees. *Didn't she understand she knocked out the only person that could help him?* It inspired a deep anger in him, but Slate fought it. Something within him didn't want to hurt Sana.

Across the room, Magnus continued slicing through Jak's guardsmen. Slate felt a distant sorrow for them, but he didn't have any desire to act. He just wanted the pain to go away. His red-hued vision was drawn to a curious sight. Behind Jak's soldiers, near the unconscious body of Rainier, Lucus began a slow dance that moved his glowing axe in a circular motion. Somewhere in Slate's muddled mind, the memory of a catalpa grove surfaced. Slate couldn't make sense of it, but he couldn't stop watching either, feeling it was important. The woodsman and his axe swirled in larger and faster patterns. Snow hit Slate in the face, swirling around the circular room coincident with the motions of Lucus.

Magnus cleaved through the final guardsman under Jak's command, and Villifor stood before him, facing him head-on. Tommy and Annarelle cast small spells that would have stunned a normal attacker, but Magnus went right through them. Jak tried to work his way to the side of Magnus to flank him, but Slate could see he wouldn't get there in time. A mighty overhead swing came down on Villifor, who held his shield up to block the blow. The huge battle-axe cut through the upraised shield and Villifor's armor like it was made of tin and the spike of Magnus' axe imbedded in Villifor's shoulder. He ripped the axe out of Villifor's body as Villifor cried out in agony. Magnus began to swing again.

Sana continued throwing darts as fast as she could while retreating from the Furies. She was slowed by Slate, who moved along with her only because of her prodding. He didn't want to have any more pain...the pain in his head was already more than he could take. Oh well, it was obvious to Slate she was fighting a losing battle anyway. He wished she would quit prodding him so he could finally get help from Lattimer.

Lucus finished his dance and thrust the axe skyward. Suddenly, the wind hitting Slate increased tenfold and he was lifted from the ground, swirling upward. As he tumbled through the air, he saw that Sana was still with him. Villifor had been lifted up just as Magnus' killing blow met empty air. Rainier's body tumbled lifelessly in the wind. Jak tried to land a final blow on Magnus as he was torn away. Annarelle and Tommy reached for each other and locked in an embrace as they floated upward.

Only Lucus was left below with the Blood Mage and the Furies. The glow of his axe faded and he knelt to the ground in fatigue. The woodsman stared at his friends as they escaped his fate. He smiled up at them with pride and hope as Magnus attacked. The battle axe descended upon Lucus' neck and the look of serenity never left his face.

CHAPTER TWENTY ONE

INCOMPLETE DEFEAT

Slate tumbled through the cold air like the snowflakes falling onto the city of Ravinai beneath him. With his red-hued vision, the winter's first snowfall rained blood onto the helpless citizens below, but his head hurt too much to comprehend or care. Ispirtu was a combination of smoke and flames, with the armies of Villifor and Darik constructing a new bridge to reach Brannon's tower. It would be completed soon and Lattimer would have his army.

He tumbled farther through the city and saw the lights on in nearly every home. The battle within the city had inspired fear. Fear made people keep the lights on. The anger within him rose at the ineptitude of the citizens. If they chose to hide from their fears instead of attacking them head on, then they deserved to die when those fears were realized. Light wouldn't save them.

Slate left the confines of Ravinai and floated toward the catalpa grove that Lucus favored. Why were they going there? They should be trying to reach Lattimer. He was the only one who could help. He looked around at the people he thought were his friends. They were trying to take him away from the help he needed. The anger rose. He needed to get away from these people and get back to Lattimer. He took out his staff.

"Slate, what are you doing? We escaped! You'll be ok now!" Annarelle saw him grip his staff and pleaded with him. He wouldn't be swayed by her lies. He tumbled through the air and met Jak as they descended into the Grove.

"He's turning, we need to hurry!" Sana screamed. Jak defended himself from Slate's blow and the collision of their weapons thrust the two apart. Slate hurdled toward Tommy, who prepared a spell. As Slate was about to reach him, he released a concussion wave that sent Slate into the trunk of a catalpa tree with startling speed.

"Restrain him, but keep him awake. If you knock him unconscious, his brain will stop fighting and we'll lose him." Slate slid down the tree trunk, determined to escape. Villifor had landed softly within the catalpa grove and sprinted to meet him. The injured soldier raised his broken shield with his good arm, ready to pin Slate against the tree trunk. Instead, Slate planted his feet and pushed, propelling himself over Villifor. Annarelle was there to meet him with a concussion wave, but instead of the spell pushing him away, the wave hit his back. It flattened him against the ground where Jak and Tommy pinned him to the grass before he could flash away.

Annarelle and Villifor each grabbed a leg, and between the four of them, they temporarily constrained Slate. He struggled mightily. If he could just headbutt one of them, he'd be able to break free, but his arms and legs were pinned and they stayed out of striking distance.

Sana appeared with a grapevine coiled over her shoulder. She cast a spell and the vines wound around him, securing him to the trunks of several catalpa trees. At her command, the grapevines tightened, lifting his body into the air and suspending him between the trees. Slate snarled and growled in frustration. Then Sana left him struggling as she went to the oldest catalpa tree in the grove. She bowed her head and placed her hand upon the trunk of the great tree. Slate felt the pressure in his head decrease slightly as he let his aggression take over. It was tempting to give in to it, but he remembered he was supposed to push against the pressure... he just couldn't remember why. He roared, trying to release all his pain and confusion through his lungs, but it didn't help. Where was Lattimer?

Sana removed her hand from the tree and withdrew a catalpa throwing knife. She plunged it into the trunk of the tree and then ran to Slate. Slate felt the familiarity of her probing and she gasped as she reached whatever was pressuring his brain. Whatever she had found, he knew she couldn't help him. She was wasting his time. He struggled against the vines holding him suspended amongst the trees of the grove. It was senseless. He couldn't reach Lattimer to get the help he needed and he couldn't hold out much longer. Maybe it was time to give up. He relaxed his muscles and closed his red eyes, fighting as long as he could within his mind.

Sana withdrew a second catalpa knife and drew blood from Slate's arm, creating a deep enough wound to produce a trickle of blood. The blood flowed over his skin and touched the vines holding his hand. Sana placed similar cuts on his other hand and her own hands. She knelt over Slate and placed her bleeding hands over Slate's opened hand.

Sana probed his mind and tried to envelop whatever was attacking him. He also felt a tugging at his arm similar to the transfusions Ibson administered in the arena, but this time blood was taken out of his body. A second later, blood entered from where Sana held his hand. What was she doing? Something changed and whatever created the pressure in his head was pushed out, little by little. His own blood was used to attack his mind. Sana pushed his blood into the catalpa tree and replaced it with her own. The pressure steadily decreased, but Slate refused the temptation to *draw* on the spell. He had learned the consequences of his Perceptor abilities and he didn't want that to happen to Sana.

The slow process was bearable only because of its effectiveness. Sana probed fewer and fewer areas in his head, but her spell weakened as time wore on. She drew from his own energy for her spell, just as she did during healing, and fatigue set in. Sana's probe stopped as Slate reached exhaustion. He shut his eyes...

A cloth cooled his forehead and memories came back with each refreshing wipe of the cloth. He had wanted to kill his friends. Lattimer had gotten away. He had failed. He kept his eyes shut, not wanting to face his failure. Then he thought of Lucus, who had offered up a true sacrifice to save his friends. He cast the spell of his own accord when Sana signaled it was their last hope. Lucus' sacrifice needed to count for something.

Slate opened his eyes and saw Sana sitting over him. His other friends sat nearby, watching closely. They flinched when his eyes opened. Jak drew his sword. "What's wrong?" Slate asked, too tired to defend himself.

"Your eyes...they belong to a Fury." Rainier answered. It was good to see him alive.

Slate shut his eyes again and let out a slow curse. At least the hued vision had left. The beauty of the world disappeared when viewed through a bloody lens. "How do you feel?" Sana asked.

"Much better...I'm sorry everyone. I didn't mean to..." I didn't mean to try to kill you? These people risked their lives for him and that was the best he could articulate?

"Say no more. You held out long enough for us to get you here."

"What did you do?" Slate asked Sana.

Sana was hesitant to say. "Do you remember the scene sketched into the hilts of my catalpa knives? It shows a man rising within a catalpa grove. There was a legend that catalpa trees had healing powers, but the spell had been lost. I found it... in my father's personal library."

"...amongst the Blood Magic texts?" Slate questioned.

"It was the only way to save you...and it worked. At least, it mostly worked."

Slate forced himself to sit up. "What do you mean? Every time Blood Magic is used there have been unintented consequences. What happened?"

"I asked permission from the tree to send your blood into it. The catalpa trees absorbed the illness from the blood into their own veins. They don't so much destroy it as much as they contain it. Your blood is killing the catalpa tree." Slate looked over and saw the once mighty tree wilted and sickly. Sana continued, "And there is one other thing..."

"What's that?"

"I wasn't able to get all of your blood out. I could only give so much of my own blood and I couldn't use someone else's because I needed to maintain my probe to direct the blood flow. When I got too weak, I had to stop. I don't know what the consequences will be..."

Slate didn't know either. "Thank you, Sana... or should I call you Rose?"

Sana blushed. "My name is Rosana Regallo, the only daughter of Brannon Regallo and sister to the first Blood Mage to terrorize Malethya in ages. I was assigned to Ispirtu when I entered the Crimson Guard, but the Sicarius headmaster convinced me that I could serve the kingdom best through Sicarius. I had a falling out with my father and the Sicarius headmaster arranged for my departure from Ispirtu and my father's care. Brannon never knew where I went, but he never looked for me either. My father was a very hard man..." She said the last sentence with a mixture of emotions. "The Sicarius headmaster taught me personally and upon his death, I took his place at the head of Sicarius. My little brother returned home to find I had left. I knew he would take it hard, but I didn't know how deeply it affected him. When I heard rumors of magical attacks starting in the villages to the north, I sought more formal training in magic. Lucus was accustomed to being alone and didn't mind absences if I needed to take them. He turned from a teacher into a confidant. Before the final battle, I met him here to stash my supplies and confess to him that the student he knew as Sana had previously been Rosana Regallo, and that I was known throughout Malethya as the Sicarius headmaster. Lucus had been friends with my father and had a hard time believing Brannon could be capable of Blood Magic. He encouraged me to speak with him. I was able to enter Ispirtu because the security orbs still registered my face as a member of the guild despite my disappearance. With the Sicarius mask, I found my way to Brannon's office. I took off the mask and questioned him as his daughter. He knew there was a Blood Mage, but he didn't know who it was or how the documents got placed in his personal library. He was being set up. I became convinced that he told the truth, so I fought at his side as the Sicarius headmaster."

Suddenly Slate could see through the confusion of the battle in Brannon's office. Brannon hadn't paid attention to the Furies, but it was because he knew the Blood Mage was present and he was trying to buy time to figure out who it was... and Slate had taken that time from him by knocking the scepter from his hand. "We failed."

"None of us knew who the Blood Mage was, Slate, and Lattimer didn't get everything he wanted. He didn't get you to lead his armies." Annarelle tried to comfort him.

"It may not have been a total failure, but we still lost. If it hadn't been for Sana erupting in a shower of electricity and Lucus' sacrifice, we would all be dead or turned into Lattimer's minions." The thought made Slate shudder, but his curiosity was too great to hold in his question. "How did you do that? I've never seen a wizard cast a spell like that. Spells are always just fireballs, concussive waves, and roiling dirt... it almost looked like your shock stick."

Sana grabbed the shock stick from her robes and tossed it to Slate. It was a carved and painted piece of wood. "I'm the shock stick. I haven't had formal training in Ispirtu, but Lucus found a natural ability for me to manipulate electricity. I use the wood carving to hide the fact that I was casting a spell." Sana let solemnity appear on her face. "All my tricks didn't save my father though..."

Slate could almost hear the words she left unspoken: "...because of you."

"I'm sorry, Sana. It was my fault." Sana did not forgive Slate, but maybe silence was all he could hope for right now.

"If this is anyone's fault, it is mine..." Villifor spoke with guilt lacing his voice. The Bellator headmaster sat with his shoulder wrapped in a bandage, grimacing in pain. "Brannon correctly labeled me as a traitor to my people. I fought alongside the real Villifor against the Disenites and during the Civil War. He was a true hero, rallying his troops and inspiring people to reach for something more than they currently had. He gave impassioned speeches about what man could accomplish without relying on magic. His resolve pushed us through Brannon's forces and we reached the walls of Ravinai. I looked upon the walls with uncountable numbers of wizards and fell victim to the inevitability of our demise. I gave up Villifor's attack plans in exchange for the safety of anyone that surrendered during the attack and the opportunity to lead Bellator under the guise of Villifor. Villifor attacked and Brannon's defense was perfect... they didn't have a chance." Slate knew this much from Brannon's journal.

"That was a long time ago..." Jak consoled his headmaster.

"Please let me finish. Villifor chose to surrender rather than sacrifice his people. Darik sent them to the farthest corner of Malethya and ordered them to work off their debt of disloyalty to the King. He created the village of Pillar in an uninhabitable rocky corner of the kingdom, took away any weapons they possessed, and charged them to start mining the stony mountain. Villifor agreed to forsake his name and took up the name Severance to gain leniency for his people by paying homage to the King's punishment of lifelong servitude." Slate remained quiet and fought the anger that was rising within him. "I came to think of myself as clever for adapting to the situation. I condemned Villifor as obstinate and simple-minded. It was only recently that I learned of Brannon's deception during the Civil War, creating the appearance of far more wizards defending the walls of Ravinai than there truly were. Slate, I tried to train you to help make up for my offenses, but more than anything I wanted to get back at Brannon. I gave the purple fabric with the lions on it to Magnus who pretended to find it in Minot. We then altered the story to convince Darik to attack Brannon. I thought that would avenge my friends in Pillar. Now I know I provided the means for Lattimer to make his move. I'm sorry..."

Slate felt the need to say something, "Villifor..."

"Don't call me that. I don't deserve the name."

Slate held his tongue. Finally, he thought of what he needed to say. "Each one of us could have done something differently to prevent the situation we are currently in. Lattimer has taken control of King Darik and will control the entire army by morning. I am too weak to attack him and we are too few. I don't know how we will stop him or even if we can. I do know that I saw Lucus' face as he sent us here to escape. It was the look of someone who knew we would find a way. What do you think? Can we beat an all-powerful wizard with an army of Furies at his command?"

"I'll die trying." Jak answered, followed by agreement from Sana, Tommy, and Annarelle.

"You have my sword to do your bidding... whether you decide to take my life in retribution for the harm I have caused or not." Villifor stated.

Slate pushed down his own personal anger at his father's betrayer. He was the last person to judge someone else's mistaken actions. "My father and the people of Pillar are gone. Help me to avenge their deaths. I will take your sword but only if you also keep the name Villifor and strive to live up to all that it stands for..."

Villifor nodded to Slate with renewed purpose.

Rainier was the last to speak in the group. "My biggest fears have been realized. The nomadic tribes believe in no greater evil than Blood Magic. It is past time that I return to the Tallow clan and let them know of our failures today. I must leave, but I will not leave you alone. I will come back with my people's aid." He got up to leave, but Sana stopped him.

She went to the wilted catalpa tree and cast a spell. It opened up to reveal her cache of supplies. She reached in and pulled out a Sicarius mask and a stratego medallion. "You have earned the mask, Rainier, and the medallion will help us find each other again. I hope to see you soon." Slate and Sana hugged their friend and wished him farewell. Rainier shook hands with everyone else and left the group.

"What should the rest of us do?" Annarelle asked, and Sana answered as a wizard.

"We need to get to another catalpa grove so that I can repeat the spell on Slate and clear him of any lingering effects."

"No" Slate said. He knelt beside the sickened catalpa tree. "The sickness is spreading...look..."

The catalpa tree wilted and the sickness spread along the clinging vines to neighboring trees within the grove. Slate brushed aside the newly fallen snow. Blades of grass slowly wilted, spreading the sickness slowly outwards. Even the pods and fallen leaves of the catalpa trees seemed to be effected, their color draining of whatever life was left within them.

Sana started, "It's a small price to pay for..."

"No, Sana." Slate said with authority. "Blood Magic has a way of corrupting things. I appreciate your efforts to save my life, but I will not allow you to cast that spell on me again. Probe the tree and see if there is anything you can do to fix it. I think you'll find that it is beyond your skill." Sana did probe the tree and her silence affirmed Slate's intuitions. They had unleashed a slowly spreading blight that would wilt any plant it contacted.

"I wasn't able to heal everything. I have no way of knowing what the lingering effects will be..."

"I will have to figure out what those effects are... and I'll need to do it alone." Surprise filled the group. "I would have killed each and every one of you when the spell had me in its grip. I can't risk that happening again. I will travel to the northern territories and explore my limitations. If I'm not mistaken, Lattimer will come looking for me. I'll have plenty of opportunities to test out my skills on Furies. We don't even know how to fight them yet... if I get some experience, we'll learn how to get to Lattimer."

"So you are just going to leave us?" Annarelle challenged, but Slate held firm.

"No, I will need every single one of you. Right now, I need Villifor and Jak to properly train Tommy in the ways of Bellator fighting. I also need them to sneak into Bellator tonight and recruit any guardsmen they trust before Lattimer tracks them down and subjugates them. Sana, I need you to train Annarelle in the ways of Sicarius and restart the guild. We'll need to fight this war from the shadows. I also need your network of sources to contact the Wizard Council and alert them to the truth. Lattimer will hunt them down and assimilate them into his army once he has solidified his power. Finally, I need more information on Ibson. He trained Brannon, Lucus, and had the texts that Lattimer stole. Can you give me more information about him?"

Sana transformed into the persona of the Sicarius headmaster. "That makes sense, but you'll need someone to help you. If you won't let me go, then take this medallion." Sana handed him a new Stratego medallion.

"You gave Rainier one as well. I thought it was just a game to learn the ways of Sicarius."

"In addition to that, it's enchanted. I know the location of anyone that carries one. It allows me to gather information much more efficiently. Your original one lost its enchantment after the tournament. If you need me, just crush it with your stonehand. I'll know your last location before it was crushed and will come to help you." Sana took a few Stratego coins from her supplies. "All of you should take one. It will be the easiest way for me to gather the group back together once Slate finishes his vacation."

Jak, Villifor and Tommy grabbed coins and armed themselves from Sana's supplies. "We're leaving right away. Bellator will likely be Lattimer's first stop after he secures Ispirtu. We'll need to hurry if we want to leave a few surprises for him." Villifor smiled as he tossed an exploding orb in the air. They left in the darkness of night.

Annarelle gave Sana back the original medallion she had carried. "How many of these are there?" she asked thoughtfully.

"I gave those to all the Sicarius members for training. They alerted me when one of them was coming to try to kill me and take my place as headmaster." Sana handed Annarelle a Sicarius mask while cautioning her that if she used it for any purpose other than Sicarius business, it would be a fatal mistake. Slate smiled inwardly. He still wasn't sure if Sana the wizard's apprentice would ever look at him the same way again, but Sana, the Sicarius headmaster, was someone that Slate needed at his side. Lattimer had won the battle, but there was a lot of fighting left to do. Sana put her Sicarius mask back on, completing her transformation. The alternating voice commanded, "Let's go, recruit. We need more shadows in the night."

REFLECTION OF REGRET

Slate stood in the middle of the village street, awaiting the hoof beats of horses and the Furies they carried. He had chosen the location of his defense carefully. Outside the inn a series of low stone walls served as stalls to tether horses and stow traveling packs as you visited the inn. For Slate they served as protection.

The squadron of soldiers reached the edge of town. Slate counted twenty Bellator Guardsmen supported by five Ispirtu wizards. Slate addressed them. "I am Slate 'Stonehands' Severance. I am Slate the Bloodless. I am the Shadow of the night. I am the Blight-bringer, and you will die at my hands."

The guardsmen charged at his declaration, their eyes burning red with hate and aggression. The wizards concentrated as they prepared spells. That was what Slate wanted. He hid behind the first stone wall, ready to flash. The first fireball hit, then the second and third in rapid succession. He dove behind the second wall as the first was hit by a concussion wave. Finally, the last fireball hit and Slate had his dance of destruction.

Bump...ba-bump, bump...bump. Slate left the temporary security of the stone stalls, heading into the open. He flashed in concert with the spells. Flash...fla-flash, flash...flash. The aggression of Ispirtu Furies caused them to cast spells as fast as they could, and thus they formed a repeatable pattern. If he could learn the melody, he could dance with it.

Slate moved amongst the charging horses, avoiding spells and striking with his staff as he flashed by. Fireballs landed in his wake, causing huge damage to the Bellator Furies. Flash...fla-flash, flash...flash. Slate passed through the initial charge and the soldiers couldn't turn their mounts in time to defend the wizards. Flash...fla-flash, flash...flash. Slate reached the first wizard, greeting him with his staff. The second wizard was crushed by his stonehand. Flash...fla-flash. One of the wizards had chosen to turn himself into an exploding orb, killing the remaining two wizards.

Slate turned his attention to the Bellator Guardsmen. He jumped out of their reach, striking from on high as they passed below him. He tripped one of the horses, causing the guardsman to fall and be trampled by the Furies in his wake. A lucky blow cut into his shoulder and Slate turned to punch the guardsman, collapsing the plate armor on his chest and killing him. He flashed to gain space and remove the sword. The pain was great, but pain he could live with...that was a gift from Primean. A slow trickle of blood came from his shoulder and he threw his head back and laughed.

There were two remaining guardsmen. He planted his staff in the ground and launched himself into the air, flipping high and killing both horsemen in one fluid blow. He landed on one knee and flourished his staff.

Slate stood up, collected his things and left town. He didn't expect thanks from these people. He was the subject of campfire stories meant to scare children. He was the last Severance in this lost kingdom... and he would save them all.

ACKNOWLEDGMENTS

No one has supported me more in the past years than my wonderful wife Leah, who continued to encourage the writing attempts of an engineer despite a busy household and a distinct lack of interest in science fiction or fantasy. You are wonderful and I promise to continue watching HGTV to make up for all the times you've heard me talk about this book.

A handful of early readers gave me higher praise than I felt I deserved, but hearing their comments gave me great joy and greatly improved the manuscript as a whole. Specifically, I'd like to mention Chad Quill, Mary Jo Quill, Luann Sieben, Paige Ahlborg, Matt Traylor, Jerry Justice, and Gina Horkey. My brother spent several late nights at the campfire with me talking about the existing story and tinkering with a bunch of ideas, some of which will show up in the coming books. I have to give special recognition to the ice-fishing crew of Josh Labau, Nick Shish, and Nate Russel, who took time for the world of Malethya while busily focusing on emptying beer cans and ignoring tip ups - may the tradition (and fish bocce) live on forever.

Then I'd like to thank the people that helped turn this story into a book. Ben Barnhart provided the editorial feedback for me when he wasn't dropping a bunch of knowledge on his writing students, and Abby Haddican did the amazing cover art. I quickly learned to trust anything she said. She also designed the website, and Josh Labau built the bones of it so that it runs as good as it looks (please visit www.jllorenquill.com). I'm extremely lucky to have found a team of people that can act professionally without sucking the fun out of everything. I can't thank you enough and look forward to working with you again.

Finally, I'd like to thank you - the reader. I've tried to write the type of book I like to read and if I succeeded, please tell me (email), your friends, or the millions on the internet by graciously writing a review. Even if I failed in some regards, please let me know and I might do better next time. I had so much fun writing Severance Lost that I kept writing my next book in the Fractal Forsaken Series. Please enjoy the sample chapter and consider purchasing Shadow Cursed (available now). Did you notice the available now comment? That's because I didn't publish this book until I knew how the whole story plays out. I can't wait to share it with you!

OTHER BOOKS BY J. LLOREN QUILL

Shadow Cursed – Fractal Forsaken Book 2

Please enjoy a sample of the prologue and first chapter from
Shadow Cursed

PROLOGUE

Hunger. Farmers fight hunger during a long day working the fields. Travelers fight hunger with carefully packed rations. Gluttons fight hunger with eager excess. Like the land of Malethya, hunger inspires people to fight. They fight for different reasons, but they all fight.

Rosana Regallo contemplated hunger while examining the plate before her. The blight had spread to the southern provinces and it was difficult to find food untouched by the disease. Spots of wilted brown lifelessness mottled the fresh red tomatoes. The speckled rot touched everything on her plate and she carefully carved around the sickened food with her throwing knife, conscious of the fact that all of this was her fault. She had used blood magic to save Slate Severance and blood magic had a cost. This time it was the blight. Even knowing the consequences of her actions, she would have made the same decision again. Her brother ruled the Kingdom and enslaved the minds of all those who opposed him, and she needed Slate's help to stop him.

If the people of Malethya needed to pick at their food and fight hunger, it was a small price to pay. Their concerns paled in comparison to Sana's hunger. Food could not quench her hunger. She set the tomato down and pushed the plate away. Her hunger ran deeper.

Some people had the slow, burning hunger for power or wealth, insatiably striving for more and more. Theirs was the hunger of greed. Her hunger ran deeper.

Others fought the hunger of addiction. Their hunger changed to a physical need, a necessity of life that must be fulfilled, but even they could fight and overcome the hunger within them.

Sana looked at her hand. Black specks periodically interrupted the smoothness of her skin. The blight slowly devoured her from within. The inevitable hunger of the blight devoured all that it came in contact with and spread until there was nothing left. The hunger could not be satisfied. The more it devoured, the hungrier it became. It would kill her, and she bore this burden by choice. It was the only way to save Malethya. If she were given the chance, the opportunity, to relive those decisions, she would make them again. The Sicarius Headmaster did what needed to be done, because others lacked the strength to do so...

CHAPTER ONE

DECEPTION OF THE INFIRMED

"Who are you today?" The infirmary wizard in charge of her care asked. Rosana contemplated that same question with every sunrise.

Rosana sat in her padded room and obediently answered. "I am the sister of the blood mage that rules Malethya from the shadows." Rosana could convincingly play the part of many Malethyans, but the truth was often better than a lie. "He is controlling King Darik and will bring ruin to this land."

The wizard from the mental health unit of the infirmary scribbled some notes on a piece of paper. He had introduced himself as Master Meikel, and he had been in charge of Rosana's care since her admittance. Meikel raised an eyebrow slightly while writing. Rosana read the mannerism as part academic intrigue mixed with pity and the slightest bit of contempt for his inferiors. After contemplating the mental state of his patient for a while, Meikel delivered his professional, slightly exaggerated smile that he reserved for masking his emotions while addressing the insane. "There hasn't been a blood mage in Malethya in centuries. They are terrors from campfire stories told to frighten children. You have nothing to worry about."

"You are right." It was impossible to argue with someone that thought you were insane. "If I'm not the sister of a blood mage, who should I be?"

"That is a question for you to answer. I am here to listen and to help. All I can tell you is that you appeared at our doorstep several days ago with symptoms of schizophrenia. So far you have claimed to be the lost relative of a blood mage, a former member of a covert spy ring, an assassin employed by the king, and the lover of a notorious criminal. After observing you, I worry that your mind has been lost to your own fantasies." Meikel thought for a moment and then came to a decision. "Treatment will begin tomorrow. Maybe then you will regain enough of your faculties to tell me your name."

The summary of her life did reek of fantasy, but she never anticipated that it would get her labeled insane. Rose Regallo was the compassionate sister of Lattimer, but as she grew up, she rejected becoming Rosana Regallo, splitting the older version of herself into a different part of her mind to keep the compassion of her youth alive. Her father, Brannon, noticed her internal conflict and enlisted the aid of his Ispirtu wizards to heal her. After months of experimentation, rumors of the troubled Regallo child reached the Sicarius Guild and the Headmaster got in contact with her. He viewed her condition, one in which she could split her personalities but access either of them at a given time, a rare and wonderful gift. Rosana escaped to the Sicarius Guild and became Malethya's most deadly assassin. The necessity and brutality of her craft troubled Rosana and Rose, so she created the Sicarius Headmaster, a nameless figure who did what needed to be done regardless of the means. During the travels of the Sicarius Headmaster she met Lucus, a wizard searching for an apprentice and, seeing the opportunity for training outside of Ispirtu's walls, created the personality of Sana, whose logic and attention to detail helped her studies in pattern-based magic. Now she was Rosana, Rose, Sana, and the Sicarius Headmaster. Her personalities changed based upon the situation although disagreements between herselves did arise occasionally. Right now, Sana's plan required a diagnosis that kept her in the infirmary, and jumping between herselves while talking to Meikel was a simple way to execute the Sicarius Headmaster's mission.

Rosana leaned forward in the chair that was bolted to the floor to show her eagerness for treatment. She quietly gripped the front of her shirt in feigned trepidation and pumped the infirmary wizard for information by asking, "What type of treatment? Will it help me?"

"The infirmary has made dramatic strides in the areas of mental illness by applying variations of our techniques for healing other parts of the body. For typical injuries, like stabbings or blunt trauma, we use probing spells to diagnose injuries to muscle or bone and then heal the patient. We cast these spells and move very methodically through the injured tissue without lasting consequences to the patient. In our studies of the human mind, we have discovered that some patients with similar cases to yours can benefit from probing spells conducted at high frequencies. It won't hurt, so I recommend you get a good night's sleep and try to relax."

Sana was intimately familiar with probing spells due to her training under Lucus, but she wasn't familiar with this technique. It sounded like the infirmary wizards used the probing spell to jump back and forth within the brain to scramble the signals. When the spell stopped, hopefully whatever signals were crossed in the schizophrenic mind became untangled. Sana didn't want to find out what the spell would do to her brain. *Rosana, Rose, and the Sicarius Headmaster agreed.*

Rose looked out the locked window of her room into the courtyards surrounding the infirmary and admired the immaculate gardens with their flowers in full bloom. It reminded her that a full winter had passed since her brother, Lattimer Regallo, seized control of the Malethya. He was the first blood mage in Malethya for centuries, and he grew in power with every second that passed. *But he was the little brother who snuck into my room at night during storms because the thunder scared him. I don't want to think of him as the blood mage who has subjugated King Darik's mind and controlled the kingdom's armies from his Ispirtu tower, choosing to rule through Darik and keeping the citizens unaware of the danger they faced.* Sana looked at the beauty of the flowers in the gardens. *How long will it be before darkness covers the land. Time moves too quickly. The Sicarius Headmaster needs to act before all the beauty in the world disappeared.*

Rose asked Master Meikel with sweetness and innocence in her voice, "Could I take a walk in the courtyards? I'm nervous about the treatments tomorrow and walking through the gardens may help me relax."

Meikel smiled at her, and this time Rosana knew it was genuine. "We believe in many forms of healing in the infirmary and encourage our patients to explore our gardens as a holistic form of therapy. I will ask an orderly to escort you there." Rose smiled in gratitude as the wizard left the room.

In her few moments alone, the Sicarius Headmaster hurried to her bed. A room in the mental ward of the infirmary provided precious few opportunities to hide anything, but the frame beneath the feathered bed had a small recess where the rounded pieces of wood formed together. In that recess she had hidden a length of string painstakingly chewed from the drawstring of her hospital-issued pants after the lights went out at night. She then remade her bed and sat in her chair when the orderly knocked on the door.

The orderly came in, looking at her chart. He said, "Good evening, Miss…umm…" He scanned her infirmary records for her name and blushed after failing to find it.

"I would like to take a walk in the gardens. Would you escort me?" Rose asked politely. The orderly held the door for Rose and led the way to the courtyard entrance. Rose stepped out into the failing light of day and headed toward the gardens. The orderly followed her until they reached the garden paths and then Rose requested some privacy. Sana's plan required it. "Will you wait here for me? I start a new treatment tomorrow and would like to spend a few moments by myself. I just want to stroll through the gardens and watch the setting sun." Politeness went a long way with orderlies accustomed to behavioral issues in the mental ward.

The orderly appeared conflicted. "I'm required to accompany you, but if you stay within my sight at all times, then I think it will be ok."

Rose thanked the orderly and walked casually through the gardens, stopping to smell flowers and idly gaze at the setting sun. The centerpieces of the gardens were a hedge of rosebushes that encircled a catalpa tree. Sana scanned the branches inside the hedge and found the object of her search. Deep within the thickest part of a rosebush was a small bag. The Sicarius Headmaster plunged her arm into the thorn covered bush to retrieve the bag while Rosana maintained a look of tranquility so as not to alert the orderly. When she pulled her arm back, the thorns had scratched and cut her forearm up to her elbow. The superficial wounds were just deep enough to draw blood and look serious.

Sana tucked the bag into her pants and secured it with the drawstring. She then tied the string she retrieved from her room to the rosebush. Simultaneously, she lowered her head to smell a nearby flower to maintain appearances. With this stage of her mission accomplished, she walked back to the orderly at a casual pace while squeezing her arm above the elbow in an alternating pattern to increase the blood flow. She returned to a normal, if slightly hunched walk as she exited the rosebushes in the gardens and came back into full view of the orderly.

He caught sight of her bleeding arm and rushed into the gardens to help. "You're bleeding! What happened?"

Rosana looked down at her arm soaked in blood and answered for Rose, who hated to lie, "I didn't notice. Isn't it pretty though? It looks like the roses in the garden." Politeness had its uses but so did insanity. The orderly concentrated on Sana's arm so much that he never noticed the slightly hunched posture she used to hide the bag in her waist. After rushing her back to her room and dressing her arm, the orderly left her alone again while mumbling about finding a new job.

Once he left, Sana stashed the bag and pressed her ear against the wall. From the adjacent room, she heard a man singing softly. The room belonged to Ibson, a famous wizard throughout Malethya who had suffered a tragic fall that left his brain permanently impaired. Ibson's legendary intellect was reduced to simple rhymes and a childlike demeanor. The song Sana heard through the wall had perfect pitch and a melody too complex for such a condition. Sana's resolve hardened, and she waited for her medications to arrive.

In short order, a new orderly brought in a dark liquid. Sana knew what it was before he explained. "This is wormroot. We give it to all our patients with the ability to perform magic. The wormroot temporarily blocks your ability to access the spark and prevents you from accidently casting a spell that could harm you or those around you. Please drink it." Sana pretended to swallow and smiled with a closed mouth. The orderly left the room and Sana spit it out. By the time the infirmary wizards discovered the small pool of wormroot on her floor that signaled her disobedience, she would no longer be a patient in the infirmary.

With her last visitor gone for the night, Sana retrieved her stashed bag and laid the contents on her bed: a lock pick, a knife, and a piece of smoothed wood that fit nicely into the palm of her hand. Only the lock pick was functional. The knife collapsed when she applied pressure to the dulled blade. People throughout the kingdom feared the piece of wood known as a shockstick, but it was a tool of deception. The shock that people feared came from a spell cast by Sana, a spell she couldn't cast if she had swallowed the wormroot.

Sana ran through her plan in her head and listened against the wall for the singing to stop in the adjacent room. Long after the stars were the only light in her room, the singing turned to silence and finally the silence turned to snoring. It was time.

In the mental ward, doors locked from the outside, so the Sicarius Headmaster used the lock pick to exit. It was a standard lock, and she made quick work of it. A soft click signaled her success and she opened the door slowly, peering into the hallway. Orbs lit the hallway, but the orderlies had finished their rounds, so the corridor was empty. The Sicarius Headmaster slipped into the hallway, entered the adjacent room, and left the door slightly ajar to expedite her exit.

Inside the room, the sound of snoring and the familiar layout of the room led her silently to Ibson's bed. The Sicarius Headmaster pressed the knife against Ibson's throat, rammed the shockstick into his stomach, and whispered, "Listen to what I say or die. I know you drank wormroot and are completely defenseless. You are at my mercy." *That last part was a lie. Any mercy that Ibson received would be from Rose.*

Ibson's eyes went wide and his body went rigid, fighting his instinct to bolt upright because of the presence of the knife. He stammered,

> Knives are mean,
> Knives are scary,
> My soul is clean,
> Don't kill...

The Sicarius Headmaster interrupted his poem, "Save the nursery rhymes Ibson." Then she changed the inflection of her voice to alternate between high and low octaves. "Do you know who I am?"

Recognition of the distinctive style of speech invoked a fear that broke through Ibson's façade. "Yes. You are the Sicarius Headmaster and the wizard's apprentice that I once knew as Sana. What do you want from me?"

"Your life means nothing to me, since you have failed to live it. You choose to hide your recovery and ignore the world. Information, however, is valuable to me, and I believe you have been hiding information." The Sicarius Headmaster spoke. *Rose tried not to think of the deeds the Sicarius Headmaster had carried out in the pursuit of information.*

Ibson protested, "If you need information from me, then I am in no danger until I tell you what you want to know…"

Sana appreciated his deductive reasoning, but she countered with her own. "I disagree. You locked yourself away and pretended to be mentally ill to protect yourself from the threat of a blood mage. You value your life, and this knife can take it, regardless of my motives. Stand up slowly. We are leaving." Ibson rose from bed slowly but didn't try to resist. He was an old man, and he fought with magic. Without the spark, he was simply old. "Take the knife," Sana commanded. A surprised Ibson reached for the knife at his throat. Before he reached it, Sana applied some pressure to the blade and caused it to collapse. "Don't get any ideas. This knife is harmless and you still have a shockstick in your stomach. Just play the role I tell you to play." Ibson grabbed the knife and nodded. Sana twisted so that her arm was behind her back but still pressed into Ibson's gut. "Grab my waist and hold me tight against you. Place the knife against my throat with your other hand. Now walk out the exit to the gardens. If anyone tries to stop you, threaten to kill me."

Sana, the hostage, led Ibson to the door and opened it. Ibson walked dutifully toward the exit, while Sana pretended to struggle against him. Ibson's wide-eyed, frightened stare even passed for a crazed hostile attacker. Halfway down the hallway, an orderly rounded the corner. Before Ibson could speak, Sana yelled, "Help, help me! He has a knife!"

The orderly turned and ran. Sana said to Ibson, "You are now committed to this ruse. You are a mentally ill patient holding a knife against someone's throat. No one will believe otherwise." Somewhere ahead, the orderly triggered a security orb and the alarm rang throughout the infirmary.

They rounded the final corner and saw three infirmary wizards barring the exit to the gardens. Master Meikel was in the lead and tried to reason with Ibson. "Put the knife down. You are a good person. Whatever you are dealing with right now, we can help you through it. Just let the girl go."

Ibson played his role to perfection by saying.

Step aside,
Step aside,
The girl won't die,
If my words you abide.

Sana tried to influence the critical decision in front of the wizards. "Do as he says. He's not himself. He could do anything…"

Master Meikel assessed the situation and commanded the infirmary personnel. "Allow him to leave. We can't risk harm to the girl. He has taken wormroot, so we can follow him safely. He won't get far." They stepped aside and cleared the path to the gardens. Ibson backed through the doorway, shielding himself with his hostage as the ruse demanded.

The wizards followed them into the darkened gardens with the infirmary alarms fading behind them. Ibson whispered to Sana, "Now what?"

"Head toward the rosebushes and get behind the hedge." Ibson obliged as the infirmary wizards continued their attempts to talk down Ibson from a distance. Sana strained her eyes in the darkness and saw that the string she placed earlier in the day had been removed. *Help was here.*

A figure appeared on the roof of the infirmary, outlined by the ambient light from the building below but shadowed by the night sky. "Ibson belongs to me!" The pitch of the figure's voice alternated between words and pierced the night sky. A second later, a thick cloud of smoke enveloped the infirmary wizards.

The Sicarius Headmaster mimicked the alternating tones of the rooftop figure, "I am the Sicarius Headmaster!" Dense smoke reflects sound and makes it difficult to pinpoint the direction of the source. By speaking from two directions, Sana knew it would be virtually impossible to identify her or Ibson's location. She turned to Ibson and whispered, "Our extraction point is in that direction. Move as fast as you are able. I will catch up shortly." Sana pointed toward a tall building just outside the infirmary grounds, within the capital city of Ravinai.

From the rooftops, Sana heard, "I defy King Darik by my continued existence. He tried to kill every member of Sicarius, his sworn servants, but I am not so easily killed. Now I serve the people of Malethya, although they are blinded to the dangers they face. I rule the world of shadows. Follow me tonight and you will never see the light of day again."

Following that bit of theater, she chased after Ibson, catching the old man quickly. The infirmary wizards were too disoriented and busy coughing from the smoke to give chase, but the real danger still awaited them. Up ahead, the Headmaster located a tall, balconied building and quietly commanded Ibson, "Head for the alleyway just left of the building." The Sicarius Headmaster could hear the distinctive sound of soldiers marching toward the infirmary in response to the building's alarms, but they were still a few blocks away. *They had made it.*

Inside the alleyway, Sana threw a canvas cover off a wooden platform. "Get on," the Sicarius Headmaster commanded Ibson. He climbed onto the platform while Sana unhooked a rope hidden amid the intricate architecture of the tall building. The rope attached to the four corners of the platform and disappeared somewhere above. The Sicarius Headmaster climbed aboard the platform holding a second rope that led to a knotted anchor against the alleyway. "Hold on tight. It might be a little bumpy at the top." She pulled on the rope which released the knot and the platform started to rise immediately, gaining speed at an astounding rate. Halfway to the top, the counterweight passed them, plummeting to the ground. Their speed continued to increase and the Sicarius Headmaster jumped gracefully onto the building's balcony just before the counterweight smashed into the alleyway below. The sudden end to the platform's rise jarred Ibson, but the Sicarius Headmaster reached out to steady the suspended platform as it swung from a pulley overhead and helped the old wizard onto solid ground.

"You played your role well, Ibson." Rosana complimented the wizard. She wanted to establish authority over Ibson, and compliments for following orders reinforced the hierarchy.

"You left me little choice. Why did you go to all the trouble of breaking me out of there? I was perfectly happy avoiding the world." Just then, the Sicarius Headmaster saw motion on the rooftops. The figure jumped gracefully from rooftop to rooftop and crouched above their balcony.

"Hello Annarelle." The Sicarius Headmaster greeted her protégé, dressed in her likeness. The series of black wraps blended into the night, allowed for a great deal of flexibility, and most importantly, innumerable folds and pockets for darts, knives and other tools of their craft. Annarelle also wore a Sicarius mask that made it difficult to look her in the face. The mask absorbed all light, creating a void in the visual signals the brain normally interpolates. The brain fills the void using information surrounding the mask. In practicality, this meant that the wearer of a Sicarius mask would be seen as a servant if they dressed in servant's clothes, a wizard if dressed in robes, or a soldier if dressed in armor. The Sicarius Headmaster was used to both wearing and interacting with others wearing the mask, so its unsettling effect was muted. "Your timing is impeccable. I take it you found my string?"

"I left the package in the rose bush the night you were admitted and checked at sundown every evening for a signal. When I found it, I contacted Villifor, and he had his rebels occupy the army's attention tonight." Sana looked at the skyline of the city and saw smoke from several fires burning, which probably slowed the response time of the troops when the alarms at the infirmary were raised. Annarelle continued, "I'm happy it didn't take longer than a few days. How did things go inside the infirmary?"

The Sicarius Headmaster thought of the ease in which she had been diagnosed and admitted to the infirmary. *It all went according to Sana's plan, but she decided against describing how easy it was to get a diagnosis and be admitted.* "I located and extracted our target before they tried to administer therapy to me."

Annarelle laughed. Most people would mistake the meaning of her laugh as jest at Sana's fear of therapy. Only a fellow Sicarius Guardsman would know the laugh's real meaning. The laugh indicated Annarelle's relief that Sana didn't have to kill the wizard who attempted to treat her.

Ibson tried to take control of the situation by demanding answers. "Pleasantries aside, when do the questions start?"

Rosana waved Ibson toward the infirmary-facing railing of the balcony while Annarelle bounded away to scout for approaching trouble. Below the balcony, the shining armor of soldiers scoured the infirmary grounds in response to the alarms. Rosana addressed Ibson, "The Crimson Guard represents justice throughout Malethya. The armor of the Bellator Guardsmen reflects the starlight in proud proclamation of their place in society. The robes of the Ispirtu wizards are hidden in the darkness, but you can almost see them scurrying around in a righteous display of power. I once stood in their company as a stanchion of Malethya and protector of the kingdom. Now the very people I strive to protect fear me. You let this happen."

Ibson responded, "It's true that I suspected a blood mage in the Malethya, but you can't blame me for your troubles. I was put in charge of investigating how our friend, Slate Severance, the Tournament Champion, ended up with iron in his hand during his championship bout. During my investigation, it became apparent that he was a victim of blood magic. The blood mage attacked me in the Arena and nearly killed me. I hid my recovery to protect myself, so that the blood mage couldn't come back to finish the job."

"You didn't hide from the blood mage," The Sicarius Headmaster scolded. "You hid from the world. You hid from responsibility."

Ibson shook his head in bemusement. "Responsibility is always shared, but self-preservation is the right of every man. Besides, I listened as you, Slate, Rainier, Lucus and Lattimer worked to identify the blood mage. Slate found evidence implicating Brannon Regallo and stormed Ispirtu. I hear Brannon has been defeated, the threat of blood magic is ended, and the people of Malethya are safe. If your actions resulted in the loss of the Sicarius Guild, then the responsibility lies with the Sicarius Headmaster. Don't delude yourself."

The Sicarius Headmaster knew her own failures and Rose mourned the loss of the Guardsmen every night. "People that fail to act are often adept at identifying fault in the actions of others. I will not take criticism from you." The Sicarius Headmaster's scorn permeated her words. Groups of Bellator Guardsmen and Ispirtu wizards combed the infirmary grounds below, searching for the notorious Sicarius Headmaster. Rosana explained to Ibson, "You are as blind as the rest of Malethya. We didn't defeat Brannon the blood mage. We defeated Brannon Regallo, the Ispirtu Headmaster and protector of Malethya. I stood at his side and fought with him before he was killed by his son Lattimer. Lattimer took control of Ispirtu and the mind of King Darik through the use of blood magic. The armies loyal to Darik fight for their king, unknowingly doing the will of Lattimer. Meanwhile, Lattimer has been growing his own army of loyal subjugates. They look and act like normal soldiers until they attack. Then their eyes turn red and they attack with pure, unbridled aggression. They attack as Furies."

Ibson blanched at the mention of Furies, foot-soldiers from the days of Cantor when blood mages fought incestually. Ibson refused to accept Rosana's story. "No, Brannon was the blood mage. Lattimer was never clever enough to accomplish what you say. It is an impossibility that he controls the kingdom and an army of Furies. Besides, Furies are mindless. Their aggression stems from a single desire to kill placed in their head by a blood mage." He pointed to toward the soldiers in the infirmary grounds. "Those soldiers aren't mindless."

"No, they are not. They attack with the aggression of Furies but the training of Bellator Guardsmen and Ispirtu wizards."

Sana paused to let the reality of that threat sink in.

"I tire of your lies. Let's end these questions," confronted Ibson.

"I have told you the truth. As for questions, I have yet to ask one. However, you did ask me when the questions would start, and I have avoided answering in the hopes you would believe me. Since you refuse to see the truth, the questions will start just as soon as you wake up." The Sicarius Headmaster reached out with her shockstick and Sana cast a spell that sent a small jolt of electricity through the wizard. Ibson fell to the balcony floor.

Annarelle rejoined her and picked up Ibson's legs. "I hate this part of the operation."

Sana, Rose, and Rosana agreed with Annarelle, but the Sicarius Headmaster knew it was part of the job. "We are Sicarius Guardsmen. We need to move and hide bodies once in a while."

As they prepared to move Ibson, a large contingent of Guardsmen and wizards entered the city grounds. At the head of the pack, a wizard walked with an arrogance that dwarfed the gaudiness of his robes and the scepter he carried. Even if Lattimer wasn't her brother, she would have recognized him from a mile away. It was Lattimer's first public appearance since seizing power, and he had apparently taken up their father's sense of fashion as well as his air of authority. *Despite the physical similarities to her father, his appearance only inspired hate. Lattimer had killed her father. He was responsible for the deaths of Lucus and Slate's parents through the actions of Magnus. Now he enslaved hundreds, if not thousands of soldiers to do his will. For any of these atrocities, he deserved to die.* The Sicarius Headmaster pulled out a throwing knife while Sana cast a spell with the pattern of a diving falcon. The knife flew straight and actually sped up as it neared Lattimer, reaching the speed of a falcon right before its talons grasped its prey.

At the last second, the knife flew off course and embedded in the ground at Lattimer's feet, harmlessly diverted by whatever magic Lattimer surrounded himself with. The blood mage looked down at the knife and then directly at her, locking eyes with his sister. He pointed at her as the soldiers and wizards around him turned to Furies. The soldiers sprinted toward their building and the wizards readied fireballs. Lattimer himself readied a spell and the Sicarius Headmaster didn't want to wait to find out what type.

"Go! Now!" She yelled to Annarelle. They flung Ibson's body onto the next rooftop. Beneath them, the building started to shake. Lattimer planned to take down the whole building. Annarelle and the Headmaster jumped onto the adjacent rooftop just as the building was hit with a series of fireballs. It collapsed a split second later in a cloud of rubble that mixed with the smoke of wizard's fire.

They gathered Ibson and used the smoke and dust as a screen to mask their escape. When they were safely away from the collapsed building, they took the time to carry Ibson more comfortably. "Well, we learned one thing tonight. My throwing knives are useless against Lattimer."

"And if we get close enough, we run the risk of being captured and subjugated like King Darik. We need Slate. He is the only one to ever resist Lattimer." Annarelle talked while she unwrapped a portion of her outfit around her leg. It had two long straps on either end of a fine mesh of fabric in the middle to form a makeshift stretcher.

"Slate could only resist Lattimer for a short period of time, but you are right. It would be long enough to attack him. Unfortunately, he hasn't recovered fully from his first encounter with Lattimer. We need Slate, but we need to fix him first. Maybe Ibson will hold the key." They rolled Ibson's body atop the middle portion of the stretcher, and Annarelle slung two straps over her shoulders. The Sicarius Headmaster tied the other two straps around her waist and the two set off with their cargo.

They carried him across the rooftops of Ravinai, and while the Sicarius Headmaster handled the physical exertion, Rose and her other selves were free to look at the city anew. *Rose's heart warmed to the sounds of merriment that floated up from the taverns below. Rosana knew it wasn't the sounds of drunkards spending their last dime on a drink but the laughter of citizens with extra change in their pockets. Sana noted the clean streets and the quality goods displayed in the store windows. The alleyways were clear of the homeless and new construction confirmed the affluence of the citizens. Ravinai's prosperity brought conflicting emotions. When Lattimer seized power, he promised to recreate the Golden Age of Cantor with his unlimited power. It appeared that he was living up to his promise, but Sana knew the golden ages ended in bloodshed with the blood mages subjugating citizens and using them as mindless weapons in their never-ending thirst for power. Rose hoped she could get answers before the prosperity ended and the bloodshed began.*

With the fear of the future refocusing her efforts, the Sicarius Headmaster checked on Ibson. He was still unconscious as they approached an abandoned warehouse. The Sicarius Headmaster had a network of safe houses and informants in Ravinai and throughout Malethya. When King Darik destroyed the Sicarius Guild, she relocated her headquarters to this warehouse, one of her more secretive locations. The warehouse's proximity to the infirmary's morgue proved to be an advantageous location for some of Sana's needs.

The Sicarius Headmaster and Annarelle hauled Ibson's body onto the rooftop of the abandoned warehouse and toward a ventilation shaft that served as the hideout's entrance. The ventilation shaft hid a ladder and a winch. The winch was for supplies or, in this case, a body. They hooked the straps of Ibson's stretcher to the winch and lowered him into the darkness until the winch stopped. The Headmaster and Annarelle descended the ladder to a small platform that inconspicuously hung from the rafters of the warehouse.

Annarelle lit a small oil lamp that lit their entrance while giving dim glimpses of warehouse below them. The floor of the warehouse was covered with row upon row of shelving that once served as a distribution center for the king's supply of grain and stores. The offices suspended from the warehouse ceiling, so that the king's clerks and foreman could oversee the workers below and keep stock of warehouse supply. The stairwell that originally connected the offices to the warehouse floor was destroyed in a fire that was extensive enough to cause the building to be abandoned. The result was the perfect hideout – the warehouse offices were isolated and difficult to infiltrate. They were also heavily modified to fit her needs.

Sana reached up to a pulley system that connected the platform to the offices. She hooked Ibson's stretcher up to the pulley hook before disconnecting him from the winch. "Annarelle, can you welcome our guest?" Annarelle smiled and swung freeform across the rafters, easily bridging the gap between the platform and the offices while Sana worked the pulley system. Ibson's body hung lifelessly as it traversed the span into Annarelle's waiting arms. She disconnected him and the Sicarius Headmaster swung across the rafter's to join them. "His room is prepared for his arrival. Please tie him to his chair and meet me in the anatomy room."

Made in the USA
Lexington, KY
19 April 2017